SKETCH

SKETCH

Ros Hill

Published by Ros Hill, 2026
SKETCH

First edition. July, 2026.

This book is a work of fiction. The names, characters, and events in this book are the products of the author's imagination or are used fictitiously. Any similarities to real people, places, or events are entirely coincidental.

ISBN 979-8-9992513-0-5 Paperback
ISBN 979-8-9992513-1-2 eBook
ISBN 979-8-9992513-2-9 Audibook

Book and Cover Design by Glen M. Edelstein, Hudson Valley Book Design
Cover art by Michael Gellatly

In memory of my daughter, Brookney.
You were a superhero in so many ways.

PART I

Chapter 1
ORIGIN

Ancient Egypt, 450 BC

Beneath the Egyptian sun, three falcons circled in the sky, riding the thermal updrafts that lifted them over a thousand feet above a temple. Below, Khepri, an artist of average build, wearing a loincloth and sandals, carried a small clay bowl of black ink as he walked through the courtyard. He was headed to a small building where his primary subject to paint was the sun god Ra, believed to be the creator of all forms of life and who was the sole deity worshiped at the temple.

But Khepri stopped, startled by the wailing sound of the falcons. Holding the bowl of ink in one hand, he shielded his eyes with the other, squinting as he looked up. The birds took their turns wailing in a repeated fashion, continuing to glide in their circular motion.

Soaring falcons were always a welcome sight, as they held Khepri in awe of their predatory prowess. On this particular day, though, it was not their hunting dominance that was so impressive, but rather, something unexpected and so powerfully spiritual, it could only be interpreted as magical.

Khepri remained still as he felt a slight vibration coming from the bowl. He removed the lid and saw the ink swirling, then cupped the bowl with both hands, trying to steady its peculiar motion, but the ink continued. Setting the bowl on a stone bench, he stepped back, his face troubled, unable to decipher what was happening.

The wailing continued, but was now twice the volume as before. Khepri saw not three, but six falcons circling. Looking back at the ink, the swirling motion had also increased. He took another step back, his dark eyes becoming larger as the kettle of falcons continued to grow, more birds flying in from all directions, joining the spiral that darkened as the formation grew tighter. Twenty…thirty…fifty…then hundreds of falcons joined the wailing tornado, spinning faster, growing louder, until it became a maddening scream.

Khepri pressed his hands tight against his ears to silence the compounding sound piercing them like sharp acoustic knives. The ink swirled faster with not a drop spilling out. Its speed and direction were reflective of the falcons, as the bowl remained steady on the bench.

He closed his eyes tightly in an attempt to shut out the unnerving fury. Dropping to his knees, his hands slapped against the earth, then clawed into the dirt. In a final moment of uncontrollable emotion, he screamed, "RAAAA!!!!"

Then…silence.

He looked for the falcons, but there were none. There was nothing more than the sun, burning through a quiet blue sky. On the bench, the surface of the ink was motionless.

Khepri cautiously approached the bowl, staring into it, hesitant to pick it up. But as the minutes passed, he came to believe the one thing that must have happened:

The sun god Ra, creator of all living things, had not only arrived, but had anointed the ink.

Khepri's hands quivered as he carried the bowl, without incident, into the drawing room whose walls had square openings to allow sunlight in. Setting it on a waist-high stone table, he opened a nearby wooden crate, taking out a papyrus paper scroll. The scroll was about a foot tall and two feet long after unrolling it on the table. He placed four stones, one at each corner, to keep the paper flat.

Alone on the temple grounds, he tried to make sense of what had just occurred. For several minutes the falcons' wailing rang in his ears, until slowly fading, then becoming nearly inaudible. After a few minutes, all that remained was a wavering distant hum, as if a presence had taken refuge in the deep caverns of his mind. The hum calmed his nerves and relaxed his hands. It was Ra, was it not? Why else would so many falcons have gathered like that? For centuries, early drawings had depicted Ra as a human figure with a falcon head. Certainly, the falcons weren't merely coincidental.

Removing the lid from the bowl, Khepri braced his hands against the edge of the table, then leaned forward, staring at the ink. It looked ordinary and undisturbed, no different than it was before the falcons had arrived. But Khepri knew that was not the case. He knew it had undergone a change, that it was different than before. He just had to figure out how different.

The scroll contained a drawing that he had started on the previous day, but had run out of ink. It was of a king walking beneath four suns arching overhead, representing the four seasons. He had intended to include a queen walking beside the king, but on this day his focus to draw the queen was disrupted, skewed by the spiraling falcons.

Khepri opened a small, rectangular wooden box on the table, and took out a thin reed pen that he had fashioned from bamboo, having cut the end of the reed at an angle to create a pointed tip. Again, he stared at the ink, anticipating even the slightest swirling motion, but it remained still. Listening for the return of the falcons, he stood motionless, looking up, as if trying to see through the ceiling. Then the silence was broken, but by an unexpected sound. A dog barked from off the temple grounds followed by a woman's terse voice. As the barking continued, once more, the woman's voice struck sharply. Was the dog barking at falcons? Khepri honed his focus on anything resembling a wail, but silence had returned; even the sounds of the dog and woman had faded into the distance.

He returned to the scroll and tried to restore his concentration. His plan was to draw the queen wearing a sheath adorned with beadwork, but as he dipped his pen into the ink, the distant dog barked one final time. It was a stronger, more piercing bark.

Khepri stood tall and alert. Something clicked in his mind. The confusion that had amassed since arriving at the temple grounds began to dissipate, clearing an opening for his thoughts, as he now sensed his role with the ink. Something inexplicable was taking place. Ra had anointed the ink, and it was now Khepri, unbeknownst to him, who had been selected to use it.

Touching the tip of the reed pen to the papyrus paper, he began drawing the outline of a slender dog with pointed ears that stood erect. The dog had short black hair with an oval patch of white centered on its back.

But that was all he drew. At first he was uncertain of what he was hearing, but then recognized the sound. And the breath—he could smell its breath.

How is this possible? How can this be? The door had been closed. From where did it come? Khepri put his pen down next to the scroll, then slowly turned his head to a dog panting behind him—it looked exactly as he had drawn it.

"Spirit dog!" said Khepri, cautiously extending his hand to touch the dog's head. "Are you born from my pen?"

The dog stopped panting, cocking its head left and right, then gently licked his hand.

"It is true! It is true! The ink…it lives!"

The dog sat down, lifting its left paw to Khepri, who then shook it.

"And you are kind! Smart and kind!"

Khepri looked back at the scroll. "Yes, you are my drawing, from the ink of Ra. But you are alone and need a companion. A person of the ink."

He gently kneaded his fingers into the fur of the dog's throat. "A queen!! I shall give you a queen!!"

He returned to the scroll, picked up the pen, and began to draw the queen he had intended to draw before, but there was one exception: he placed her next to the dog, and not the king. Finishing the outline, he included the sheath and…

"My faithful companion," a woman said from behind Khepri, as she spoke to the dog.

Khepri turned, wide-eyed, speechless. Dropping to one knee, he bowed to her.

"My queen! Oh, my queen! The ink speaks truth!"

The queen stepped forward, touching him on the head. "Khepri, I am not a queen to bow to, but rather someone who owes you a great gratitude. After all, you gave me life."

"You know my name?"

"Of course. I was born with knowledge. It is part of the magic of the ink."

The queen bent over and cupped the dog's head in her hand. Then, looking into his eyes, she said, "My four-legged friend, welcome to eternity."

Chapter 2
ARRIVAL

1967

Sunset neared as Charles sat at his drawing table with the sketch book and red pen that Heba had given him the week before while visiting Egypt. A gooseneck lamp arched above the table, illuminating a blank page as he prepared to draw a superhero whom he envisioned being much like himself, but older: in his early 30s, six feet tall with an athletic build.

For thirty minutes Charles toiled with his superhero's identity—his signature clothing and superhero name. On a separate page he experimented with different designs he had considered during his travel back to the States. After several renderings using colored pencils, he struggled to find the right colors. Either his selections weren't complementary, or he felt his designs were mimicking those of other comic book superheroes.

After the sun slipped beneath the horizon, giving way to the advancing darkness, two miles away crowds of people began forming at the city park, staking their spots, unfurling their blankets or setting out lawn chairs in preparation for the City of Lehman's July 4th fireworks display.

Charles examined the shape of his pen, particularly its fine-pointed, spade-shaped nib, and thought about drops of ink. Within that observation though, he found himself on the brink of discovery, realizing how his superhero was to be identified. He wore a black mask, long-sleeve red bodysuit, silver boots, and dark gray briefs with a silver belt. On the chest, Charles kept things simple, drawing the shape of a large black ink drop, tapering to a point at the top.

He positioned the pen tip just above the blank page, poised in its final moments prior to conception—prior to bringing his drawing to life. After all, the pen contained ink that was not only twenty-four hundred years old, but was magical.

When paired with something called his imaginative energy, drawing with the red pen would bring a supernatural being to life. He would be creating immortality. He had proven himself capable with the butterflies Heba had asked him to draw in Egypt, but was a human truly possible? She had reminded him to let his imagination be his guide, to will as much power into his drawing as he could. She had also issued a warning:

"The Frenchman who calls himself the Finger Gunman—he cannot be trusted. I witnessed your brief conversation with him. I know a snake when I see one. He is of no good, thriving upon evil. When willing the superpowers into your drawing, you must also will the knowledge of the threatening existence of the Finger Gunman. That is critical."

Charles closed his eyes, blocking out his surroundings as he prepared to draw, but his acute concentration was momentarily interrupted. Within a few seconds, he had fallen asleep, then snapped out of it with a quick, reflexive jerk. The compounding effects of his trans-Atlantic travel had returned. Charles was exhausted, and struggling to stay awake. Shaking his head as he repeatedly blinked his eyes, he regained focus, lowering his pen to the paper.

Using colored pencils with the magic ink, the drawing took very little time to complete as his superhero stood solid and confident with arms akimbo. He made the facial characteristics similar to that of himself: slightly wavy brown hair, brown eyes, and a square jaw line. His athletic stature evoked an indestructible durability. The inner workings of physical features and personality would be assigned by the pairing of the magic ink with Charles' imaginative energy. He zeroed in on nothing other than willing his superhero to come to life, willing it to defend what is good, and protect against what is evil. Willing it to slaughter the Finger Gunman if the time ever came.

And then, in an outwardly, expressive voice, Charles exclaimed, "Sketch! I shall call you, Sketch!"

He set his pen down, remaining focused on his drawing, but listening—waiting for a footstep, a shoulder tap, a breath, a voice, even a cough. Something, other than the surrounding silence.

Beyond his window, two miles away, beneath the now darkened sky, the first firework took flight, exploding into a brilliant display of red, white and blue sparkles. Charles turned in his seat and looked around his room. Nothing. Nobody. He returned to his drawing, looking at it with purposeful intent. And then…he yawned. Fatigue had, again, encroached. Or maybe it had been there the entire time he drew, just beneath the surface, harbored in his subconscious, impairing his ability to remain focused.

He listened for a final minute before conceding to the weight of his tired eyes. He turned off his drawing lamp and crawled into bed as a cluster of distant fireworks kaleidoscoped the night sky. Within seconds Charles sailed away into a deep sleep.

Where am I? Why is it so dark? Am I late?

From inside the closet in Charles' bedroom, came the soft sound of stumbling over a scattering of shoes. Sketch had come to life.

The door creaked open as he entered the room. As his eyes adjusted to the darkness, Sketch made out a shape in the bed.

"Charles?" he whispered, reaching out to tap the figure. But three successive, reverberating booms shifted his attention as he was interrupted by the fireworks seen through the bedside window.

Wearing his superhero suit and mask, he made his way around the bed and stood before the window as an explosion of bright white fireworks fell toward the earth.

"What?! What is this?!" Sketch whispered sharply. "My city! The Finger Gunman is attacking my city!!"

There was no time for introductions. No time for nice-to-meet-you. There was only time to act, to respond, to defend.

Hurrying downstairs, he gathered himself in the yard, looked back at the upstairs window and said, "Sleep well, my friend. All is safe!"

As another round of explosions threatened the city of Lehman, Sketch, in all of his bravery, tore off into a run, heading toward enemy fire, and oblivious to the fact that he had no superpowers.

Chapter 3

FIREWORKS

Pyrotechnician and fireman Andy Snell, a safety-conscious, portly man in charge of Lehman's fireworks show, had cleared the launch site for a barrage of beehive fireworks that would give the effect of a colorful swarm of stars—a guaranteed crowd pleaser that consistently earned a strong round of applause. The launch pad was an outdoor basketball court located in the city park. On one side was a parking lot with a firetruck and a crew of firemen in case things went awry. On the other side was a soccer field with barricades and police tape to keep the public from entering. Beyond that were two additional fields with an adjacent parking lot where the public congregated or watched by their vehicles. Five police officers were on duty, routinely patrolling the low-key crowd. Most of the college summer school students had gone home for the long weekend, which left a crowd comprised mostly of local families.

"Clear!" cautioned Andy, checking that no one was on the court. He then lit the fuse, hustling away before the firework shot into the night. The beehive exploded high in the air with a flash of brilliant white swarming stars darting in all directions, illuminating the crowd before fading into gray streaks, then floating away on the evening breeze.

That's when Andy happened to turn his head to the crowd, and, in that moment of illumination, he believed he saw a figure running across the field directly toward him—a figure being chased by two policemen.

"POLICE!! STOP!!" yelled one officer.

"POLICE!! STOP!!" repeated the other.

Andy stood his ground, placing himself in front of the launching equipment and containers of fireworks. It had been thirty years since he played high school football, and now, here he was, a linebacker on a basketball court, preparing to tackle the moron charging toward him. He craned his neck forward, puzzled by the dark figure closing from forty yards out.

Who the hell is this? The Flash?

"STOP THE ATTACK!!" yelled the moron with a labored breath, clenching his fists as he prepared to take flight like a human missile, straight into the gut of Andy Snell.

Thrusting both arms into the air as he leaned forward, Sketch took off on one leg. For a moment, within his heroic cause, he was airborne, serving justice, saving his city from attack. However, gravity pulled him down to earth, clumsily chest-planting him into the grass.

He had flown, maybe, four feet.

Andy may have been right: he was nothing more than a moronic grown man dressed in a superhero Halloween costume.

The two chasing officers hoisted him up by his arms, and escorted him off the field to a nearby patrol car where two other officers joined, forming a perimeter around Sketch.

"Sir," said the officer, his breathing heavy, "I'm Sergeant Perkins, and…this…is Officer Montague. Is there any…particular reason why you didn't stop running when we ordered you to?"

Perkins, who was just shy of forty-five, kept fit with a regimen of fifty push-ups and squats each morning. He wore round wire-rimmed glasses and a trimmed sandy mustache. He was tall, but not too tall. Montague was half his age and slightly shorter with a proportionally similar build. It was not unusual for the two to be mistaken as father and son.

Sketch couldn't take his eyes off of Andy, who had kept the show on schedule by launching a series of multi-colored Roman candles. "Sergeant Perkins, why are you letting the Finger Gunman fire his artillery?!"

"Artillery?" scoffed Perkins. "Sir, have you been drinking tonight?"

"Hardly." Sketch shifted his eyes to Montague, thinking he might understand his urgency. "Please explain to your partner the situation."

"Sir," said Montague, killing Sketch's hopes, "what's your name?"

"My name? You want to know my name? We don't have time for names, sir! The Finger Gunman must be stopped!!"

Montague leaned in close to Sketch. "Tell me your damn name!"

"My name is Sketch. But, the Finger—"

"Shut up with the Finger Gunman! Look, just answer the question. We know you're sketchy, but what's your name?"

"I told you, it's Sketch."

Andy lit another round of Roman candles that shot from their firing canisters in rapid staccato fashion. *Thud-thud-thud!!*

"Officers, please! Stop him!"

"Listen, buddy," said Perkins, "it's fireworks, not artillery. Are you playing with me? Were you born yesterday?"

"Well, technically, today."

"You know what? I'm taking you in."

"In?"

Perkins took out a pair of handcuffs. "In. To the station. One night, Sketchy. Not going to arrest you, but you need a little time to cool off. Time to think about this little charade of yours. Now, if you'll please turn and put your hands behind your back. It's for your safety and ours. I'll take them off when we get to the station."

Sketch did so with no complaint, his sense of urgency to save the day had mellowed. "Sergeant Perkins, you're serious?"

"Yes, I'm taking you in."

"No, not about that. You said it's fireworks, not artillery. You meant that?"

Perkins chuckled, "Yes. Harmless fireworks. And that man out there is Andy Snell, not the Fingerman or whatever the name was." He opened the back door of the squad car, guiding Sketch in, before he and Montague sat up front. "Let me ask you a question, Sketch," he said, starting the engine. "Does that look like a bunch of horrified people in danger to you?"

Sketch looked out the window at the crowd now joyously applauding. Their happy faces lit up beneath multiple rounds of white chrysanthemum fireworks, whose flares they had tracked rocketing into the sky before exploding in all directions. "No, it doesn't," he said.

Montague made a quarter turn in his seat to look at Sketch. "I've got a question…what the hell are you wearing?"

"No kidding," added Perkins. "Aren't you a little old for…for whatever it is you're doing?"

Too many things were on Sketch's mind, but the predominant thought was: *What went wrong?* He'd been in existence for less than two hours, and he was already detained, being driven to the police station to cool down. He hadn't met his creator, nor could he fly, run super-fast, break free from handcuffs, or distinguish fireworks from artillery. He was a defect. A superhero by intention, but the final product had fallen short, way short. The only thing differentiating him from the common man was his outfit, which was showcasing him as a farce. He looked down at himself and suddenly felt foolish. Without superpowers, he was merely dressed for child's play.

How strange this is, he thought. Down to the tiniest microscopic details, I am here, fully equipped with knowledge and physiology, but my knowledge is just shy of knowing the time and place prior to the instant of coming to life. It's as if all of my learning and development occurred within one billionth of a second between my non-existence and existence. And at some point, within that infinitesimal fraction of time, something fragmented. What was the something that confused fireworks for artillery and resulted in an absence of superpowers? And were there other surprise defects yet undiscovered, such as lying about my name?

A hundred yards into his run from Charles' place, Sketch knew something wasn't right.

He detected nothing more than normalcy. His run had slowed to a jog. His feet felt heavy, and his lungs were tight and unable to expand. He had considered flying, but sensed it would be futile, which was later confirmed when he did try to fly. Prior to entering from behind the crowd of spectators, Sketch had to stop to catch his breath, bending over to brace his hands on his knees, his shoulders rising up and down from the exhaustion of the two-mile run.

How could he possibly face the Finger Gunman in this condition?

So, this is life.

The officers walked Sketch from the police station parking lot into Perkins' office where Montague took off his handcuffs.

"I got it from here, Montague," said Perkins, taking a seat behind his desk. "I'll call you if I need anything."

"Yes, Sarge."

As Sketch sat in a chair across from Perkins, Montague stopped on his way out. "Sketch," he said. "One last question: When we were chasing you, did you try to fly? 'Cause it sure looked that way. But, obviously, you didn't…I mean, it was like you just tripped or something. Like, what the hell were you thinking?"

There was a typewriter on Perkins' desk that suddenly became an open invitation. Sketch stared at it intently—trying to muscle it with his mind—to move it with telekinetic energy. If he could just levitate it over to Montague, then drop it on his foot. But the typewriter didn't budge—confirming he was unable to perform any such influence.

Which raised the question: *Why do I have the knowledge of possessing superpowers, yet I have none?* It was like a new house having been wired for electricity, but nothing worked because the breaker box was malfunctioning. *So, where's my faulty breaker box? Did Charles forget to install one?*

It didn't add up. Sketch knew he was a superhero, but he couldn't summon his powers into action. Perhaps he did have them, but they were dormant, hibernating, or tucked away incubating in the recesses of his development.

"Sketch," said Perkins, his voice now friendlier than the authoritative tone used after the foot chase, "will you please take off that mask?"

Sketch removed it without protest, his sweaty brown hair matted to his forehead. Wiping it to the side, his dark brown eyes were more exposed; they had more presence, more pop. His face was no longer covert, but rather handsome and neighborly, despite the blades of grass stuck to his neck. He looked like someone who Perkins felt wasn't a threat—a welcomed stranger.

"So, Sketch…just who are you?"

"My name is David Skechenski."

"I see…Skechenski explains Sketch."

"Yes, sir. Just a nickname. I'm in Lehman, visiting a friend."

"So, does your nickname mean that you're an artist?"

"An ink artist, I guess you could say."

"Well, David, were you really trying to put an end to tonight's fireworks? In all my years, I've never seen anything like this. Especially, not dressed the way you are."

"Sir, it's a complicated story to even begin to explain. It was a big misunderstanding on my part, but luckily no one was harmed. Nor did I ever have any intentions to harm anyone."

"But you're dressed like some kind of superhero. What's with that?"

Sketch smiled as he told Perkins in cloaked honesty, "Oh, trust me, Sergeant. I'm hardly a superhero. Well, I am, but I'm not. The only power I have is the ability to screw things up. And how I ended up wearing this…like I said…it's complicated."

"Fair enough. I won't press you for an answer. But what I will do is let you call someone to pick you up. It's that or stay the night here in jail. But, remember, you're not being arrested." Perkins picked up the telephone receiver, prepared to dial. "You have someone you want me to call?"

"Yes, but I don't know his number. Do you have a phone book?"

Perkins took one out from a desk drawer. "I'll look him up. What's his name?"

"Charles Sweeney."

Perkins ran his finger down the page, then found Charles' number. "Can't say I know him, but he's responsible?"

"Yes, sir."

"For your sake, I hope he's awake." Perkins paused before dialing, then asked, "Before I call, I'm curious…who's the Fingerman?"

"It's the Finger Gunman, and he's trouble."

"What's with the nicknames tonight? What's his real name?"

"I'm not sure. I just know he needs to be stopped."

"From doing what?"

Sketch glanced around the office, realizing what he was about to say was going to sound ludicrous. "He must be stopped from becoming a global threat."

"Can you be more specific?"

"Unfortunately, no. I just know he has the potential to mastermind menacing evil."

"Globally, right?"

"Yes, sir."

"And we're talking about one person?"

"Yes, sir."

Perkins cracked a smile, pulling the phone toward him. "Tell ya what, David…you've had a long day. Let's call your friend."

He dialed Charles' number, letting it ring several times until a groggy voice answered.

"Hello?"

"Hello, is this Charles Sweeney?"

"Yes, it is. Who's this?"

"Charles, this is Sergeant Perkins with the Lehman Police Department. I have a man here at the station who needs to be picked up. He says he knows you. His name is David."

"I know a David Prescott. Is it him?"

"No, sir, not Prescott. It's David—" Perkins cupped his hand over the receiver, whispering to Sketch, "Remind me of your last name?"

There was a slight pause as Sketch jogged his memory, internally reminding himself how to pronounce it. "Skechenski."

"Skechenski," Perkins told Charles.

"Um, I don't know anyone by that name."

"Are you sure?"

"Positive."

"Well, he's dressed kinda odd."

"Odd?"

"Yeah, like in a red outfit, with silver boots, and wears a mask."

Charles stood up from the sofa where he had answered the phone and carried it as far as it would go to his bedroom doorway. He turned on the wall light switch and looked at his drawing a few feet away.

"Sergeant Perkins…would you say he looks like a superhero?"

Perkins chuckled as Sketch looked on, anticipating each exchange in the dialogue. "Yes, exactly. And there's a big black drop or something on his chest and—"

"Officer," Charles interrupted. "May I please speak to him?"

"Of course." Perkins handed Sketch the receiver, stretching the cord across the desk. "He wants to talk to you."

For the first time in his life, Sketch put a phone receiver to his ear and said, "Hello?"

Charles spoke slowly with an inflection of uncertainty, "Ske-e-tch?"

"Hi, Charles!"

"Holy…shit…I'll be right there."

Chapter 4
THE STATION

Charles parked his car at the Lehman Police Station, then took a couple of deep breaths before going inside to meet Sketch for the first time. *Well, this is going to be weird.*

Entering the station, he was greeted by a middle-aged woman with strawberry-blonde hair piled like cotton candy. She stood behind a chest-high countertop, stapling papers. "May I help you, sir?" Her tone was nondescript.

"I'm here to see Sergeant Perkins."

"Is he expecting you?"

"Yes, ma'am."

"Your name?"

"Charles Sweeney."

She told him to wait, then passed through a half-door with access to the area where Charles stood. There, she unlocked a steel door that shut loudly behind her, then walked down a long hallway before entering a room. Minutes later, she returned.

"Follow me, please. Sergeant Perkins will see you now."

Sergeant Perkins was straight ahead, standing behind his desk when Charles walked in. As they shook hands, Charles' peripheral vision caught a figure in a chair to his right.

"Please," said Perkins, "have a seat next to David."

Charles turned, having no idea what to expect or what to say.

"Hey, buddy!" said Sketch, smiling and extending his arm for a hand slap.

Charles gave him a quasi-hand slap.

"Uh, hey...David."

"So, Charles...you're younger than I expected." said Perkins. "Are you attending the university?"

"Yes, sir."

"I trust you're responsible enough to drive him home?"

"Yes, but what did he do?"

"I'm going to spare you the details—I'm sure Sketch will fill you in on them. But suffice it to say, he kinda lost his mind tonight. He thought he was doing everyone a favor by saving our city from enemy fire."

Charles squinted his eyes ever so slightly at Sketch. *You told Perkins your name?* "Enemy fire?" he asked.

"He says he thought the fireworks were artillery."

Oh, my god. What have I created?

"Anyway," continued Perkins, "there was no harm done, and he wasn't carrying any weapons. Just dressed funny."

"Charles," said Sketch, "I told him...this outfit...it's complicated."

"Oh, yes," agreed Charles, "very complicated."

Perkins stood up behind his desk. "Gentlemen, I'd love to learn more about Sketch the superhero who never was, but I've had a long day and I think we should all just go home and get some sleep."

Sketch rose from his seat and shook Perkins' hand. "I promise this won't happen again, sir. Next time, I *will* be able to fly."

"Oh, Sketch," laughed the sergeant, "of course you'll be flying. I mean, isn't that every man's dream?"

Charles was becoming uneasy with the conversation, wondering if Sketch didn't come equipped with a common-sense filter. Did information—specifically, classified—flow out of him without any second thoughts of consequence? In a moment of impromptu, would he mention the magic ink? Or had he already done so? "Sergeant, thank you for your time, and I promise we're going straight to my house."

The three of them walked down the hallway, through the noisy steel door, and into the lobby, where Montague appeared from out of a restroom.

"Sketch!" smiled Montague. "Guess you got your walking papers!"

"Yes, sir."

"Well, I tell ya what..." Montague pointed to a cork bulletin board in the lobby that had thumbtacked photos of wanted criminals at-large. "I certainly hope you don't end up in the ranks of these guys. All of them are bad news. Get your head straight. And, damn it, learn to dress normal."

"You do that, Sketch," added Perkins. "Now, go get out of that silly costume."

Exiting the building, Charles and Sketch walked through the parking lot as firecrackers and bottle rockets could be heard in nearby neighborhoods. The loud booms of the city's fireworks were no more, as the traffic volume increased from the exodus of spectators.

Charles drove for two blocks, then made two turns before parking on a dimly-lit street of moderately sized homes with tidy front yards. Their windows rolled down, they could smell the lingering fragrance of Saturday: the aroma of fresh-cut lawns from the motoring chorus of afternoon push mowers.

"Sketch, before we head home, I need to understand something, like...enemy fire?"

Sketch fiddled with his mask he held in his lap. "I know. I screwed up."

"Screwed up? You didn't screw up. You got lucky. You almost got yourself arrested. Now, that would've been screwing up."

"I know. I'm sorry."

"And you're David...Skeski?"

"Skechenski. Ske-chen-ski."

"Is that your real name?"

"Nope. Made it up. Brilliant, huh?"

Charles closed his eyes, briefly shaking his head in an effort to make sure he wasn't part of some strange endless dream that had begun in Cairo. "Sketch...how is any of this possible?"

"Because I mistook the fireworks for artillery?"

"No, not that. I mean, you…how are you possible?"

"Honestly, I don't know."

"You know nothing?"

"All I know is I appeared in your room. Before that, I have no memory. Nor should I, because I didn't exist. I simply never was."

Far down the street the dark figures of teenagers waving sparklers could be seen dashing back and forth as a string of lit firecrackers erratically danced on the pavement.

"But you obviously know about the magic ink, right?"

"Yes, I do. And the only reason I'm in this car telling you this is because you created me."

"You are an impossible possibility."

Sketch laughed. "Yeah, I guess you could say that."

The group of teenagers started to thin as the last of the fireworks had been lit. The celebration of July 4th was beginning to quiet.

"So, Charles…what's wrong with me?"

"What do you mean?"

"You know…I'm not quite right. I thought fireworks were enemy fire, and I can hardly run a city block without having to stop to catch my breath. And I flew just a few feet, if it could even be called flying. What happened? I'm human, but not superhuman."

"You can't fly? I don't get it. I willed that into your drawing."

"I was like a wingless bird out there. Officer Montague said it looked like I tripped or something. So, is this to be my existence? I'm feeling more and more foolish in this costume."

Perplexed, Charles looked straight ahead at the empty street. Though Sketch's appearance was exactly as he had drawn him, Sketch was nothing more than an ordinary man. Charles had proven his ability to will the butterflies to life when he drew them for Heba in Egypt, but there was a problem when he drew Sketch: he had come to life, but he wasn't fully developed.

"So, what did happen to you?" asked Charles. "I did everything I was supposed to have done, specifically willing you to be a superhero, but you're no different than me."

"What powers did you give me?"

"I willed you the ability to fly, run super-fast, and possess super human strength."

"So, basically, you willed me to be Superman. Well, that's original."

"Yes, I did. I mean, why not? Unlike you, though, Superman is fiction. So, you'd really be the first of your kind."

"But nothing happened," said Sketch. "So, the question remains: What went wrong? I have no powers, but I'm fully aware of the Finger Gunman."

"Well, that's good. At least that worked."

"Yes, it did work. However, I think you should know that my knowledge of the Finger Gunman goes beyond what you know of him."

"What do you mean?"

"Charles, I possess knowledge of him that confirms your suspicion that the Finger Gunman is evil. What I know is the prime motivator to find and eliminate him. I know he aspires to be a global threat. Though it's true I am incomplete with no superpowers, I have a unique innate ability that allows me to detect the existence of immortal supervillains who possess supernatural powers. I cannot locate them, but I do know they exist."

"How many are there?"

"One. The Finger Gunman."

"What are his powers?"

"That's what is so interesting. He has none, and yet I can detect him. Perhaps he used to have powers, but something happened, and I'm not sure what. But the fact that you willed an urgency of the Finger Gunman's existence into my drawing, concerns me. May I ask, what was it that he said to you?"

"He mentioned unleashing a fury upon everything he detested, and said the world would never have seen such a thing, whatever that means."

"I'm not sure what he's up to, but he must be stopped."

"If you are aware of his existence, might he be aware of yours?"

"No. Supervillains are not given that privilege by the ink."

Charles sat quietly as he recalled drawing Sketch, from start to finish. He had set out his inks, pens, colored pencils, and sketch book, while considering different superhero outfits and various super powers. He could hear the distant BOOM of fireworks through his bedroom window. Soon his focus narrowed, and the world did begin to disappear as he slipped into a prioritized and near-hypnotic state of creativity. How he would draw Sketch had become quite evident. But in the final moments before his pen touched the paper, the reason for Sketch's ordinary outcome became clear.

Urgently fumbling for his keys, Charles found them wedged in his seat, started the car, and pulled away from the curb.

"You okay?" asked Sketch.

"I gotta get back to your drawing, and make things right."

"And make what right?"

"Why you're the way you are. Sketch, you didn't screw up. I did. Right before I drew you…I fell asleep."

After passing through a couple of traffic lights, Charles turned onto a country road that would take them to his garage apartment. Overhead, a full moon hung in the sky like a giant eye watching the world below. Sketch looked up at the moon and wondered out loud, "Do you think I'll ever be able to fly?"

"I certainly hope so, because if the Finger Gunman is as evil as you say, then it's going to take a fully-equipped superhero to defeat him."

Both sides of the road were lined with miles of cornfields, their stalks basking in the moonlight, seemingly inching taller toward the stars.

"Charles," said Sketch, watching the moonlit fields pass by, "how did you come to possess the magic ink?"

"Well, I guess you could say it all began a week ago when a young girl dropped a glass lantern in Cairo, Egypt…"

PART II

Chapter I
THE MARKET

One Week Earlier

It had been more years than she could remember until she finally discovered Charles. There had been others who came close, but no one like him. And it wasn't that he was being sought after, it was never like that. To her it was kismet. Not to say that other chance encounters weren't out there, not by any means. But Heba knew she had to have hope that one day his path would serendipitously cross with hers.

It was the end of June. She was a street peddler in Cairo, Egypt, appearing to be in her 50s, and dressed in a traditional black abaya, draping her from neck to toe. A tan hijab framed her round, likable face as she sat on a wooden stool behind a small fold-out table. She was a smiley person. Even her voice seemed to smile, warm and welcoming. A canvas awning provided shade while she watched shoppers milling about Cairo's Khan el-Khalili open-air market. It was first created in the 12th century, and was a labyrinth of streets, alleys, and meandering, narrow cobblestone walkways, one of which she was on. The market, encased by the rising towers of centuries-old mosques and historic Islamic sandstone architecture, was abundant with spices, perfumes, sparkling trinkets, swathes of exotic fabrics, and everything else that made up the cornucopia of middle eastern wares. Lingering on the summer breeze were incense and the aromas of traditional Egyptian cuisine wafting from the small booths and local cafes.

She sold handwoven baskets that were indiscriminately stacked around her tented area that backed up to the stone wall of a limestone two-story building. Heba's soft voice had a way of authenticating that her baskets were handcrafted and not from an outside source.

As the sun hit its apex, the shopping traffic thinned—always a welcome reprieve. A British couple stopped by to purchase some small baskets, doing so in fleeting fashion—in and out, no questions asked. Others inspected her baskets as if undergoing an audit. Gauging a basket's weight, weave tightness, symmetry, functionality, and even smell. And then came the price haggling, the age-old art of working a deal, from both sides. Seller starts high, buyer starts low, and somewhere in between the two compromise and part ways without injury. Like a strategic tennis match, ending with a handshake across the net.

Heba retrieved a sack from beneath her table and removed a small container of hummus and some pita bread which she ate with a cup of tea. The market was pleasant during these downtimes. But the calm broke not long after it started.

The shatter of glass came from down the walkway. Heba stood up and saw Charles kneeling on one knee, comforting a crying child who had dropped a glass lantern. The young man, in his early 20s, kept eye level with the young American girl, assuring her everything was fine. "Hey, it's ok, everybody breaks things. Even I do."

The girl sniffled and asked, "You break things, too?"

"Well, sure," he said, smiling. "Even me. Accidents happen."

"But it was my mom's."

Charles looked around. "Where is your mom?"

The girl shrugged her shoulders. "I don't know. She told me to hold the glass thing. She was with some man."

"Is your dad here?"

The girl shook her head. "He's gone."

Charles knew her answer could have meant a number of things, and there was no need to ask. "Look," he said, pointing, "there's a man coming with a broom. He'll get this cleaned up."

"I don't like the man," she said.

"It's okay. He's just here to clean the broken glass."

"Not him. The man with my mom."

"What do you mean?"

"She met him yesterday. They drank last night, and—"

"Angie!" her mother hollered from down the walkway, moving with short, quick forceful strides. She saw the broken lantern as the man continued sweeping. "What did you do this time?!"

"It was an accident," the girl said, sheepishly.

A mid-30s Frenchman trailed behind the woman. Wearing sunglasses, his black hair was greasy slick and combed straight back, seemingly manicured into perfectly neat rows. He wore three gold chains that hung within a partially unbuttoned red satin shirt tucked into tight white slacks, and wore shiny black shoes. Coming up next to her he said, "You're right, baby. It's always something."

"She didn't mean to drop it," said Charles. "She feels bad that it happened."

"And who are you?" said the mother, leaning forward, her demeanor wrought with tension.

"I'm Charles."

"Well, Charles, she should feel bad. It's inexcusable. She can't be trusted."

Yanking her arm, the mother whisked her away, her little strides trying to keep pace with her mother's. The man remained, tilting his sunglasses at Charles. "Next time, mind your own business."

"Sir?"

"You heard me."

"I was only trying to help."

"Perhaps you didn't hear me."

"Sir, I—"

The man moved towards Charles. "Dammit, boy!" he said, whispering sternly with rank breath. "Stay out of it!" Pointing in the direction the mother and daughter had left, he added, "I'm buying time with those two. Once I get what I need, I'm gone. But the last thing I need is some punk like you stepping in my business."

"I'm sorry I've upset you."

"Sorry? I don't need an apology. Silence. There should only be silence."

Charles was ten years the man's junior, and his aggressive behavior made him feel diminutive, incapable of standing up for himself. Or maybe he was capable, but didn't want to test a dangerous situation.

Then again, maybe Charles didn't want to walk away with an unanswered question, so he asked, "What is it you need?"

The man rocked his head side to side. "What I need is for you to understand that I will one day unleash a fury upon everything I detest. But since I'm confident you can't wrap your brain around that, then I am certainly wasting my time talking to you."

"A fury?"

"Like nothing the world has ever seen before."

"Just who are you?"

The man sighed agitatedly, then made a gun out of his index finger and thumb, aiming it at Charles. Winking, he fired one shot. "I am the Finger Gunman," he said, then walked away.

Heba had watched the entire scene, up to the final moment when Charles had escaped injury or death of the finger bullet. And what a loss it would have been, she thought, had the gun been real, had the bullet torn through his heart and dropped his body with a fatal thud. Why does a young man doing the right thing have to walk away feeling defeated? Why does the young girl have to suffer with the constant weight of her mother's persistent condemnation? Why do good deeds of good people have to go unappreciated? Why must these things be? Answers to these questions had often riddled her in the broad spectrum of everyday life. Not just this little girl, but so many others trapped in a world where there seemed no escape from their intolerant mothers. And boys, no different with their ruling fathers. Time and time again, over the years, she had witnessed the public displays of unfair parenting. And each time, even though on a small scale, they reaffirmed one reality: that evil was everywhere.

Despite all the injustices she had witnessed during her life, from blatant public humiliation to physical torture, evil was evil, and one of the bigger challenges of life was doing one's best to minimize or avoid it. But that is easier said than done. If evil wasn't lurking in the shadows then, like the scene with the little girl, it could be in your face in broad daylight. Though the mother's harsh impatience with her daughter was hardly high on the list of serious injustices that have plagued humanity, it was enough to remind her that evil needed to be avenged.

And it was that single thought that stirred Heba's curiosity: Was it possible what she just witnessed with the little girl was, somehow, a test? Had the mother and the man been planted in the sequence of events by some unknown to trigger an unforeseen response? Maybe their ugliness was something far greater and more beautiful than anyone could have imagined. And maybe this street peddler was now the beginning of that unforeseen response.

For that matter, she thought, maybe evil, regardless of its intensity or wherever it reared its ugly head, was designed to bring out the good—the rescuers and protectors; an opposition, to reduce the tension and restore the calm. And that was exactly what she saw in the young man—a compassionate soul with only good intent. There was something about him, an aura of sorts, that told her he was the one. He would be offered the ink.

But there was something about the Frenchman that she couldn't pinpoint. She had stared at him, drawn in by his French accent, contemplating the possibility that, as strange as it seemed, she recognized him. But she had never seen him before, of this she was certain. Still, what was it that seemed familiar? The last time she had been to France was to talk to Genevieve, to offer her the ink, which she accepted. But it was also the last time Heba would ever hear from her.

The Frenchman…just who was he?

Charles stood before Heba, turning a small basket in his hands. "These are nice," he said, "nicer than most around here."

"Thank you. I have been making them for a long time."

He looked back to where he encountered the girl. "Did you see that? I thought I was helping her."

"You were. I saw it all."

"But her mother…what was with her? And that man. He told me he was the Finger Gunman. What's that all about?"

"I am not sure. I have never heard of anyone referred to by that name. He concerns me, though, but I do not know why. For some reason I am reminded of Shakespeare when he wrote 'All the World Is a Stage'".

"You know Shakespeare?"

"You seem surprised."

"I'm sorry…I just…"

"It is okay. I understand. I sell baskets on the street in Cairo, Egypt. What could I possibly know about Shakespeare, right?"

"It was a foolish comment, I'm sorry. Please don't take it as judgment. I was surprised, that's all."

Heba smiled. "Hardly an issue my friend. I will not hold it against you, unless you do not buy that basket."

The crowd was beginning to pick up, the familiar sound of haggling was slowly returning. An old dog rose up from beneath the table next to Heba. She fed it a cracker, then patted its head.

"This is Khaldun. He is as loyal a dog as I could ever ask for."

"Dogs are the best. And you are?"

"Heba." She extended her arm and shook his hand.

"I'm Charles…Charles Sweeney. It's nice to meet you."

"So, Charles Sweeney, what brings you to Egypt? I am assuming you are a long way from home."

"Yes, ma'am," he said, nodding. "I go to a university in America and major in art. My class is here on an international art history studies trip."

Heba's eyebrows lifted. *What kind of art? Surrealism? Abstract? Humans…could he draw humans?* "Sounds exciting. Of course, there is plenty of history here."

"The Egyptian Museum is fascinating, not just for its collection, but how intact the art is. Drawings on papyrus paper over two thousand years old. It's crazy."

Khaldun pawed at Heba's abaya, and in return she gave him another cracker. "Watch out, Charles," she said, "street beggars come in many forms."

"How old is he?"

"Old. As old as I am."

"I won't ask."

"Ah, a true gentleman!"

There had been a light breeze that set off a pleasant sound of nearby wind chimes. Charles noticed a red book on her table hand-titled in different languages: *And You Are From?*

"A guest book?" he asked.

"Yes, feel free. Signatures from around the world."

"I'll only sign if I buy," he said, selecting a small lidded, light brown basket. "I'll take this one." Charles paid her above price, insisting she keep the change.

And those were the small cues that she picked up on. Gracious and courteous with not a hint of being aloof, and a kind demeanor sincere to the bone. Of course, they were qualities that many possessed, but a necessary foundation for someone to receive her gift—something that few in the entire history of civilization had ever received. With each passing minute of their conversation, she felt more and more confident that Charles might meet her qualifications. But one quality that held more importance than any other came without asking. Charles opened the book to the last person's entry, which was at the bottom of a left side page, allowing him to use the entire right page. "Do you mind if I sketch something?"

"Of course not," she said, handing him a pen. "Take your time."

As he fluttered the pen above the page, she studied him: athletic, six feet tall, with brown hair and brown, engaging eyes that seemed to listen all on their own.

A feeling ran through him—an unexpected spark of inspiration, triggered by the encounter with the young girl and her mother.

Replaying the mother's frustration with her daughter, he sketched a girl standing on the palm of a giant hand. At her feet, and scribed in the palm, he wrote, "ATWAS".

"I know no one's going to understand the meaning of this," he said, turning the guest book to Heba.

"This is the girl from earlier, is it not?"

"Yes, it is," he said, handing back her pen.

"And A-T-W-A-S?"

Charles smiled. "All the world's a stage."

Heba gave an approving nod and said, "Clever!"

"I see the hand as a metaphor of protection that the young girl is going to need in order to ward off the hardships delivered by her mother, as well as that other creep, if he stays with her. It also represents the earth, our stage, where all of our drama is played out, by us who are merely players."

"And all of this came to you as you sketched?"

"What can I say?" he said, shrugging his shoulders. "Shakespeare inspires."

Yes, he does, she thought, and so do you. You have unexpectedly appeared with no warning whatsoever, and you have no idea the impression you are currently making on me. Nor do you know—nor would I expect you to know—that I have a history that spans centuries, having circled the globe several times. I've lived through horrific wars, worldwide sickness, brilliant inventions, great philosophers, mathematicians, and Michelangelo. I exist because of someone's imagination many, many years ago. Except for the one thing that can end my life, I am eternal. And that, my friend explains why I am familiar with the world being a stage. It is not because I plucked a book from a library shelf. But rather, in 1599 when Shakespeare wrote *As You Like It* in London, I was in the city at the same time, and ended up watching the play in the Globe Theater. I was there, and had the privilege to shake his hand afterward. I managed to hold it for just a little longer than normal as I praised his work. But I was only buying time. I was looking into his eyes, beyond them and into his creative being. And what I saw was, indeed, an inspirational creative genius.

It was like his eyes had deep wells of creativity—ocular portals leading directly into his personality. Much like you, but there was one exception: he could not draw, but you can.

Heba was closing in on Charles, sizing him up for selection. So much of her decision making was based on gut and pure intuition. If he crossed the lines or misled her, it was only he who would suffer the consequences, while her toll would be the fallout of disappointment.

Looking at his drawing in the guest book, it was becoming quite evident that Charles had the gift. In such a short amount of time, he had not only captured a close resemblance of the girl, but had done so with a minimal amount of pen strokes that had effortlessly danced around the page, composing without hesitation. The drawing offered the girl hope, and did so from a compassionate heart. In addition to being a highly talented artist, it was crucial that he execute his drawings with good intent.

"Are your classmates out here? Are you alone?" she asked, calculating if she had enough time to continue talking.

"We're on a two-hour break, then we head back to the museum. I'm here alone."

Heba bent down to separate a few extra baskets piled at the rear of her booth. Behind them, there was a burlap sack secured at the neck with twine. She untied it then reached in and pulled out a second smaller burlap sack and untied it. From that second sack she pulled out an old wooden black box, about four inches square with a small brass latch.

"Charles, may I ask you a personal question?"

"Of course."

"Do you believe in magic?"

"Like does it really exist? Or do you mean magician magic, like illusions?"

"I mean real magic."

"Honestly, I'm not sure I've ever seen real magic. Though I once went running in the woods and a deer came up from nowhere and we kept stride for stride for nearly a quarter mile. He was close enough to touch. All I could think was what is this? What is happening? It might have been pure coincidence, but I say it was more of a magical coincidence."

"Yes," said Heba, tightly clutching the box. "Coincidences can often seem more than they really are, especially when we cannot explain them. But, Charles, the magic I am talking about can be explained, to an extent. And, trust me, it is not trickery; it is quite real."

Charles noticed her hands were positioned firmly around the box. "I'm assuming, there's something to do with magic inside that?"

"Very much so, yes. But you must understand something…" Her expression shifted from friendly and casual to serious, her eyes pinpointing on his. "Inside this box is something that very few people have any knowledge of, let alone have ever seen. It is, without question, magical. And it is also something that must be understood. By that I mean, it can read you. It knows good intent. If your intentions sway even the slightest, the magic will cease to exist."

"I don't know what to say. I mean, whatever is in there, why me?"

"Because my instincts and observations have told me that you are the recipient. As they say, it is a gut call. This is no scam or hoax. This is not some sleight of hand magic trick. You must believe me. This is real."

Heba looked down at the box, then lifted her eyes back at him. "Charles, are you prepared to experience the supernatural? How would you like to create a superhero?"

Chapter 2
BUTTERFLIES

Heba took out from under her table two large canvas sheets that she used to cover her baskets whenever she went on break. There was really nothing more required than that. In all her years at the market, not once had a single basket ever been stolen.

"What do you mean," said Charles, "create a superhero?"

"I will explain everything soon. But first, come this way." Carrying the box, Heba guided Charles away from her booth and down the cobblestone walkway, as Khaldun walked alongside her. After a couple of turns, they ended up in a dead-end alley leading to a wooden door. From a side pocket, she took out a key and unlocked it.

"It is ok. You are safe," she said, turning on the living room light. "This is my apartment. Trust me, this is not a trap."

The walls were thumbtacked with geographical maps of the world, from continents to small towns. Some maps had handwritten notes on them; others included arrows denoting travel routes.

Within the room was a collection of historical artifacts or souvenirs—a small replica of the Statue of Liberty, an old rusty trowel with a splintered handle, a buckshot rifle, Hawaiian leis, a framed black and white photo of two fighting sumo wrestlers, a jar of foreign coins, crudely shaped pottery bowls, a pair of moccasins and buffalo horns bound together by leather straps, and a medieval mead stein.

Original artwork was displayed around the room, some on easels, others on the floor leaning against a wall. Surrealism, abstract, charcoal and graphite nudes, quick sketches, pen and ink, cartoons, acrylic, oil, watercolor, etchings, sandstone, and, of course, Egyptian drawings on papyrus paper.

"You live in a museum," said Charles, touching a display of peacock feathers protruding from a large floor vase.

"You could say that," smiled Heba. "I am a collector."

"These maps, are they from your travels?"

"Yes, they are, but that is a story for another time."

She sat down on a worn, green corduroy sofa, inviting Charles to take a seat across from her on a wicker chair. Khaldun circled a few times before lying next to her feet. Between them was an old wooden coffee table inlaid with a thick sheet of tin upon which was printed: "Kathmandu." Heba set aside a stack of manuscripts that had been written in old style calligraphy, then set down the wooden box. She leaned over to an end table and grabbed a black sketch book, setting it next to the box which she unlatched. Taking out a red fountain pen, she slid it over to Charles along with the sketch book.

"Charles, you are about to experience what should be impossible, if not inexplicable. I want you to open the book to any page and draw a butterfly. It need not be perfect, just a sketch. However, I have only one request: as you draw, it is critical you do so with the intent to give the butterfly life. But, understand, it must be able to fly."

"Repeat that," said Charles, understandably puzzled.

"Which part?"

"All of it. Like from the beginning, when you asked me outside if I believed in magic."

"I know this must sound ridiculous. Who would not question my request? But I am asking you to bear with me for just a few more minutes. It will be worth your time."

"You want my drawing to fly? Like, literally fly?"

"I want you to *will* it into the air, and I want you to trust me. There is already some ink in the pen. Please, gather yourself, then draw."

"But—"

Heba rested her hand on his forearm. "Charles, I know none of this makes any sense to you, and that I must be playing a game. But that is not so. Please, draw a butterfly and you shall see."

"But what about a superhero? You asked if I wanted to create one."

"That will be later. And that cannot be rushed. Charles, please…a butterfly."

"You promise this isn't a trap?"

"I promise."

The room fell silent as he stared at the page. *What was it about Heba? Her tone, the gravity in her request. There was so much to grasp: the mystery of her, the objects in the room, the artwork. What are the odds that this butterfly will actually fly? Is there a bigger picture here?*

He sketched two symmetrical wings protruding from a narrow thorax and an abdomen with two antennae. "Fly!" he commanded. "I say, fly!" The drawing remained nothing more than a drawing.

"Nothing happened. It's not—"

Then…noiseless, erratic, and primarily blue. The sketched butterfly hadn't moved, but the one in the room, the one making intermittent stops, sure looked like the one in the drawing.

"What's that?" said Charles, puzzled.

The butterfly took off from the top of a painting's frame, then landed next to the butterfly sketch.

"That, my friend, is your drawing."

"I don't understand. My drawing is still here."

"Correct. Your drawing is still there. It has not moved. But what did move was its energy. It is called imaginative energy. May I ask if you willed it to be blue?"

"Yes, I did."

Heba rolled back into the sofa, applauding his performance. "Perfect, Charles!! Perfect!!"

The butterfly took off, seemingly exploring the objects of the room, taking short flights here and there in repeated fashion.

"Ma'am, this is a lot to take in, let alone believe. And you're saying this butterfly happened because of this ink? How do I know you didn't just free it from your pocket or somewhere?"

"I understand, you are skeptical."

"Of course I'm skeptical. I'll give you credit though. It's a neat trick."

Heba figured it would come to this, that the only way to get him to believe her would be by destroying the butterfly. There was no other option. She stood up, then cautiously moved toward the butterfly that had landed on top of a lampshade. With her thumb and forefinger extended with a slight separation, she slowly reached out, closing in on the backside of its motionless wings. In one quick motion her fingers pinched the wings, successfully capturing it. Heba left the room momentarily to return with the butterfly securely contained in a lidded glass jar. She also carried a pair of scissors.

"Ok," she said, setting the jar next to Charles. "I understand you did not witness its instantaneous appearance out of thin air. But perhaps I can make you a believer by having you witness it vanishing *into* thin air."

"Oh, this should be good," scoffed Charles.

"Now bear with me, and understand that what you are about to do will cause no harm, for the butterfly within this jar is not real as you might think it to be. It has the physiological characteristics of a real butterfly, but with one distinct difference: it is supernatural. It is a product of your willing it to exist."

Heba set the pair of scissors on the coffee table, then nudged them to Charles.

"I want you to cut your sketch paper right up to your drawing, then stop."

Charles followed her instructions as Heba moved the jar close to the sketch, but just off the paper.

"I am going to count to three," she said. "Then I will say cut. At that moment, I want your eyes on the butterfly as you cut. That is all you have to do."

Charles nodded. "I'm ready."

"Ok...one...two...three...cut."

The scissors snapped, and the butterfly vanished, leaving behind no trace of its existence. Its disappearance was practically too fast to observe.

"It's not possible!" said Charles, stunned. "Where'd it go?"

"It went nowhere. It merely ceased to exist."

"How is this possible?"

"That is a difficult question to answer. It is all in the ink. So, do you now believe me?"

"I don't know what to say. It happened so fast. It's all so strange: the little girl and her mother, meeting you selling baskets, then being led back into this small apartment where I've been told to draw a butterfly to prove I am its creator...and destroyer. It's like I'm in the middle of a puzzle, but I'm not quite sure how the pieces fit together."

"Charles, I need you to turn to a new page and draw the jar, just sketch it. Then draw a butterfly inside it. As you make the final stroke of the pen, watch the jar. I know you are confused. I know this seems impossible. But, please, do as I say. And remember: draw with the intent for it to come to life."

She couldn't afford to lose him. She feared that nonsense was building in his mind. That the ink was nothing more than a well-crafted illusion. That there was some sleight of hand involved. But she knew whomever she found, it wouldn't be easy convincing him or her of the power of the ink. Of course it was normal to have doubts. So, she watched him draw the jar, then the butterfly within it.

He stopped as she had requested, just shy of completing the final wing, pausing momentarily to set his eyes on the empty jar that stood next to his sketch. For whatever it's worth, he thought, then with one final quarter inch line of ink, he finished the butterfly.

It was a defining moment that she would never forget. With his mouth agape, and his eyes wide open, the pen fell out of his hand. His eyes grew large. And the loss for words caught in the icy cracks of a cerebral freeze. All except for one small opening of pronunciation as he grabbed the jar and took off the lid, setting the butterfly free.

Charles lifted his head to Heba and said, "Imaginative energy… it's real!!"

During its first flight of discovery, the butterfly made its way around the room, as curious as its predecessor, with brief landings on Heba and Charles' shoulders, as if acknowledging them for its existence.

"Born from ink," said Heba, "and no cocoon, it is incredible, is it not?"

Charles was tracking the butterfly's every movement, in awe of its physiological perfection. "Yes, it is, though incredible seems like an understatement."

"You gave it life, Charles. You willed it into this world."

"And let me guess…you now want me to cut this butterfly sketch in half and basically kill it?"

"No," smiled Heba. "Let us let this one go."

"Go where? It's not real. Or is it? I'm confused."

"I understand your confusion, but there is much to tell you about the ink. And it is important you understand everything, meaning its origins and limits."

"Limits?'"

"There is only so much that you can draw to life. One animal and one human."

"Wait a sec'. I can create a human? So, this is where the superhero comes in, right?"

Khaldun had fallen asleep beside Heba's feet, his legs twitching from a dream. The butterfly landed on the dog's nose, but he remained unbothered.

"Yes," she said. "A superhuman. Someone with abilities far greater than we know. Someone to fight evil."

"You can't be serious. Like Superman or Flash?"

"In a way, yes, except they are fiction."

"You're serious, aren't you?"

"Completely."

"So, how am I supposed to control a superhuman? Let alone, how does someone become superhuman?"

"There is so much to explain to you. So much personal experience to share. When do you need to return to your class?"

"About an hour." Charles stood up and began walking around the room, taking a closer look at the paintings and objects. "Earlier I asked if all this was from your travels, and you said yes, but that it was a story for another time. Well, I think we've reached 'another time'."

"I cannot disagree with you." She got up and walked over to Charles, who was looking at a small sandstone sculpture of a bird. "That is a falcon," she said. "One of the most prized possessions in this apartment."

"Why's that?"

"Partly because of its age."

"How old?"

Heba picked up the sculpture, securing it in two hands.

"As old as I."

"And you are?"

"So, you do want to know."

"Well, I am curious."

"Charles, I have no proof of my age. There are no documents, no birth certificate, no letters of correspondence with anyone to indicate how far back my life goes, or the eras I have lived through. No proof of meeting Shakespeare. No proof of experiencing the advent of electricity. No proof of walking under a full moon in the 1700s along the Baltic Sea coastline, in what used to be called East Prussia. And no proof of tending to the ill during the pandemic of Europe's bubonic plague. The only proof of my history is the collected objects in this room, all of which anyone could acquire. There is no proof of my childhood, and certainly not of my birth. After all, I was never born. What you see in this room, I collected everything from my travels. That table—I had it made to fit the sign that came from a market in Kathmandu. I had stayed in the city for a couple days before trekking with a sherpa guide to the base of Mt. Everest. That was in the mid-

1800s. And I know this is very difficult for you to believe, especially when I cannot provide any proof of my life." Heba set the falcon sculpture on the table, then continued. "But, Charles, what I can do is prove that I am supernatural. I want you to understand who I am. Please, wait here."

She left the room, soon returning with two band-aids, then entered the adjoining kitchen, fingering through a utility drawer of miscellaneous items, until she came across a small case of sewing needles. She selected the smallest needle available, then searched in the drawer one more time until she found a book of matches. Securing the eye of the needle between her lips, she struck a match, then held the needle to position it so the flame engulfed the tip, sterilizing it.

Charles moved into the kitchen. "You're going to give me proof with that needle?"

"Yes, but not in any way that, even you the artist, could ever imagine."

Heba opened a cabinet door and took out a small porcelain ramekin. She then sat on a stool and set her left hand palm-side up on the kitchen countertop, while her right hand held the needle. "Charles, please, come closer."

If her instincts were right, she would never regret her decision to completely confide in Charles. She would never have to worry about his passing on the deepest secrets about her and the ink to wrongful people, or anyone else for that matter. For her greatest fear was if someone found a way to anoint evil into the ink, altering its properties, and then managed to corrupt it to execute nefarious motives. This would not be accomplished through the creation of one villain, but rather an army of them, drawn by an entire gang of artists with bad intent. It was critical, she knew, that for the sake of mankind, the ink must never pass into the wrong hands.

"I am going to prick the tip of my finger several times," she said, "and then let the ink drip into the ramekin."

"Ink?"

"Charles...welcome to my world. For over twenty-four hundred years I have held this secret, never divulging what courses through my veins. I am the result of an ancient Egyptian's sketch. I was the first person created with the magic ink. And once created, there is no blood, only ink. I was told to never tell a soul, for it can be assumed that I am cast from an evil lot. And I found this to be true as there were times when I had to be particularly careful. When witches were believed to exist, if someone were to see me bleed from a cut, and assume that my blood was black, it could send me to the gallows or burned at the stake. My life is eternal as long as I avoid the ways people die: fatal accidents, lack of oxygen, loss of blood, or, in my case, ink. For whatever reason, due to the unknown properties of the ink, I am immune to illness of any kind. Diseases, disorders or cancer will never inflict me. I am eternal. However, there is one other way I can cease to exist, as you witnessed earlier when you cut the butterfly sketch. I too can quickly lose my life. Be it fire, shredding, tearing, or at the mercy of a pair of scissors, the destruction of the original sketch from which I was created can terminate my life."

Charles stood silent, stuck in the middle between believing or not believing. Not sure which camp to side with. It was a state of shock, blindsided by—who would've thought—two supernatural butterflies and a woman as old as dirt.

She gave five quick jabs with the needle, not wincing once, then hung her finger down, letting the black ink drip into the ramekin.

"Shit!" burst Charles. "That is ink!"

"As dark as night, yes." Heba used her free hand to apply pressure to the punctured finger, increasing its flow, then opened up the band aids, and secured them over the needle marks.

Charles stepped back. "Who are you?! What are you?!"

"I am good, not evil. I am not human. I am not an alien either, so do not run. I am not a witch, who is only a storybook creation and nothing more. Charles, Khaldun and I were the first created with the magic ink. We are supernatural. Our creator was an Egyptian artist named Khepri, which means 'to create'. The ink was anointed by the god Ra. Have I lost you? Are you in shock?"

"No, I'm fine. It's just a lot to take in."

"Of course it is. Welcome to the supernatural."

Chapter 3

MORAL COMPASS

Charles had three more opportunities to visit Heba before he returned home. She expressed the importance of secrecy regarding the ink, and of keeping loyal to it.

"Telling of its magic or its existence will normalize the ink," she said. "It will also terminate that which has been created by the ink, as well as end your access to its magic. That means you must not tell anyone."

"My girlfriend included?"

"Especially a girlfriend. You are in college. It is not unlikely your relationship will one day end."

"But she's different," he said, vouching for his girlfriend who was half a world away.

"It does not matter. The rules do not bend, not even for love."

"Even though she's an artist?"

"It does not matter."

"But what if—"

"There are no what-ifs. It is just you, Charles, and only you."

He shifted in his seat, inching slightly forward, then said, "What about blood relations?"

"Sorry, but no one is an exception."

"Not even my son?"

"You have a son?"

"Not yet, but on the way. My girlfriend, Tennie, is due in a couple of months."

"And you know it is a boy?"

"Well, it's a gut feeling. Kinda like you have about me."

Heba smiled at the comparison. "And what if your gut is wrong? Will it matter if it is a girl?"

"Not in the least. A healthy baby is all that I hope for." Charles stood up and walked over to an original painting of a seaside village.

"A street artist painted that," said Heba, "in Vernazza, Italy—a quaint, colorful fishing village. I never did get his full name. 'Pierre' is how he signed it."

"He was so talented. Why didn't you select him?"

"For the same reason I have not approached countless other artists: he had a history of malice. He betrayed his wife and children for selfish reasons. The ink has no tolerance for that. Charles, I believe you do not have those flaws, and that is an important reason why I picked you."

He continued scanning the painting, studying the details of the oil brushwork. "What if my newborn grows up like me, and has my traits…would that be an exception?"

"I would not suggest telling your son or daughter, no matter how talented or good you may think he or she is deserving of the ink. Otherwise, you will put your artistic privilege in jeopardy."

Charles returned to the Kathmandu table, sitting in the wicker chair that creaked of old age as his weight settled. "You said you'd like me to create a superhero. You want me to create one to fight evil, right?"

"Yes. And I will be honest, this would be the first superhuman ever created. It really was not until the 1930s that superhero comics became known. Before that time, I never knew it was an idea to pursue. It is not like there are highly qualified artists on every street corner. And the ones that I did find, many had good intent, but they just did not possess enough imaginative energy."

"So, are there other ink people like yourself walking the earth?"

"That is hard to answer, although I know people have been sketched and willed to life, I have no knowledge of whether or not their drawings are still intact. It is quite possible there could be sketch books packed away in boxes of artists who have long since passed away, but I really do not know."

"So, even you weren't given superpowers?"

"Me?" laughed Heba. "Oh, no. I was just a line drawing on papyrus paper. Neither Khaldun nor I have powers of any kind."

"Just how much evil can a superhuman fight?"

"That is an unknown. There will be limits, I am sure, of how much power the ink can provide. But my advice is for you to will as much power into your drawing as you can. Let your imagination be your guide."

"So, we're talkin' Superman and Flash, right?!" There was excitement in Charles' voice.

Heba had no definitive answer. Without question, comic book superheroes had influenced her vision and hope of what such a person created by ink might be capable of, but she also knew it was silly to be swayed by make-believe. Still, she thought, if an artist can create a flying insect, then why not a flying human? After all, it was not so much the insect, but rather defying the impossibility of flight that was so astounding. Then, perhaps, creating something greater than a normal human might be possible.

"I have no idea what superpowers to expect," she said, "but I do know however you draw the superhuman, thoroughly think it through. The ink will only allow you one human."

"Wouldn't you have better luck by having a comic book artist draw one, instead of me? Wouldn't they be more qualified?"

Heba looked at a clock on the kitchen wall, noticing that there were only ten minutes left until Charles had to go.

"It is not about having experience drawing superheroes," she said, "It is beyond that. It is about having the gift to be able to bring things to life. And as you have proven, you have that gift. Besides, I like an underdog."

The last day they met, sitting at the Kathmandu table, she served Charles tea along with some flatbread. She took him back to the very beginning of her creation, when she looked down to meet Khaldun for the first time, and in the ensuing minutes of her new life, Heba had her first conversation with her artist creator. Khepri had explained to her as much as he knew about the ink. "In its own mystical way," he told her, "it understands you. It reads you. It feels you. It responds to good intent and declines deceit. It cannot be fooled."

"Charles, from the moment I watched you interact with that little girl, I had an instinctual feeling that you are not only artistic, but you have a moral compass that recognizes wrongs in need of correction."

"But that's not an uncommon trait. I'm hardly alone."

"True, but you possess something that sets you apart: your neurology is very different. I would not have pursued your innate skills had I not detected your uniqueness. Remember, my ink is my sixth sense. You must understand that you are a rare find. The ink only responds to those it can trust. I am the only one who can pass on the knowledge of the ink. I am sure it has to do with my being the first created, the details of which even I do not fully understand. I am what you might call a talent scout."

Heba went into the kitchen to get the tea pot, then refilled Charles' cup. "There was an artist I met about three years ago who lived in a small village in southern France. Her name was Genevieve, and she possessed all the qualities that you have. I had first encountered her a year earlier at an art fair in Paris where she painted impressionistic portraits of tourists in a style like Van Gogh's. She was also quite capable of creating quick portraits using only a fountain pen. Also, like you, Genevieve never hesitated to help someone in need."

"How long did you watch her?" asked Charles.

"Long enough to finally realize she was worthy of the ink. If you watch someone in public long enough, even from a distance, and study their social interactions, you can observe a lot that defines that person's character."

"So, you gave Genevieve the ink?"

"Eventually, yes, after I got to know her, I gave her a pen, just as I have for you."

"Did you have her draw a superhero?"

"Yes, I did. But I have no idea what came of that. It was a busy time of her life, but she said she would do it in about a week."

Charles' curiosity piqued. "So, there may be a superhero flying around France right now?"

Heba laughed. "I guess it is possible."

"And you have not heard from her since?"

"Nothing. I have written letters and called. Not a word. I find it odd, and worrisome in a way."

Charles took a couple last sips of tea. "Do you think something happened to her?"

Heba stared into her cup, jostling it slightly with both hands. "I am not sure, but I do wonder."

"Wonder what?"

"If something went wrong."

When their time came to an end, she gave Charles the red pen with the magic ink, wrapped in a soft cloth, and secured in a small burlap sack. She put it in a satchel containing the sketch book, which had her name and phone number written on the inside of the front cover. There were only two jars of magic ink in existence, both of which she kept.

"From this point on, you are in control." she said. "I wish you well. If you have any questions of any kind, feel free to contact me anytime. If anyone asks what is in the box, tell the truth…that it is ink, and nothing more."

"What about the butterfly?"

"I could use some extra company, so it will stay here."

"Its life is eternal?"

"As long as the drawing is intact, yes. Keep in mind that the butterflies you created were test sketches. The ink knew my presence was involved, that I was training you. But now that you are on your own, the trial is over. Remember: one animal, and one human is the limit. If either of their sketches are destroyed, you never get to create another one again. So, choose wisely before you begin."

After giving her his contact information, he hugged her goodbye, thanking her for entrusting him with the knowledge and privilege of using the ink.

"Stay true to who you are. That is the key," she said.

Before he left, Heba reached out, cupping his hands in hers. "I cannot read the future, but I wish you well. And, Charles…do you remember that Frenchman from the other day?"

"The man who called himself the Finger Gunman?"

"Yes."

"What about him?"

"Watch out for people like him. There is too much evil in this world. And what we do not want is for evil to rule our lives—to instill an irreversible and uncontrollable fear that we cannot correct. The time for a superhero is now."

"I understand," assured Charles. "I will thoroughly think it through before I bring him to life."

How quickly she had entrusted him with the ink. Heba had no second thoughts, though. She was completely at ease with her decision since the ink had a foolproof property of losing its magical quality if an artist tried to manipulate it for selfish reasons.

After Charles left her apartment, Heba heated some lentil soup on the stovetop, then sat at a small kitchen table, dipping chunks of naan into the soup, sponging the savory broth. She looked around the room at some of the objects and paintings that Charles had admired. In particular, the small sandstone sculpture of the falcon caught his eye most. Mere coincidence? she wondered. Why the falcon? Of all the pieces in the room, why was he most drawn to the one thing that was not only closest to her heart, but also closely linked to the god Ra who created the ink in the very beginning?

She saw it as an omen assuring her that Charles was, indeed, worthy of the ink.

That night, after a hot bath, she settled into her bed, gazing up through a window that gave a star-filled view above the silhouette of the neighboring two-story building. She looked at the stars before falling asleep with Khaldun curled up beside her, never realizing that this day had been the last time she would ever see Charles Sweeney.

Chapter 4
BRAINSTORMING

It was July 4th when Charles landed in Chicago after sixteen hours of travel from Cairo. With layovers in between, he was worn thin from having had little sleep along the way. The flights were full, with little leg room and endless chatter amongst his classmates. Positioned between his feet was the satchel containing the red pen and sketch book. He was eager to begin sketching superhero ideas with a regular pen of his own, but knew it might create unnecessary attention and curiosity if seen. Complete secrecy was critical, so he resisted the impulse.

He had one flight remaining that would take him to his hometown of Lehman, Illinois. With a ninety-minute layover, he found a payphone and called Tennie who was visiting her parents for two weeks in Oklahoma. Her pregnancy, which was entering its sixth month, had not been planned, though having been together for three years did help soften the unexpected news. In fact, the pregnancy was more of a welcome than not, since they had talked often about wanting to start a family soon after getting married.

"Charles! You're back!"

"Hey, Ten! Not quite home yet. I'm in Chicago with one flight left to Lehman. Man, I miss you."

"I miss you, too. The past ten days have seemed like forever. I received your letters. Loved reading them!"

"I thought of calling you, but international calls are outrageously expensive."

"Yes, they are, and we need to save what we can for this new baby."

"You been feeling okay?"

"Actually, yes. This baby is starting to rock and roll," she chuckled. "I swear she's doing summersaults."

"I suppose baby boys will do that."

"And so will girls," she laughed.

As their conversation continued, Charles couldn't help but recall Heba's words of warning: "Tell anyone of its magic or its existence and your privilege to its magic is over." Outside of surprise gifts, there was nothing he kept secret from Tennie. Nor did he ever have any reason to. But now he did.

"Charles?...Charles? Are you there?"

"Hey, I'm here. Must've been a poor connection."

"I was asking if they spoke much English?"

"Yes, there were some locals who spoke English...Hey, I need to start making my way to the gate. They'll be boarding soon."

"Ok. Well, call me when you get home. Oh, and things are fine here with my folks. Just a lot of pregnancy questions, and what are our plans for the future. You know parents."

"Sure do," he said. "And, yes, of course, I'll call when I get home. I gotta go, Ten. I love you tons."

"I love you, too. Have a safe flight. Bye, bye."

Is this what it's going to be like living with the ink? Dodging suspicions. Dusting trails to conceal his secret? Was it worth creating a superhero? During his last few visits with Heba, there were particulars that she had shared with him regarding creating a superhuman.

"It does not matter if it's a superhuman or normal human," she had told him, "they share five primary traits:

"They are completely fluent in the creator's language.

"They are fully equipped with knowledge.

"They do not require food, but they can eat, such as might be needed in certain social settings.

"They do not require sleep, but they can.

"They are completely loyal to their creator."

"But if I create a person," asked Charles, "am I responsible for their actions?"

"No. Once they are brought to life, they have their own autonomy. But they will act upon your request as long as it is of good intent."

"So, is there ever the chance that they might turn against me?"

Heba answered emphatically, "Never."

Sitting at the gate, waiting for the boarding to begin, Charles looked out the large windows and watched the planes taking off and landing. The technology developed to fly people around the world fascinated him. Thrust, propulsion, aerodynamics, fuel conversions, everything, even down to the plastic moldings of the stowed food trays—every detail intrigued him. But he was an artist and not an aeronautical engineer, and so the science behind flying was completely foreign to him. But who needed science to fly? Couldn't pen and paper suffice? And who needed a plane? Superman didn't. And who needed fiction when reality was just a few pen strokes away?

As the excitement of being in the position to create a living human from his imagination began to grow, the uncertainty of how to keep his secret from Tennie began to fade. He would cross that bridge when it was time. But for now, he was at the helm of what should be impossible. The greatest magicians and illusionists of all time couldn't hold a candle to him. He was not only going to bring two-dimensions to life, but, quite possibly, set it on a course of eternity.

There was enough room around him at his gate so he could conceal his sketching from curious eyes. He took out the sketch book and a personal pen, then focused on a blank page as he conjured the initial thoughts of envisioning his superhero. It would be a male, but with what powers? It was one thing to want to assign certain powers, it was yet another to be able to will them to life. And what would his hero wear? A cape? Mask? A signature emblem? Colors? What would his name be?

He thought of the origins of Heba, thinking some aspect of the superhero's outfit or character should reflect her creation. Ancient Egypt brought to mind the pyramids which he simplified to a triangle. He toyed with the idea of having successive triangles becoming smaller and smaller within each other until the final triangle was practically a dot, but the design was too busy, and the comical candidates of Pyramidman or Triangleman were nothing but lost causes. Then came another failed attempt of commemorating Heba: Basketman would save the world by hurling handwoven baskets at supersonic speeds at evil doers. Camelman was the worst of the lot, being a man with two large humps on his back who could spit blinding acid into the eyes of his foes. Eternalman was a boring farce. And Hebaman was a complete disrespect.

He began sketching a male figure holding a massive boulder above his head. Accentuating the muscles under tension didn't necessarily mean he was contemplating drawing a visually muscle-bound character. Instead, he was warming up his hand, finding the feel of the pen, allowing the creative groove to conceive a superhero.

Over the intercom an announcement alerted passengers that boarding would soon begin. Charles closed his sketch book and returned it to the satchel.

On the flight, he sat next to an overly-talkative businessman. Stock market trading, a house on a golf course and one in the Rockies, three outstanding Ivy League children, and a list of celebrities and politicians he had dined with—there was no stopping him. Charles made three trips to the restroom to take a breather from his arrogant babbling. Before boarding, he had been on the fringe of formulating a superhero, but the narcissistic motormouth had now made that a postponed anticipation.

Chapter 5

ILLINOIS

Charles arrived mid-afternoon at his garage apartment on the outskirts of Lehman. He rented the detached apartment from Gordon Metz, a robust 72-year-old property owner, who had picked him up at the city's regional airport. He was a corn farmer who kept a tractor, various farming implements, and a large collection of dumbbells in the garage. Gordon and his wife, Peggy, lived in a two-story whitewashed wood house with a wrap-around porch. It was just a stone's throw away from the garage, and both sat atop a knoll that rose from the center of the property's six-hundred-plus acres of corn. It gave a full view of the skyline of Lehman two miles in the distance, its tallest buildings belonging to the local university that Charles attended. The corn crop was a couple of months away from being harvested, then standing almost ten feet tall in its verdant green prime. On summer nights Charles would open his bedroom window, framing a perfect view of the skyline, then fall asleep to the crackling cornstalks swaying against one another in the breeze.

"It's good to have you back," said Gordon, as they got out of the car. "You going to the fireworks tonight?"

"I don't think so. I've gotta catch up on some sleep. It's been a long haul."

"Can't blame you. But keep in mind, we've got some leftover

meatloaf in the fridge, courtesy of Mrs. Metz. If you want some, feel free, anytime."

"Thank you, sir. I might take you up on that."

"And when does Tennie return?"

"Back from Oklahoma in two weeks."

"She's doing ok, I assume?"

"Yes. I talked to her in Chicago. I think her nauseous days are over."

A flight of stairs ran up the side of the garage, unseen from the Metz's house. Inside, the kitchen and living room shared the same space, adjacent to the enclosed bedroom which had a drafting table where Charles drew editorial cartoons for *The Insider*, the university student newspaper. The table sat opposite his bed. Thumbtacked to the wall facing the table were newspaper clippings of his editorial cartoons, quick sketches of new ideas, and random lists of editorial topics. There were also photos of him and Tennie: barbecuing at her parents' house in Oklahoma, attending a university football game, building a snowman, and a nighttime Halloween photo, dressed as scarecrows standing amongst towering corn stalks.

Putting away his clothes and toiletries from the trip, he placed the red pen with the magic ink on his drawing board, then took a shower in a small bathroom located in his bedroom. Feeling hungry, he decided to take Mr. Metz up on the meatloaf offer, then returned to the apartment and lay down on an old sofa in his living area. He put the telephone on the floor next to him, and called Tennie.

"Hello?" It was Tennie's mother, Laura.

"Hello, Mrs. Nelson. It's Charles. Is—"

"Charles!" her voice elevated. "Welcome back! Tennie said you had called earlier. You have a good trip?"

"Yes, ma'am. But it's good to be home."

"Wonderful! Hang on. Let me get Tennie."

A minute passed as he momentarily closed his eyes, feeling fatigue creeping in.

"Hey, honey," said Tennie.

"Hey, Ten. I meant to tell you earlier, happy 4th."

"You, too. Any plans tonight?"

"Sleep. And lots of it. You?"

"Pretty much the same. I'm sleeping for two you know. Sleeping and eating. Feels like I could sleep for an eternity."

Eternity. The word brought back the memory of Heba draining ink from her finger into the ramekin, then telling him that she was eternal. Given all that he had learned and experienced over the last week, he had no problem believing her.

The way he saw it was that his art class abroad had been an insignificant secondary excursion compared to his unexpected immersion into the supernatural. And the more he thought about it, the more he questioned his own mortality. If the ink were dependent upon his imaginative energy to will two-dimensional things to life, then would it be unreasonable to assume that he is supernatural? There had been others over the millennium who had proven their ability. Were they, too, supernatural? Was it something that humans were physiologically and psychologically wired with, and they just had to tap into it the right way with the right resource to evoke its potential? All his life he had grown up with superheroes. Scores of them in comic books, as well as Superman on TV, but not a single one real. And here he was, in the driver's seat, on the cutting edge of what any artist could only hope for.

He certainly didn't want to blow it by telling people of the ink and its supernatural properties. Heba had insistently warned him of that. But Tennie had mentioned eternity, and as bad as he wanted to carry on a conversation, he knew that even attempting a roundabout way to discuss eternity could be risky. So, he did the next best thing, and talked about the baby.

"Ten, do you realize how close we are to being parents?"

"I know. It's kinda scary."

"Thank God, our parents are so supportive."

"No kidding. It'll be nice moving out of that garage apartment, and into the first floor of the duplex. Even with summer school, apartments rent out so fast in town. Your dad really pulled some strings."

"Yes, he did. Always good to have a realtor on your side," said Charles, looking out a window at the Metz's house. "But I'm gonna miss this place. A lot of my inspiration comes from here. There's something about the acres of corn that opens my mind. Even when the fields are plowed and empty, I'm inspired. There's sort of a mystical connection I get from the farmland that triggers my ideas. Sounds crazy, I know."

"No, not crazy. I think it sounds magical. So, tell me, did you draw in Egypt?"

He didn't know how to respond. Could the ink really read him? Was everything Heba had told him, true? He didn't want to lie to Tennie, but he was on the cusp of doing something unheard of with his artwork, and didn't want that jeopardized. He chose to answer honestly, but generically.

"Yeah, I drew a little bit, but most of the time was spent in museums or viewing private collections."

"That must have been fascinating seeing art that is thousands of years old."

"All of it was impressive, for sure."

"What did you draw?"

Keep it honest.

"I drew a young girl. She was in a market, and she dropped a glass lantern that upset her mother who briskly yanked her daughter's arm and then took her away."

"Interesting. And from that you decided to draw her?"

"Well, yes, but there's more to it than that. I met a basket maker who had a guest book. And I ended up drawing the girl in her book."

"You drew her in a guest book?"

"Like I said, there's more to it. If I told you that the basket maker and I discussed Shakespeare, and how that inspired the drawing of the girl, you might be confused. Am I right?"

"Perhaps. But you've always acted upon the moment, so I can see that happening. Very cool."

Had he really come that close to sharing Heba's identity with Tennie? There was no lying in not telling her about going to Heba's apartment. So, he kept it simple, only telling Tennie about the basket vendor in the market, omitting the details of the Finger Gunman.

"Ten, I'm starting to nod off. I need to get some sleep."

"I'm sure you do. Well, call me tomorrow and we can talk about the baby. Happy 4th, Charles."

"You too, Ten. Love ya. Bye."

The sun was a couple hours from the horizon, where it would set behind the silhouette of Lehman's skyline, framed within his bedroom window. His circadian rhythms completely out of sync, jet lag had blanketed his brain.

He dozed off for an hour, then his eyelids bounced intermittently in and out of sleep, as one particular thought—small but impactful— brought him to full consciousness.

The Finger Gunman.

It was the pivotal moment when he realized that, as Heba had told him, evil was everywhere.

Charles stood up from the sofa, and made his way to the drawing table.

It was time to draw his superhero.

PART III

Chapter 1
THE TRACTOR

Coming to the end of their drive from the police station, Charles turned off the headlights as they crept up the long, moonlit caliche driveway, trying to minimize the rocky crunch beneath his tires that might awaken the Metzes. It was midnight and no lights were on in the farmhouse. After parking the car, he and Sketch quietly closed their doors, then headed up the side staircase and entered the apartment.

"Welcome home," said Charles, turning on a ceiling light, then setting his keys on a small kitchen table.

Sketch walked over to the sofa and pressed his hand into a cushion. "You know, I don't remember this sofa, but I know it. This is where I sleep, and yet I've never slept here."

"So, you know everything about this apartment?"

"Yes, everything."

"And do you know you're a mess? Look at you—the grass stains and dirty scuff marks on your outfit. We need to get you cleaned up. Take a shower and I'll get you some clothes to wear."

"What about my powers though? Weren't you going to try to fix things?"

"I am. I just need a little time to think it through."

Charles took a seat at his drawing table and turned on the lamp. He hadn't closed the drawing book when he left for the police station. As his superhero took a shower, Charles stared at his rendering of Sketch. He was certain that fatigue from his long flight had impeded his concentration as he drew, yet here he was, still having slept very little since Mr. Metz brought him home. But he was alert this time with a greater motivation that was keeping the fatigue at bay—superpowers.

How do you give a superhero powers, when you failed to give them the first time? Searching for an answer to rectify his mistake, he recalled Heba's emphatic reminder to fully will his drawing to life. "Do not fall short of your ability to fully create. To give superpowers, you must invest all of your focus into the ink."

Into the ink, he pondered. *Into...the ink.*

INTO...the ink!

The shower stopped running and soon after, Sketch emerged barefoot from the bathroom with a towel in his hand and wearing blue jeans with a white t-shirt. His hair was damp and ruffled.

Holding the red pen with the magic ink, Charles turned in his seat to face Sketch. "Does the name Heba ring a bell with you?"

"I can't say it does. Why?"

"I met her ten days ago in Egypt. She's a street peddler who gave me the magic ink to create you—the ink that's in this pen."

"Interesting. How did she come across the ink?"

"She, like you, came from the ink. She was the first person to be created. An artist named Khepri drew her."

"Wait!" recollected Sketch, "She was a queen, right?"

"Yes! Exactly!"

"And she has a dog?"

"Yes! So, you do know her?"

"I can't say I know her, but I know of her. If, in fact, she's the queen I'm thinking of."

"But you don't recognize her name?"

"I don't," said Sketch, patting the towel around his head, then hanging it on a hook inside the bathroom door. "But, maybe, like the fireworks and artillery, it's just part of the cloudiness in my head. The unfinished me."

"And that's why I'm mentioning her. I believe Heba gave me clues. I think she said some things that were deliberately intended for me to figure out."

"Such as?"

"Shakespeare."

"Who?"

"Wow, you really are unfinished."

"Who's Shakespeare?"

"He wrote plays back in the 1600s. Probably the greatest playwright of all time."

"What does he have to do with me?"

"When I first met Heba, she said, 'All the world's a stage.' It just came up in our conversation. It's a quote from a Shakespeare play, and one from which I had memorized the first four lines a couple years ago:

All the world's a stage,
And all the men and women merely players;
They have their exits and their entrances.
And one man in his time plays many parts."

"I'm afraid I still don't follow," said Sketch, taking a seat on the side of the bed closest to Charles, then, for the first time, noticing his drawing. "Hey, that's me!"

"Yes, it is. The real deal."

"I look so…so…like I'm all there. Like I should have my powers."

"And that's why I'm telling you about Shakespeare. I think I figured out something Heba wanted me to discover on my own."

"I'm not sure I follow, but enlighten me."

"Heba and I had a few lengthy discussions about the magic ink and creating superheroes. She said that in all of her centuries of traveling and issuing the ink to worthy artists, no one had ever been able to will superpowers into their creations, no matter how focused they may have been."

"Just like you drawing me."

"Correct."

"So, what did you figure out?"

"That there was a reason for discussing Shakespeare. But the reason was riddled. Those lines that I memorized are from the play *As You Like It*. They tell us that our existence is like theater where we, the players, all have our roles. We have an entrance and an exit—we are born, we live, and then we die. But Heba added a further explanation. She stressed the importance for actors to truly know their lines—to not veer from them, because each word that Shakespeare wrote mattered. During that same discussion, Heba stressed the importance of willing powers into the ink. 'Like theater,' she said, 'do not veer from your lines, because that is where the magic is.'"

Sketch shrugged his shoulders. "I'm still confused."

"Heba was very particular about who is given the ink. You have to possess certain qualities; the primary one is being a person of good intent. What I'm getting at is this: I don't think fatigue from my trip has anything to do with your not having powers. I think the secret is not veering from the lines—the ink lines. Heba stressed the necessity of putting all of my focus *into* the ink. What she was telling me was in order to give superpowers I must exactly trace the original lines. I must literally keep the pen tip in the ink of the lines in the drawing."

Sketch stood up and began slowly pacing around the room. "So, Heba knew you might run into difficulty creating my powers. But, in order to see just how worthy an artist you are, she left you with a sort of puzzle to solve to prove your worth."

Charles snapped his fingers toward Sketch. "Exactly!" he said. "Don't veer from the lines, because, just like Shakespeare, the lines matter!" He stood up and went to the kitchen window to look through the curtains at the Metz's house. It was still dark with no signs of movement. Returning to his seat, he readied himself with the red pen, preparing to precisely trace his drawing and will the powers into the ink.

"Well," said Charles, "do you feel anything?"

Sketch extended his arms, looking at his biceps for some kind of obvious change in the size of his muscles. "Not really," he said.

"Try picking up the bed."

"All of it?"

"Sure, try it. Just grab the bed post with one hand and lift the entire bed off the floor."

"But that's impossible."

"Nothing's impossible if you're a superhero."

Sketch made his way to a front bed post and knelt down, securing it with a firm grip. Looking up at Charles, he said, "You traced the lines exactly, right?"

"Exactly, yes. Now, lift!"

The bed didn't budge. Not even an inch. Sketch tried several times, but it remained stubborn and unmoving.

"This can't be," said Charles, puzzled. "This simply can't be." He began pacing about the apartment, indiscriminately tapping on countertops and furniture. "I traced the lines exactly with every bit of focus I could summon. I know I did!"

Sketch followed him into the living room, taking a seat on the arm of the sofa. "Maybe we should go down into the garage and mess with the dumbbells."

Charles stopped tapping. "You know about the dumbbells?... Well, of course you do...you're Sketch. You're five hours into existence, and this is no fairytale or comic book story. You're real, and you know so much, but you're incomplete. And I'd ask you to take off from the steps outside the door and fly into the night, but I'm almost certain you'd break your neck the moment you'd try, by just falling to the ground. And you're suggesting to go lift dumbbells? For what?"

"To gradually add weight. Maybe the bed was too much weight too soon."

"I'm up for anything. It can't hurt to try."

They entered through a side door where Charles turned on a bare yellow light bulb that occasionally flickered as it hung from the center of the ceiling. It cast a soft glow for the better part of the garage before tapering into darkness around its perimeter. There was a row of heavily dust-caked windows across the top of the double wooden garage doors, but their opaqueness made it difficult for the light to be seen from the outside. The garage was occupied by a rusted tractor, an abundance of tools, farm implements, gasoline cans and containers of motor oil, a washer and dryer, and a set of dumbbells ranging from five to sixty pounds each. Dust gathered in every possible crevice of the garage which smelled of tilled soil and the collective aromas of metal, steel, and iron drawn out by the damp, summer humidity.

It was one in the morning, and Charles and Sketch stood before the rack of dumbbells, looking down at them with a bit of uncertainty, not exactly sure where to begin.

"Well?" said Charles.

"Well, what?"

"What do we do now?"

"I guess I'll just start lifting."

The cast iron dumbbells had hexagon-shaped ends embossed with the number of their weight. Sketch's hands hovered over the 30-pound set. "Start with these?" he said.

"Might as well," said Charles. "Pick 'em up and let's see."

Sketch pulled both dumbbells off the rack, then held them by his sides.

"Well," said Charles, "what do they feel like? Balls of cotton? Like nothing's there?"

"No," said Sketch. "More like thirty pounds each."

"Good lord. Then lift them above your head and see if it changes anything."

"But they're already kind of heavy just holding them."

"Sketch, I don't know…I'm just hoping some superhuman strength will switch on."

Sketch snatched the weights overhead, locking his elbows to hold the extended arm position. "No. No cotton here," he said. "They feel like thirty-pound dumbbells."

"Then try the sixties." Charles said, frustration seeping into his tone.

"The sixties? There's no way."

"Sketch, you gotta believe."

"Oh, I believe. I believe none of this is going to work. I believe nothing has changed. I'm still ordinary."

Charles walked over and tugged on a sixty-pound dumbbell. What was he thinking? Nothing magical was going to unveil itself by going heavier with the weights. Nothing was going to spark a change in his strength. He sat down on a nearby wooden bench, propping his elbows on his thighs while clasping his hands together. "I don't know, Sketch. I just don't know."

"Let's call it a night. It's late, and you've been awake for a long time. I bet fatigue is the reason I have no powers. I'm going upstairs to get my outfit and bring it down to start a wash."

He made it five steps toward the side door when Charles said sharply, "Sketch! That's it!"

"What's it?"

"It's your outfit! Go change into it, then come back down. You're about to meet your superpowers!"

"Are you sure about this?"

"Absolutely. The outfit completes you. Without it, you're just a guy in blue jeans. But with it…you're Sketch! Now that I've traced the lines, put it on and come lift."

The intermittent flickering of the ceiling light increased as Charles heard Sketch walking above through the apartment. He stood up from the bench and walked over to the garage doors where he wiped clear a small eye-hole on a window, and confirmed that the Metz's house was still asleep. The upstairs door could be heard closing followed by footsteps coming down the stairs. The side door opened, and there, entering from the dark side of the garage opposite of Charles, Sketch appeared, in full uniform with his mask on.

"Moment of truth," said Charles. "Do you feel any different?"

"Well, I feel like—"

Those were Sketch's last words before the great fall. Before the defining moment that settled both of their curiosities. Before both realized this was the beginning of not just something new, but something greater than they had ever hoped for. Before the light flickered one last time and went out. Before the room went entirely dark.

That's when Sketch not only tripped, but fell, extending his arm with his hand landing firmly against the nose of the tractor.

His fall was as ordinary as anyone else's might be, with one exception: the two-and-a-half-ton tractor ignored its parking brake, skidding fifteen feet across the concrete floor, before crashing through the bolted garage doors, knocking one completely off its hinges, shattering three windows, then coming to a stop.

Moonlight now flooded the garage, casting itself over Sketch who lay on the floor, smiling as he looked up at Charles and finished his answer:

"—a superhero!"

Chapter 2
OKLAHOMA SLIP

Gordon Metz abruptly sat up in bed, alert and focused on the noise that came from outside his open bedroom window. He shook his wife, waking her from a deep sleep, snorting as she breached consciousness.

"Peggy!" said Gordon, in a hushed tone. "Did you hear that?"

"What?" she said, groggily and muffled.

"I'm not sure. Like an explosion or something."

"It's the 4th of July, hon'. Go back to sleep."

"No, it was different. Like something crashed."

"Probably just Charles—"

"Shhhh! Listen!...voices...did you hear that?"

"Yeah, I'm sure it's just Charles."

"Peggy," he said, throwing the covers to the side, then pivoting out of bed in red plaid pajamas, "something's going on out there." He opened a drawer from his bedside table and took out a flashlight, turning it on as he walked over to the second-floor window. He hovered the light over the yard below, then directed it further out toward the garage until its wide beam captured the tractor with Charles sitting at the steering wheel, his body turned, waving to Mr. Metz. "Good evening, sir! Sorry to wake you. Bit of an accident down here. But I'll pay for it."

"What the...?" Gordon squinted his eyes, not quite sure what to make of one garage door lying flat on the ground, and the other unhinged at the top, hanging at an angle against the side of the tractor.

"Gordon, what is it?" said Peggy, now sitting up in bed.

"I'm not sure. It looks like…hey, Charles…my garage doors… what the hell?"

"Just a little mishap, sir. But I'll get it all fixed, don't you worry!"

Gordon saw something move inside the garage. He panned his flashlight to the left, capturing a figure that seemed to be pacing. "Who's that?" he asked.

"Him?" said Charles, playing down Sketch's presence. "Oh, he's David—a friend of mine visiting from upstate."

"Uh, huh…hey, David, do you mind stepping out here?"

Sketch did as requested, squinting as he looked up at the flashlight. "Evening, sir," he said. He was dressed in blue jeans and a t-shirt. The two had agreed he needed to quickly change out of his outfit. "Sorry we woke you up like this."

"Boys, I don't even know what to say. I'm flabbergasted. How in the hell did you manage to do this?"

"Well—" began Charles, but was interrupted by Gordon.

"Hang on a sec'. I'll be right down," he said, then turned to his wife. "It's a shambles down there. The garage doors are all messed up. How they did this, I have no idea."

"Well, I'm awake now. Guess I'll join you," said Peggy, reaching for her robe, then followed her husband downstairs.

"Now what?" said Sketch to Charles. "Are you sure your plan will work?"

"We don't have much choice," said Charles, anticipating Mr. Metz's imminent arrival. "Just go with the plan. Getting you out of that outfit was job number one. I'm just hoping the ink will forgive me for not telling the truth. But no one can learn of the source of your powers."

The Metzes appeared from the side door facing the garage. Gordon, wearing brown slippers, turned on the overhead light which flooded the area, including the tractor. Peggy came out wearing pale pink slippers, matching her full-length quilted robe.

"Oh, my," she said, approaching the garage, "How did this ever happen? Charles, have you been drinking?"

"Oh, no ma'am, no drinking," he said from atop the tractor. "Not a drop."

His arms crossed and feet spread apart, Gordon stood defiantly, though his pajamas and slippers did soften the edge. "So, boys, what happened?"

"It was all my fault, sir," said Sketch, now standing next to the tractor. "I pushed it through the doors."

Charles looked down at Sketch, nervously pinpointing his eyes directly at him, into him, through him—trying to get his attention to stop whatever he was going to say next. This was not the plan!

But Sketch continued...

"I know it sounds crazy, but Charles mentioned there were some weights down here, and I just thought it'd be fun to workout. I know, it's one in the morning...who does this kinda thing? Two guys bored and awake on the 4th of July, I guess."

"Back up a sec'," said Gordon. "You said you pushed the tractor through the doors?"

"Yeah, like Superman."

"It's David, right?"

"Yes, sir. David Skechenski."

"David, as much as I'd like to believe you had that kind of strength, it looks like Charles and the ignition key beat you to it."

"Yes, sir," said Charles, glaring at Sketch. "I fired up the engine, just for kicks, not even thinking that it might wake you. Then, only God knows why, I put it in reverse. And then...this happened."

"But to blow a door off its hinges," Gordon pondered, "that's quite an acceleration."

"That's what I thought. It just jumped. I've driven it so many times helping you farm, but this was different."

"Like when I pushed it?" said Sketch.

Gordon shrugged, chuckling, "Sure, Superman. Just like the way you pushed it."

"I think we should all get some sleep," said Peggy. "Obviously, it's an accident, and we can talk about it some more in the morning."

"Agreed," said Charles, stepping down from the tractor, then pausing momentarily as he heard his telephone ring.

"Expecting a call?" said Peggy.

"No, not this late."

Was it Sergeant Perkins? What would he want? Was there now some sort of criminal investigation? Had Sketch really done something wrong? The phone stopped ringing, then moments later began again. Charles double-stepped his way up the stairs, then entered the apartment in time to answer the phone. "Hello?"

There was silence on the other end, then a sniffle. More silence, then a series of gasping sobs. The voice struggled to say his name. But when it did, there was a noticeable change in Charles' stature, a slump in his posture, as if his body had lost strength. This was the second fall of the night, but, unlike Sketch's, this one wasn't something to celebrate. This fall held uncertainty. This fall was down a flight of hardwood stairs in the safe haven of a cozy two-story where accidents aren't supposed to happen. "Oh, Charles," said Tennie's mother, "I should never have polished the floors!" Then a sobbing outburst: "The baby, Charles! The baby!"

When the call ended, Sketch entered the room and saw Charles drop his head into his hands. Sketch sensed an unforgiving weight of despair and said, "It's Tennie, isn't it?"

Charles looked up, his eyes watering.

"Yes, she's in an ambulance. I need to get to Oklahoma."

Chapter 3
THE OWL

Charles sat on his sofa at 2:00 a.m., taking another call from Tennie's mother, updating him about her daughter's condition. Sketch was seated at the kitchen table with a pencil and some plain paper, attempting to draw a superhero of his own design.

"Five fractured ribs," said Mrs. Nelson, "a broken tibia and wrist, a concussion, and lots of bruising."

"And the baby?" asked Charles. "How is the baby?"

"The baby is doing well. It was quite a tumble down the stairs, but, miraculously, the baby was unharmed."

"And, Ten? She's okay, right? You know…she's talking okay?"

"A big headache and painful to move, but she'll heal."

"And you're sure the baby's okay?"

"Yes, the doctors feel very confident the baby wasn't harmed." Mrs. Nelson paused, gathering herself as her emotions returned to the surface, crying as she spoke. "Charles...it could've been so much worse...she fell hard…I was downstairs in the kitchen when I heard her falling. She was coming down to grab a snack, and just slipped. She was in socks, and...why I had to polish the floor and stairs…I mean, what was I thinking?! There was no time for her to react."

"You can't blame yourself. Accidents are always going to happen. Look, I'm going to try to catch a flight to Tulsa today."

"Oh, Charles, are you sure? It's not going to be cheap."

"I already talked to my parents, and they're going to help me out. It's critical that I be there to support her."

"Thank you, Charles. We already consider you like one of the family. Let us know your flight details, and we'll pick you up at the airport."

After the call ended, Charles slumped into the sofa. "I'm exhausted."

"I'm sure you are. There's been a lot to process," said Sketch.

Charles lifted his head up slightly as he took notice of Sketch. "Are you drawing?"

"If you can call it that."

"Let me guess…a superhero?"

"Actually, yes."

"Seriously?"

"Yes. But he's pretty pathetic looking."

Sketch held up his drawing, depicting a large, masked circular head atop a short oval body with disproportionately long arms and legs that seemed as if they were missing elbows and knees. There was a squiggly black lightning bolt on the chest of the superhero's white outfit. "Told ya I can't draw."

"I've seen worse," laughed Charles. "What's his name?"

"Scribble. He'd be my cousin."

"I like the idea. And what are Scribble's superpowers?"

"He can foresee the future one day ahead of the present."

"Anything else?"

"Nope, that's it."

"Well, I like Scribble. That's not a magic pencil, is it?"

"I hope not. The last thing I want is some superhero competing with me."

Charles stood up to pour himself a glass of milk from the fridge. "But what if he didn't compete? What if he teamed up with you?"

"Do you think it's even possible that I could create my own character?"

Charles finished the milk in one drink, then poured himself another. "You're asking me? You mean, *you* don't know the answer?"

"I really don't. What about your Egyptian lady friend, Heba… did she say anything about superheroes creating superheroes?"

"No. And looking at your artwork, I don't think you have a

chance of doing so." Charles rinsed out his glass then set it in the sink, before heading to his bedroom. "Sketch, I'm gonna try to get some sleep. I'll set my alarm clock for six."

"And then what?" asked Sketch, now stretching himself out on the sofa.

"Then we'll see if you can fly."

Just before dawn, they stood on the backside of the garage, hidden from the Metz's house. Sketch was dressed in his dirt-stained superhero outfit and mask, and Charles was in gym shorts, a college t-shirt, and flip-flops. To the west, darkness still remained, while at the sky's apex a palette of aubergine coated the top of the eastern half where it blended into indigo before meeting a thin line of fiery red at the horizon.

"Sure is pretty," said Sketch.

"Yes, it is. This is what I love about early mornings. The sky shifts colors by the minute."

Before them was a sea of corn gently sloping downward away from the Metz's house. Below, in the distance, they could barely make out the telephone poles that marked a county road. Beyond that the land continued its undulations of neighboring cornfields. As far as the eye could see, this was the land that fed the world.

Charles turned to Sketch. "You feel like flying?"

"Like right now?"

"Well, it's why we came out here."

"I know, but, honestly, I'm not sure what to do."

"That's not exactly the answer I was hoping for."

"Sorry. Guess I could just run and dive into the air. But the last time I did that, I was taken to the police station."

"Look, you shoved that tractor with no effort, then certainly you must be able to fly. I focused all of my imagination and willed your superpowers into the ink. Besides, you're wearing your superhero suit."

"Then guess I better try before the Metzes wake up."

"Exactly!" said Charles.

Sketch widened his stance, then began torso rotations as he swung his arms side to side on a horizontal plane. Jumping jacks were next, followed by some in-place high knee runs, then extended arm flapping.

Charles bewilderedly stared at him. "What are you doing?"

"Warming up to fly."

"With calisthenics? Come on, Sketch, give it a go."

"Okay, but if I fall out of the sky, you only have yourself to blame."

They say timing is everything, being at the right place and at the right time. The owl was on night patrol, perched on a high sycamore tree limb at the backside of the Metz's house, giving it a clear line of sight to the two men across the way. It had been listening for field mice, but their conversation interrupted any chance of locating prey. The owl didn't move, though. It stayed and studied. It shifted its head at different angles, observing the one in the red outfit, with the bird eyes and small beak. The one flapping its arms. The one that, however it was translated in the owl's mind, looked hesitant.

"You've got this!" Charles encouraged. "You were created for this!"

Sketch took a runner's starting stance with one leg positioned ahead of the other. He focused on the tops of the cornstalks. He had to clear them or his feet might catch. One final deep breath and he was off, racing toward the corn. But everything was ordinary, nothing superhuman. For a moment, he considered aborting the effort, surrendering to failure, giving up on the supernatural properties of the ink. But failure was not an option.

Launching itself from the tree, the owl stealthily swept down from behind, passing directly over Sketch and tapping his shoulder with her wing as she soared past. She cut to the right, ascending above the corn, then turned her head to see him. He accelerated through speeds much faster than normal, and, just before liftoff, caught her eyes that said to him, "Follow me!"

Which he did, waving to the owl as he rocketed past her, and then flew out of sight.

Chapter 4
BLUEBERRIES

Twenty minutes had passed, and still no sign of Sketch. The fiery red horizon was now orange, gradually shifting to a soft yellow with scattered buttery-white clouds.

Charles could only guess where he might have gone, which could be anywhere. He could be miles away, or, if things continued the way the night had progressed, he might have flown straight into a tree or a highway billboard.

"Charles?" It was Mr. Metz walking over from his back yard in his pajamas. "Looking for something?"

"Oh, no. Just admiring the sunrise."

"It's a pretty one." he said, looking the same direction as Charles who was experiencing an onset of anxiety. The last thing he needed now was Sketch coming in for a landing.

"Yes, sir, sunrises are the best."

"Is David up?"

Is David up? Where is David? That's a really good question. Would you believe he's flying? Of course not. Just like you didn't believe he pushed the tractor through the garage doors. The fact is, I don't have a clue where Mr. Skechenski is. But what I do know is that he followed an owl up into the air, and then shot off like a missile, and basically left me in a state of high anxiety. "I think he went for a walk," said Charles.

"Early riser, eh?"

"Yes, sir."

"Well, I'm gonna go take a peek at those doors. They actually might not be that hard to fix."

"I'm really sorry about what happened," said Charles scanning the sky. "It was just a stupid mistake."

As Gordon turned to walk to the front of the garage, Charles caught sight of Sketch about two hundred yards away, skimming just above the corn that moved turbulently in his wake. He then sped away and circled two large oak trees, weaving a figure-eight pattern several times in a matter of seconds before hovering in mid-air like a large hummingbird and, with a big smile, waved to Charles.

Are you kidding me??

"Hey, Charles!" hollered Mr. Metz. "Come on in here. I want ya to see somethin'."

Charles walked to the corner of the garage and saw Mr. Metz inspecting the garage doors. When he looked back, Sketch was nowhere to be seen.

"Yes, sir," said Charles, nervously walking toward him.

"In here," said Mr. Metz, leading Charles inside the garage where soft, early morning light began filling its interior. "Look at this'." He pointed to the floor at the two skid marks that lined up with the tractor's tires. "I know you said you accidentally backed out the tractor, but this just doesn't make sense."

"Hmmm. Are you sure they weren't there before?"

"Positive. And even if that were the case, how could an old farm tractor like this one possibly lay down skid marks like that?"

"Maybe because I pushed the tractor," said Sketch, entering the garage from behind them, wearing jeans and a t-shirt.

"Morning, David," said Gordon, "How was your walk?"

"My walk?" Sketch looked at Charles who stared at him with big eyes.

"Yes. Charles said you were walking."

"Oh, yes...sorry, misunderstood. Yes, I just got back."

"How far did ya go?"

"To Missouri. Did you know the Saint Louis Arch is as wide as it is tall? And what a view!"

"David, you're a mess," said Gordon, shaking his head. "But since you're here…do you have any idea about these skid marks?"

"Well," said Sketch, "like I said—"

"Mr. Metz," said Charles, "sorry to interrupt, but that call I had last night…it was Tennie's mom. Tennie's in the hospital. She had a bad fall. I'm hoping to catch a flight out today."

"Oh, no. Is she okay?"

"Seems to be pretty beat up with some broken bones. She fell down some stairs."

"And the baby?"

"So far, the baby seems fine. I just need to get to Tulsa. And these doors—I'll pay for them, I promise."

Gordon put his hand on Charles' shoulder. "Look, this can wait. It's nothing. If you can't find a flight out of our airport, then I'll drive you to Chicago."

"Is everything okay, boys?" It was Mrs. Metz walking out from the house, still in her robe.

"Tennie's in the hospital, Peg," said Gordon. "She had a bad fall. Charles is going to catch a flight today."

"Oh, Charles, I'm so sorry. You must be exhausted. If there's anything we can do, don't hesitate to ask."

"Thank you, you're very kind."

Charles and Sketch went back into the apartment where Charles sorted through his clothes to take to Oklahoma. He would have to piecemeal sleep throughout the day in order to catch up.

Sketch stood in the doorway of the bedroom as Charles packed a small suitcase. "I had no idea about Tennie," he said, "Sorry I rambled out there."

"Don't worry. You didn't know."

"You're sure she and the baby are okay?"

"Yes. She just took a rough tumble," Charles said, putting toiletries in the suitcase. "My god, Sketch, you can fly!! Did you really go to the Arch?"

"Sure did. They're all here, Charles…all my superpowers are here."

"What's it like? I mean what's it feel like, inside?"

"Honestly, it feels like it's a normal part of me. Like walking or running…there's no thought to it. The flying is simply effortless. But, damn, I can go fast!"

"Well, yeah! You went on a hundred and fifty-mile trip in twenty minutes. Hell yes you're fast!"

As the sun broke the horizon and brought the summer morning into bloom, Charles and Sketch had cereal and toast for breakfast. Charles washed and dried Sketch's outfit, then began making calls to book a flight to Tulsa. He found an evening flight that originated from Lehman, flying to Chicago where his connecting flight then went direct to Tulsa.

"Would you mind if I went to the airport with you?" asked Sketch.

"Of course not. You're more than welcome."

"I've never seen an airplane before. I know of them, but haven't seen one in person."

"They're fascinating. But just not as fast as you."

Sketch stood before the drawing table and studied the college newspaper clippings of Charles' editorial cartoons that were pinned on the wall.

"You know, I arrived equipped with knowledge, but as I look at your drawings, it's dawning on me there are some things I don't know."

"Such as?"

"When did you learn to draw?"

Charles stepped over to the drawing table. "All of those cartoons, and anything I've ever drawn before has been self-taught. I'm majoring in art at the university, and I've taken art classes in high school, but honestly, they've had no influence on how I draw. I've always had the skill."

"So, even as a kid, you could draw well?"

"Yes. Of course, it developed over time. But I began drawing younger than my childhood days, too."

"Younger?"

"Much younger." Charles paused, then said, "Sketch, come to the kitchen. I want to share something with you about my past."

Charles took out a container of blueberries from the refrigerator and set them on the kitchen table.

"When I was ten years old, my mom said that when I was a baby she had a bunch of friends over one night for dinner. She said she'd placed frozen blueberries on my high chair because they were my favorite snack. After the guests had left, and I had been put to sleep, she went to clean my food tray, and said it looked like someone had painted a bird with the blueberry juice. She figured her friend Janice had painted a hawk.

"She didn't think anything of it until a week later when my parents took me to a lake with a wet sandy shoreline. She said she saw some children gathered around me yelling, "Bird! Bird! Bird!" She went over to see what the excitement was all about. And there it was…the image of a hawk in the sand. Keep in mind it wasn't drawn well by any means—I was very young—but good enough to make out what it was."

"So how old were you?" asked Sketch as he began eating a handful of the blueberries.

"About a year old."

"And you could draw a hawk?"

"It's crazy, I know. But to answer your question…no."

"I don't understand," said Sketch.

Charles scooped out a few blueberries for himself. "There was a third drawing, except it wasn't a hawk. My mom had taken me for a check-up at the doctor's office. I was just beginning to walk, and in the crowded waiting room I began drawing on a chalkboard. Mom said she was flipping through some magazines when she noticed people starting to talk and point at me. That's when she realized the blueberry painting wasn't something her friend Janice had created, but rather I had—a one-year-old. And that was also when a parent in the waiting room said, 'That's a falcon! Your child has drawn a falcon!'

"My mom had no idea what to make of the three drawings. And to this day, when on occasion the story comes up, she still doesn't have an answer."

"But, do you?" asked Sketch.

"Yes, I do. Thanks to Heba. I related all of this to her last week. She's convinced it was a sign, like a stamp of approval that I possess the innate qualities to be worthy of the ink. She said this was common with all the artists over time whom she had given the ink to. At some point in their lives prior to meeting her, each person had drawn three falcons. And all said they never remembered consciously doing it. The drawings came from a spirit within."

"Did Heba say why you drew your falcons at such an early age?"

"Yes." Charles went to his bedroom and got his backpack. Inside, he pulled out a ball of cloths, and carefully unwrapped them. There he held the sandstone falcon sculpture from Heba's apartment. "She wanted me to have this as a reminder of where the ink came from. She said I had drawn my falcons at a much younger age than any other artist. I had been destined early on to one day receive the ink. She said the three falcons represented the three that circled high above Khepri before the ink was anointed."

"And here I am," smiled Sketch.

"Yes, here you are," said Charles. "And can you please do me a big favor while I'm in Tulsa?"

"What's that?"

"Don't let the Metzes see you flying. Ok?"

Sketch laughed, "I'll do my best."

Later that day, Sketch and Charles loaded into the Metz's car and headed to the airport.

Chapter 5
THE CALL

Fifteen minutes into the night flight, Charles felt the vibration through his feet, as if someone beneath in the fuselage had taken a steel mallet and gave it one good swing to the underflooring. It was different than a turbulent bump. He looked around from his window seat to see if anyone else had felt it, but everyone seemed unbothered. A mother and her young son continued smiling as they pointed at pictures in a children's book. The businessman three rows back didn't flinch while he read the newspaper. And an elderly woman across the aisle kept bobbing her hanging head in and out of sleep. The Douglas DC-3 flight out of Lehman had been smooth from takeoff, but Charles wasn't at ease. His flights to and from Egypt were nearly flawless, with only a few brief stretches of turbulence. But this flight…

It was just a bump. Just a bump. Let it go.

He took a deep breath, exhaling slowly, trying to calm his nerves. The seat next to him was empty. He reached over to the unbuckled seatbelt and twirled the slick nylon strap between his fingers. He found some assurance thinking about the pilots in the cockpit. Vibrations were nothing to them. Occasional bumpy rides came with the territory. After all, they were well-trained and experienced. And all those dials and numbers on the instrument panel—so much necessary information, all designed to safely guide the aircraft and passengers to their destinations.

The second vibration was more noticeable. A bigger bump. A bigger mallet. The mother stopped reading and instinctively clenched her son's hand. The newspaper folded as the businessman tilted his head, his eyes squinting, concerned and curious. The elderly woman, abruptly awakened, was the first to speak. "What was that?"

Charles looked outside his window, cupping his hands around his face to block out reflections from inside the plane. The propeller engine was in sight, filling the plane with its constant buzz-like roar. But something wasn't right with the wing. It seemed to have an abnormal amount of bounce to it. He looked back at the other passengers, as a rise in concern had spread throughout the plane.

There was no third vibration, but rather a cluster of them. A hundred mallets pounding against the flooring. The plane tilted to Charles' side as he hurriedly reached beneath his seat for his satchel with the sketch book. Plates and drinks spilled into the aisle. Screams cried out. The pilots corrected the plane back to normal as the engines roared louder. The distraught mother and son held each other tightly. The businessman was nothing less than horrified. And the elderly woman extended her arm across the aisle to Charles. "Help us," she pleaded. "Your friend, I overheard him...what was it he said? The call can save you?"

Though not knowing what Sketch had been referring to, she was right.

Before he had boarded the plane, and while Mr. Metz had gone to the restroom, Sketch had told Charles:

"You have an ability to summon me. No matter how far away you may be, you have the ability to call me. By that I mean if you encounter a problem that needs my help, I want you to quick-sketch me. It doesn't need to be detailed. Just needs to suggest that it's me, with a rough sketch of where you are or what the problem is. But it's critical that you will a sense of urgency as you draw. That's the call, and it can save you. My intuition will connect the dots and act upon it immediately."

"Please!!" begged the woman. "Whatever it was your friend was talking about...please!!"

The plane tilted again as the pilots struggled, but managed to correct it a second time. Retrieving the satchel, Charles frantically took out the sketch book. His fingers fumbled deep inside for his drawing pen. "Jesus! Where's the pen?!" Seconds seemed like minutes, but soon he extracted the pen, flipped the sketch book to an empty page, and began to draw. All he needed was a minute. No details required, just a sketch.

Horizontal lines of water raced across his window as the plane entered a mass of rain clouds. As long as it maintained a reasonably level position, there was hope. However, if the nose dipped too sharply, if objects in the aisle began to tumble and slide toward the front, then forget the holidays, forget birthdays, forget the pay raise, forget all the simple, priceless pleasures that warm our hearts...Tennie and the baby...forget it all. When a plane pitches downward like the drop on the roller coaster you wish you hadn't buckled into, it's over.

The combination of weather turbulence and the plane's structural issue further escalated tension and fear. The mother anticipated the worst, holding her son tightly as she restrained her words.

But the boy saw something outside his window. A human figure that could only be one thing. He craned his neck up to his mother, who bent down to hear him as he spoke.

"Hush!" she said sharply. "Hush!"

"But it is!"

"Stop it!!"

Thirty seconds later the plane did pitch, and the sketch book flew from Charles' hands and into the aisle. It was too dangerous to stand. He stretched his leg out, but couldn't reach. The elderly woman tried as well, but to no avail. The nose of the plane dropped even further, then again tilted to Charles' side, maintaining one big spiraling descent. The sketch book was now nowhere to be seen, lost in the chaos.

Into its free fall, the pilots fought to save the flight, exhausting themselves, white-knuckled hands glued to their yokes as they spun toward the earth.

"MAYDAY!! MAYDAY!! MAYDAY!!"

It was beyond their capabilities, but there was no giving up. Breaking through the clouds, but still caught in the downpour, the plane spiraled faster as the lights of a city came into view. Who were the unfortunate souls below caught in their path? Accelerating into the descent, the pilots helplessly watched as a neighborhood rose up towards them. How many children? How many lives cut short? No way to warn of their impending doom.

And no need to.

Later, one of the pilots described it best: "We were lifted by a greater power." For a moment he had thought they had been spared the horror of impact and had passed into the afterlife. He said he could feel the g-forces of the aircraft as it rose. "I was pushed deep into my seat, as if I were four times my normal weight." And then, as the plane leveled: weightless. But how? A hand of God? Something atmospheric? Whatever it was that they had relinquished to, it was real and something that they couldn't identify. Their wives and children didn't flash before their eyes out of fear that they'd never see them again, but rather they knew they would.

Charles retrieved his sketch book, and returned to his seat where he held it tight against his chest. He then closed his eyes and smiled.

He had drawn enough.

The call had been answered.

Chapter 6
THE CALL RECEIVED

"Please!!" the elderly woman had begged as the plane tilted. "Please!!"

While willing a sense of urgency, Charles quickly drew Sketch in a flying position near an airplane with a bent wing. It took less than a minute to complete a rough drawing to convey the emergency, to make the call. And as he finished, the plane rocked and pitched downward, launching the sketchbook into the aisle then disappearing from sight.

Ten thousand feet below the aircraft, Sketch had just returned from the airport to the garage apartment with Mr. Metz. He had rounded the back of the garage and was about to walk up the stairs, when the call arrived.

It was an inner feeling that radiated from his spine, as though his vertebrae were wrapped with a heating coil. His chest rose and shoulders retracted as a wave of heat instantly flowed outward through his body, before breaking the surface of his skin and dissipating into the air. A flash of bright white light then shot through his eyes, unseeable by anyone but himself, as if the flash were something he had imagined.

But he hadn't. He saw the quick sketch clearly, alerting him of its urgency: himself flying toward a troubled and crippled airplane headed to nowhere but its fatal impact with the earth.

Stripped of his jeans and t-shirt, and wearing his superhero outfit, Sketch left in a blur, racing into the night as the ink within his body—in its own mysterious way—guided his trajectory directly to the falling aircraft.

There was no concern as to whether or not he could save the airplane. There was no second guessing the capability of his strength. There were no doubts of any kind, because the properties of the ink worked. The system worked. Select the artist who meets all the requirements to create the right kind of superhero and watch a fully-loaded passenger aircraft falling from the sky be rescued by that superhero. Watch as he sweeps in between the deafening roar of the plane's twin engines, centering his hands on the plane's underbelly, then guides it safely back to the Lehman airport, despite one of its wings noticeably angled down so that the wingtip nearly touched the ground at landing.

The pilots, speechless as they lived through the last-second correction of their aircraft, lowered the plane's landing gear as it approached an impossible level landing with a broken wing. When the tires touched the tarmac and the plane rolled to a safe stop, they knew they didn't deserve the cheering applause coming from behind them. And until the day they would each die of old age, they would forever wonder what it was that saved their lives.

Chapter 7
TRAGEDY

Strewn throughout the plane, along with emotional tears of elation, were cups, bottles, broken glass and plates, silverware, luggage, purses and their contents, books, magazines, toys, and scattered food items. Muscle strains, bruises, and minor cuts were also prevalent, but nothing broken, nor any fatalities. A total of forty-eight passengers, some moving gingerly, exited the plane as they were helped down the portable stairway in the rain, assisted by emergency crews, flight attendants, and the pilots. Three passengers were taken away by ambulance, the rest were led into the airport where they were examined by paramedics, doctors and nurses. Many were crying, overcome with emotions, unable to make sense of what they had miraculously survived.

Inside the terminal, a nurse sat next to an elderly woman—the nurse's arm around her, holding her close and speaking calmly, assuring her that everything was going to be alright. But the woman, her eyes bloodshot, wept in her hands, repeating, "He saved us! He saved us!"

"Who saved you?" asked the nurse.

"The young man."

"What young man?"

The woman looked up and saw Charles who happened to be walking by.

"Him! Him!" she hollered, pointing.

Charles walked over to the woman and knelt on one knee, smiling as he held her hands. "We're alive," he said. "We made it."

"But you saved us! You drew something. I watched you. And after that, it happened."

"What happened?" asked the nurse.

"The plane… it stopped falling. It just stopped falling."

"Do you know her?" said the nurse, looking at Charles.

"Only that she sat across from me."

"Well, whatever you did, it made an impact. So, thank you."

"And thank you for your help tonight." Charles leaned in to the elderly woman. "You're in good hands, ma'am. Take care."

He made his way to a row of ticket counters where passengers were using the telephones to call friends and family members. He called Mr. Metz who had already heard the news that was being broadcasted on TV and radio. Word was out that a commercial airplane had landed with one wing, which wasn't too far from the truth.

"Charles, are you ok?"

"Yes, I'm fine."

"What the hell happened?"

"I'm not sure. But it was bad. Really bad."

"Is it true your plane had one wing?"

"Not exactly, but it was bent. We went into a downward spiral."

"Well, your pilots did an amazing job. Just amazing."

"Yes, sir…it was truly amazing."

Charles could hear Mrs. Metz talking in the background. "Yes, he's fine," said Mr. Metz. "Charles, we're going to get in the car in just a few, then head your way. I'll let David know. I'm sure he'll want to come."

"Is he there?" asked Charles, feeling the return of anxiety, suddenly wondering if Sketch might be in the apartment, but still in his outfit.

"Why wouldn't he be?" said Mr. Metz. "We came straight back from the airport."

"I don't know. I mean, he loves to walk."

"In the rain?"

Sketch's whereabouts could be anywhere. He could be back in St. Louis celebrating his successful heroic effort with a bottle of champagne atop the Arch. Or he could be taking a long hot shower. Anywhere.

Under an umbrella in the light rain, Gordon knocked on the apartment door, and Sketch answered in his jeans and long sleeve work shirt.

"David, sorry to bother but we need to go back to the airport to get Charles. He's fine, but his flight almost crashed."

"Are you serious? What happened?"

"I don't know the details, but there was a problem with one of the plane's wings. Like it was bent or something."

"And it landed?"

"I heard it on the radio. One of the pilots said he felt like the plane was flying itself. He said people were thanking him, but he said he didn't do anything. David, how do you explain something like that?"

"I'm not sure, but it does sound strange, if not impossible."

Mrs. Metz was now standing outside. "Honey, I'm getting in the car. The rain's supposed to pick up. Ready when you are."

Mr. Metz directed his voice upward, "We're coming! Be there in a sec, Peg!"

Sketch sat in the back seat on their way to the airport. Beneath his jeans and work shirt he wore his superhero outfit. His mask was tucked in a rear pants pocket. The intensity of the rain increased as strobes of lightning flashed within the dirty-gray clouds. Looking out the window, the night felt reminiscent of riding in the police car some twenty-four hours earlier, when he sat in the back seat just two hours fresh into the world. Had there been lightning on July 4th, he wondered if he would have confused it for artillery like he had the fireworks.

Within such a short period of time, though, he had now become a different person. He was complete with his superpowers intact. He fully understood the purpose of his existence: to protect from harm, to rescue from danger, and to combat evil.

When he had approached the airplane during its spiraling descent there was no problem with the driving rain, the weight of the aircraft, or any difficulty positioning himself. Because all that mattered was saving lives and, in particular, saving Charles. After all, if Charles were to perish, then also would the essence of Sketch.

There were two police cars at the airport's entrance when the Metzes and Sketch walked inside, making their way past the reservation counters, then down the terminal corridor. At the end of the corridor was the gate where the crippled airplane was parked.

A group of aviation accident investigators had arrived from Chicago. Equipped with flashlights, cameras and clipboards, they gathered beneath their umbrellas as they assessed the plane's damaged wing. All of the evening flights had been cancelled.

"Hey, there's Charles!" said Peggy, excitedly.

He was using a phone at a ticket counter. He acknowledged their presence then returned to his call. Distant thunder could be heard as lightning bolts flashed across the sky, signaling more stormy weather to come. "If the weather's okay, I'll catch a flight out of Chicago tomorrow, I love you so much. Bye, Ten."

With his satchel slung over his shoulder and small suitcase in hand, Charles made his way over to the Metzes and Sketch, and gave Peggy a hug. "Oh, Charles, you must have been horrified...absolutely horrified."

Charles sent a nodding smile to Sketch. "It did get pretty hairy up there, but then something happened...and...I don't know...we were no longer falling...I knew we were in capable hands."

"Well, my friend," said Sketch, giving Charles a welcoming hug, "it's good to see you made it down safely."

"Jesus," said Gordon. "How could it have landed in that condition?" He was walking toward the end of the terminal where he could see the plane and the team of investigators. A TV crew was reporting on the scene and a newspaper photographer was taking pictures. Gordon noticed that the plane's wing was clearly as damaged as the media had been reporting. "I mean, look at it," he said. "The tip is nearly touching the ground. How's it even possible?"

Passengers continued being treated along the terminal, most of whom were emotionally shaken, sharing the common denominator of confusion—unable to explain the moment the plane leveled off from its free fall. News reporters worked their way around the area, conducting interviews in an effort to find an answer to the predominant mystery.

Sketch, Charles, and the Metzes stood before the large plate glass windows, looking out at the plane as Sergeant Perkins and Officer Montague, dressed in long yellow raincoats entered the area through a nearby emergency exit door, when Montague spotted Sketch.

"Hey, Sarge. Look! It's David from last night."

"Well, it sure is. Staying out of trouble, David?" smiled Perkins, as he made his way toward Sketch.

"Sergeant Perkins, good evening. Yes, sir…all good. Charles was on that flight."

"Good evening, sir," said Charles.

"Is that so?" said Perkins. "Well, they're calling it the miracle landing. How in the hell did it not crash?"

Conversations around them were full of people speculating just how was it that the plane landed. The two pilots were off to the side conducting interviews with the media. They were being heralded as the heroes of the century, but all they did was pray and fear for their lives. They did all they could do, but they knew it had amounted to nothing. So, what was it? What really did save them? Was it God? It seemed like the obvious answer, or was it an answer they knew people resorted to when no other pieces fit the puzzle?

However, there was one piece that did fit, but it just seemed too far-fetched to believe. Talking about it would be preposterous, so no one did.

Except one person: the little boy who was traveling with his mother.

Accelerating into the descent and amongst the roar of the engines and helpless cries, the boy had looked out his window as his mother constrained him, and said to her, "It's Superman!"

"Hush!" she had said sharply. "Hush!"

"But it is!"

"Stop it!!"

And that's when everyone—as the pilots had later said—felt like four times their weight as their bodies sank into their seats. Then weightless. Then flying level and landing with a broken wing. The mother relaxed her arms and looked down at her son who smiled and repeated excitedly, "It was Superman!!…Superman!!" Everyone on the plane had heard him, but it was too ridiculous to consider. And certainly not worth mentioning to the media. He was a kid being a kid.

"It's going to be very interesting what they come up with," said Perkins, looking out at the group of investigators inspecting the plane. "I mean, Charles…you must have been thinking, this is it."

Charles glanced at Sketch and said, "I had faith."

"Well, glad you made it down alive."

"Thank you, sir. Me too."

"You all have yourselves a good evening. We're heading back to the station."

Perkins paused, though, and said, "I do have one question…David, what was it you called yourself last night? Was it Sketch?"

Here we go again, thought Charles with trepidation.

"Yes," said Sketch. "A nickname."

"I thought that was it. Well, Sketch, last night when you were in your costume, you had said, 'Next time, I will be able to fly'. And later, after I went home, I thought, what an odd comment that was… like who says that kind of stuff? And I thought about your costume…and that mask…and then I saw this plane tonight, and the impossibility of it landing…and I thought…Sketch??"

"Excuse me, sir," said Sketch, "but are you implying that I had something to do with saving that airplane?"

"No," said Perkins as he chuckled. "I think what I'm implying is I'd have to be crazy to believe such a thing. You all have a safe evening. Goodnight."

As the two officers walked away, Gordon Metz turned to Sketch and Charles, and said, "What costume?"

"I'll explain it in the car," said Charles, as another wave of storms approached.

TV news reporter, John Stills, and cameraman, Freddy Sanchez were en route to the airport in a Chevy station wagon. Stills, best known for his curly red hair, was driving while Sanchez was in the passenger seat, cleaning the lens of his video camera and fitting it with a protective rain cover. They were running behind to cover the story of the damaged plane.The event was being unanimously dubbed as "The Miracle Landing" by the media who were already reporting from the scene. All except for Stills and Sanchez.

Five miles from the airport, they were traveling northbound at 65 mph into the thunderstorm that was gaining intensity. Their windshield wipers struggled to keep up with the heavy rain, leaving a watery obscurity with each sweep. John had a penchant for having a heavy foot, no matter how dangerous the driving conditions.

"Remember," said Freddy, "it's probably not a bad idea to arrive at the airport in one piece."

"All under control. I'm not going to put us at risk. It's just these damn deadlines they give us. It's like no matter how fast you go, you're always behind."

Freddy paused from cleaning his camera, and looked out the windshield, the visibility only worsening as the rain machine-gunned the car, causing them to raise their voices. And then the first of the swirling winds arrived, followed by a barrage of hail, instantly deafening the interior of the car.

Approaching them in the southbound lane, were two shimmering watery headlights moving erratically side to side. The pelting hail drowned out the horn which was blowing from the oncoming vehicle that had suddenly fishtailed across the divider line. And as it fishtailed, two more headlights appeared that had been traveling closely behind.

"JOHN!!!!" screamed Freddy, just before impact.

"Damn, I hate this weather," said Perkins, as he drove with Montague southbound, away from the airport. "And to think that that airplane was caught in this, spinning to the earth with a broken wing. That's gonna puzzle me 'til I die."

"You don't think the investigators will find anything?" asked Montague.

"I think it's doubtful. I'm no physics wiz, but I do know a plane takes two wings to fly."

"So, what's your guess?"

"Look, call me crazy, but—"

Lightning splintered down from the sky, stabbing a plowed field just off the highway, as thunder cracked and rumbled like a demon's cry.

"Damn, I hate this weather!" Perkins repeated, tightening his grip on the steering wheel. "Yeah, call me crazy, but I think Sketch is different."

"Different?"

"Yes. Like he can do stuff that we can't."

"But last night—"

"Forget last night. He's different tonight. Just something about him…aw, shit! Hail!"

Checking his rearview mirror, two bright headlights were annoyingly close. "And who the hell is this riding my ass? Back off, buddy!" he said, as golf ball-sized hail battered the squad car, shattering the top emergency strobe lights.

Just as Perkins was beginning to decelerate, there was a loud BOOM!! as the driver side front tire blew, shredding it to the rim that hit the road, sending the car into a fishtail.

"WE'RE GONNA HIT!!! WE'RE GONNA HIT!!!" screamed Montague, as Perkins laid on the horn.

John Stills had tried his best to avoid the collision with Perkins, but he had reacted too late, causing the front of his Chevy to vault upward off the lowered front-end of the police car where the tire had blown out.

And as it launched, it rotated on its side, corkscrewing into the air, sailing toward the car trailing behind Perkins.

Peggy Metz always felt that her husband followed too closely behind vehicles on the highway. In their forty-four years of marriage, they had very few disagreements between them. But of the ones they did have, the highway following distance stirred the pot the most. And so, when the situation arose, she would back off the issue, tighten her lips, look out her side window, and avert her eyes from the close proximity of the vehicle ahead of them—the source of tension and anxiety.

On this particular night, as they drove away from the airport and into the pouring rain with Sketch sitting behind her, and Charles behind Gordon, she felt her husband owed a greater responsibility to all the occupants, and needed to give a little more space from the car ahead of them.

"Honey," she said, as diplomatically as possible, "you do know that's a police car ahead of us."

"Yes, Peggy, I do. And I know what you're thinking, but I'm not too close."

"Hon'...you are."

"Peg...please..."

It was a conversation that Sketch would play back for many years to come. A conversation that, had he interrupted it, he might have changed the fate of things to come. But, instead, he said nothing, and, in doing so, Gordon Metz kept his tight spacing, and the life that Sketch had come to love, quickly changed.

Swirling winds. Barrage of hail. Splintered lightning. BOOM!! A blaring horn.

And then...tragedy...

Seconds after Gordon Metz hit the brakes, he and Peggy were

killed instantly as the front end of the TV crew's station wagon speared into the upper hood of the Metz's car, shattering the windshield and collapsing the dashboard into them. Stills and Sanchez were also killed as their vehicle suffered severe damage from landing on its top after cartwheeling over the Metzes and onto the roadway.

Sketch, though, was quick to react.

Bending his right arm at ninety degrees and bracing it horizontally against the back of the Metz's bench seat, he was able to stop anything from caving in on him. Simultaneously, he extended his left arm across Charles to protect him as well. After all, in this situation, he had only one mission: to protect from harm.

Three cars. Five people dead.

The fifth was Montague, who had taken the fatal blow from the side impact with a telephone pole after their car had spun off the road.

As the hail moved on, the wreckage settled with only the sound of hissing steam and the continuing rainfall.

But there was a moan that came from Charles. A painful moan. And one that Sketch instinctually recognized as, for lack of a better word, not good.

Charles remained as still as possible, knowing that any movement would certainly worsen the situation. His eyes grew large as he looked at Sketch. He spoke cautiously, knowing that any effort to speak could intensify the pain.

A narrow, foot-long piece of steel from the door frame had broken free and knifed into Charles' chest, just missing his heart, but the bleeding was profuse.

"Sketch…is there…anything…you can do?"

Sketch then saw it and said, "I don't know. I honestly don't know." His eyes were laden with sadness.

"Sketch…" he said, scared and sensing his time was nearing.

"I'm here, Charles. I'm here."

The only help Sketch could offer was his presence. Beyond that, there was nothing.

Charles' voice became quieter. "Please…take my hand."

Sketch did so, as he felt his first-ever tears run down his cheeks. "I'm sorry, Charles!" he cried. "I'm so sorry!"

"Sketch…tell Tennie and the newborn I loved them dearly. And remember…always protect your drawing."

Before he died, Charles spoke two final words to Sketch, who remained in the car, holding his hand and crying unrestrained. He cried and screamed repeatedly, anger and confusion coursing through him. He wanted to pound the earth, shaking nearby trees as he did so. He wanted to fly to the Arch and beat it to the ground. He wanted to do so much, but it would be futile. He had failed his only friend who had created him, and nothing would ever reverse that.

And so, there he sat…once again…powerless.

PART IV

Chapter 1

$100,000

2008

The mass exodus to the Gulf Coast had already begun on a Friday afternoon as the students of Waterstone College packed their cars on the advent of Spring Break. The college sat in the heart of Waterstone, Texas—a river town shaded with large oak, pecan, and cypress trees located at the edge of the Texas hill country. If the students weren't traveling south, then they were headed to the ski slopes of New Mexico or Colorado.

It was at the end of a drawing class when art professor Wyatt Collins delivered the news.

"I know y'all are anxious to get a jump on the week, but I'm giving you one assignment to complete over Spring Break."

The classroom grumbled disapprovingly.

Collins was loyal to one wardrobe: long-sleeve denim shirts, jeans, and weathered cowboy boots. His face was worn but handsome, shaped by years of honest, hard ranch work under the Texas sun. "Oh, chill," he said. "It's something y'all actually might enjoy."

"So, it involves alcohol?" asked a student.

Wyatt laughed. "I suppose it could, but that's your choice."

The student slapped his desktop. "I love this class!!"

"Ok, now here's your assignment, due Friday after you return from the break." Wyatt distributed a handout to each student, as the grumbling continued, then read it to the class.

"Your assignment is to create a superhero who is completely original. Your character must be completed using one of (or a combination of) the following mediums: graphite, pencil, colored pencils, black ink or colored ink. Your drawing must be on sketch book paper or cold or hot press illustration board, no larger than 8-1/2" x 11". Your superhero must have human attributes, such as human language and physical features. However, he or she need not be completely human. Your character can possess animal features as well, as long as it is at least 50% human. An example would be the mythological Centaur who was part human, part horse. Your superhero cannot be a copy of one that has already been created, such as the classic superheroes: Superman, Captain America, or Wonder Woman. Your character must also possess an appearance that is unique, something more than just the average Joe. Think about skin color, fur, height, shape, clothing, multiple limbs, eyes, etc. One drawing of your superhero is all you need. Include the character's name, along with a brief description that explains what makes your character unique. Remember, create a character who is completely original. What are his or her superpowers? Perhaps your character can read minds, see the future, or throw spears of ice. The superpowers needn't be original, but there must be one overall attribute that makes the character stand apart from all others."

Wyatt scanned the classroom when he finished. "Any questions?"

A student in the back of the room raised her hand. "So, super powers are not required?"

"No, they're not. But they might add a little interest to an already creative physical appearance."

Wyatt began gathering his papers. "No other questions? Ok, then…" he paused for a moment, walking around to the front of his desk, then sat on top, dangling his legs. "I do have just one little detail to add. This is not your average art assignment. In fact, today, the assignment is being given to every college art drawing class in the country. A cash prize of $100,000 will be awarded to the top ten artists who create the most unique superheroes. I think that'll be it. Have a safe Spring Break, and I'll see y'all in ten days."

The room murmured as confused faces looked side to side. A voice from the back asked, "Professor, is this a joke?"

"It's no joke. The university has thoroughly researched the credibility of the contest, and it's legit."

"Who's puttin' up the cash?" asked another student.

"VIP Comics is sponsoring the contest which they're calling The Lure. VIP is new to the industry, but they're well-funded and are searching for superhero creators with original ideas. Their goal is to rival Marvel and DC."

"$100,000...cash?"

"Yes, every penny of it."

A girl in the front row raised her hand. "This is an assignment, too?"

"Yes. It doesn't matter if you're selected as a winner or not, it's a graded assignment." Wyatt looked at the clock on the wall. "If you have any more questions about The Lure, feel free to stop by my office. That's all for now. Have a great Spring Break, and party hard!"

As the class made their exit, Wyatt called over a student. "Mr. Welch...can you come here for just a sec'?"

"Yes, sir."

Sid Welch had a tall, lanky build, with wavy chestnut hair and dark eyes. He was a likeable, smiley 20-year-old, infused with optimism.

"It's been a while since I asked," said Wyatt, "but how's the mural coming along at Sierra Oaks?"

"Oh, I love it! It's abstract, but it's cool."

"Does it have a title yet?"

"Not yet. But it'll come. It's only about half way complete."

"We should unveil it to the class when it's done. Turn it into an event."

"Oh, I don't know if it'll be that good."

"Sid, don't kid yourself. You're damn talented."

The students had all cleared out of the classroom which had become noticeably quiet as Sid cinched his backpack snug over his shoulder.

"This contest—The Lure—I'm not sure what to draw."

"You'll have no problem. Just give it some time. Something'll click."

"A $100,000 superhero, huh?"
"Sid, if there's one artist who might have a chance, it's you."
"You think so?"
"I know so."
"Give it your best shot. Pour your imagination into it."

Chapter 2
MURAL

The Sierra Oaks retirement home sat on a thirty-foot cliff overlooking the Verde River that wound its way through Waterstone. It was an expansive facility whose five-hundred-plus residents had access to two dining rooms, a six-lane bowling alley, fitness center, lap pool, movie theater, woodworking shop, arts and crafts studio, and outdoor sport courts. There was also an on-site physician and dentist. If that wasn't enough, there was an outside perimeter walking trail, and a golf course a quarter of a mile away. Other than having to go to the grocery store across town, there wasn't much need to leave the Sierra Oaks premises.

Sid, who was in his second year of college, worked at Sierra Oaks, mostly tending to grounds maintenance jobs like mowing, weed eating, and pruning. He also worked in the dining rooms, bussing tables or helping to decorate for the holidays and special events such as live music performances.

Sierra Oaks was a three-story limestone building whose main entrance was joined by a hallway that led to a spacious atrium. Four large triangular panes of glass converged in a pyramid fashion at the top of the atrium, letting in an abundance of natural light. For the past two weeks the floor was lined with drop cloths as Sid painted his mural working atop a complex of scaffolding.

A few weeks, before the project began, Professor Collins had been asked by his long-time friend and director of Sierra Oaks,

Bryan Cobb, if he knew of any artists at the college who could create a mural. They were in a local coffee shop when the conversation came up.

"How big of a mural are you talking?" asked Wyatt.

"Well, you know the atrium there. I'm thinking the top half of one of the walls, up to the ceiling windows."

"Subject matter?"

"Honestly, I'm open to anything. It could be Texas-themed, or even reflect Waterstone."

"How about abstract?"

"Yes, but not too weird."

Wyatt laughed. "That's all in the eye of the beholder."

"Oh, you know what I mean. Sometimes abstract art is just too far out there. I remember at one of your class exhibits there was a piece titled, *Absence of Time Bruised*. And I was like, what the hell does that even mean?"

Wyatt bowed his head, shaking it ashamedly, as he stirred creamer in his coffee. "The painting that was entirely dark purple except for the small alarm clock and blurry boxing gloves in the middle? The student had intentionally damaged the canvas repeatedly with a hammer."

"Yes! That disaster. Wyatt, what are you teaching these kids?"

"You're right, it was a disaster. In fact, I failed that student. I can't disagree. Sometimes they're just too far out there."

"So, you have someone in mind for the mural?"

"I sure do. And you know him. He works for you. It's Sid."

"Sid Welch? My grounds worker?"

"Yes, sir. I haven't seen a student with his kind of pure talent in a long time, if ever."

"Sid, huh?" said Bryan, sipping his coffee. "I knew he was studying art, but I just never thought to ask."

"Well, ask him. I think he'd do a good job."

"Ok. I will."

"And the reason I asked if abstract art interests you is because he's done some incredible abstracts himself. He's got a real eye for evoking mood with color. The kid can paint and draw anything."

On Saturday, the first day of Spring Break, Sid and two other grounds keepers arrived at the Oaks around noon to plant snapdragons bordering the parking lot. They then added fresh black mulch and rid the area of stubborn weeds.

Afterwards, Sid took a late sack lunch break on a tree-shaded picnic table at the back of the building. When he finished, he made his way to the atrium and began preparing to paint, mixing his acrylics, selecting brushes, and securing a wide-spray nozzle on an airbrush. At the bottom of the mural and working its way up were different shades of greens blending into light blues before gradually becoming darker. As Sid positioned himself on the scaffolding, Bryan Cobb entered the atrium. He was a balding, middle-aged man with a pooched tummy, dressed in black slacks and a blue button-down shirt.

"Sid, it sure is looking good."

"Thank you, sir. That's my goal, to create something that's soothing."

"How long do you think it'll be before you're finished?"

"By the end of the week, I hope. I've got a few surprises coming."

"You're not going to make it weird, are you?"

Sid laughed as he stirred titanium white with ultramarine. "No, sir. Nothing weird. Just some subtle geometric shapes."

"Well, Professor Collins was right. You're a pretty talented kid. I'll let you be, Sid. Have a good day."

"You, too, sir."

As Bryan turned and walked away, and as Sid poured his acrylic mixture into the airbrush paint reservoir, Dwight and Lola Kellogg passed through the atrium. It was a brief appearance in which neither noticed Sid above on the scaffolding.

"Jesus, Lola! Did you have to say yes?"

"But, they're—"

"But, they're what? Friendly? Fun? You know I can't stand them."

"Dwight, please. I didn't mean to—"

"But you did. You said yes. And now we have to go to the damn dinner!"

"Dwight, please…"

And off their voices trailed as they left the atrium, then headed out the main entrance.

Sid stood silent, feeling sad for Lola. Her husband was a tyrant. An oppressive asshole. He had witnessed him too many times in action. Storming out of the dining room in a fit of impatience. Raising his voice at Lola during shuffleboard. Or not holding a door open for her. But his disgruntled attitude surfaced elsewhere. He complained loudly in Bryan's office. He belittled waiters. He would use subterfuge to win a tennis match, serving an older ball that had less bounce, making it more difficult to return. He would tee up his golf ball on a second stroke when no one could see him. Dwight was rotten to the core, and poor Lola just kept taking the hits.

Sid turned on an air compressor and began air brushing the light ultramarine in a back-and-forth pattern, layering the paint with each stroke. But Dwight was stuck in his head, and so was Professor Collins. There was a sort of collision of the two as Sid recalled the art contest Collins had announced. *Unique. Superhero. Remember: create a character who is completely original. $100,000!* But where was he to begin? He wasn't sure, so he stayed on the scaffolding and worked on the mural for two more hours, then went home, upset with Dwight Kellogg.

Chapter 3
KRYPTONITE KOMICS

Kryptonite Komics was a comic book store in Waterstone that had been around for over thirty years. It had quite a following from the locals, college students, and enthusiasts from small satellite towns, as well as those making the hour trip from either Austin or San Antonio. The store's inventory covered the entire spectrum of comics from rare, limited-edition collectibles to newly released Japanese anime. Posters of Archie, Dick Tracy, Dracula, the Fantastic Four, Pokémon, Superman, and a multitude of other characters covered the walls. Wooden bins divided by labeled and colored cut-to-size poster board housed the comics that were separated by genres. The store smelled of a stale odor, of a vintage era before modern technology began eliminating paper. It was a time of turning and not swiping pages. And that was much of its lure. Entering Kryptonite Komics was like passing through a portal where time froze, and the imagination of years gone by returned to life.

It was Monday evening, and Sid had come to the store to get some ideas for his art assignment. Two long days of grounds work, and more time spent on the mural had left him exhausted. He had thought of a character named Tripod, whose three legs telescoped to such heights that he could touch the clouds, but the concept just didn't fully impress him.

He hoped that by going to Kryptonite, something might catch his eye. It could be anything: anatomy, hair style, eyes, superpower, outfit, or even a character's motor vehicle. It could be a detective, vampire, werewolf, or alien. There were no genres that he wouldn't consider. He knew it had to be something he'd enjoy creating. Though Tripod was unique, Sid wanted something more than just someone walking above skyscrapers or being able to straddle the Himalayas and put a Christmas star atop Mt. Everest.

As prolific an artist as he was, Sid's creativity was at a standstill.

"Good evening, Mr. Roberts," said Sid to the store's owner, a middle-age man who was wearing a black t-shirt with a yellow Batman insignia on the chest.

"Evening, Sid. Aren't you supposed to be at the beach?"

"I wish, but I need the money. Gotta work."

"I understand. College is big business. It ain't cheap."

"No kiddin', sir."

"Can I help you with anything tonight?"

"I'm just looking around. I've got an art assignment due next week. I'm supposed to create an original superhero, and I'm stumped. So, I thought I'd come here to get some ideas."

"Take your time. You're bound to come up with something in this place."

Sid flipped through bins of X-Men, the Atom, Green Lantern, and Ice Man comics, paying attention to not just the artistic technicalities, but the stories as well. Development of the superhero's arch enemy always interested him. Cityscapes, night scenes, and the different visual perspectives were equally intriguing.

Making his way around the room, he passed by a glass cabinet that contained comic memorabilia, including a child's Wonder Woman purse, a Thor hammer, "WHAM!!" and "BAM!" stickers, and superhero figurines. The cabinet was set against a wall where a framed newspaper article hung. Within the frame was a drawing of an airplane on a piece of paper.

"That's new. I put it up yesterday," said Mr. Roberts, finishing checking out the purchases for a father with his young son, before walking over to the cabinet. "I've actually had this frame at my house for years. Then a couple days ago I was going through some boxes and came across it."

"So why hang it here? What's so special about the airplane?"

A bearded man dressed in jeans and a flannel shirt emerged through a door that led to a back room from behind the checkout desk. Looking across the room, he said, "Sid?"

"Mr. Tisdale. I didn't know you worked here."

"You two know each other?" asked Mr. Roberts.

"Yes, sir," said Sid. "I basically clean his dishes at night."

"Well, I wouldn't put it that way," chuckled Mr. Tisdale. "Sid works at Sierra Oaks, bussing tables at dinner time."

"So, do you work here?" asked Sid.

"Now and then, but it's volunteer work. Retirement can get really boring. So, Jack, those boxes in the back…you want me to flatten them for recycle before I leave?"

"Yes, Henry. That'd be great."

"Ok. Nice seeing ya, Sid. Oh, and Jack…you need to swing by Sierra this week and check out his mural. It's really coming along."

"Will do. You leaving through the back door?"

"Yes, sir. I'll see ya next time."

As Henry went to the back room, Sid returned to the frame, reading aloud the newspaper article's headline.

"*MIRACLE LANDING!* So, what happened? What's the significance of this article?"

"Give me one second," said Jack, who then went to complete two final sales, then flipped the OPEN sign to CLOSED before locking the front door.

"Sid, if you have a little time, I want to share something with you. Something that I've kept quiet for quite some time. And I don't know why, but it just seems right telling you."

"By all means, Mr. Roberts. I'm in no rush. Is everything ok?"

"Oh, everything's fine. I just need to tell you about this article. About that photo of the airplane."

"Sid, my father, who died a few years back, owned a comic book store in Lehman, Illinois. He ran it for over twenty years, and it was much like this one. There's an airport in Lehman, and in 1967 one of the planes that had taken off to go to Chicago experienced mechanical issues. I want you to look closely at that photo of the plane. Does anything look odd or just not right?"

Sid leaned in for a closer look. "Yeah. The wing…it looks broken. The tip is touching the ground."

"Exactly."

"It flew like that?"

"Yes."

"But…that's impossible."

"Exactly!"

"So, how'd it land?"

"No one knows."

"But the pilots must've—"

"Sid, the newspaper that had this article was left at the front door of my dad's store with that drawing tied to it. I'd like you to read what's written at the bottom of the drawing."

Sid leaned forward again and read what was written in capital letters:

THE LITTLE BOY ALMOST GOT IT RIGHT.
S

Sid looked up. "Who was S?"

"No one knows. But this is where things get strange. If you'll notice, the plane in the drawing looks very much like the one in the photo. And it, too, has a broken wing. But under the plane, though it's rather small, is a human figure, as if it's holding up the plane."

"Or, perhaps, flying it?" suggested Sid.

"Yes…perhaps flying it."

"Well, obviously, someone was pulling your dad's leg."

"Or, perhaps not."

"Mr. Roberts, you don't seriously think that—"

"Sid…this is going to sound crazy. You're going to think I've lost my mind, but hear me out. In the article, the pilots are quoted as saying they felt like the plane was flying itself. The plane was spiraling toward the earth, nose down…with a broken wing, and the pilots said something lifted it up, leveled it, and took it in for a landing. But no one believed them. No one knew what to believe. The only thing the passengers knew for certain was that they survived.

"And so…here's where things get crazy. The wing was clearly broken. And in the sketch, there is a human figure holding up, or flying an airplane that looks strikingly similar to the one in the photo. And, if you read the article, a mother who was interviewed mentions that her son said he saw Superman outside his window. Of course, the comment was in jest. Or was it?

"Sid, for years my dad beat his head, trying to figure out who left the paper at his business. Who drew the airplane? And who was S? I, too, could never figure it out. Is it possible…is it actually possible that S is Superman? I know! I know! I work in a place full of superheroes—fictitious characters with superhuman strength. But is it possible? Or maybe not even Superman, but someone else? Like the note said: almost got it right. Was it some other superhero, who even the comic book artists and writers didn't, and still don't, know about to this day?"

Sid couldn't take his eyes off the drawing. He kept looking closer and closer at the figure beneath the plane. He found himself intrigued by everything Mr. Roberts was suggesting.

"Mr. Roberts…"

"Yes?"

"I'm not sure why, but I don't think you're crazy at all."

Chapter 4
TRES HALCONES

On Thursday afternoon, Sid completed the mural. During the two-week production, he had witnessed Dwight Kellogg pass through the atrium a dozen times, and not once did the man show any sign of appreciation or interest. Whether he was alone or with his wife, Lola, his signature crabby tone was always on display. But Lola did take notice, and she did compliment Sid. "It's a masterpiece! We are so privileged to have you!" She would give him a smiling thumbs-up as they passed, while Dwight wallowed in his crotchety mumbling manner.

Near the end of the mural's completion, Bryan Cobb expressed nothing but gratitude as he and Sid stood in the atrium.

"Sid, the residents love it! I've heard only great comments. It's abstract, just as you said it would be. But it works, it really works. It has a feel-goodness about it."

"Thank you, sir. It means a lot to hear that."

"I do have one question, though," said Bryan, looking up at the ceiling windows. "I know you said the green transitioning into blue represents grass and sky, but up there, close to the windows…what are those three light-brown and whitish triangular shapes?"

Sid smiled. "Funny you should ask. The shapes came to me unexpectedly. It was strange. It was as if I painted them subconsciously.

And then…I was finished, and there they were. They're the title of the mural."

"Which is?"

"Tres Halcones."

"Which means?"

"Three Falcons."

Chapter 5
BATTERY

A steady rain moved into Waterstone on Friday morning, saturating the ground and cancelling any mowing that Sid had been assigned to. Instead, he tended to the final clean-up at the mural, disposing of wads of blue masking tape and plastic drop cloth, storing the ladder and extension cord, and boxing up his paints, brushes, and airbrush. A rental company was scheduled for the afternoon to dismantle and remove the scaffolding.

Sid asked if there was any extra work he could help with, but there wasn't. Nor had anyone called in sick, which was the norm on a Friday, so he was free to go home.

After loading the car with his supplies, he turned the key in the ignition switch, but it didn't turn over. The red battery light dimly flickered, then faded. He waited a few seconds, then tried again. Nothing. He waited a minute. Again, nothing. He dropped his head to the top of the steering wheel, resting it there for a moment, then went back into the building.

He thought of asking Mr. Cobb for jumper cables, but he was dressed too nicely to have to be out in the rain, as were the other people in the front offices. There was an elderly couple shuffling through the lobby, but they were an obvious "no." He tried the kitchen, but it was unoccupied.

He went back to his car where he had left his cell phone, and began calling his friend, Devin, but then hung up as he remembered he was at the beach.

Sid's attention was focused on his windshield as tracks of water streamed down and joined with each other to create larger streams. What a strange way to occupy oneself, he thought, but it was interrupted as a car pulled into the parking space next to him. The water running down his windows obscured the view of the man hurriedly getting out with a plastic bag of groceries. Sid emerged from his car, and said, "Excuse me, sir, but…Mr. Tisdale?"

"Hey, Sid! Good morning!"

"Sir, I hate to bother you in this rain, but my car's dead. Do you have any jumper cables?"

"Sure do. Hang on…" Henry set the groceries back in the car, then opened his trunk and retrieved the cables. "Sid, you do realize it's raining, don't you?"

"My bad, sir."

Henry laughed. "C'mon, let's get this done."

They propped open their hoods as the rain fell steadily, and the first sign of thunder rumbled in the distance.

"Here ya go," said Henry, water now rolling off his beard as he handed one end of the cables to Sid, who looked at them as if someone had handed him a problem to solve for advanced calculus.

"Sir, I don't know what to do."

"You kids, I swear. Okay, first, I'm going to clamp my red to my positive terminal, then you're going to clamp your red to your positive. But, first, hang on a sec'…"

Henry grabbed two rags from the backseat of his car, handing one to Sid. "Make sure to dry off any moisture on the clamps."

Sid did so, then attached his red clamp. Henry continued, attaching his black clamp to his negative terminal.

"Now, I want you to attach your black to a piece of metal."

Sid looked perplexed, not quite sure where to secure his clamp.

"Right there," said Henry, pointing to the alternator bracket. Sid connected the clamp, but in a more confined area than Henry had intended him to. It would do, though.

Thunder rolled again, appearing to travel completely around them. A slight wind picked up, as did the rain.

"Ok, Sid, cross your fingers. I'm going to start my car first. I want you to stand back. I don't trust batteries. Give my car about thirty seconds to send some juice, then I'll tell you when to start yours."

"What do you mean, you don't trust batteries?"

"If it were to spark. I'm just being cautious, that's all."

Thirty seconds later, Sid turned his key and the Civic fired up. Henry got out, and went to Sid's side of the car, shouting with an okay sign, "Keep it running!"

Sid watched Henry disappear behind the hood. He could see the cables swing between the two cars, then Henry reappearing as he took off the clamps from his own vehicle. But as he returned to the Civic, Sid noticed a peculiar movement, like a sudden jerk of Henry's body. At the same moment, he heard Henry yell, muffled through the din of the rain, "DAMMIT!!" Henry jerked again, as one fist pounded Sid's car. "DAMMIT!!"

Sid cut the ignition and ran to the front. "Mr. Tisdale! What's wrong?!"

Henry's head hung down with his beard soaked against his chest. His left hand covered his right hand as heavier rain began to fall.

"Was it the battery?"

"No. It's nothing, Sid. I'm fine."

But it was something—something Sid had never seen before. "Mr. Tisdale…what is that?!"

Henry raised his head, slowly shaking it side to side, then paused. Sid moved closer, extending his hand to Henry's, but Henry pulled away.

There was a cut that ran several inches from just above the wrist toward the knuckles. He was unable to completely cover it up.

"Sir, that's not blood! That's black! You're bleeding black! What is that?!"

He was cornered. There was no escaping this. There was no story he could tell that would hide the truth. The time had come.

"Sid," said Sketch, "I have much to tell you."

Chapter 6
GRANDFATHER

Sketch wrapped his wrist and hand with the rag used for the jumper cables, then he and Sid closed the car hoods, turned off their vehicles, and went inside the building. In an effort to avoid residents, they took the stairway to the third floor where they entered Sketch's room.

"Please take off your shoes," said Sketch, doing the same after he closed the door.

A short entryway led to a shared kitchen and living room space divided by a gray granite kitchen island with countertop stools. Two bedrooms, a small office, and a bathroom were located down a hallway accessed from the living room. The apartment was modestly furnished and accented with a large handwoven African wall tapestry and a variety of African wood carvings.

"It's not my first cut," said Sketch, running water over the wound in the kitchen sink. "It'll heal quickly."

He shook his head side to side, silent for a moment, and frustrated that he hadn't been more careful under the car hood. "Sid," he said, "I know this is going to sound cliché, but I think you need to take a seat."

Their clothes wet from the rain, Sketch spread out a towel on a brown weathered leather sofa for Sid to sit on. He did the same for himself on a matching leather wing chair. Between them was a wooden coffee table that stood on a zebra hide.

"I don't know where to begin. I really don't."

Sketch had folded a few paper towels, compressing them on the cut with his free hand. "You were right when you said this wasn't blood."

"I don't understand."

"I wouldn't expect you to."

"Then what is it?"

Sketch lifted the paper towel to check the cut's healing progress. There was now barely any stain on the towel, the cut having nearly disappeared. "It's ink."

"Ink? What do you mean, ink?"

"Like drawing ink."

"This doesn't make sense."

"I know it doesn't."

"Then tell me the truth."

"I am, Sid. It's ink."

"Certainly, your blood is just dark. A disease?"

"No blood, Sid. It's ink. And look…" Sketch removed the paper towels. "It's practically healed."

"I…I…don't—"

"Of course, you don't understand." Sketch moved to the edge of his seat. "But if you were to look at the ink under a microscope, you wouldn't see any blood cells. Because there is nothing but ink."

"Then who the hell are you?"

"My name is Sketch."

"Where are you from?"

"A young man's imagination. He was your age."

Unable to process, Sid stood up, as a look of unease crossed his face. "Sir, I think I should go."

"Sid, please. I know this must sound—"

"Crazy? Yes, it does. Mr. Tisdale…Sketch?…or whoever you are…I'm beginning to feel uncomfortable."

Sid made his way to his shoes and began putting them on as the familiar voice of Dwight Kellogg could be heard passing by in the hallway, complaining about something to do with Sierra Oaks and not enough covered parking.

"Look how wet I am!" Dwight barked, moving down the hallway.

Lola, trailing behind, spoke in a hushed tone. "Shhhhh! Dwight, please....you're being too loud."

"That guy is such a pain," said Sid, as he finished tying his shoes. He then opened the door, at which point Dwight slammed his door at the end of the hallway. A few seconds later Lola quietly entered their apartment, as Dwight's complaining projected into the hallway.

"He can be a real monster," said Sketch, as Sid walked toward the stairway.

"And what's that make you?" said Sid. "Please tell me you have some sort of rare blood condition. Otherwise...what are you?"

Sid walked down the stairs, leaving Sketch behind, silent and not knowing what to say.

For forty years he never had to explain to anyone who he really was. And now, because of a careless accident, he was being questioned. He was jammed in a position where he had to show proof to explain his existence. He believed that his hopes of himself ever regaining his superpowers had vanished the moment Charles died. He believed that he would never again fly to the Arch, blaze through a cornfield, or have the strength to bend solid rods of steel like Superman.

Then, on this particular rainy day, Sid's car battery died, and the potential for Sketch to regain his superpowers became an actual possibility. Perhaps a long shot, but still a possibility.

The thought occurred to him when he realized he wasn't just a product of Charles' imagination. He was much more. He was a product of Charles! Even imagination must be encoded in the DNA of the genes that are unique to each human. Charles hadn't passed on biological traits, but he had passed on traits through his imagination. And the magic ink was the vehicle that transported those traits into the supernatural.

Sketch hurried back inside his apartment and looked out his living room window that had a view of the parking lot. Sid could be seen exiting the building and getting into his car, but it wouldn't start. The headlights struggled to brighten after each subsequent turn of the key. It was the break that Sketch needed, buying him the necessary time needed to change clothes, and make one phone call:

"Hello?" A woman's voice answered.

"Hey, everything's alright, but I had a little accident. I cut myself, and Sid saw the ink seeping from my wound."

"Are you okay?"

"Oh, I'm fine, but Sid's a little frightened. He doesn't know what to think."

"That is understandable. I guess the time has come. Either by accident or being confronted, he eventually had to find out. Are you going to talk to him?"

"Yes."

"Just go easy. He has to earn your trust."

"And if he doesn't?"

"I think he will."

"How do you know?"

"Because he reminds me of Charles."

"Got it," said Sketch, affirmably. "I need to go. I love you, Heba. I'll see you in a couple of days."

"I love you, too. We may be closer to bringing your powers back to life. Goodbye."

The rain had stopped as the clouds began to thin, and a clearing in the sky pushed its way through Waterstone. Once again, Sid laid his head on top of the steering wheel, letting out a surrendering breath. As he looked up, the one person he didn't want to see was coming his way. It was Sketch, wearing a pair of jeans, long-sleeve blue t-shirt, Nikes, and Charles' satchel strapped over his shoulder.

Reluctantly, Sid opened his door. "It's your lucky day, sir. My car won't start."

"Sid," he said, slowing his walk as he neared, "I know this is very confusing but, please, just hear me out."

"Ok. I won't run off this time."

Sketch made his way around Sid's open door, while maintaining a reasonable distance so he wasn't encroaching.

"The other night at the comic book store, Mr. Roberts was talking to you about the airplane that landed with the broken wing."

"Yes," said Sid. "It was the miracle landing newspaper article. And there was that sketch of the airplane, too. Mr. Roberts wondered if it were possible for someone like Superman to have saved the plane from crashing."

"And what did you think when he said that?"

"At first, I thought it sounded crazy. And then I remembered thinking, for whatever reason, that...maybe...he's on to something."

"Sid, he is on to something." Sketch pulled back the sleeve of his shirt, exposing where he had cut himself. "It's healed. The wound is completely healed."

"How is that possible? The cut was deep."

"Sid...I'm caught in a difficult situation of having to prove who I am. And, so, I'm asking you to please bear with me."

"I promise, I'm not going anywhere. You have my attention."

Sketch looked around the parking lot that had been quiet, barring the short stop of a FedEx delivery truck. He took out the sketch book, opening it to the original drawing Charles had done of the plane with a broken wing, diving nose-first, and Sketch flying toward it.

"Anything look familiar?" said Sketch, handing the book to Sid.

"It looks like the same style of drawing I saw in the frame at the comic store. Same size page, too."

"Turn the page, and you'll see where the page you're talking about was torn out."

"I'm confused." Sid turned back to the airplane drawing. "Who tore it out? And who was the artist?"

"I tore it out, and the artist's name was Charles, and he created me."

Sid looked up from the sketch book. "*Created* you?"

"Like I said...please, bear with me. In a most unusual way, you and I are somewhat related. We are not linked biologically, but we are imaginatively."

Recognizing Sid's urge to interrupt, Sketch held up his hand and continued. "The young man who created me was someone you've known of, but never met. He was your grandfather, Charles Sweeney."

"But he—"

"He died, yes. Two days after the beginning of my existence. And even now, forty years later, I'm still grieving over his death."

Sid sank into his seat, calm but confused. The man who stood before him had a noticeable cut on his forearm and wrist just thirty minutes earlier, and it was now completely healed. From that cut he bled what appeared to be ink. The man had handed him a sketch book containing artwork that looked exactly like the sketch at Kryptonite Komics. The man also professed to be mourning the loss of his grandfather, who, he says, created him. And the reason he now referred to him as the man and not Henry Tisdale, was because Sid wasn't sure who he was dealing with anymore. Could it be possible that Mr. Roberts was right?

Another delivery truck entered the parking lot. It stopped at the front entrance. Two men got out and went to the rear of the truck where one lowered an automatic lifting platform. The truck was full of large boxes of furniture. The hydraulic lift was noisy, and the truck blocked any view of Sketch and Sid from the front office windows.

"Sid," said Sketch, "obviously, there's a lot to explain to you, and I'll get to that. But you know that project you're working on for your art class—trying to create a superhero?"

Sid rolled his eyes up to Sketch. "Yesss..."

"Well...I have an idea."

Chapter 7
HE'S IN YOUR BLOOD

The hydraulic lift of the delivery truck squealed, moving up and down as the workers dollied boxes of new furniture into the building and brought out the old. Being a college town, traffic dropped significantly during Spring Break, and the scarcity of vehicles in the Sierra Oaks parking lot seemed no different.

"I can stand here all day," said Sketch, facing Sid who remained in his car, "and tell you about who I am and how I came to be, but I'm afraid those are just words that will amount to nothing but being perceived as a fabrication, or even insanity. I practically had this same conversation with a police sergeant on the night your grandfather died."

"You were at the car accident?" asked Sid, holding the sketch book now closed on his lap.

"Yes."

"Grandma Tennie told me about it, but only once. She said it devastated her."

Sketch paused. "Yes, it did. She was very much in love. I was sitting in the back seat with Charles when the car hit us."

"Wait—you were with him?"

Sketch aimlessly looked around the parking lot, trying to divert his attention away from the well of emotion rising within him. It had been years since he had touched the subject of Charles' death, and now he found himself trying to circumvent the choke in his throat that made it difficult to talk.

"Mr. Tisdale...sir...are you okay?"

Sketch let out a long, calming sigh. "Yeah, I'm good. It just hit me. I think it always will."

Sid was becoming more relaxed in the car, no longer feeling threatened by so much that still didn't make sense. He had a myriad of questions, but only one stood out. "Sir, how did my grandfather create you?"

"He drew me with magical ink."

Sid tilted his head with a somewhat muddled expression. "Like the ink in your body?"

"Yes."

"You said you had an idea. Does it have to do with the ink?"

At last, thought Sketch, he was making headway. Sid was inquiring about the ink in a tone that wasn't antagonistic or skeptical, but rather simply curious.

"It has everything to do with the ink. But talking about it, telling of its history and ability is pointless, unless I prove to you just how magical it is."

"And how will you do this?"

"Sid...you will do it, not me."

Sketch reached into the satchel and took out the red pen that contained the magic ink, then handed it to Sid. "Here," he said. "This is where you begin. But first, understand, you're sort of being thrown into the fire. So, if at any point you want to stop, you have complete freedom to do so."

Sid rotated the pen in his hand, inspecting it at different angles. "You want me to draw something?"

"Actually, trace. Sid...in the back of the book there is a drawing of me. The page is loose, so please be careful. I'd like you to take it out."

Sid did so, taking out the original drawing of Sketch. "Looks like a superhero. Like the one I saw flying under the airplane at the comic book store."

"It is a superhero. And, yes, the same one."

"It's cool! My grandfather drew this?"

"Yes, he did."

"Why was he drawing a superhero?"

"Because the qualities that Charles possessed were the ones necessary to create a superhero who could combat evil. He was offered an extremely rare opportunity…to be able to, literally, create the supernatural. Sid, when I say that Charles created me, I mean it. You are holding the original drawing that he made of me. And once he finished, I then came into existence. That pen that you now hold, contains the magic ink, and it's the pen he used. He's the one who gave me the name, Sketch. I am the superhero. And I believe that you, my friend, have the potential to continue where Charles left off.

"I need you to pay close attention to what I'm about to say. I want you to know that I have been observing you for quite some time. You are a near replica of your grandfather Charles. So much about you reflects who he was. You're optimistic, kind, you have sincere intentions, a good eye for discerning right from wrong, you have a sound moral compass, and you're a great artist. I'd say Charles did a pretty good job of passing on his genes to you. I believe it's possible for you to return my powers."

"Powers?"

"Yes. Flying, running super-fast, and possessing superhuman strength."

"Flying? You want me to believe that you once could fly?"

Sketch scanned the parking lot. There had only been two cars, one entering, and one leaving during their conversation. The furniture movers were plenty busy, moving at a fast pace, as if they were required to finish the job within a certain amount of time. He pulled up his long-sleeve shirt, exposing his superhero outfit beneath. "Does this look familiar? Do you see a similarity between this and the design that your grandfather Charles drew?"

"Well…yes. It does look the same, but it's just a costume, right?"

"It's much more than that. It's my identity."

"Identity?"

Before lowering his shirt, Sketch pointed to the insignia on his chest. "Charles designed my identity. It's an ink drop. That airplane in the newspaper article—the one with the broken wing—Charles was on that flight. It was spiraling toward the earth. He did a quick sketch of his situation and of me coming to the rescue. It's known as a 'call.' Charles called me. I felt his desperation. I felt the rapid beating hearts of forty-eight passengers. I felt their fear, their sadness, their cries, their helplessness, all believing they were about to die. And the heart I felt more than any was that of Charles. It's nearly impossible to imagine that I had time to save them from death. But, Sid, I am supernatural. I brought that plane down safely, and only because Charles called me. Then, a few hours later, he died next to me in the car accident. I thought I had protected him, but I made a mistake."

Sketch looked up into the trees, and wiped away some tears. He took a couple of deep breaths, collecting himself, then continued.

"I didn't have my eyes on him. I was looking at the Metzes who were in the front seat. I watched them die with their necks bent at ungodly angles. And as that happened, a piece of steel speared into Charles' chest, just next to his heart...and soon after...well, that was it. Had I kept my eyes on him, I could've prevented his death. That was forty years ago, and I can't help but still carry the burden of having failed him. I considered suicide soon after, but I got lucky and chose to live."

To Sid, the conversation had become strangely serious, and eerily believable. Why would Mr. Tisdale be exposing the topic of the ink and the supernatural if it were all just a hoax? What was the benefit of taking something this far? After all, it wasn't like they were buddies. The only answer he could think of was that he would simply have to be a crazy man. It was that or he was a pro at pulling off practical jokes. But nothing was indicating those possibilities, especially considering how quickly his wound had healed. That, alone, was supernatural.

"Sir...Sketch...can I call you Sketch?"

"Yes, of course you may."

Sid did a quarter turn in his seat, extending his left leg to the pavement. The rain had moved to the east, the canopies of large live oak trees that dotted the parking lot were teeming with various species of vocal birds.

"I honestly don't know what to believe. But there are several things adding up in my head that are making me wonder if what you're saying is true—that you were once a superhero. I can't believe I'm saying this, but what is it you want me to do?"

"Sid," he said abruptly, "I need you to use that pen and precisely trace over the lines that your grandfather drew of me. I cannot stress enough when I say precisely."

"I can do that, sir…Sketch."

"Well, there's more to it than that. Listen carefully…you must will my superpowers into the lines as you trace them. You must put all of your focus *into* the lines. If your mind travels elsewhere, none of this will work. I know this sounds like lunacy, but trust me, it can only be done this way."

"So, you want me to think about you being able to fly, run super-fast, and have supernatural strength?"

"No," said Sketch, being direct. "You cannot just think about the powers. You must *will* the powers into the drawing. You must believe in your intent for me to reacquire them."

"And you want me to do this here? In the parking lot?"

Sketch looked around the lot, and along the length of the building at the apartment windows which were empty. The surroundings were quiet except for the delivery workers who still had a few dolly trips to go. "Yes, it's fine here. The truck is blocking the front offices."

"Excuse me for asking, but what could they possibly see? The only thing I'll be doing is tracing in my car."

Sketch chuckled. "Sid, if this works…well…you'll see."

Sid swung his leg back into the car, then sat tall with the sketch book closed on his lap, and the page of Sketch's drawing placed on top of it. As he did this, Sketch took off his shoes, using one foot to assist the other.

"You're taking your shoes off?"

"Trust me, Sid. There's a reason."

"Those aren't socks, are they?" asked Sid, continuing to look at his feet. "What are those? Silver boots?"

Sketch looked down and chuckled. "I know…lunacy."

"Sir, you promise this is all real, right? Just asking that makes me look like a possible believer. But you're being sincere, right?"

"As sincere as I could ever be. Understand that this is something that is very real. If you choose to be a part of this, you must remember you cannot tell anyone about the ink. You cannot speak a word to anyone about its magical properties. To be honest, I'm not even sure if my speaking to you about the ink is safe. By doing so, I might be jeopardizing my chances of regaining my powers. But this situation is unique. I am not a creator. I am merely someone who has been created. However, because you're of Charles' bloodline, it might make this situation an exception to the rule. The worst that can happen is that the ink just won't work."

"I don't know, Sketch. This is sounding a bit too far out there to believe."

"You have every reason to feel that way. But if you were given the chance to restore my superpowers, would you? Keep in mind, if you do this, the supernatural, meaning me, will never harm you, and will forever be loyal to you. The ink doesn't allow it."

Sid reached over the passenger seat and picked up a bag of comic books that he had purchased and left in the car the night he talked to Mr. Roberts.

"Sketch," he said, pulling them out of the bag, "you're saying you're like one of these? Except you're a real-life superhero?"

"Yes, I am."

"And that if I trace your lines exactly, and focus my will into the lines as I trace, your superpowers might return."

"Yes," said Sketch. "But only you can do this. I believe you are my only chance."

The delivery workers had returned for a final trip of dollying furniture into the building. There was very little chatter between them, just a sense of urgency to finish the delivery. After all, it was Friday.

"Those guys will be wrapping up their job soon. It'd be best to trace now, before they move the truck. Are you good to go, Sid?"

Sid shrugged his shoulders, smiling. "You're quite the salesman, Sketch. Sure, let's give it a go."

"Can you trace sitting there?" asked Sketch.

"Yes, sir...I'm comfortable."

Before he took off the cap of the red pen and began tracing, he selected a comic book from the bag, held it facedown, then asked Sketch, "Guess who my favorite superhero is?"

"Ummm...Superman?"

"Nope," said Sid, turning the comic book over to show to Sketch. "The Falcon."

Sketch's eyes grew big. "Sid, you really are the one."

"The one?"

"Yes, the one. Sid...it's time to trace."

And so, he did as requested, pushing aside any stray thoughts that might distract his focus. Though he had been leaning toward not believing what was being asked of him, he knew he had nothing to lose by giving Sketch the benefit of the doubt.

As he traced the lines with the red pen, Sid grew excited knowing he was tracing a drawing that his grandfather had created forty years earlier. Or so he had been told. Perhaps it was true, though, as he found it surprisingly easy to will his thoughts into the lines while his hand effortlessly maneuvered the pen. It was as if he were mimicking the exact way Charles had drawn—as if he could trace it blindfolded. Or, as if Charles, in some spiritual way, was with him—guiding him into the supernatural.

Fly!...fly!...fly!...be strong!...so strong!...so very strong!...run fast!...so fast!...so very fast!

Sid repeated the words in his head, immersing himself in their intent. Committing himself to the possibility that they might come to life. Over and over, he repeated them, just as he believed Charles had when he created Sketch. If, in fact, this were all true.

"There," Sid announced, ending with a sigh as he finished. "I'm done."

He looked up from his drawing, but Sketch was gone. His jeans and long sleeve shirt were piled on top of his shoes. Sid looked around the parking lot, but there was no sign of him.

"Hey…Sid…"

He heard Sketch's voice, but couldn't locate it. He turned his head left and right in his seat, quickly looking in all directions, almost bird-like, but he was nowhere to be seen.

"Sid," the voice repeated, hushed but firm. "Up here."

Sid tucked the drawing back into the sketch book, then set it and the pen on top of the bag of comic books in the passenger seat.

He leaned outside, bracing his left arm against the open door, and looked up.

"Sketch?!…you're—"

"Suspended in mid-air?"

Sid rose from his seat, standing with his head tilted back as he watched Sketch, wearing his mask, hovering twenty-feet high, just below the tree canopy. "My god! You can fly!"

"It worked, Sid! It worked! Somehow Charles is alive. Not physically, but spiritually, for sure. He's in your blood!"

"I…I don't know what to say."

"Of course you don't. Welcome to the supernatural."

The surrounding oak trees rustled in the breeze, their branches interlocked, causing the canopies to move as one. Sid watched Sketch move higher into a canopy, positioning himself out of sight as the delivery workers exited the building for the last time. They stowed the noisy hydraulic lift so it was flat against the back of the closed rear doors, then drove away.

"You really can fly," said Sid. "The ink is truly magical."

"Yes, it is," said Sketch. "But you know what? I'm probably the first superhero with a beard."

The two laughed as Sketch floated down to the ground, unseen by anyone.

"I can't believe this," said Sid. "I really can't. It's so surreal."

"Sid, there's so much to tell you, but this is neither the time nor place." Sketch picked up his shoes and clothes, and set them in his car, along with his keys. He retrieved his cell phone which had been in his jeans pocket, then went back to Sid where they exchanged phone numbers.

"I'm going to cut out of here and test my flying skills. It's been decades since I've flown, and I can tell things are a bit rusty. I'll be back later tonight."

"And what am I supposed to do?" asked Sid, still dazed with disbelief.

Sketch smiled. "Check your phone. I'm gonna send you a selfie."

"But—"

And like that, he took off, shooting through the canopies, a blur streaking across the sky and quickly disappearing from sight.

Minutes later Sid's phone alerted him with a text message ding. It was Sketch's number. He tapped it to see a photo of Sketch smiling exuberantly, with the St. Louis Arch far below him. The text read:

Look where I am! Let's meet up tomorrow. Lots to discuss. In the meantime, you know that Dwight Kellogg guy, the prick? It's time he learned a lesson. :)

PART V

Chapter 1
LOW POINT

1967

"Sir?...Ma'am?...Can you hear me? David, is that you?"

"Yes Sir. They're dead, sergeant. And so is Charles," said Sketch speaking through the opening where the windshield used to be. The shifting wind blew rain into the car, and a blanket of hail covered the road and surrounding fields.

"Montague's dead, too," said Perkins. "And so are two reporters from the local station. My front tire blew. There was nothing I could do. What a fucking mess."

Perkins limped around the car to Sketch's door, tugging on it, but it wouldn't open. "Jesus...these poor people. All of them...their kids, spouses, families. Just tragic."

"It wasn't your fault, sir."

"I know. It's just so sad."

Sketch let go of Charles' hand, then carefully avoided broken glass as he began maneuvering himself over the back of the Metz's bench seat. He then made his way through the mangled frame of what was once the windshield and out onto the cratered hood of the car.

"I radioed for help," said Perkins. "Emergency crews will be here soon."

Coming off the hood, Sketch stood in the rain, looking at Charles slumped to one side with his head down. So, this is how mortal life ends. An immediate emptiness. Fully functioning organs one minute, then the next, becoming cold and stiff. Sketch had knowledge of the human spirit that was presumed to live on after death, but had no inclination of his own. It seemed he knew more about mortals than he did about himself. Perhaps he was more human than he thought. Perhaps his eternal design was just a microcosm of who he really was—a person with true feelings, a person whose sorrow over the loss of his only friend was as real as the hole in his heart, the depression in his grief.

Sirens could be heard beyond the horizon where the road disappeared into the pulsing red glow of emergency lights.

"I'm really sorry," said Perkins. "I don't know what to say."

"There is nothing to say."

"Unfortunately, in my job I see this more times than I ever care to."

"He was such a good kid," said Sketch.

He wanted to say more, to go deeper, to divulge what only he and Charles knew had rescued the plane. But could he tell Perkins the truth? Or would doing so only be looked at as pure nonsense? If only he could fly or rip a telephone pole from out of the earth, he could prove how heroic Charles really was, how it was his "call" that made the difference. It would prove that the drawing in the sketch book was the primary reason the plane didn't crash. There would be no need for doubt or debunking, because the fact that he could tell the story while hovering in mid-air, twenty feet above his listeners, would be proof enough.

But that was now impossible. Sketch would look foolish to say such a thing, for the instant Charles died, was the instant Sketch lost his superpowers. It was an irreversible property of the ink.

Three ambulances, a fire truck, and three police cars arrived on the scene. All six occupants were officially pronounced dead. After investigators collected their needed information, tow trucks took away the three totaled vehicles. Broken glass and debris were then cleared from the roadway.

Perkins told his fellow officers that he would take David home, then meet them back at the station.

As they drove, Sketch sat in the front seat, his clothes entirely wet. He held Charles' satchel, intact with the sketchbook and pen. On the backseat, he had set Charles' suitcase. The rain had finally passed through as the clouds began to separate, offering small patches of stars. Sketch looked up as they drove, and wondered about heaven. Was Charles already there? Or was there some delayed movement in his body bag? Perhaps a faint pulse had been overlooked. Were these typical thoughts that mortals had? A final desperation clinging on a wing of hope.

"He was my best friend."

"I know, David…I'm really sorry. How long did you know him?"

Sketch continued looking up at the sky as the clouds separated further from each other, opening up a larger star field. He had lost Charles. What else was there to lose? Just tell him the truth. "Two days."

Perkins turned to him. "Two days? That's it?"

"Yes, sir."

"And he was your best friend?"

"Yes, sir. I grew up with him."

Perkins' brow scrunched, momentarily confused, but then he gave a short, suppressed chuckle, and started nodding his head as if realizing something finally made sense.

They turned onto the county road that took them to the Metz's farm. At the top of the caliche driveway, Perkins put the car in park, then cut the engine. Ahead of them, dark cornstalks swayed and crackled in the wind like hardened shadows.

"David…"

"Yes, sir?"

"That nickname you go by…may I call you Sketch?"

"Sure."

Perkins looked to his left at the Metz's house. Dark, silent, and undisturbed—a place Gordon and Peggy would never return to. "Sketch…there's an odd strangeness about you. I've never been able to quite pin it down, but...you're different."

"Sir?"

"You know what I mean. You're…different."

Sketch paused within their mutual understanding. "I can't disagree."

"Look, I saw it in you at the fireworks. I heard it in your voice at the police station. This thing you seem to have with flying."

"Sir—"

"Please, let me finish."

Sketch nodded.

"Tonight…as you stood outside the car, I was looking at where you sat, and I noticed nothing collapsed into the back seat. Nothing. But the Metzes were crushed. Had it not been for that piece of steel, Charles would have survived. And as I look back on the events of the past forty-eight hours, you're present at each one. You wore a strange superhero outfit, you talked of flying, your best friend survived an impossible landing, and he should've survived the car accident, just as you did, but he died in such a way that even you couldn't prevent as you braced the seat with your arm and kept it from collapsing."

Perkins paused, taking a deep breath.

"Sketch…you brought that plane down to safety, didn't you?"

The clouds had all blown away, and the wind began to calm as Sketch looked at the panorama of stars. "Yes, sir, I did. But because Charles is dead, I cannot prove a single thing. My superpowers are forever gone."

Sketch unbuttoned his shirt, exposing his outfit.

"Yes, this costume allowed me to run super fast, fly, and have superhuman strength."

"But you failed to fly at the fireworks," said Perkins.

"Only because I wasn't fully developed."

"I don't get it."

"Sir, I can sit here and tell you all I know, but what good is it if I can't prove anything? Yes, you're onto something, but until the day comes when I can prove my superpowers, it's inevitable that you'll begin to have your doubts."

For a minute, they sat in silence, then realized it was time to go.

Sketch got out of the car, and slung the satchel over his shoulder, then reached in and shook Perkins' hand.

"Sketch...are you going to be ok?"

"Yes, sir. Just sad, that's all. I'm not used to this."

"Well, if you need anything, you know where to find me."

"Thanks. Goodnight, sir."

Sketch stood silent inside the garage apartment, looking at all of Charles' belongings: the sofa, kitchen table, bed, photos with Tennie, drawing table, and the thumbtacked college newspaper sketches. Every single item now no longer existed in Charles' present, but only had a past memory. Inanimate objects that once thrived with a purpose, now seemed as lifeless as the owner who would never return. Tennie would sort through what she needed, then leave the rest behind.

He took the sketchbook out of the satchel and opened it to the original drawing that Charles had done of him. He carefully tore the page out, then set the book open on the drawing table.

And there he stood, holding the page with both hands...contemplating.

The idea had never entered his mind until this moment, when he realized eternity would be a very lonely place to live. The door was open to the closet, so he stood there, looking in. This was his womb, where his existence began. It was as if he was born into this world through a slivered opening in the air, so thin that only Charles' imagination could direct him through.

The loss of Charles had changed everything, though. This was no longer a place where he cared to be. He didn't want to live forever. He wanted out.

Holding the page, all he had to do was tear his image in half—tear it right down the middle, and he'd be gone.

And that was his plan. He was so close to the edge. So close that he even began to tear the paper, slowly and with intent.

But, as a breeze blew in through the bedroom window, and flickered the pages of the sketchbook on the drawing table, he remembered Charles' final two words that he had whispered before he passed—the two words that would now save Sketch's life and, also, give him a purpose.

"Find Heba."

Chapter 2

THE ARCH

It had been two hours since Sergeant Perkins had dropped off Sketch at Charles' garage apartment. The unshakeable vivid details of the accident clouded Sketch's mind as he collected the items necessary to begin a journey into the unknown: two sets of Charles' clothes, a pair of tennis shoes, his superhero outfit, and the satchel containing the sketch book, pen, and the sandstone falcon sculpture. He took a shower, got dressed, laid down on the sofa, and fell asleep.

In his dream he was in the Metz's car with Charles who was looking out his window as Mrs. Metz was urging her husband to slow down. Although Sketch knew how the accident was about to unfold, and he knew he was in a dream, he found there was nothing he could do to reverse time or alter the fatal events. He even kept a close eye on Charles, preparing himself for the piece of steel destined for Charles' chest, but the nightmare blocked his efforts each time as the fatal sequence kept looping over and over again. In the middle of the night, Sketch woke up in a cold sweat, his t-shirt drenched, his heart pounding. He had no idea that he was capable of dreaming. Was the dream revealing why he couldn't save Charles—that he was a little more mortal than he thought?

After a second shower, Sketch changed into another set of clothes, returned to the sofa and, again, fell fast sleep.

He woke up to the early morning light, had some toast and orange juice, then packed his clothes and satchel with its contents in Charles' small suitcase.

And then he stopped. With a slight twitch of his head, he realized he was able to prove to Sergeant Perkins that he had superpowers. At the time, what he had done seemed trivial. But now, as he looked back on his first flight into the dark, early morning hours, what he had done with one single penny might have paid off.

Setting the phone on the arm of the sofa, he stood before the window facing the Metz's house and dialed the police station.

"Lehman police, how may I help you?" said the receptionist.

"Is Sergeant Perkins available?"

"I'll see. He just stepped in a few minutes ago. Your name, please?"

"David Skechenski."

"Skechenski? Aren't you the guy who wore the Halloween costume?"

Sketch rolled his eyes, acknowledging that his grand entrance into this world wasn't all that grand. "Yes, ma'am. That's me."

"Please hold."

A couple of minutes passed as Sketch looked out the window at the Metz's house. Just knowing its inhabitants were deceased evoked a feeling of despair. And the apartment he now stood in seemed no different.

"Sketch?" said Perkins.

"Good morning, sir. I'm sorry to bother you, but I was wondering if you had any time to talk?"

"Maybe. There's going to be some follow-up questions after last night's mess. I'm working on the report now. I've already spoken to Montague's wife. He left behind three kids with her. He was a great husband and father with a good sense of humor. He will certainly be missed. I'm sure Charles is just as much of a loss to you. One of our investigators made the call to his parents. It's one of the worst parts of being a cop. So, how are you holding up?"

"I'm doing okay, but I'm so sorry about Montague. His wife's situation. I can't imagine…" Sketch paused, looking at a framed photo on an end table of Charles and Tennie smiling with the Grand Canyon behind them. "Yes, Charles is an enormous loss, and in ways you will never understand. But last night I sensed something from you that gives me hope I can confide in you and share information about myself that only Charles knew. Obviously, this isn't the best time to talk, but could we meet later? I could come to the station."

"Sure," said Perkins. "A little later should be fine. How about one o'clock?"

"Works for me."

"Sketch, are you going to need a ride?"

"No, thank you. I'll walk."

"You're sure?"

"I'll be fine, sir. It's probably best I get going now. I'm sure family members will be showing up soon. I'd rather walk anyway. I could use the fresh air."

"But don't you want to see Charles' parents? Certainly you know them, being as close as you were to Charles."

Sketch picked up the framed photograph of Charles and Tennie and put it in the suitcase that was open on the sofa.

"Sir..."

"Yes?"

"I don't know anyone."

"What do you mean?"

"I mean…I don't know anyone. Charles was the only person."

"But—"

"Sir, I have been in existence for three days. Just three days. I am supernatural. Yesterday, I was able to fly, and today I can't, and probably never will again. But if there's one person I think I can convince what I'm telling you is true, it'd be you. Are you still there?"

"Yes, Sketch, I'm listening."

"After things settle down at the station today, I'd like to take a little road trip with you, if it's possible."

"To where?"

"The Gateway Arch in St. Louis, sir."

"Why the Arch?"

"Because all the proof you need is there."

It was a familiar road he was on. Just two days prior he had run here, on a mission to save the city of Lehman from enemy fire, and utterly clueless of his inability to do so. He was now a vagabond, walking on the shoulder of a county road, and with nothing to do but think.

Though the road was lightly travelled, he thought about the cars that passed by, moving in the opposite direction. Were they related to the Metzes or Charles? And if they were, it wouldn't matter if they saw him, because nobody knew Sketch. They would only see a wandering man with a small suitcase. And the chance anyone would recognize the suitcase was slim.

Making his way into town, he passed by a couple of restaurants, a hobby store, hair salon, and gas station before coming to Lehman Comics. The store was closed, so Sketch cupped his hands around his face and looked inside through the large front window. There were long fold-out tables supporting numerous wooden crates of comic books. It was a small store whose lackluster aesthetics were nothing more than a few posters of superheroes thumbtacked to the walls. But what it lacked in interior design, it made up for being known as a collector's paradise.

Sketch viewed it differently, though. He saw it as a kind of morgue—a place where the unborn supernatural resided. Unborn in the sense that they never breathed air, or stepped foot beyond the pages. The comic store was a place where superheroes were stacked amongst one another, only known for what they did on paper. Of course, no one but Sketch could see it that way, because only he had entered the world of the living. Short-lived, but he had done it. And now, stripped of his superpowers, he thought: Just make a comic book of me, and tell my story. The closet, the fireworks, the tractor, the owl, the Arch, the airplane, and, yes, the car accident. Lay me to rest in this morgue of fictitious entertainment, never to be known that my story was real. And if someone should buy me and take me home, then so be it. But that will most likely be a far worse ending, as I'll eventually be forgotten in a box in the attic or perish in a garbage truck, soiled with coffee grinds, damp napkins and orange peels, destined for the county landfill.

Getting bogged down in the idea of a superhero morgue was a sinking ship he needed to abandon, so he picked up his suitcase and walked further into town, until he came to the public library. There, he spent the rest of his time parked in a cushioned chair, reading magazines and watching the clock.

It was a short three-block walk to the police station, where he checked in with the receptionist, her strawberry-blonde hair piled high as usual. She greeted him less nondescript this time, and with more empathy.

"Good afternoon, David. I want to apologize for my Halloween comment over the phone. I shouldn't have said it. I mean…last night…just so tragic."

"It's ok. I wasn't offended."

"Well, just know you're in our thoughts."

"Thank you, ma'am."

"Please," she said, motioning to a chair in the lobby, "take a seat. It shouldn't be long. He's got one last investigator with him."

Five minutes later Perkins and a heavyset man in a suit entered the lobby through the hallway door.

"Sir," said Perkins. "This is David. He was in the Metz's car."

Sketch stood up and shook the man's hand.

"You walked away scratch-free from that accident, didn't you?"

"Yes, sir," said Sketch. "I got lucky."

"My team investigated the crash site. Your seat was the most confusing. I mean, nothing caved in on you."

"Like I said, sir…I got lucky."

"I guess so. Well, glad you're ok. And my condolences for the loss of your friend."

"Thank you, sir."

Perkins walked Sketch back to his office and closed the door as Sketch took a seat, setting his suitcase next to him.

"Sergeant, you've obviously had suspicions about me, that I'm… well, unusual. That there's something about me that's different."

"Yes, you're correct on that."

"Sir, I need to show you something." Sketch opened up the suitcase and took out the drawing book from the satchel then laid the original drawing of himself on Perkins' desk."

"It's you!" said Perkins. "So, you like to draw?"

"Hardly," chortled Sketch. "Charles drew that. It's the drawing that brought me into existence."

Perkins picked up the drawing to inspect it more closely. "Existence? As in you being supernatural, like you mentioned on the phone?"

"Yes, sir. Exactly."

"But what does a drawing have anything to do with—"

"Sir, do you have a knife?"

"A pocket knife."

"May I use it?"

"I suppose, but what for?"

"Nothing much. Just to prick my finger with the tip of the blade."

"Are you serious?"

"Yes."

"And what will this accomplish?"

"It'll prove that I'm supernatural. It's something I learned from Charles when he told me about a woman named Heba who did the same thing for him."

Perkins opened his top desk drawer, and within its clutter of miscellaneous items, took out a pocket knife and handed it to Sketch. "Here ya go. Work your magic."

"May I have a sheet of typing paper, too?"

Perkins handed him one which Sketch laid on the desk.

"Oh, and a band-aid, too. If you have it."

The sergeant went to a bathroom down the hallway and brought back a first-aid kit, and gave him a band-aid.

Sketch then steadied the blade just above his index finger which was positioned over the sheet of paper.

"Sergeant, please don't be alarmed."

With one quick grimacing stab, the finger dripped black ink onto the paper.

"What is that?!" asked Perkins.

"It's ink. Magic ink."

Perkins' eyes grew wide and inquisitive as he leaned in for a closer look. He tapped the droplets with his finger, then smeared them across the paper. "It's ink! It really is!" Looking up at Sketch, he said, "Who are you? Where do you come from?"

"I am the product of Charles' imagination. I entered this world the moment he finished my drawing."

"And you said on the phone that you've been alive for three days, right?"

"Yes."

Perkins swirled the ink in a figure-eight pattern. "So, why are you telling me this?"

"Because I need someone I can trust," said Sketch, opening the band-aid package. "And I need your help. I need to get to Egypt. But first, we need to visit the Arch."

"And what's going to happen when we get there?"

"You'll buy a ticket and take the tram car up to the top. Once there, you'll go to the center-most window that faces the Mississippi River and look to the far southeast. As far to the right as you can."

"And then what?"

"You'll see."

"I'll see what?"

Sketch wrapped the band aid around his finger. "Sergeant, all I can say is you need to discover it all on your own. I think it's best that way."

"You know," said Perkins, "I've never come close to being in a situation like this. But, then again, you're made of ink, so why would I? I must admit, though, that I have had my suspicions about you for the past couple of days. And here I am now, having just witnessed ink flowing out of you which definitely puts you in the non-human category, and for some reason I'm not tremendously surprised. Sounds strange, I know, but it's almost as if all of this is something that I'm supposed to accept without hesitation. But ok, I'll do it. So, yeah, I'm good to go."

"Thank you, sir."

"We can actually leave in about thirty minutes. I need to go to the TV station in St. Louis where the cameraman and reporter worked. You can join as a civilian ride-along. Will that work?"

"Perfect." said Sketch, unwrapping the band-aid, exposing his freshly cut finger which had now completely healed.

Prior to leaving for St. Louis, the local newspaper had been delivered to the police station. "I'm gonna take it with us," Perkins said to the receptionist. "I'll be back later tonight."

The drive to the Arch was occupied by nothing more than conversation regarding everything related to the magic ink, including Heba. And there sat Sergeant Perkins, manning the wheel with Sketch next to him who claimed to be only three days old and with not a drop of blood flowing through his body, only ink.

And he was listening intently to every word of it.

As they made their way through the farmland of southwestern Illinois, Sketch sat with the newspaper on his lap, the front-page headline reading, *MIRACLE LANDING!!!* "It even surprises me that I brought the plane down safely, that I knew its exact location. Do you realize the weight of that plane? The difficulty involved? And had it happened four days ago, it would have crashed, killing everyone, because there wasn't even a single molecule of me in existence. But here I sit, unable to run faster than this car, unable to soar with the eagles, and unable to crush a rock in my fist. I am supernatural, but, in a way, I am now as ordinary as you."

"I guess I don't fully understand why you want me as your confidant."

Sketch lifted the newspaper to show Perkins the front-page photo of the crippled airplane. "You and I are the only people who know what saved the plane. But I need you to have no doubt in your mind that I could fly. The Arch will prove that. But I don't want to turn into some kind of freak show if things were to go public. I don't want to have to keep proving myself and stabbing my fingers to drain ink."

"So, what do you want?"

"I want to meet Heba. And if the world discovers who I am, then eventually Heba will be exposed. And if that happens, then

I'm afraid the unknown properties that empower the ink will be no more. The ink is powerful, but fragile as well."

Five minutes later they came to a rise in the roadway, opening up a panoramic view of St. Louis as the stainless steel Arch towered and glimmered in the sunlight at 630 feet tall.

"There it is," said Perkins. "I'm not quite sure what I'll be looking for once I'm up there, but you think I'll see it, right?"

"As long as you look out the center-most window facing the Mississippi, you'll see it. Remember, look as far to the southeast as possible."

It was a relatively quiet afternoon on the grounds of the Arch with moderate tourist activity.

"I'll be down here waiting," said Sketch, as they stood outside beneath the Arch.

Sergeant Perkins entered the Arch ticket office from where the tram cars departed. *I'm an Illinois cop being told to look out a window of the St. Louis Arch, by an ex-superhero who's three days old. Is this really happening?*

It was a four-minute ride to the top in the tram car. Exiting through the car's automatic doors, Perkins made his way along the arcing walkway dividing the east and west viewing windows. Positioning himself at the center-most window, he did as instructed and looked to the far southeast. He recognized the Poplar Street bridge and a railroad bridge spanning the Mississippi River. After that there was the small Illinois town of Cahokia, beyond which the land became an indistinguishable blending of trees, farmland, and small communities that eventually morphed into a white cloudy summer haze at the horizon.

He was looking as far to the southeast as possible, but nothing indicated any clues of someone having flown. This search for the answer to Sketch's flight made no sense. Was there supposed to be a sign in the mighty Mississippi? Perhaps something to do with a river barge? All that was out there was the state of Illinois.

Look as far to the southeast as possible. Sketch had stressed the word "far". So, Perkins looked as far as possible, right up to the edge of the outside window frame. Right to the...edge...

Perkins' eyes widened as he chuckled upon his discovery. He didn't know what Sketch had used, but one thing was for sure... you'd have to be able to fly in order to do it.

As far to the southeast as possible...where the Mississippi River disappears into the metal window frame...Sketch had found a penny and etched vertically into the frame:

S
K
E
T
C
H

W
A
S

H
E
R
E

As his tram car began its descent to the bottom of the Arch, full clarity encompassed Perkins' mind. It wasn't a crazy idea after all to travel to St. Louis, because the man who had claimed to having been in existence for only three days, had not only been speaking the truth, but he had flown as well.

Perkins exited the tram car, then passed through the ticket office lobby before going outside, where he found Sketch anxiously waiting.

"Well?" said Sketch.

"Well, what?"

"Did you see anything up there?"

"Sure did," said Perkins, smiling. "I'm gonna get you to Egypt!"

Chapter 3

THE TRAIN

As they crossed the Mississippi and headed into Illinois, Sketch turned in his seat and looked back at the Arch. He felt a sense of accomplishment, having proven to Perkins just who he was, and that he had been able to fly. If he hadn't been able to substantiate his immortal qualities, then each day that would pass from here on out would be like marking off time in prison. Eternally shackled.

"Sketch, what's it like to fly?"

Sketch pondered the question as he watched the Arch diminish in size. He remembered Charles once asking the same question. "Complete freedom," he said. "I know I have mass, but I feel weightless. It feels like what you'd expect being supernatural should feel like...almost heavenly."

"Did you ever fear that you might fall, plummet to the earth?"

"Never. Once I took flight it became as natural as walking. Fear of the ground collapsing beneath my feet just isn't a consideration."

"And you believe you'll never fly again?"

Sketch turned in his seat to face forward, watching the miles of cornfields pass by. "My flying days are over. Charles died, forever ending any chances of me flying again."

"I don't know if I'll ever completely grasp the fact that you're supernatural. You're not human, but you're real. Are there others like you?"

"Heba had told Charles there were possibly others, but no one has ever had superpowers like me. There was, however, a talented young French artist named Genevieve whom Heba had encouraged to create a superhero. But she never heard back from Genevieve, nor was she ever able to contact her."

"You've mentioned Heba a couple of times before. What's her importance?"

"Heba—Queen Heba, officially—was the first created by the ink." Sketch smiled briefly, recognizing a needed correction. "Actually," he said, "her dog, Khaldun, was created moments before her."

"A dog?"

Sketch nodded. "And it's believed she was created after the dog to be the dog's companion."

"So, she's like you…an ink person."

"Yes, but she's far older…over two-thousand years old."

"She must look horrid!"

"Actually, no. Ink people don't physically show their age beyond fifty."

The police radio began picking up crackling static as they drove further into Illinois, some forty miles from Lehman.

"Sergeant…why did you choose to be a cop?"

Perkins chuckled. "My dad was a cop. His dad was a cop. And his dad was a cop. I certainly didn't want to mess with tradition, so I became a cop."

"Was it just tradition or did you want to fight crime?"

"Well, there's not much crime in Lehman to fight, unless you're running down some nut who thinks fireworks are some kind of enemy invasion."

Sketch shook his head. "Rub it in, Sarge."

"Oh, you'll never live that one down. But, yeah, seriously, protecting citizens from criminals was always my reason for joining the force. And I had plenty to deal with, working the streets in Chicago. We sure could've used a superhero back then. Hell, even today."

Sketch fell silent for a moment as they passed through a small one-stoplight town.

"I miss him, Sarge."

"You always will. Just like I do Montague."

"But I should've stopped that piece of steel."

"You can say that all day long, but the fact is you didn't stop it. And as supernatural as you are, you can't reverse time. You never will. I could've possibly turned the car away from that telephone pole, but I just wasn't quick enough. And, so, I too feel the guilt and grief that you're feeling. Today's trip has been a welcome distraction, but going up in the Arch…it was all Montague in my head."

They were interrupted by the radio dispatcher mentioning something about a stalled semi-trailer truck at a railroad crossing, but the static made it difficult to make out the location. "All units, please respond…all units, please respond. Over."

Perkins picked up the microphone. "This is Sergeant Perkins. Please repeat the truck's location. Over."

The dispatcher's voice was clear this time. "At the College Avenue crossing. Over."

Another voice joined in. "This is Officer Johnson. I'm two minutes away. Over."

"Calling all units!" alerted Perkins. "I repeat…all units…go to the other crossings with your flashers on. Be prepared to wave down any approaching train headed toward College Avenue. Over."

Five patrol cars scattered, each to a different crossing. All was clear, but the big rig remained stalled on the tracks where officer Johnson had just arrived. "I've called for a tow truck. Over." he said.

As Perkins and Sketch continued towards Lehman, the officers reported their locations. The dispatcher announced a minor accident at a grocery store parking lot. Perkins told everyone to hold their positions.

Sketch listened intently as the officers kept each other informed of their status. There was no unnecessary talking. Everything was succinct and professional.

"Train approaching Mitchell Street. Over," alerted an officer furthest away from College Avenue.

A 55-car freight train moving at 30 mph crossed the western boundary of Lehman. The cop on Mitchell Street positioned his car just behind where the railroad arms fell. His emergency lights were flashing as he stood in clear sight, crisscrossing his arms while facing the oncoming locomotive.

That was when Sketch felt the sting. A sharp pulse of heat radiated from his spine, coinciding with a white flash in Sketch's mind that momentarily blinded his view of the passing farmland. Within the flash he saw the train, and the cop frantically waving his arms as it rushed by. A second flash and he saw a tow truck backed up to the stalled semi, and heard the train's horn in the distance. These weren't just random snapshots of what his imagination was gathering from the police radio, but rather, were composites of a call. But how was it possible for Sketch to be receiving a call if no one had drawn anything? Or was it possible that someone had? Charles? Was Charles communicating from the afterlife? It was a curious thought that, when weighed against the backdrop of his eternal life and past supernatural abilities, might not be too far-fetched to believe. He squeezed his fists, driving his fingers hard into the palms. There was no doubt he felt stronger than normal. But as the police continued their updates on the radio, and as the situation intensified, for whatever reason, the flashes stopped, and the super strength in his clenched fists had subsided and returned to normal.

Ultimately, there was no call, but only fragments of one. Like nerves that continue to twitch after a snake's head has been severed from its body and both ends keep moving, Charles had been cut off from Sketch, but there were still receptors in Sketch's call sensors that hadn't completely perished. Perhaps the receptors did whatever they could to respond to the dire situation, regardless of whether or not a drawing had triggered the call. The severed receptors would react to anything, even a police radio. The only problem was they basically had no life left in them. Sketch saw the two flashes, then that was it.

"Hey, buddy," Perkins said, nudging Sketch in the shoulder. "You okay?"

Sketch blinked his eyes a couple times, shaking his head. "Yeah, I'm good. What's up?"

"You didn't hear? The tow truck pulled the semi off the tracks, just in time. That train just barreled through. I don't even think he saw my men."

"I saw the tow truck."

"Saw it?"

"Yeah. Like a call."

"Your superpowers are back?"

"I'm afraid not. I think it was just a fleeting sensation as my instincts reacted to the situation. Something like that."

"You never know," said Perkins, excitedly. "Want me to pull over to see if you can fly?"

"Not a chance," laughed Sketch. "Whatever it was, it's gone now."

They continued the drive in silence for the next ten minutes. Just the sound of the tires thumping over the concrete seams in the highway, and minor announcements from the dispatcher. Perkins took an exit to gas up the car and use the restroom. As they got back on the highway, Sketch brought up a topic that had been on his mind since the morning.

"Sergeant Perkins, I have a dilemma. I didn't want to bring any of this up until I was able to prove to you just who I am, but...I have no money and no place to stay, so I—"

"Sketch, say no more. The money's not an issue. And I have a guest room. I'm recently divorced, so I live alone. You're more than welcome to stay. I know what you need. Getting to Egypt is going to require a little effort since you're not a normal person. But I've got ya covered. In my line of work...trust me...I have contacts. I used to work in Chicago, and dealt with a couple of key confidential informants—criminals who are too vital to arrest. Obtaining a passport and driver's license...I can make it happen."

"I can't thank you enough, sir. Who would've ever guessed that a superhero would need this much help?"

"Well," said Perkins, "I say keep your head up. You never know what the future holds."

Sketch turned in his seat and opened his suitcase that rested behind him. He took out his sketch book from the satchel and carefully tore out the page on which Charles had drawn the call, consisting of the airplane and Sketch flying toward it. He retrieved the newspaper from the seat then set it on his lap along with the drawing.

"If you don't mind," he said, "I'd like to go to the Lehman comic book store tonight, after they close. I need to make a little anonymous delivery."

"Sure," said Perkins. "May I ask why?"

"Because this drawing needs a home. It needs a place where it will have meaning. I see it as a sort of family heirloom, and I want to pass it on to those who would welcome it. I think the comic store is best."

"Why not deliver it to a TV news station?"

"Because they don't understand superheroes."

Chapter 4

S

Sergeant Perkins parked his patrol car at a closed hardware store a few buildings down from Lehman Comics. A single light post illuminated the central part of the parking lot, attracting crickets and moths that erratically flew around and bounced off the hot bulb.

Sketch sat in the passenger's seat with the newspaper and Charles' emergency airplane drawing that he had taken out of the sketch book. After adding a brief handwritten note to the drawing and newspaper, he bound them together with some twine that he had found during a quick stop at Perkins' house. Dinner consisted of canned potato soup with some canned mixed vegetables. "I suppose you can tell I lost my cook in the divorce," said Perkins, with an admissive hint of sarcasm.

"I wouldn't know," laughed Sketch. "I haven't had too many relationships these past few days."

Perkins had parked in the shadows of a far corner of the hardware store's parking lot to best conceal himself from the street. All of which he found to be strangely ironic, as he was not only a police sergeant assisting an immortal being, but he was also quite willing to obtain a counterfeited driver's license and passport for him as well.

"You're sure you want to get rid of that drawing?" asked Perkins.

"Yes, I'm positive."

Sketch stepped out of the car, and made his way to the front door of Lehman Comics. There was a wooden planter box to one side where a small shrub grew. He pulled it out from the wall just enough to comfortably lay the twined newspaper so as to not disturb the drawing and note that were tied on top.

He saw the three articles as a sort of gift, comprised of clues and a possible solution to the miracle landing mystery. Whoever would pick up the bundle in the morning would share it with the staff and certainly see the similarity of the sketched airplane and the airplane in the photo—both showing a broken wing. The drawing, however, showed Sketch flying toward the plane.

And then there was the ambiguous note:

THE LITTLE BOY ALMOST GOT IT RIGHT.
S

Ambiguous, until the newspaper article was read with the note's reference to the little boy's quote. All except for S. Just who was S? What were the chances that the little boy had, indeed, seen a superhero? Did S stand for Superman? Possibly, but he was fictional. The superhero in the drawing was a one-of-a-kind. Other than a practical joke, why would someone go out of their way to make this up? The plane's wing was literally broken. Given the unimaginable life-threatening stress at the time of the plummeting flight, and given the fact that planes cannot fly with broken wings, it would be unlikely that the boy would have lied. It would be more likely that he saw S outside his window.

Why a comic book store? Because people who worked there wouldn't just wave the twined bundle off as fodder. Given the unusual facts and puzzling pieces, there was a possibility that something supernatural had occurred.

Sketch now put aside his preconception that a comic store was more like a morgue of superheroes who never crossed the chasm between fiction and non-fiction, and began to see superhero comics as a sort of close genetic link to himself. After all, his superpowers were attributable to their existence, as Heba had been inspired by them and encouraged Charles to will them to life.

So, there he stood, staring at the bundled newspaper he had placed behind the planter box—a mystery delivery, but also a final farewell to Charles' drawing. Feeling satisfied, Sketch turned and walked away.

Chapter 5
BURIAL

Charles' burial was held in Groveton, Illinois, a small rural community an hour east of Lehman. A Celebration of Life was held earlier at the Methodist church, which had overflowed with family and friends.

Being Perkins' day off, he drove Sketch to the cemetery in his personal car. They stood a fair distance behind the small seated group, as Sketch wanted to maintain his anonymity. In attendance were Tennie and her mother, Charles' parents, a sister, grandparents, aunts, uncles, and cousins. Sycamore trees towered above, their leaves flipping in the afternoon breeze. Their swaying motion added a comforting serenity to the ceremony, as if the trees were paying homage to the deceased.

As the minister conducted the ceremony, Sketch looked on, realizing the human burial, including cremation, was something he would never be the subject of when he died. The end of his earthly existence would be to vanish into thin air, without a trace of his physical being. For the vast majority who would never learn of his immortality, his permanent absence would only be understood as him being a missing person—a case never to be solved.

Sketch found it peculiar that he had no knowledge of whether or not he would enter an afterlife if his existence were to end. Nor did he have any knowledge of having a soul or spirit. He assumed that his life was kind of a two-for-one deal, that living eternally was his heaven as well. But what happens if my drawing is destroyed and I vanish? Is there a soul that lives on? Is there a possibility that I will somehow reconnect with Charles, regardless of my immortality? Sketch found it frustrating that for someone who was supernatural, answers to these questions were not a given.

At the end of the ceremony, the minister asked everyone to bow their heads and offer Charles a moment of silent prayer. Charles' father and mother leaned into each other as they sorrowfully cried for the loss of their son. "So young," was the common murmur. "So, so young."

The group exchanged farewell hugs and handshakes, then began their departures. Sketch recognized Tennie from the apartment photos. She was visibly pregnant and walking with crutches, a precaution from her stairway fall. She appeared shorter than in the photos, of average height, but just as slender. The added baby weight was just that: all baby—a large ball sitting between her hips. From her backside, it was hard to tell that she was carrying.

She and her mother had parked away from the main line of vehicles, which made it easier for Sketch to meet them at their car. Tennie held a handkerchief, dabbing her bloodshot eyes and streaks of mascara. They moved slowly, in a grieving manner, their heads hung in sadness.

Sergeant Perkins hung back as Sketch approached Tennie.

"Excuse me…Tennie?" He spoke softly as he neared.

She looked at him with unsure eyes. "Yes?"

"I'm sorry to bother you, but my name is Sketch…I was a friend of Charles. I just wanted to tell you how sorry I am for—"

"You're…" Tennie began to cry, then walked over to Sketch and hugged him. "Mother," she wept, "it's Sketch!"

He couldn't have foreseen any of this coming. He was blindsided by her knowing his name. What had Charles shared?

"Sketch," she said, taking a step back to dab her eyes again. "Charles spoke of you, only a few times, but with great admiration."

"Well, I admired him, too."

"It's funny, because I never heard of you before. He talked like you'd been friends for years. But I know that wasn't the case."

"So…he told you?"

"Yes."

Sketch was uncertain what her answer entailed. "May I ask what he said?"

"He said you were on the flight with him—the one with the broken wing. He said you helped everyone get through it. I wasn't quite sure what he meant by 'everyone', but thank you for whatever you did."

"I did my best to give everyone hope."

"Well, thank you." Tennie paused to sniffle. "At least you gave him a few more hours of life."

Tennie's mother moved closer, gently patting her back, as she helped her to the car.

"Tennie," said Sketch, "may I ask you a question?"

She turned, giving him her full attention.

"Would you mind if I stayed in contact with you? I'd love to know how the baby's doing."

"Certainly. Call anytime."

"Thank you. That means a lot to me."

"I'll be moving back to Oklahoma. I'm going to need help with the baby. I know it's not exactly around the corner, but feel free to stop by if you're ever in the area."

Sketch opened the passenger door and helped her in, holding her crutches as she maneuvered herself into the seat.

"This damn leg," she said. "I still can't drive."

"It could've been worse," said Sketch, laying the crutches down in the back seat.

"True. So true."

Tennie rolled her window down after Sketch closed the door. She wrote her address and phone number on a piece of scrap paper and handed it to him before saying, "Is Sketch your real name?"

For just a moment, he contemplated, then said, "Yes, it is."

"Is it a family name?"

"No. Just a name I was given when I came into this world."

"What a strange coincidence—your name being Sketch and Charles being an artist. What are the odds?"

Sketch smiled, then said, "Tennie…I think you should know…" He knelt down so he was eye level with her. "I was sitting next to Charles when he passed."

Tennie dropped her head, sobbing into her hands while her mother, in the driver's seat, reached over and held her hand.

"I'm telling you this so you'll know that he didn't suffer. He went peacefully."

"But they said a piece of steel stabbed his chest, near his heart."

"That's true. But he could still talk. I held his hand. Tennie, he told me to tell you he loves you, and the baby. Not loved, but loves."

The giant sycamores continued swaying in the wind, as Tennie reached out and took Sketch's hand, linking the three of them together. It was at that moment when Sketch was convinced he, unequivocally, felt the spirit of Charles.

Chapter 6

JIGSAW

Sergeant Perkins and Sketch made the two-and-a-half-hour drive to Chicago to obtain a passport for Sketch. Making their way through the suburb of Cicero, they reached their destination—a small modest grey home at the end of a cul-de-sac that sat in the afternoon shadow of a neighboring textile manufacturing plant.

"I'll wait out here," said Perkins. "You go ahead. You'll be fine, he's expecting you."

Moments later, a large-framed man opened the door, letting Sketch in, then gave Perkins a thumbs-up.

Jigsaw was "the man" as they say. Just under six-feet tall and weighing over 300 pounds, he consistently wore blue denim overalls, and gnawed on a popsicle stick instead of the traditional toothpick. He was a reclusive Chicago forger whose impeccable work had never failed the test of real-world security points or places requiring proof of identity. After a three-year manhunt, a Chicago Police Department task force, led by Sergeant Perkins, tracked him down, but did not arrest him. He was too valuable to keep behind bars with his inside knowledge of Chicago-based mafia and other nationally-known crime organizations. Under the condition that he would provide the identities of key criminals who used his services, the CPD hired him as a confidential informant. Jigsaw's work location was never stationary. In Chicago, renting a small home with a basement was his choice location for operating his business. He had a good reputation with the underground crime syndicates as someone who could be trusted. Little did they know he was a snitch.

Needless to say, he was the perfect fit for Sketch—reliable, professional, and always willing to help out a cop, especially Perkins.

"Without a doubt," said Jigsaw, when he and Sketch were in the basement of Jigsaw's rental home, "you're a very unique client, having no prior identification, including no knowledge of your social security number."

"That is correct," said Sketch.

"You weren't issued one at birth?"

"No, sir. It's complicated."

"How complicated?"

"Very."

"And your name is Sketch?"

"Sir, I don't mean to be problematic, but are these questions necessary?"

Jigsaw smiled. "Just a formality, I guess. But you're right, they're not necessary. You're just an unusual case, that's all. Sketch is catchy. Kinda like my name. And I like it,"

They were seated across from each other at a wooden table laid out with Jigsaw's tools of the trade: X-acto knife, scissors, glue, colored pens, ruler, and a gooseneck magnifying glass allowing him to work hands-free. On the floor next to Jigsaw sat a half-full box of stolen passports, one of which he had selected for Sketch.

"I've scoured through my entire collection, including that over there," said Jigsaw, pointing to a stack of boxes in the corner of the room, "and I think our best bet will be this guy." He slid a passport across the table to Sketch.

"Henry Tisdale?" said Sketch, opening it to the ID page. "He doesn't even look like me."

"No worries," said Jigsaw. "I'll take a photo of you to replace his. It's an easy switch. Everything else will stay the same. It's a routine job. Just make sure you remember his name and birthdate. Say it over and over for a few days. You want it ingrained in your memory so when someone questions you, you don't have to think twice. A successful passport forgery is all about minimizing suspicions."

"So, where is the real Henry Tisdale?"

"Unknown. But you'll be fine. All that international customs agents will be checking is that your face matches your photo. And trust me, my work is flawless."

"But if I get caught?"

"You won't."

"You're certain?"

Jigsaw shifted his heavy weight in his chair, then rested both elbows on the table, interlocking his fingers beneath his chin. "Sketch…your new identity…what's your name?"

Sketch answered without hesitation, "Henry Tisdale."

"There ya go," chuckled Jigsaw. "You're off to a good start."

PART VI

Chapter I
GENEVIEVE

1966

One year before meeting Charles, Heba was visiting the Mediterranean coastal city of Montpellier, France, when she came across a sidewalk artist named Genevieve who was doing quick-sketch charcoal portraits. She was six-feet tall, and beautifully proportioned with a round, happy, pinkish face and brunette hair that she tied back in a bun. Her ankle-length, white summer dress had a weightless comfort about it as she stood at her easel.

When Heba traveled, she made sure to pack a couple of pens containing the magic ink, but never too much ink as it was a rare commodity whose supply only declined and was never replenished. On this particular day she carried the pens inside a satchel containing a sketch book, all of which were what Charles would one day receive. It was important that Heba's selected artists were the cream-of-the-crop, otherwise one misjudgment on her part regarding an artist's talent or character would only amount to wasted ink. Since the beginning of Heba's existence, worthy artist selections had always been critical. There was no room for error. And so far, since Queen Heba had been distributing the ink, her success rate was a solid 100%.

Then along came Genevieve, and, as they say…all hell broke loose.

When Heba first spotted her in Montpellier, it wasn't Genevieve's artistry that initially caught her attention, but rather witnessing her actions, just as she would later witness Charles and the little girl breaking the glass lantern in the Cairo market.

It was a busy Saturday afternoon, and Genevieve was at her easel sketching a young girl, who sat before her, with a balloon tethered to her wrist. As she drew, Genevieve noticed a woman in the background brush up against another woman, then slipping her hand into the woman's open purse, and stealthily stealing her wallet. The thief then turned around, putting the wallet into her canvas shoulder bag, before casually blending into the crowd as she scanned for her next victim.

"Excuse me," said Genevieve to the little girl. "I'll be right back."

Her long dress floated like a pleated cloud as she trotted up behind the thief, deftly reached into her canvas bag and extracted the stolen wallet. She returned to a trot until she caught up with the woman whom the thief had targeted, and gave the wallet back to her. The victim graciously thanked Genevieve.

When Genevieve walked back down the sidewalk, she approached the thief, whispered something into her ear, then returned to her easel, and continued sketching the girl with the balloon.

Later, Heba introduced herself and paid Genevieve to draw her portrait. Heba told her she had witnessed the wallet incident and asked, "What did you say to the thief?"

"I asked her if she was missing something and left it at that."

"You did not scold or accuse her?"

"No."

"Why not?"

"Because, she's my sister."

"Your sister?"

"Yes," she said, as she made the first few strokes of charcoal outlining Heba's face.

"What a unique situation," said Heba, keeping still in a fold-out chair as she faced Genevieve. "But I must say, you looked pretty skilled yourself, the way you retrieved the wallet without your sister knowing."

Genevieve paused, lowering her hand with the charcoal stick. "That's because I was once a thief myself. But not by choice."

"I don't understand."

"We used to live in Paris. We were poor, very poor. So, my father taught us how to pickpocket and shoplift. My sister and I were too young to know any better, so we did as told."

"Do you continue to steal?"

Genevieve laughed, returning to Heba's portrait. "Oh, no! I'm twenty-three, and I gave that up years ago. Once I moved out, I was done. My conscience couldn't take it anymore."

"And your sister?"

"She's younger and struggling, but she's doing it less often. That fool just forgot I was here today."

"So, your thievery is over?"

"Oh, very much. If I could turn back time, I would return all the money to the people I stole from. It is unfortunate that we live in a world that must be on the lookout for evil."

Genevieve's statement was not monumental, but had just enough punch in it to elicit one major image in Heba's mind…a superhero.

"Genevieve…" said Heba, "after we are done here, may I buy you lunch? I have something I would like to share with you."

"Why, of course. I'd love to."

During the two preceding days, Heba had been periodically watching Genevieve draw, and at no point did she have any concerns about her artistic abilities. The more they talked at lunch the more Heba understood that Genevieve's impoverished childhood was fully corrupted by her father's ill will. She had always wanted to escape the corruption, but that was unfortunately dependent upon the slow progress of her growing older. When she did finally break free, she stayed with friends, relatives, and trustworthy strangers, and never once looked back. And that was when Heba decided to explain all about the magic ink. She took from her satchel a pen and sketch book and set it on the table. "Genevieve, it has been a turbulent world, especially for France, when just twenty years ago this country was being invaded by Germany. It takes time to rebuild from such a horrific period, but your country has rebounded and pressed forward. And with that, the arts have come alive. I am a seeker in search of artists who must fit very specific criteria. And I believe you are such a person."

Heba opened up the sketch book, and set the pen on the first page. "Genevieve, I want you to draw a butterfly. It need not be perfect, just a sketch."

Chapter 2
ROGUE

Four months before Heba discovered Genevieve, a pair of peregrine falcons found a cliff ledge seven-hundred feet high in the French alps. A two-foot-deep recess formed a small cave-like shelter that would protect their chicks from inclement weather. Resting on her breast, the mother repeatedly pushed her feet back, scraping the substrate until an indentation had been made—a sort of shallow bowl in which to lay her eggs.

Four days later, and for three consecutive days, she laid three mottled brick-red eggs. By the thirty-sixth day, the eggs had hatched. The hatchlings whistle-chirped in the scrape as they wobbled and fumbled into each other, their heads too heavy to steady, their legs too weak to stand, and their wings nothing more than feeble appendages. Born blind for the first few days, they were altricial, being completely dependent upon their mother to survive.

Over the ten-week period as they grew and gained sight, feathers, and strength, their time to take flight from the cliff neared. On the day the three fledglings were preparing to fly, the mother and father circled below, anticipating their takeoffs. The siblings teetered on the cliff's edge, not quite sure if this was to be their day, flapping their wings now and then to keep balanced. A cluster of fir trees grew above the bird's small cave, their branches whistling in the gusty wind. The sound was eerily melodic and seemed to intensify as a line of dark clouds moved in. Thunder rumbled once, but that was all—a warning in disguise. An asp viper—a thick, two-foot long, grey venomous snake with a black, broken zig-zag pattern—slithered down into the nesting cave from a rocky corner entry where the ground above formed the cave's ceiling. It entered quietly and unnoticed.

This asp was no ordinary viper.

After Heba was drawn into the world, Khepri had warned her to be on the lookout for signs of Apep, the serpent demon God who thrived in darkness and chaos, and was the polar opposite of the god Ra. Though it was believed that Apep had lost a battle to Ra and forever existed in the underground, never to surface into mortal life, Khepri wasn't completely sold that this was true. His fear, he told Heba, was that Apep was, in fact, waiting in the underground. "When you least expect it," he said, "I believe Apep will rise and strike. Since Ra created the magic ink, Apep will try to find a way to corrupt it."

There had been no signs of any such strike in Heba's existence, which gave her solace that, perhaps, Apep had been defeated by Ra. But what if, she thought, Apep's evil spirit lingered? What if Khepri was right and he hadn't been completely defeated? What if Apep wanted possession of the magic ink, but needed the perfect opportunity to make it happen. If so, what would that entail? How would it be accomplished?

The viper was the demon in the details.

It moved slowly, approaching the three fledglings from behind. The vertical slits of its eyes were silver, which was unusual for its species. It could only strike one at a time, so it honed in on the closest bird—the one on the left that had coincidentally stepped backward. And the timing couldn't have been better. In an instant, the viper struck. The two siblings hadn't noticed, as they were looking down to the right. It was quick and silent as its fangs sank into its neck. An immediate paralysis took effect while the snake slowly dragged the bird to the back of the cave.

The mother and father continued gliding below in a circular pattern as the fledglings remained on the ledge.

But it was only a matter of time until the fledglings did notice their sibling was missing. As they looked back, there was no opportunity to locate it, for the viper had returned—closing in on them—preparing for a second strike with its triangular head raised and ready to jab.

Unprepared, the fledglings screamed off the cliff and tumbled through the air, the land and sky spinning in their disorientation as they fell past their parents. The mother folded her wings against her sides and dropped like a dart, splitting between them and wailing as the earth approached. Extending her wings, she managed to break each bird's tumbling motion, offering them a chance to save themselves. The young falcons' instincts took over as they opened their wings, then swooped perilously close to the ground, and landed like seasoned raptors.

The two siblings gone, and the snake having slithered away, all that was left in the cave was the stricken bird, now standing upright with no sign of injury or pain. It flapped its wings and hopped to the ledge where, far below, it saw its family on the ground, and its mother looking up.

But it was no longer one of them. The snake had changed it, injecting a silver venom that altered nearly every aspect of its being. Blinking its newly-colored silver eyes, it took flight, soaring up and over the mountain, flying farther and farther away.

This falcon had now gone rogue—a servant of Apep.

Chapter 3
ZENATOR

A month after meeting Heba, and having been given the satchel containing the sketch book and pen with the magic ink, Genevieve was house-sitting for a family at their modest chateau in Chamonix, France. A resort town that catered to skiers in the winter and hikers in the warmer months, Chamonix sat at the base of Mont Blanc, Western Europe's tallest mountain.

Twice a year, Genevieve stayed at the chateau for two weeks while the family went on vacation. It made for some of the most treasured times in her life. Each morning, she would curl up in a creaky, wooden rocking chair on the back deck, and sip on fresh brewed coffee while the sun cast its early morning yellow on the stunning views of the eastern face of Mont Blanc.

The month leading up to her arrival had been a busy one, working double-shifts waitressing at a restaurant with no time available to focus on creating what Heba had encouraged: a superhero.

"I am convinced," said Heba, "you have the gift. You have the imaginative energy. You can make it happen. I watched how easily you willed the butterflies to life. I have never come across an artist like you. I do not think your creating a superhero is out of the question."

"But what powers should I give my superhero?"

"That is entirely up to you. I do not want to influence your decision. Everything must come from within you."

"And this person will live forever?" she asked.

"For as long as the drawing is not destroyed. But, Genevieve, I do not know how much power you can will into a drawing. This is all new territory for me. As you know, this was all inspired by superhero comics of the late 1930s and 40s. Up until then, the idea of willing superpowers into drawings never occurred to me. I know that it takes a very gifted artist to accomplish what I am asking. I have watched you, and I believe you are capable. I could be wrong, but we will not know until you try. Understand this, though...you must be fully invested. If your heart is not into it, your imaginative energy will be weak."

"How much time do I have to think about it?"

"As much time as you need."

"Once I have settled into the chateau, I will create a superhero, and one that is loyal to its cause."

She had no doubts that this was something she was actually capable of, and that Heba wasn't some fly-by-night con artist pandering to her gullibility. Genevieve had drawn and witnessed the creation of her two butterflies, as well as their terminations. When asked to create an insect of her choice, she sketched a caterpillar and willed it to move fast, which it did, rapidly inching its way across a tabletop.

Folding her legs beneath her, Genevieve positioned herself in the rocking chair with the sketch book on her lap. Holding the magic ink pen, she took in a deep breath and calmly exhaled with closed eyes. She repeated this several times, envisioning her future superhero dressed in everyday clothes: jeans, sandals, and a white t-shirt with a black peace symbol on the front. She called him Zenator and his superpower would be the ability to convert criminal minds into peaceful ones.

Peace was the prominent quality of Genevieve that unfortunately ran concurrent alongside her father's criminalities. It was an undeniable virtue that struggled against his coercive pickpocketing insistencies. But at age eighteen, she escaped the criminal influence of her father and, at last, lived under her own remorseful terms.

Expending her imaginative energy willing a superhero to fly or possess super human strength or x-ray vision was of no interest to her. Creating someone who could influence world peace and harmony was more her style.

She took off the pen cap and began to draw the wavy black hair and endearing appearance of Zenator. As easy as the peace symbol t-shirt and jeans were to draw, she fastidiously took her time willing every morsel of peace into the lines of magic ink. However, she felt the lines looked unfinished and proceeded to precisely trace over them. Doing so not only resulted in a sharper drawing but, for Genevieve, it unknowingly brought Zenator's powers to life.

When she finished, without delay, he was standing next to her.

"Hello, Genevieve."

She jerked in her seat, leaning away from him. "You!" she gasped. "You…it is you…it is really you! Zenator!"

"Sorry to startle you," he said. "I had no idea how I was going to arrive."

"You were somewhere else before here?"

"No. It is hard to explain. I mean, I have been here for less than a minute, and yet it feels like a lifetime."

"And you are real, right?" asked Genevieve, standing up to face him.

"Yes, I am. Not in the way that you are real. But I am living, existing in your reality."

"It's so strange."

"Yes, it is. To the point that neither of us will ever be able to fully understand it. We immortals have our mysteries too."

Smiling, Genevieve looked him up and down, then circled him before reaching out to pat his hair and gently poke his shoulder. "Amazing. You are exactly as I drew you. Exactly."

"You draw well," he said, returning the smile.

"And you are a messenger of peace, right?"

"Yes, I am."

"So, my drawing worked!"

"Yes, but to what extent I do not know."

"Well," she said, "I am just happy you—"

They both heard it as they simultaneously looked up. Three peregrine falcons circled in the sky, wailing in a discordant order.

"Falcons!" said Genevieve, excitedly.

"Yes, they are." Zenator's voice was cautious and foreboding.

"Is everything ok?"

Zenator paused, shielding his eyes as he observed the birds. "I am not sure. Something is different."

"What do you mean?"

"Dangerous. It is a warning."

"For what?"

"Us."

"Are we in danger?"

"I think so."

"From what? Can you use your Zen superpowers?"

"I am not sure. I cannot figure it out."

"You're scaring me, Zenator."

Two more falcons joined the trio, all spinning faster as a group, as the wailing grew louder.

"Stay close to me, Genevieve."

Genevieve was still holding the drawing pen. She opened her hand so it was resting on her palm. "It is vibrating. I can feel the ink moving inside."

The five falcons maintained an even distance between one another while they circled, as if they had practiced the choreography many times before.

"Why is my pen vibrating?"

"I am certain it is a warning," said Zenator, then pointing away from the birds. "Look!"

A sixth peregrine appeared in the distance. It flew silently, but directly on line with the circling group, picking up speed as it neared. Four months prior it had been bitten by an asp viper, under the guise of the serpent god Apep. Its vile purpose had been put in motion. Indistinguishable from below, the approaching falcon narrowed its silver eyes…then…

The first two falcons had their necks broken instantaneously in the quick lethal grip of its talons. It then attacked a third falcon, crippling its wing, sending it into a fatal spiral.

The remaining two falcons fled, both narrowly escaping attack. The rogue tucked its wings against its sides, and accelerated into a vengeful dive toward the two figures standing on the chateau's deck.

Zenator yelled, "Grab your sketch book! We must get inside!" But their rushed attempt to beat the falcon's attack, failed. Even when Zenator aimed his fists at the falcon, and emitted wave-like pulses of tranquility, the bird blew through them, unaffected.

The chaos of the moment was too great. The falcon opened its wings, braking itself to a perfect landing on Zenator's arm, where it then sank its talons deep into his flesh. Genevieve swatted at the bird, grazing its back. A second swat solidly hit its side, but the falcon maintained a tight grip as its talons pivoted ninety degrees, causing more flesh to be torn.

She attempted to strike it with her sketch book, but failed. Keeping entrenched in Zenator's arm, the falcon lowered its head and lunged forward, stabbing Genevieve in the throat with its beak—dropping her and the sketch book to the deck. With a harrowing shriek and victoriously raising its head to the sky, it released its talons from Zenator and flew upward.

"Please," said Genevieve, her throat throbbing in pain and her voice faint, as she held her palm firmly over the severed, bleeding artery. "Get me a towel from the kitchen."

Zenator dropped to his knees next to Genevieve, but not to assist her. Something unfamiliar was happening to him—something chemical, like an infusion. He felt dizzy and impaired. He couldn't conjure a will to fight or protect. Instead of standing his ground, Zenator succumbed, his hands shielding his head as he cowered, fearful the falcon would return. He trembled, knowing he didn't have a chance to survive. How could he be a superhero if he was showing this much fear? Why wasn't he aiming his fists and emitting pulses of peace and tranquility?

"Genevieve..." He spoke hesitantly, then said nothing more. He looked at his arm, perplexed, where the talons had sunk deep. Black ink pooled within the wounds, but a change was occurring rapidly. Thin swirling lines of silver ink began to appear, quickly multiplying like cellular division. What was this? He was created with innate knowledge, but this was beyond his scope of understanding. It was foreign for sure, but the more the silver ink infiltrated his system, the more the feeling of unfamiliarity grew.

And the more pronounced the change in him became.

Zenator had been created with good intent, but the tables had now turned. And one falcon gone rogue had made all the difference. He rose to his feet and stepped away from Genevieve. Looking up to the circling falcon, he raised his punctured arm to the sky, smiling and embracing who he had now become all due to the changing composition of the ink flowing within him. He tilted his head back and screamed with primal emotion as silver ink, not black, seeped from his wounds, and streamed down his arm.

Evil had found its way into the ink.

"Zenator…" Genevieve pleaded, blood coating her hand and soaking into the neckline of her shirt. "I created you. Please, help me." But the moment she saw him look down—his face aglow with a sickening happiness—she knew he was no longer a messenger of peace, nor was he loyal.

"Zenator," he said, "is no more."

Genevieve could feel herself fading. How unexpected and quickly her life was coming to an end. "The falcon poisoned you," she cried.

"Perhaps," he scoffed, "but do not meddle in my affairs."

Genevieve noticed the sketch book was open to her drawing of Zenator. All she needed to do was grab it and tear it in two, and he would vanish. But just the act of reaching out for the book was insurmountable. She tried, though, but her attempt simply lacked strength and coordination. She did, however, manage to hold onto the magic ink pen.

Zenator bent down and calmly picked up the sketch book. "All mine," he said.

In a moment of resurgence, Genevieve shouted, "Heba will destroy you!"

"Who is Heba?"

"The first created. Queen Heba! She holds the ink. She holds the power. She will destroy you!"

Zenator's curiosity piqued. "She holds the ink?"

It was an irreversible blunder that Genevieve knew she had made, caught up in the emotion of her final minutes. A costly slip of the tongue in a moment of angst that gave Zenator the single most important lead he could ask for. "You fool!" he said. "You ratted her out!"

A small porcelain planter sat on the deck just to the right side of Genevieve. Her right hand had been compressing her artery. She had, at most, a minute to go. There was no time for obsessing over the regret of her blunder.

Letting go of her neck, she rolled to her right, extended her right arm and summoned all she had to grab the planter. With her left hand she dropped the pen and, just as Zenator realized what she was doing, she crushed the pen with the planter, splattering the ink on the deck, making it impossible to collect.

Genevieve died with a faint smile.

"Goodbye, Genevieve. And don't you worry. I will find Heba."

Walking away, he curiously opened the sketch book and read an inscription inside the front cover:

Heba
Kahn el-Kalili Market
Cairo, Egypt

"You fool!" he laughed, looking back at Genevieve. "You utter fool!"

And with that said, he made a gun out of his index finger and thumb, firing an imaginary bullet into her heart.

The Finger Gunman had arrived.

Chapter 4
SIBLINGS

The murderous falcon hadn't flown more than half a mile out of sight from the chateau when it met its end. And it was of no surprise when the attack did happen. After all, it had just killed three falcons and made an attempt to kill two others. But so goes the life of a martyr who knows the penalty of its actions will be death. And, subsequently, sooner than later.

Its beak stained with the blood of Genevieve, and its talons black from Zenator, the rogue flew peacefully toward the pristine snow-covered backdrop of Mont Blanc. It was a strange heavenly sight having departed from the hell it had just created.

It could hear them approaching from behind, and knew exactly who they were. There would be no evading, only acceptance. It had served Apep, and that was all that mattered. And so, realizing there was no escape, the falcon stopped flapping its wings and, instead, opened them wide and glided through the air with its silver eyes closed.

In pursuit of the rogue and closing fast, were the two falcons who had earlier avoided injury or death. They were the siblings of the rogue who, as fledglings, had escaped the asp viper. One would break the rogue's neck while the other tore into its heart—a quick team effort—before releasing their talons, and dropping the corpse to the earth.

Unfortunately, though, the rogue had won the fight, long before it had started.

Chapter 5

I DON'T LIKE HIM

Like Sketch, the Finger Gunman needed a passport in order to roam about the world. He needed a skilled forger like Jigsaw to do the job. Using the money he collected from Genevieve's purse inside the chateau, he took her car and made his way to Paris, along with extra clothing and various odds and ends that he gathered from the homeowners' belongings. He also took a handgun and a box of bullets that he found in a bedside table. The chateau sat on several acres, which made leaving inconspicuous. Once he arrived, he parked at a grocery store, locked the doors, tossed the keys in a trash can, and walked away.

He frequented bars late at night in both the shady and nice parts of Paris. It didn't take long until he began to socialize with the city's underground network, and discovered who were the most reliable forgers. Of course, their services came at a cost, but were easily afforded thanks to teaming up with a group of car thieves to generate some easy cash.

His forger, who went by the name of Flip, wore a long grey beard and black suit, and was well into his seventies. He operated in the back room of a money-laundering flower shop located next to a cathedral. If there were two things that didn't smell of crime, they were roses and God.

He and the Finger Gunman were seated at a steel-top table sprinkled with white and blue hydrangea petals. As Flip handed over the forged passport, his advice was no different than Jigsaw's.

"Your new name is Claude Fontaine. Memorize the hell out of it. If you pause when asked, well, it's a dead giveaway, and don't come running back to me if you get caught. I'm too old to nurse your wounds. Understand?"

"Clear as a bell."

"So, where are you headed?"

"Egypt."

"And why can't you obtain a legal passport?"

"You wouldn't believe me if I told you."

"Obviously, you're up to no good," smirked Flip. "Not much different than I, though. But it's how I make a living."

"I'm meeting a woman there."

"Ah, romance!"

"Hardly romance."

"Revenge?"

"Not that either. She has something that I want."

"So, you're..."

"You are asking too many questions."

"I am only curious."

The Finger Gunman stood up with his passport in hand, lightly tapping it against his other palm. "This is the last time you will ever see me," he said. "I want to thank you for your services. However, I trust you won't concern yourself with my visit to Egypt. I am a different breed. There is no need to have me followed. If you do, the wounds you'll suffer will be impossible to nurse. Goodbye."

The flight to Cairo had a layover in Athens. Everything ran smoothly for alias Claude Fontaine with no hiccups going through customs. He took a taxi from the airport to a hotel located about a mile from the Khan el-Khalili market, then found a small restaurant and had an early dinner.

Returning to the hotel he noticed a woman in her thirties

with blonde hair thumbing through a pamphlet by the front desk. Wearing a sleeveless, knee-length floral dress and sandals, she had a slight scowl across her face that he found both interesting and appealing. He walked over to her and took a pamphlet from a small acrylic display.

"Excuse me," he said, "is there anything of interest in this?"

"It's pretty much the museum, the bazaar, and the pyramids," she said.

"I've never been to any of those. This is my first time here."

"Are you from France?"

"Oui, madame. Guess my accent gave it away. And you are American, oui?"

"Yes, American."

"Are you here alone?"

"No, my daughter is with me."

"And your husband?"

"He left yesterday. We had a big argument."

"I'm sorry to hear that," he said, not the least bit sorry. "He went back to the States?"

"Yes."

"It must have been a big argument."

"It was. But they're nothing new. I think he wanted to argue. I think he wanted things to get out of control, which they did, so he could go back. I'm pretty sure he's seeing someone on the side, so he needed a reason to leave. Excuse me for a second."

She walked over to a nearby woman's restroom, opening the door and shouted inside, "Angie, are you done?!"

A small voice replied, "Coming, mom."

Her scowl grown larger; the mother walked back to her spot. "I have very little patience with her. She's either taking forever or she's just careless. I know she's young and I should have more patience, but, damn, that child really gets under my skin."

The Finger Gunman was enjoying the tension within the mother's family. Hearing about the unstable marriage and her snapping at her daughter brought him a sense of twisted comfort.

Angie emerged from the bathroom. She was six years old, blonde like her mother, and wore a similar floral dress. "Sorry, mommy. I had to wait for a lady until she was done."

"No worries," said the Finger Gunman, smiling at Angie. "You're just a kid."

"Who's he?" said Angie cautiously, sidling up to her mother.

"My name is Claude." He extended his hand, but she inched away. "It's nice to meet you, Angie."

"Go ahead, shake his hand," said the mother. "He won't bite."

"But what if he does?"

"Angie, don't act like that." The mother shook his hand. "My apologies, Claude. I'm Amanda. It's nice to meet you."

"It's nice to meet you as well," he said, behind a false smile.

Feeling emboldened, Amanda asked, "Would you care to join us for a bite to eat?"

"I have already eaten, but I don't mind going back to the same restaurant and having a glass of wine or two."

"Sounds good," she said. "Let's meet back here in thirty minutes."

Genevieve would be so proud, he cruelly thought. Within a matter of minutes, he had charmed Amanda into inviting him to dinner. How easy was that! It wasn't something he had strategically planned, but had simply evolved. If he could keep them on his good side, it might create an image of normalcy to shroud the deceit lying within him. But Angie, he knew, had her suspicions. She was wary of him.

The conversation flowed freely over dinner as the Finger Gunman continued surprising himself by how quickly Amanda was enjoying his company.

"You know, Claude, you're more than welcome to join us tomorrow. We're going to tour the museum then go to the market for a couple of hours."

"Sure. I'll tag along if you don't mind."

"But, mom," said Angie sitting next to her in the booth, "I thought it was just going to be you and me."

"Angie, hush!"

"But—"

"He's a nice man. It'll be fun. Claude, I'm sorry."

"It's okay. I understand." But the Finger Gunman knew it wasn't okay. Nor did he expect it to be.

Angie was skeptical of him because there was reason to be. She could sense he wasn't a nice man. She couldn't articulate it, but the feeling was there, like a dog heeding to the signs of an approaching storm. Conversely, her mother felt a sense of excitement and courtship the way this outsider was giving her attention—buying her dinner, opening her doors, and pouring her wine. The great divide between her and her husband was widening; Claude was a welcome surprise that was filling the gap.

"Angie," her mother said, later in the hotel room as she leaned close to the bathroom mirror, applying red lipstick. "I'm going to Claude's room for just a little bit."

"Why are you putting that on?"

"Just for color, that's all."

"Do you like him?"

"Angie, stop with the questions. I won't be gone long."

"I don't like him."

"Well, I don't know why. He's been a real gentleman."

"Does dad know?"

The mother shifted her eyes in the mirror to look at Angie. "You listen to me, little girl! Your father needn't ever know of this. Do you understand me?!"

"Yes, momma. I understand."

And with that, the mother put on an extra layer of lipstick, then headed to Claude's.

Chapter 6

CLOSING IN

The following morning, the Finger Gunman met Amanda and Angie in the hotel lobby. He wore clothes he had taken from the chateau: white slacks, a red silk shirt, shiny black shoes, and three gold chains. The slacks and shirt fit him tightly.

"Are those yours?" asked Amanda.

"What do you mean?"

"I don't know…they just look a little small."

"Guess I put on a few pounds since I bought them. Should I change?"

"Oh, that's up to you."

He wanted to tell her to shut up. He wanted to point emphatically at her and tell her to mind her own business. The anger erupted inside him from nowhere, turned on like a switch. He was fully aware of who Genevieve had drawn him to be, but the peaceful soul of Zenator had been completely extinguished. All that remained was his physical appearance. He had to learn to tame his anger, to suppress it at times in order to work things to his advantage. He couldn't care less about Amanda, but he needed her in order to create the facade of happiness. The irony was that Amanda appeared to have an anger switch as well. That's when he would chuckle at the thought that maybe, deep inside him, there was a little bit of Zenator wanting to keep the peace.

They took a taxi to the Egyptian Museum and strolled through the exhibition halls that housed colossal granite figures, sarcophagi, funerary art and the contents of various tombs such as jewelry and ornaments, all dating back to over four thousand years.

They were passing by a smaller room when the Finger Gunman noticed a group of people listening to a tour guide standing near a display of paintings created on papyrus paper. There was nothing of grave interest to him, until…

"Through years of studying painting styles, we believe one artist created all of the works in this room. His name is beneath many of their images along with a small rendering of a falcon. Thus, we have named this The Khepri Collection."

The guide pointed to a rolled-out scroll of papyrus encased within a wall display behind thick glass.

"As you can see, this drawing depicts a woman and a dog walking ahead of a king. As far as we know, this is the only drawing of her. But what is interesting are the falcons flying overhead. It is believed that this is a spirit connection to the god Ra. After deciphering the written Egyptian characters beneath the drawing, we know her name was Heba…Queen Heba."

The Finger Gunman craned his neck forward, squinting as he listened intently, but uncertain what he thought he had just heard. "Excuse me," he said, approaching the tour guide. "Did you just say Queen Heba?"

"Yes, sir."

"I don't mean to interrupt, but you're certain that is an original drawing?"

"Yes, sir. Quite certain."

Amanda walked over to the Finger Gunman and stood by his side as the tour group moved on. Looking at Heba's drawing she asked, "Are you familiar with Queen Heba?"

"Sort of. A friend of mine had once mentioned her."

"Is your friend an archeologist?"

"No, an artist."

"In France?"

"Yes."

"It's interesting that your friend would know of this queen."

Her interrogation irritated him. Without thinking, he snapped at her. He shouldn't have, but he did. "What does it matter?!"

"Why the outburst?" she asked.

Contain it, he thought. Get a grip and control yourself. He could feel the silver ink ebbing and flowing within him, his skin warming in response. And somehow this physical change was encouraging him to fire back at her, to unleash who he really was and no longer feel restrained. No longer put on the act.

But he did hold back and kept himself in check. And Heba was responsible, if, in fact, it was her drawing behind the glass. What were the chances that it was her? The tour guide had said Queen Heba. It must be her! There was hope. A sense of solace and contentment stirred within him. The possibility of obtaining the magic ink seemed evermore within his grasp.

He put a gentle hand on Amanda's shoulder. "I'm sorry," he said, "I don't know why I did that."

"It's ok. I do it too."

"Let's go to the Khan el-Khalili market," he said. "You never know what you might find there."

At such a young age, Angie had no idea that the lamp she was about to break would bring things perilously close between the Finger Gunman, Charles, and Heba. None of them knew each other's identities, but it would be enough of a close encounter to trigger their curiosities.

It was close to noon when the Finger Gunman, Amanda, and Angie arrived at the market. There was a mix of locals and international tourists making their way through the network of alleyways and streets lined with shops and street vendors. The Finger Gunman scanned the area, looking for Heba, though not knowing what she looked like. All he had to refer to was a twenty-four-hundred-year-old drawing. But he knew the properties of the magic ink. He knew she would never physically age beyond fifty years old. Unfortunately, there were many women who fit that description, and nearly all were fully clothed in black abayas.

"Angie," said her mother, later paying for a glass lantern at a shop sparkling with colored glass, "hold this lantern. I'll be right back. I need to find Claude. He's somewhere nearby, I'm sure."

Angie nodded, enjoying her reflection in the lamp. As her mother disappeared down the cobblestone walkway, she stepped out from underneath the shop's awning, to hold the lamp in the sunlight. But she stubbed her foot on an uneven section of the cobblestone, losing hold of the lamp which slipped from her hands and shattered on the walkway. She began crying, her head lowered as she looked at the colorful pieces scattered about.

That was when Charles walked over and knelt in front of her. "Hey, it's okay," he said. "Everybody breaks things. Even I do."

"You break things?" she asked, sniffling.

"Well, sure. Even me. Accidents happen."

"But it was my mom's."

Charles looked around. "Where is your mom?"

"I don't know. She told me to hold the glass thing. She was with some man."

Soon after, Amanda walked into the scene, followed by the Finger Gunman. She berated Angie for dropping the lamp, and didn't soften her tone regardless of Charles' attempt to console her. The damage was done, so she pulled her daughter by the arm and escorted her away.

Left alone, the Finger Gunman tilted his sunglasses and made a gun out of his index finger and thumb, aiming it at Charles. He winked and fired one shot. "Next time, mind your own business," he said, then left.

And there Heba stood, down the walkway, under her tent canopy, watching Charles for the first time, picking up on his wonderful innate qualities and unaware of the fact she was the sole object of the Finger Gunman's reason for coming to Cairo. She was sixty-feet away from Genevieve's creation, with not even an inkling that she had ever created anything, let alone someone who would be so deeply rooted with evil.

The sinister serpent of Apep was closing in.

Chapter 7
CELEBRATION

"We'll be gone for four days?" asked the Finger Gunman, surprised and not thrilled.

"Yes," said Amanda. "It'll be fun. A riverboat cruise down the Nile. We leave the day after tomorrow."

"But isn't there a shorter cruise, like two days or something?"

"No. Besides, the tickets are paid for. My husband was going to go, but that's obviously not going to happen."

"And your plans tomorrow?" he asked.

"Nothing much. Angie and I are just going to hang out by the pool."

And that was the opening he was looking for—an opportunity to venture out alone, to return to the market and search for Heba. He had been with Amanda and Angie for only a day and a half and already his geniality was running thin. He wasn't equipped for lengthy periods of politeness. He had a vested interest in the art of disruption. Promoting peace was not his forte. Keeping a cushion of normalcy around him was exhausting. A break from mother and daughter was desperately needed. How he was going to survive four days on a boat on the Nile was beyond him. But, like it or not, he needed them to give the appearance of a happy family.

The next day, he met Amanda at the hotel pool. She was lying on a sun chaise next to a kiddie pool where Angie was playing with a small hand-sized plastic dolphin, somersaulting it into the water.

"I'm going to head over to the market," he said.

"Anything you're looking for in particular?"

"Not really. Just whatever catches my eye."

"Well, if you should find a grocery store, do you mind picking up some aspirin? In case I get headaches on the riverboat."

"I'll be happy to."

It was late morning when the Finger Gunman arrived at the market. He figured Heba must have been a merchant since the market, and not an address, was written beneath her name in Genevieve's sketchbook. Though the market covered a large area, and was teeming with thousands of merchants, it was not impossible to track someone down. All it took was a little asking around. He began questioning store owners if they knew of a woman by her name. There were some leads, but they only led to other women named Heba.

Persistence paid off, though, two hours into his search when he found himself on a cobblestone walkway, scanning the stores and small booths, looking for anyone resembling the woman in the drawing at the museum. A woman walking ahead of him was wearing a black abaya, and a hijab that obscured her face. She was just another Egyptian woman, except for the dog—slender and black with pointed ears and a large white spot on its back. It was an older dog, but kept pace with the woman.

"Khaldun," she said, turning left into a narrow alleyway. "Come on, boy."

The Finger Gunman stepped aside next to a display of carpets that hung lengthwise at the front of a textile store. Blending in with the shoppers, he kept his eyes on the woman with the dog, who unlocked a door and, just before entering, took off her hijab.

It was her profile, and that was her dog, and this was Heba! Queen Heba! What were the chances?!

"May I help you?" said the shop owner, dressed in a traditional full-length brown jibbah and turban.

"I'm just looking, but thank you, sir."

"If you have questions, please ask. All of the carpets are made in Egypt."

The Finger Gunman lifted a section of a large dark blue and sand colored carpet. "They are impressive, to say the least."

"Thank you."

"Actually, I do have one question."

"Please, ask."

"Not about these, but do you know a woman named Heba who works in the market?"

"Why, of course. If she is the Heba I believe you are talking about, she is a basket maker who works at a small tent back that way." The man pointed in the direction the Finger Gunman had come from. "Near a store that sells lamps. You cannot miss it."

"Ah, I was at the lamp store yesterday."

"But, my friend, if you cannot find her, then try that door down this alley. That is her apartment."

Instantaneous surges of happiness filled the Finger Gunman as he smiled and said, "You have been most kind. I would like to buy this carpet. In fact, I would like to buy ten of them. May I come back in five days to give you the shipping details?"

"Why, of course!" the man said, jubilantly. "Thank you, sir! Thank you for your business!"

The Finger Gunman shook his hand, then walked away.

He had found Heba, and had already formulated a plan of attack. The magic ink was near. This was the cause for a much-needed celebration.

A twisted celebration.

The Finger Gunman took a taxi to a clothing store several miles away from the market and the hotel. From there, he walked a couple blocks to a small grocery store.

He had found Heba. Although the ink was not yet in his possession, knowing where Heba lived was a critical part of his plans, and that was worth celebrating. Of course, bubbly champagne and confetti were not to be called for. He needed a different kind of celebration. Stir up some trouble. Create some chaos. After all, the Finger

Gunman was feeling confident and at the top of his game.

The grocery store was the place to celebrate, to break open a bottle of evil.

A kindly old man with a narrow face and prominent bony features was working the cash register, checking out a customer at the front of the store. "Thank you, and come back again," he told the exiting customer, then patted his forehead with a handkerchief while four dusty ceiling fans, wobbling with age, struggled to keep the warm air moving.

"May I help you with anything, sir?" he asked the Finger Gunman.

"Yes, you may. Why don't you explain to me why I am with two annoying females."

"Sir?"

"The mother and that terror of hers. Am I crazy? I met her in a hotel lobby two days ago. She was flirty. So, we had a little fun that night. I told the girl to wait in the lobby until we were done. And now, they are just a ball and chain. I am so sick of—"

"Sir, excuse me. I am sorry for your frustration, but perhaps—"

"Perhaps? Perhaps what?" The Finger Gunman pressed himself against the edge of the counter, leaning forward with narrowed eyes. "Perhaps, you should let me finish. And if you can't, then maybe this will help."

He lifted the bottom of his shirt. There, tucked into his pants, was the handgun he had taken from the chateau. With a menacing almost snake-like smile, he quickly pulled it out and brandished it in the air, before replacing it into his belt line. "Now," he said, "may I finish my story?"

"Please, sir," said the cashier, nervously opening up the register's drawer. "There is not much. Please, take it all."

"What do you take me for?! A robber? A thief?!" The Finger Gunman, incensed, retrieved the pistol, then, keeping an eye on the cashier, locked the door's deadbolt and lowered the window blinds.

"No, sir. I just—"

"You're a liar!! You have no idea what I'm capable of doing!! Give me the money then, and I shall be what you think I am!"

"Please, do not shoot me. Please!" The old cashier wiped tears from his eyes. "I have children and grandchildren."

"And now you think I am a murderer? That I would kill you just for money?"

"No, sir, I do not think that."

"Well, you're wrong. Now put the money in a paper sack, then I want you face down on the floor right where you are. Put your hands on your head."

His hands trembling, the cashier did as ordered, then lay down, sobbing behind the counter.

The Finger Gunman walked around to the cashier's side of the counter, then extended his arm and aimed the pistol at the cashier whose crying intensified at the sound of it being cocked. "I have been known to snap," he said. "I have what I call an anger switch. If you believe in the afterlife, know that your children and grandchildren will one day be with you again in heaven, so maybe this is not that bad after all."

The cashier cried harder, begging for his life as he told his family goodbye.

"Understand, old man, that you are powerless against my hands of evil. There is nothing you can do to alter the inevitable outcome. For the final moments that remain of your existence here on earth, find your most cherished memories and relish them throughout eternity as I shall do with this one. My friend, once I have the ink, I shall find the best artists to create the most powerful super villains who will rule the earth as I wish."

"Ink? Super villains?" the cashier sobbed.

The Finger Gunman placed the tip of the muzzle against the back of the cashier's head.

"Quiet, my friend…it is time…"

In the Finger Gunman's mind, the sound of the single shot screamed through the store, sending a shockwave through Cairo. But in reality, there was no bullet. He had replaced the gun with his finger, then said "BANG!!"

"It's okay," he laughed, walking to the door to leave. "I just wanted to take you to the edge, where death awaits. Feel free to celebrate. You live another day."

Chapter 8

FOURTEEN RINGS

Six-thousand miles away and eight hours difference in time, Sketch sat at the kitchen table in Perkins' house. He was hesitant, staring at the telephone he had set on the table, as if it were some foreign contraption requiring operating instructions. Behind him, Perkins entered the kitchen after taking out the trash.

"Still haven't called her?" he asked.

"I don't know what to say."

"Well, you could try hello for starters."

"Very funny. What if she's already in bed?"

"Are you kidding me? Look, Cairo is eight hours ahead of us. That means it's six at night there."

"So, she could be asleep."

"Are you just looking for reasons not to call her? Don't be silly. Now go ahead, make the call."

Make the call.

What an interesting role reversal, he thought. Here he was using language that had once described summoning him—the superhero. But that communication was a thing of the past, since he was no longer the superhero. Instead, it was he who was making the call—just an ordinary phone call—and it was as simple or common as opening a door or walking the dog.

"Look," said Perkins, "it's not like you're asking her out on a date. It's just a call."

"I know that."

"Then what's the issue?"

Sketch ran his fingers over the scratches and indentations in the tabletop—a story behind each mark. "She's immortal," he said. "I've never met one of my kind. And I don't know why, but…"

"But what?"

"I don't know how she's going to take the news."

"You mean about Charles?"

"Yes."

"I would imagine she'll be sad, but that's to be expected."

Sketch stood up and poured himself a glass of water from the sink. "It's not that, Sarge."

"Then what is it?"

"It's that she'll blame me for not saving Charles' life."

"Sketch. We've gone over this. Stop blaming yourself. You did all you could do."

"But—"

"Sketch…"

"Yes?"

"Make the call."

When Sketch finished dialing Heba's number, the line sounded hollow—like monotone white noise traveling through an empty steel drum, and the ringing was mechanical and choppy. After the twelfth ring, he hung up.

"What are you doing?" asked Perkins.

"She didn't answer."

"Maybe she was just entering her home. Maybe she was going to the bathroom, or taking a shower."

"Or maybe she's not there."

"Maybe," agreed Perkins. "You should try again. You never know."

Sketch called a second time. After ten rings, he started to hang up the receiver.

"No. Not yet," ordered Perkins. "Let it ring."

“But—”

“Sketch, let it ring.”

On the fourteenth ring, a voice answered.

“…Hello?”

“Hello, Heba?”

“Who is this?”

“My name is Sketch…”

Chapter 9

INTRUDER

In an effort to find the magic ink, the Finger Gunman had pulled every drawer out of its cabinet or desk, emptying the contents onto the floor. Mattresses and cushions were flipped, furniture shifted, pots and pans scattered about, pottery broken, and shoes and clothing tossed in every direction.

He had pried open Heba's apartment door with a screwdriver that he stole from a maintenance closet on the riverboat. The four-day cruise was nothing more than a test of his patience. By his measures, there was also far too much evening gaiety. There were excessive amounts of laughter and social pleasantries. It became a challenge to see how well he could stave off the urge to sink the boat, which was inspired one night as he dreamed of an iceberg adrift on the Nile, and of a drunken captain so bewildered by such an arctic phenomenon that he, like the Titanic, rammed the boat into the deadly floating berg of blue ice, killing all the passengers onboard. In a twist of irony, the dream lifted the Finger Gunman's spirits.

Much to his dismay, the river cruise went without incident. Though, on a trip to the restroom, he did "accidentally" bump into a waitress carrying a large serving tray of entrees, causing them to cascade off the shoulder of a gentleman seated at a party of eight. The entrees crashed onto their table, splattering Egyptian cuisine and wine into everyone's laps. He immediately came to her assistance, selling an apology that granted him collective empathy from the guests. He hardly slept a wink that night as he proudly replayed his performance over and over again.

Searching through Heba's apartment was making him angry. He was having no luck finding the ink, which the success of his eternal life depended upon. The Finger Gunman could perform evil acts all day long, but nothing would ever match the evil that could come from corrupting the magic ink. In the last dying minutes of her life, Genevieve had leaked Heba's name. He was certain it wasn't a final game she had played with him. But the ink wasn't surfacing. Of course, it could be with Heba at her booth, but he felt it was best to try her apartment first.

He moved aside the heavy wooden Kathmandu table, making room to upend the sofa where Heba had sat while Charles drew his butterflies. He looked for any kind of hidden compartment that might be beneath the furniture or carpets, but he was unsuccessful. And so…emotions took over, and he lost control.

In a rage, he raked paintings down from the walls, toppled over table lamps, emptied the refrigerator and freezer contents onto the floor, broke numerous historical artifacts she had collected over the centuries, and tore every travel map in half.

Then he walked out, and made his way toward Heba.

Genevieve was deceased and Heba knew nothing of it. She had created a wonderful, peace-loving superhero, and Heba knew nothing of it. Genevieve's greatest mistake was uttering Heba's name to the Finger Gunman, and Heba knew nothing of it.

But what Heba did know, or at least suspected, was that the Frenchman she had told Charles to be leery of—the one now approaching her booth—was bad news.

"Good afternoon, ma'am. Are these baskets your work?"

"Yes, they are," she said, unenthusiastically.

"Well, they are very impressive!"

What was it about him? What was she sensing? It was the same feeling when she first saw him approach Charles after the girl had dropped the lamp. She wanted to give him the benefit of a doubt, but her instincts were telling her otherwise. Still, she thought, let us see where this goes. "Thank you. I have been making them most of my life."

Khaldun appeared from beneath the table and lapped at his water bowl behind Heba.

"Ah, your assistant," chuckled the Finger Gunman. "How old is he?"

"I have lost count."

"But if you had to guess…decades? Centuries?"

"No dog lives that long."

"Unless…"

"Unless what?"

"Unless they are immortal."

He was not fishing, she thought. He was reeling her in. Bringing immortal into the conversation wasn't coincidental. He was playing her.

"My name is Claude. And you are?"

She was hesitant. "Heba."

"Heba, it's nice to finally meet you."

"Finally?"

"Why, yes. I've heard about you."

"From whom?"

The Finger Gunman looked around, inching closer to the table. "Heba, have you ever travelled to France?"

Another moment of hesitancy. "Yes."

"Montpellier?"

Her response was immediate. "Who are you?"

"I am no different than you."

"Sir?"

"Heba…we share some things in common."

"What do you mean?"

"We have a common friend."

She felt a surge rise within her. A frightful foreign feeling, tracing back to her initial intuition of him. He was her counterpart, an immortal up to no good. He was French, and so was…

"Genevieve," he said. "Does her name ring a bell?"

Heba stepped back. "She created you, didn't she?"

"That she did. And I was Zenator, a superhero of peace. I was all that you would have been so proud of. But things didn't go as planned. An insane falcon attacked me, infected me, forever changed me. It was the perfect circumstances I needed to be the ultimate evil creation that I am. And here I stand before the great Queen."

"You must be an agent of Apep."

He proudly smiled, nodding gently. "Don't make this complicated," he said. "Give me the ink, and I will let you live."

She moved forward, then whispered slowly and emphatically, "N E V E R!!"

"Don't be as foolish as Genevieve."

"What do you mean?"

"It doesn't matter."

"What happened to her? She has not contacted me in months." Heba's voice grew louder. "Tell me!"

"She's resting."

"Resting? Did you kill her?!" She was drawing attention from shoppers and merchants who kept their distance, more intrigued than concerned.

"No, I did not. Now listen…I know where your drawing is. I've seen The Khepri Collection. All I need to do is detonate an explosive, and your life is over. So, give me the ink and eternity is yours. Life or death? It's your choice."

"Did you really think it would be this simple? To just swoop in here with your threat, and off you would go with the ink? The fact is if you kill me, you will never find it. And only I know where it—"

The Finger Gunman lurched forward, snatching her forearm with one hand, then pulling her against the table. "Listen to me!"

Unable to break free, she yelled, "Khaldun!!" The dog quickly spun out from under the table, showing its teeth with a sustained, threatening growl.

"You are too old, ancient dog!!" the Finger Gunman yelled, waving his free hand at Khaldun.

Old yes, but full of fight. His neck hairs bristling and mouth gaping, the enraged Khaldun sprang from his hind quarters, launching himself up onto the table. Sharp inhalations preceded more aggressive growling as he slowly crouched closer to the Finger Gunman, who had relented and decided on a different approach, backing away and letting go of Heba.

"POLICE!! POLICE!!" she yelled.

It was now too risky for him to stay. He had no choice but to flee. "This is just the beginning!" he said, as he turned to run. "Just the beginning!"

Chapter 10
THE TABLE

"We must hurry, Khaldun!" said Heba, gathering her essential belongings from her booth, preparing to leave everything else behind. It was going to be a long time until she returned to the market, if she ever did.

An insane falcon infected him—what did he mean by that? Infected meant blood, but in his case, blood was ink, which must have meant that the crazed bird had torn into his skin. But falcons weren't crazy, so what happened? It was a mystery for another day. Right now, she had to get to her apartment and secure the ink, because the last thing she needed was him finding out where she lived.

But when she arrived with Khaldun restrained on a leash, Heba froze, standing before her apartment door that was cracked open, the door frame gashed and splintered.

Slowly opening the door, she poked her head inside, then cautiously stepped into her ransacked home, shocked by the overall devastation. She froze again, listening for any kind of movement or sign of human presence. "The police are coming!" she hollered. Moving gingerly, she navigated through the rest of the apartment, stepping over clutter strewn about the kitchen, before determining no one was there. Her immediate concern was not the condition of the centuries-old artifacts or that her privacy had been breached, but rather the safety of the magic ink.

Taking a seat in the living room wicker chair, Heba reached under the coffee table and dragged her fingers along its edge. When she felt a quarter-size indentation, she pressed it firmly, actuating a spring-loaded mechanism that flipped up the inlayed "Kathmandu" sign, exposing a hidden compartment in the table.

She reached inside and pulled out the burlap sack containing the box of magic ink and pens. How close he had come!

"His heart is wicked cold," she said, looking around at the destruction of original artwork. Not a single piece made it unscathed.

Realizing sunset was a couple hours away, and that he might return, she began packing a small suitcase with the needed necessities.

Then the phone rang.

It sat on the kitchen countertop. She stared at it, frightened by the possibility that he had found her number. It was written on the phone's receiver. Of course he had taken note of it. Of course it was him. Very few people had her number. She let it ring until it stopped.

Heba moved urgently, collecting her things, double-checking that she wasn't leaving anything important behind—passport, toiletries, snacks for Khaldun, and banking information.

The phone rang again.

She toiled with the indecision of whether or not to answer, but on the fourteenth ring, she picked up the receiver…

"Hello?"

"Hello, Heba?"

"Who is this?"

"My name is Sketch."

"You must have the wrong number. Please, do not call me ag—"

"Heba…" interrupted Sketch. "Charles created me."

The line hummed during a brief gap of silence.

"Is he there?"

"No." Sketch looked up from the kitchen table at Perkins who was leaning against the sink. "Charles died."

"Died?"

"Heba, I'm so sorry."

"But I was with him just last week." Her voice softened from its guarded tone. "What happened?"

"It was a car accident."

There was another gap of silence.

"How do I know I can trust you?" she asked, sniffling. "How do you know my name and number? Did Charles tell you?"

"Heba, I'm in the US. I was created from the magic ink. I have his sketch book with your contact information."

"I need more. I need proof you are who you say you are. I am in a very difficult situation right now, and I don't know who to trust. I don't have much time to talk. Tell me something about me that only Charles would know."

Sketch closed his eyes, replaying his and Charles' conversations; searching for the common threads that connected him and Heba. His lips pursed, he stared at the floor. Searching…searching…then snapped his fingers. "Shakespeare's *All the World's A Stage.* You told Charles to always stay within the lines."

The faint buzz of white noise filled another gap in their conversation.

"Heba…are you there?"

"I am here." Her voice was tearfully sad, trapped in a sobbing outburst. "Oh, Sketch…what happened?"

"It was a tragic accident. And I feel responsible."

"For his death?"

"Yes."

"Why? Were you driving?"

"No. I was sitting next to him."

A quick succession of memories suddenly replayed before Sketch's eyes. The hellish violence of the collision. The Metzes without a prayer. And the irreversible piercing by the rod of steel.

"Heba…I am…I *was*…the superhero you had encouraged Charles to create. I had it all. I was exceptionally strong and fast, and I could fly. I saved his plane from crashing. I saved Charles. I saved everyone on board. It had a broken wing—"

"Sketch! You were the Superman the little boy in the newspaper article talked about!"

"You heard?"

"Of course! The story of the miracle landing was heard around the world!"

Sketch rose from the table and grabbed the phone's cradle as he aimlessly paced in the kitchen. "Heba, I have a passport. May I come visit you?"

"Of course you may. But do not come to Cairo. It is very dangerous here. I am leaving soon. There is a mad man searching for my magic ink. He is pure evil. I have no time to tell you the details. Listen closely…I am going to Grenoble, France. There is a hotel there called Le Grand Hotel. I will be there in three days. I will wait for you."

"It might take me a week, but I'll get there."

"Thank you for calling, Sketch. And remember, keep your original drawing safe. After all, your life depends on it. I will see you in France. Goodbye."

After they hung up, Perkins said to Sketch, "So, you're going to Egypt?"

"No. France. And if there were ever one time, I wish I had my superpowers."

"Why France?"

"Because it sounds like there's a mad man on the loose."

Chapter 11

LA CONQUÊTE

"Henry Tisdale...Henry Tisdale...Henry Tisdale..." Sketch repeatedly rehearsed his alias aloud, cementing it into his memory so there would be no hesitations raising suspicions if authorities ever asked for his name to verify his passport. And how ironic, he thought, that he was a supernatural being created as a superhero to fight evil, and he possessed a forged identity. He had funded criminal activity, but without the passport he could not travel, so there was no option. It wasn't like the government had a clause declaring "immortals as exceptions to the rule" requiring passports.

Two days after his phone call with Heba, Sketch landed in Paris. The flight was arranged and paid for by Sergeant Perkins. By his standards the transatlantic flight was exceptionally slow. Despite the advances in modern aviation improving jet engine efficiency and speed, the technology would never come close to the propulsion that Sketch had been able to generate. And how that propulsion was attained would forever be a mystery. After all, the secret lay within the ink. It was something that even Sketch had no complete understanding of, other than flying simply began with an inward thought like a meditative focus or a visualization compressed into a milli-second. Whatever Charles had willed into him, every magical molecule had remained active. If he wanted to fly, the thought alone was all it took. There was no science behind it. Merely magic.

He took a six-hour bus ride from Paris to Grenoble, then taxied to Le Grand Hotel, arriving mid-afternoon. It was a small historic establishment with a big name, completely furnished in classic French style.

"Good afternoon, sir," said a petite, well-dressed older woman at the front desk. "Welcome to Le Grand. Do you have a reservation?"

"No. I'm meeting a friend here. Her name is Heba."

The woman opened a guest registry, dragging her finger down the page with the recent entries. "And what is her last name?"

"I don't know. I don't even know if she has one."

"You're not sure if she has a last name?"

"Well, I suppose she does. I've just never known it. But she has a Middle Eastern accent. She's Egyptian."

"Ah, you must mean Ms. Habib…the woman with the dog."

"Yes! That's Khaldun, and she's Heba."

"Her entry was just 'H. Habib'. May I call her room to tell her you're here?"

"Yes, please."

"Your name?"

"My name is Sketch. She'll know it."

Three minutes later, he stood with his suitcase in hand before Heba's door. He had no idea what she looked like and could only piece together fragments of her personality from their phone call, and what little Charles had shared. He felt anxious, unsure of what to say. Perkins was right, though—when he had hesitated calling her, it wasn't like he was asking her out on a date. Still…

Hi, I'm Sketch! I know, weird name.

Hi, I'm Sketch! You do not look twenty-four hundred years old!

This is insane.

Seconds after he knocked, Heba opened the door as Khaldun stood obediently next to her.

"Hi," said Sketch, "I'm—"

"Sketch! You made it!" She gave him a quick hug, then went back into the room, packing her suitcase that was on the bed. She wore khaki shorts, white tennis shoes, and a light blue blouse. Her dark hair fell to her shoulders. Khaldun remained at the doorway, sniffing Sketch's leg. "We must go now," she said. "We must get to Genevieve before the Finger Gunman does. Something terrible happened. She created a superhero who somehow became the Finger Gunman, and is after the ink so that he can corrupt it. He confronted me in Cairo. He destroyed my apartment. It all happened so suddenly. If, in fact, he is telling the truth—and I believe he is—then he is a very dangerous man."

Sketch took a few steps into her room. "So, where are you going now?"

Heba paused packing. "We need to go to Chamonix to talk to the owners of a chateau where Genevieve told me she would draw her superhero."

"You don't know where Genevieve lives?"

"Unfortunately, no. But we must hurry. I have a friend who will drive us. We can be on our way within twenty minutes."

"Why haven't you already been to the chateau?"

"Because I am afraid."

"Of what?"

"The unknown."

There was a brief silence between them, until Sketch said, "Heba…"

"Yes?"

"I understand your sense of urgency regarding the Finger Gunman, but I'd like to take just a moment to say it's finally nice to meet you."

Heba stopped packing, visibly taking a deep breath. "I am sorry. You are right…it is nice to meet you, too."

"You're really twenty-four hundred years old?"

"Every single day of it," she said, smiling. "And you are a couple weeks old?"

Sketch returned the smile. "Yes, ma'am. Every single day of it."

"Sketch, we have much to talk about, and I am excited you are here, but we must hurry."

"The Finger Gunman is as dangerous as you say?"

"Unfortunately, yes. A venomous snake in the grass."

💧 💧 💧

The drive to the chateau was fairly quiet as they refrained from discussing anything pertaining to the magic ink in the company of their driver. The mountains appeared to grow taller, reaching higher and higher into the early evening sky as they neared Chamonix on the drive from Grenoble. A week earlier Sketch would have been able to punch a cavity into Mont Blanc's snowy peak. But now he could only dream about it.

There was a middle-aged woman tending to a flower garden in front of the chateau when they pulled into the driveway. Their driver and Khaldun stayed in the car as Heba and Sketch got out. The woman stood with a trowel in her hand, tightening her grip as the two strangers approached.

"Please stop," she said.

Doing so, Heba said, "I have come looking for a friend."

"Pierre!" The woman yelled toward the front door. Moments later, her husband of like-age emerged.

"I must ask you to leave," he said.

"We do not mean to bother you," said Heba. "We are only trying to find—."

"We know who you are," said the man. "The investigator was here yesterday."

"Investigator?" asked Heba.

"Yes. He asked if a Middle Eastern woman had come by."

Heba looked at Sketch and whispered, "It must have been him."

"What is it you want from us?" the woman asked, moving next to her husband who had stepped further outside.

"Want? Madam—"

"You're Heba, aren't you?"

"Yes, but I am only trying to find Genevieve."

The woman sighed heavily, her eyes at once saddening before dropping the trowel. Burying her head in her hands, she began crying, then turned and went inside.

"Sir," said Heba, "we have come only in search of Genevieve."

The husband walked forward, putting his hand up. "Genevieve is dead. We found her on the back deck. She had been decomposing for two weeks. She was brutally murdered."

Heba had suspected the news, but hearing it stung more than she had anticipated. She wanted to ask permission to enter the house and console the wife, to let her know she wasn't alone. She wanted the relationship of both of them—mortal and immortal—sharing their loss. But Heba knew she was too much of a stranger for that to happen. Dispirited, she sniffled and said, "Sir, we will leave you now. But please understand that the man who visited you yesterday…you cannot ever trust him. I do not know if he killed Genevieve, but I would not rule him out. Did he give you his phone number or show you any identification?"

"No, he didn't."

"I suspect you will be safe, for it is me he is after."

"What did you do?"

"I refused his demand."

"For what?"

"An invaluable commodity."

After Sketch and Heba left the chateau, they took a bus to the Bay of Biscay coastal city of La Rochelle, France, where they boarded the ship *La Conquête* to the US.

The bus ride was an uneasy one for Heba, as she feared the Finger Gunman might board along the way. He would go for her suitcase, knowing she wouldn't travel without the magic ink. It would be a dog fight fending him off. There were no police on the bus, so he would claw and chew as he pushed his offensive, even with Khaldun involved. If only Sketch had his powers, she thought. She would feel more at ease.

Oh, Charles, why did you have to die?

Eventually, the stress of worrying about the Finger Gunman,

coupled with the news of Genevieve's murder, exhausted Heba. Leaning against Sketch's shoulder, she slept hard the last two hours with Khaldun curled beneath her legs.

Heba's seafaring contacts throughout the centuries were numerous to say the least, as traveling on ocean vessels was not an uncommon practice for her. Five years prior, while docked in the port in Cairo, the captain of a French cargo ship spent time in the Kahn el-Khalili market, where he was drawn to Heba's baskets.

"These are yours?" he asked

"Yes, sir. All handcrafted."

"They are wonderful! I would like to buy some to decorate my cabin."

"A ship cabin?"

"Yes, madam."

"You are the captain?"

"Yes," he smiled. "You are intuitive. How did you know?"

"Your posture is tall and confident. You are well-groomed, and your clothes are pressed. Above all, though, your voice is clear and assuring. In an emergency, you have been trained to lead."

"I'm impressed, truly impressed. But tell me…am I the captain of a cruise or cargo ship?"

"Oh, that is easy. Cargo."

"How did you know?"

"Cargo ships are not glamorous. Of course, your cabin needs decor!"

"You are a treat! It is a pleasure to meet you." He extended his hand which she shook. "My name is Jacques Arquette."

"A pleasure to meet you, Captain Arquette. My name is Heba."

"Well, Heba, if you ever want to sail on a cargo ship, you're more than welcome to come aboard."

"Are you serious?"

"Very much. We allow guest travelers all the time. It's not a cruise ship, but the rooms are clean. I'll even add some of your baskets to spruce it up."

And that was how Heba found herself having guest access to traveling on cargo ships. She was likable and trustworthy, and not young and vulnerable to the male labor crew who made up the majority of the ship's labor force. There were some females who either worked in the ship's medical clinic or the galley where Heba often volunteered cutting up vegetables or helping prepare fresh baked desserts.

Heba accepted Captain Arquette's invitation to sail to Miami, where she then spent time in the States. The spontaneous decision was a luxury she possessed—one of the many perks of being eternal. On her return to Cairo, she boarded a cargo ship through the captain's referral. She was a standby passenger always in good standing.

It was early evening in La Rochelle when Sketch, Heba and Khaldun boarded *La Conquête,* a container ship that Heba had not sailed before, but had met the ship's captain—Captain Marceau—in the past through an introduction by Arquette. Once Marceau was informed of Heba's arrival, he made it a priority to accommodate her needs. And being a genuine dog lover, Marceau gave them immediate clearance to board the ship.

One night, Sketch and Heba stood on the deck at the bow, while behind them were stacks of intermodal steel containers destined for truck and railway transport that creaked and moaned as the ship rose and fell with the movement of the sea. At the stern, the ship's churning effervescent wake agitated noisily, then trailed off like a chalk line for two miles before disappearing. In the distance, far beyond the offing, where the dark sky touched the ocean, were France and Egypt—two places they agreed they might never return to.

"It's nice out here," said Sketch.

"Yes, it is," said Heba. "But sometimes the sea grows violent with swells that rock the ship like a toy."

"I can't imagine what it must have been like sailing on the Mayflower. Did you sail back then?"

"Never. Weeks at sea would have been too much for me."

Sketch looked up at the Milky Way spanning across the sky. "How long do you think the Finger Gunman will keep looking for you?"

"Since he is eternal…as long as it takes him. He will not give up."

"I suppose you're right."

"Oh, I know I am. He was created to corrupt the ink. That is the sole purpose of his existence. If he were to ever possess the ink, it is unimaginable what he might do."

"Such as?"

"Create a fleet of supervillains whose evil would make Hitler's atrocities look like child's play."

"Should we destroy the ink?"

Heba wiped away wisps of her hair blowing across her face. "I have considered it. But I cling to two things that prevent me from doing so. First, I fear he still might find some way to spread his evil without the ink. If that were to happen, it would take a superhero to defeat him. And second, I wonder if there is a way for you to regain your powers. And if so, we need the ink."

"But Charles is dead."

"True. But Charles stirred my curiosity once when he asked if he could tell his girlfriend about the ink. I told him to never do that. The ink can detect being boastful. Besides, only I am allowed to find the artists. If he were to do so, it could jeopardize his privilege. When he questioned me about bloodlines, I told him it is possible a child of his could be chosen one day to draw a superhero, but it is never a given. It must be earned.

"My curiosity, though, about bloodlines went a step further as I began to wonder if a child of his, with imaginative energy, could continue the job by precisely tracing an original drawing of a superhero if the artist-creator were to pass. And here we are in that situation, except there is no child."

Sketch turned his back against the railing. "So, why wait on me? Why not go find a new artist to create a new superhero?"

"I know, it sounds easy. And it should be. But whatever happened when Genevieve drew her superhero—however maddening things went wrong—I worry it might happen again."

"But nothing happened to me, and I was created after the Genevieve incident."

"That is true, but I wonder if you just got lucky. At this point, I do not want to take the risk."

"Are you saying wait until Charles' baby becomes an adult? Hoping the child can draw, and is born with good intent."

Heba turned her back to the railing as well, her hair dancing forward around her cheeks. "Yes, we must wait. I do not know how to explain it, but I believe there is power in Charles' bloodlines that evil cannot penetrate."

"But that would be twenty years, at least."

"A blink of an eye for us immortals."

"And if that child can't draw?"

"Then we will wait for that child to grow up and have a child who might carry the artistic trait."

"And what about the Finger Gunman?"

"We can only hope that, without the ink, he is nothing."

Chapter 12

FOR FORTY YEARS...

Under a full moon, a water buffalo moved cautiously through the brush, while a calf that had wandered from the herd stayed close by her side. A hundred yards away, positioned atop a fifteen-foot viewing platform located inside a fenced bungalow compound, Heba and Sketch lay on their stomachs, watching through their binoculars.

The buffalo froze in mid-stride, forever watching for signs of a lion—a branch snapping, movement through the tall grass, a deep humming growl, or its odor wafting downwind. Her mud-caked snout dripped wet with dangling strings of mucus. Both ears were torn lengthways, and divots of fur were missing from her back where lions had sunk their claws and teeth. Her horns were scarred from countless battles—all of which she had never lost. She lifted her head, snorting once, her eyes shifting quickly to one side. The number of lions she had gouged was large, and her kick had fractured the skulls of many more. There was no doubt, she must always be on-guard: watching, listening, smelling. There is no other option when you are the hunted. But tonight, there was no lion. So, into the darkness she retreated, proceeding cautiously deeper into the brush, guiding the calf safely back to the herd.

"Her name is Alpha," said Heba.

Sketch lowered his binoculars. "She has a name?"

"Of course."

"Did you name her?"

"No. A man named Tafari did. He was a friend of mine, but he died."

"I'm confused. I know you haven't been here in at least ten years since we left France on the cargo ship. But a water buffalo comes out of the brush, and you know her name?"

Heba grinned. "Tafari drew her. He said her name was influenced by Alpha Centauri—the closest star system to our sun."

"Wait.... Tafari drew her? That buffalo is of the magic ink?"

"Yes," she said, laughing softly as she turned over on her back. "I told you Africa was full of surprises!"

"But how do you know it's her? Could you be mistaken?"

"Her ears are split down the middle. Tafari intentionally drew her like that so she could be identified."

"Are there other buffalo, too? Or what about elephants or giraffes? Are some of those of the ink as well?"

"Actually, yes. There were a handful of African artists I chose who drew animals. Two from Tanzania, one from Uganda, and Tafari, from Zimbabwe."

Sketch turned on his side, facing her with his arm bent and head propped up by his hand. "You kept this a secret from me for ten years?"

"I have existed for twenty-four-hundred years. I do not have time to tell you everything. Besides, surprises are fun!"

"Okay, you make a good point," he said, playfully poking her shoulder. "So, did you know Alpha was going to show up tonight?"

"I knew the chances were favorable. This is her home. She is over three-hundred years old."

"What about Alpha Century?"

"Centauri...Alpha Centauri. It is made up of three stars." Heba had Sketch lay on his back, then pointed up at the sky, explaining Centauri's location. "Tafari believed the stars represented strength, wisdom, and courage. So, he willed those qualities into her drawing."

"The water buffalo is a super animal?"

"No. Animals of the ink cannot have superpowers. Willing those attributes only boosted Alpha's innate sense of survival."

"Do you know where the drawing is?"

"I do not."

"Is it possible the buffalo could become corrupted, and turn evil?"

Heba's upbeat mood dropped a notch. "There was a time I would say no. But after what happened to Genevieve, I no longer know what to believe. That is partly why I came here…to see if Alpha is different than before."

"Is she?"

"Luckily, no. If she were, I believe she would have killed the calf."

Heba shifted her position, resting her head on Sketch's chest and listening to his heartbeat that she listened to each night before falling asleep. "Sketch…"

"Yes?"

She tapped him three times on the chest, emphasizing her words at each tap as she said, "Do…not…die."

With a quirky smile, he gently ran his fingers through her hair. "Why, do you have more surprises in store for me?"

Heba looked up, her eyes forlorn, then pulled herself tight against his chest. "I mean it, do not die…ever."

Sketch returned the hug. "Don't worry. I have no plans to. But why are you saying this?"

"Because I could not bear eternity without you."

"I'll do my best."

"I need more than your best. Promise me you will not die."

He loosened his hold and gently pushed her back. "Hey," he said, "look at me."

Heba revealed her face, rolling her tearful eyes up at him.

"I can't promise, but I'll do my best. As long as you do the same."

She nodded with a crescent smile, then lowered her head back to his chest.

Of the few things that differentiated an immortal being from a mortal one, such as living eternally or being immune to disease, an immortal's heartbeat was one of them. Normal human hearts beat at a regular rhythm, but immortals' hearts beat differently:

…thuh-thump…thump…thuh-thump…thump…thuh-thump…

What was most interesting was not only did Sketch and Heba's hearts beat in perfect synchronization with each other, but so did all animals and humans created from the ink, regardless of any physical exertion that would normally raise the heart rate.

"Sketch… do you think the Finger Gunman has our same heartbeat?"

"I suppose it's possible, since he is immortal. But even if he does, what does it matter?"

Heba shrugged her shoulders. "I just do not want him like us."

"I can assure you," he said, draping his arm over her shoulders, "he will never be like us."

Lying there next to Sketch, watching a water buffalo and listening to the matching heartbeat within his chest, it was the assurance that she needed to soothe her concern. "Henry Sketch Tisdale," she said, "I love you."

If there was one thing that Sketch was certain of, it was the fact that he didn't want to grow accustomed to being alone. He didn't want to occupy himself with the simple pleasures of reading, cooking, and traveling, with no true companionship. He noticed a change in himself had occurred—a curiosity that had been triggered by watching people, especially couples. It was a curiosity of a void in his life, of years never having been lived. He was created as a man in his early 30s, but life before those years had never existed.

What is it like to be young? he thought. What is it like to grow—to fully develop from a single cell and not a drawing? What is it like to father children? What is it like to have blood?

He wasn't sure if his immortality was a blessing or a curse, or if it even mattered. What was the use of living forever if you had no true beginning? Sketch's life in this world began with the final stroke of a pen, but there was no beginning to truly identify him as human. No moment of biological conception. No womb, no breastfeeding, no learning to walk and talk. No parents or siblings. No birthday parties, and no dying days until your final breath. These voids in his life troubled him as much as anything.

But there was one other thing that was missing in his life. It was the one thing that shared no bond between his supernatural existence and those who were human. He wondered if it would ever unveil itself to him. He knew it was possible, but not with a human. It would have to be with his own kind. It was love.

Their relationship began on *La Conquête* when they sailed to the States from France. They had elected to work as assistants on the ship. Heba spent much of her time in the galley, while Sketch helped with odd jobs, from repairing faulty washer and dryer machines to regular maintenance checkups in the engine room. By the time evening rolled around, they were in their separate rooms, fast asleep. High seas often kept them below deck during their spare time, but when weather and sea conditions permitted, Heba and Sketch took advantage of calm sunny days and often spent their work breaks standing at the railing of the ship's bow. Three weeks into the voyage, Heba found herself looking out at the ocean, lost in its overwhelming enormity. "It is as if it has no end. As if it is eternal."

"Then it's something you can relate to," said Sketch.

"You as well."

"But I don't feel eternal. I've only been alive for a few weeks. You, on the other hand, have been alive for centuries."

"The feeling will come before you know it. When you look back, the years will seem to have passed like weeks."

"Perhaps, but…hey, look!…dolphins!"

Sketch pointed to six dolphins that were swimming parallel to the side of the ship, effortlessly propelling themselves in and out of the water like acrobats of the sea.

"They are beautiful," said Heba. "I have never seen them before."

"You're kidding, right?"

"No, this is my first time."

"All the years that you've sailed, and this is your first time?"

"Hard to believe, I know."

For several minutes the dolphins kept pace with the ship, then angled away, continuing to dive until they no longer surfaced, and then were gone.

Sketch had been looking at Heba as she watched the dolphins. It was something he found himself doing more often whenever their paths crossed. Not just catching glimpses, but engaging in playful small talk as well. It was fair to say they had a mutual admiration for each other. When she served food to the line of workers in the cafeteria, she took her time loading his plate. "I'm in no rush," he would say.

"I am happy I got to see the dolphins," said Heba. "Maybe tomorrow we will see whales."

"Have you seen whales?"

Heba looked down over the railing, watching the bow cut through the water, creating its wake. "Yes, but they were harpooned."

"Where?"

"Off the coast of Japan. I was not prepared. I thought it was a sightseeing boat. The whales cried in pain. Their blood leaked into the sea, surrounding them like oil. It was murder. They were creatures too magnificent to be slaughtered. I closed my eyes and covered my ears, but I could still hear the men joyfully singing in Japanese as the carcasses were hoisted up onto the boat, then butchered with cutting spades."

"I'm sorry you had to see that."

"Me too. You would think that, being immortal, the mind might have the ability to be selective about what you do not want to remember. But that is not the case. So, the whales are quite vivid."

Injecting a tone of levity, Sketch said, "So, how about we change the subject?"

Heba nodded, approvingly. "I think that is a great idea. You go first. Ask me anything."

His index finger and thumb massaging his chin, Sketch contemplated. "May I ask you a personal question?"

"Oh, no," said Heba, playfully horrified. "Not one of *those* questions! Like, are you dating anyone? Certainly, you have dated."

Sketch chuckled. "But you are a couple thousand years old! Certainly you have dated."

"I am not sure if 'dating' is the right word, but, yes, I have been in some relationships."

"Recently?"

"Why do you ask?"

"I'm just curious, that's all."

"It was forty years ago."

"Was he mortal?"

"My, you are curious." She turned her back to the railing. "Every man I have been with has been mortal."

"Were any of them artists you had entrusted with the ink?"

"Never. That is forbidden. That would ruin an artist's opportunity to create." Heba faced Sketch. "Now, it is my turn," she said. "Being a man of merely a few weeks old, I am assuming you have never been with a woman before."

"You're correct."

"You watch me, do you not?"

"I—"

"Your eyes…they follow me."

Sketch fumbled his words. "Well…yeah…I mean…"

Heba stepped toward Sketch, stopping inches away from contact. "Sketch," she said softly, "do you mind an older woman?"

He looked into her eyes. "No."

Coquettishly, she said, "And a young man intrigues me. Especially an immortal one."

All it took was one kiss.

Sketch had never experienced intimacy, except with the one who was now embracing him—the one who, also, was wondering if they were on the cusp of what would become an unbridled chemistry, an eternal intimacy. Because the more they kissed, the more the world disappeared.

For forty years their love held firm, strolling hand-in-hand as they traveled the world, and keeping in touch with the two people who mattered most: Sergeant Perkins and Tennie.

Introducing Heba to Sergeant Perkins was the first order of business once they arrived in the States. She explained the origins of the ink to him, and the early years of her existence, then walked him through the centuries of changing civilization and the highlights of what she had experienced.

Unsure of whether or not to trust exposing the ink to a new artist, they secured it in Perkins' safety deposit box in a bank vault in Lehman. It was also where Sketch's original drawing was kept.

"I trust him completely," Sketch assured Heba. "He read me like a book, suspecting I could fly, and that I brought down the plane to safety. And when he saw how I walked away from the car accident without a scratch, he knew I was different. His curiosity about me got me curious about him. With no one to trust and nowhere else to go, I needed someone with his abilities and talents. Someone who had contacts for getting me a passport and a birth certificate. Someone who had a house with no other occupants. Someone who had a good reputation and would never be suspected of sheltering or funding a superhero." Sketch then added, smiling, "Not that a superhero has ever existed for people to be suspicious of."

Contrarily, Tennie was treated differently. Not a word was spoken to her about the ink. If she were to eventually pass on knowledge of the ink to her child, that would consequently dilute the ink's magical potency, or end its magical powers altogether.

Only one other person needed to know about the ink: Anne, Tennie's newborn.

Of course, Anne would have to meet the same criteria that her father, Charles, did in order to be a recipient, such as: be a highly skilled artist, live life with good intent, and have no selfish motives with the ink. The latter could only be predicted by judging current and previous actions.

As Anne grew up, though, her opportunity for selection as a candidate for the ink grew slimmer. By the time she was eighteen, she had proven herself to be selfless and had received high acclaim at juried art shows throughout the Midwest. But things took a turn at the height of her artistic maturation, when she was two years into college.

She lost interest in art.

"But, honey," said Tennie, "you've come this far. Why quit?"

"Mom, I know this is disappointing to you, but I just don't think college is for me."

"But, you're so talented. I thought your father was a great artist."

"Mom…"

"I mean, he could draw anything, but you…"

"Mom…please…"

"Honey, what is it?"

Anne drew in a deep breath. "I guess I've become my mom." Tears began to fall. "Mom…I'm sorry…I'm pregnant."

Tennie immediately stepped forward, cupping Anne's head against her shoulder. "Oh, Anne," she cried with her, "let us make these happy tears. I was nineteen when I found out. I had to tell my mom, and she, too, understood." Tennie tilted Anne's head back. "It's going to be alright. Lewis is a wonderful young man."

"You're really not upset?"

"No. I'm really not."

"That's a relief, mom. We've known for a couple of weeks. I was just too nervous to tell you."

"Well, I'm glad you did. Are you excited?"

"Actually, yes. It was a shock in the beginning, but Lewis and I were like, well, we've always wanted a family. So, here we go!"

"You know, you can always postpone college."

"I know, but I just want to focus on raising a family."

"You'll be a wonderful mother. So, from this moment on, no worries. Ok?"

"Ok," Anne sniffled, smiling. "Thanks, mom."

Tennie pushed Anne back, holding her at arm's length. "This is just curious, silly me, but have you thought of any names?"

"Funny you should ask. We were thinking about that yesterday. If it's a girl, Cheryl. If it's a boy, Sid."

"And who knows," said Tennie, "either one might be an artist… continuing on where you left off."

"Fingers crossed, mom."

As the years passed, it became difficult for Sketch to make in-person appearances due to his immortal physical aging limit of fifty-years. And since he had only known Charles for twenty-four hours, he couldn't hold Tennie's attention with the same stories, so he stayed in touch through Christmas holiday correspondences, using a post office box address that Sergeant Perkins secured for him. Tennie composed an annual Christmas newsletter that kept friends informed of happenings in Anne's life. As Anne grew into motherhood, she continued the same Christmas tradition, and kept Sketch on her newsletter mailing list.

Happy Holidays!! 1988

"...Our two dogs now have a brother!! Sid has arrived!"

Happy Holidays!! 1990

"...Sid turned 2. He can't let go of crayons! All he does is draw!!"

Happy Holidays!! 1996

"...Sid turned 8 this year, and was selected by his elementary school to draw the school mascot...the falcon! He's got the gift!"

Happy Holidays!! 2006

"...My, how fast he's grown. It's bittersweet news, but next year Sid will be leaving the house and attending Waterstone College in Waterstone, Texas..."

Forty years of Christmas letters. Forty years of just enough pertinent information to let Sketch and Heba know the trajectory of Anne and Sid's artistic developments. Anne fizzled out, though, giving way to motherhood, and Sid's gained promising momentum each year.

Keeping abreast of Sid's whereabouts was a priority as it might lead to a geographical move of their own. Such was the case when Sid enrolled into Waterstone College. Up until that time, their home base had always been Sergeant Perkins' house. He had never remarried or settled into a lasting relationship. Instead, he preferred being single. Sketch and Heba were all he needed. The fact that his best friends were immortal and eternal forever intrigued him, and he never uttered a word about it to anyone.

Eventually, though, when Perkins retired from the police force, he sold his house and moved onto more reclusive property—twenty wooded acres a few miles outside of Lehman that included a guest cottage. The ideal come-and-go location for the ageless Sketch and Heba.

But once Sid settled into Waterstone College, and Heba and Sketch learned he was working at the Sierra Oaks Retirement Home, it was the perfect opportunity for them, and one other person, to move as well.

"Sergeant," said Sketch, "you're eighty-four years old, clear as a bell, but slowing down. Heba and I would love for you to come with us to Texas. It looks like Sid is nearing the age and maturity where we can approach him about the ink, and the possibility of restoring my superpowers."

There was no quibbling, resistance, or great divide. Instead…

"Say no more," said Perkins. "I'm on board!"

Two months later, they made the move to Texas.

As much as they traveled, no matter where they went, Heba could not escape the ominous thought of the Finger Gunman. He lingered in her head like a bad regret—always there until dealt with. Only three people knew of his potential—Sketch, Perkins, and herself. With the ink, he had the potential to mastermind a global threat unlike any other in history. Heba had no idea how such a threat might be achieved, but she did know the potential was real. "Mortal weaponry would have no chance against him," she once told Perkins when they first met. "His army of evil immortals would hold the upper hand."

"And if he doesn't get the ink?" asked Perkins. "What then?"

"I am afraid he is going to get creative. If he cannot find me, then he is going to make sure I know he is out there. Sketch must regain his superpowers. He is our only hope. And I believe the only way that can happen, started with Tennie, because she carried Charles' bloodline that created Sketch."

As Heba spoke—and though she would never hear a word of it, because it was not destructive enough to make the news—the first explosion of many to come cratered a road leading to a chateau in Grenoble, France.

Chapter 13

THE PLAN

The Finger Gunman had returned to Heba's apartment early the next morning after fleeing the market when she yelled for the police. The shops were closed and the streets and alleyways empty except for several stray cats foraging for scraps of food. Her apartment was a shambles that normally would please him to no end, but not this time—he had failed to find the ink. Scanning the apartment, he noticed something different about the coffee table. The "Kathmandu" sign was standing upright, perpendicular to the table, having acted as the inlayed top of the hidden compartment. The magic ink, he now realized, had been there all along. He had moved the table when he ransacked her apartment. How had he overlooked it? It should've been obvious! There was a bronze sculpture Arabian oryx lying at his feet. Its long, slender horns were broken after having been thrown to the floor. He picked it up, then moved close to the table. With two hands he raised it above his head and, without any concern for the tumultuous crash, he violently bashed the sculpture into the ink compartment. A vehement rage mounted within him. He needed to keep quiet. He needed to restrain the boiling within his skull. But that was impossible, so he hammered the onyx six more times until the table was nearly destroyed.

He told Amanda he had a family emergency he needed to deal with, and left almost as suddenly as the news he'd just announced.

He should've snapped Khaldun's neck when he jumped onto the table in the market. He should've cracked its spine over his knee. And if that wasn't enough, he should've put Heba in a chokehold, making her beg for her last breath. That would've made a statement. But, instead, he ran away empty-handed with not a drop of ink, and no trail of Heba to follow. Regardless of his efforts to present himself with a friendly demeanor, he had left a scar on it in the eyes of the surrounding shop owners who had witnessed Heba's fright. It would be useless to question any of them about her whereabouts. There was only one place he knew she might go to…the chateau. Certainly, she was concerned enough to go find Genevieve.

Of course it was a failed trip, having missed Heba by a day. Nor would it have mattered if it had been an hour, he had no idea where she was. He was taking shots in the dark, randomly choosing towns to visit in hopes that he might find her. But the odds were astronomically against him, regardless of the fact that he was eternal.

The way he understood it, after the rogue falcon had infused him with the silver ink, he was entirely on his own to concoct his evil rampage. It was up to him to devise whatever plan he wished to press forward with. Whether or not Apep's presence could help foster his plan was unknown to him. He had no idea how to summon the evil deity, or if Apep might arrive on his own as he had, as the asp viper. And it could be that was Apep's final appearance, and he was now forever entombed in the underground. Thus, the Finger Gunman felt it best to assume that Apep was out of the picture.

But the question was…now what? How would he find Heba? Without her, there would be no ink for him to claim. She could be anywhere on the planet. She could even be watching him—something that he occasionally considered a possibility whenever he felt discouraged. And it was then that his worries tumbled even further, as he wondered how many artists she had commissioned to create superheroes in the past. How many more Zenators were out there? She would have threatened him with one or had one called to action, right? Certainly, that would've occurred.

But she hadn't. She had fled. Still, she could be using her time to find artists to protect her.

For nearly twenty years since his only encounter with Heba, he had worked tirelessly trying to find her, using his connections to comb through airline, train, bus, and cruise ship passenger lists. The problem with this strategy was two-fold. First, it took years to formulate criminal relationships that could perform such requests, which were especially difficult to plan in countries where he didn't speak the native language. Second, obtaining the passenger lists was seemingly futile, accessing only 30% of all available lists. Needless to say, Heba's name never surfaced. Or maybe she was on a list, but a forged identity prevented her from being discovered. Though, in the end, he never came across her name, he had no choice but to give the 30% a look over.

After a year off from being burned out from too much effort and no reward, a light went on. Somewhat dim, but, still, a light.

The Finger Gunman needed a plan. Something that would fly under Heba's radar of suspicion. If he couldn't find the ink, then he would have to find an artist or artists using the ink, if one even existed. It was a long shot, but, one August night in 1990, after years of abandoning dead-end ideas, the plan came to him.

First, he established more relationships within certain criminal networks, but this time narrowing his focus of illegal activity to explosives specialists. He orchestrated detonating devices at specific locations in hopes that they might make international news—in hopes that Heba might catch wind of them, wherever she might be. Not wanting to draw too much attention to his targeted locations, fatalities were to be avoided. The last thing he needed was to be the subject of a global manhunt. The explosions occurred at night when buildings were unoccupied. Structural damage was all that was needed.

Ammonium nitrate, urea nitrate, Tannerite, black powder, picric acid, and TNT were the main explosives that did the dirty work. When they exploded, he felt they left behind fragrances. Or, as he coined it, "Perfumes of destruction."

Bali, Montreal, London, Paris, São Palo, Mexico City, and Los Angeles all had targets: ink manufacturers.

If she were in France in 1995, she might have heard the news of the first explosion that cratered the road leading to the chateau. If she were elsewhere then so be it, as it was an inaugural explosion that made the Finger Gunman happy, giddy with laughter.

Two years later, two simultaneous explosions occurred in Cairo. One, an ink manufacturer, the other, outside the Museum of Egypt. Subsequent explosions took thorough planning and travel coordination, especially with the advent of 9/11. But having the right contacts made the bombings doable over a span of six years.

The day after the Cairo explosions, halfway around the world, Heba was pouring herself a cup of hot tea in Perkins' kitchen, when Sketch showed her the newspaper article.

"It is him," she said. "I know it." She looked at the photo accompanying the article. The museum explosion blew up two cars in the parking lot. "This is the third ink manufacturer to get hit. And now the museum, too. They are suspecting Islamic terrorists, but they are wrong. It is obvious it is him, but what is he accomplishing? I do not understand what he is up to."

"Could it be a distraction?" asked Sketch.

"It is either a distraction or a message. I am not sure which. But he is up to something. I think he is making a move."

"What kind of move?"

Heba reached out and squeezed Sketch's hand. "A big one."

After the Cairo explosions, the Finger Gunman's plan took nearly three years to complete. Finalizing its details was laborious. And Sketch was right—the explosions were a distraction, and nothing more. Whether or not they figured that out was irrelevant. The explosions were just little party favors. There was only one thing that truly mattered…

His plan to create a superhero drawing contest called The Lure, and sponsored by his very own VIP Comics.

PART VII

Chapter 1
POPS

The day after Sid had traced Sketch's original drawing in the Sierra Oaks parking lot and, in doing so, had restored his superpowers, he and Sketch paid their $15 guest fee to Heavy Metal, the local weightlifting gym, for some strength testing. The gym was abnormally quiet as students were just beginning to trickle back into town, returning from Spring Break.

Sketch wore his superhero outfit concealed beneath a pair of baggy gray sweat pants and top. With a matching grey headband and black Converse basketball shoes, he looked like an ordinary fifty-year-old bearded man, with one exception—a hidden strength advantage.

"Mr. Tisdale…"

"Please, Sid, call me Sketch."

"Okay…Sketch, do you really need to be here?"

"What do you mean?"

"I mean you're a superhero. You can fly."

Sketch led Sid over to a bench press. "I'm rusty. I could tell yesterday when I flew to the Arch."

"You call flying to the Arch, rusty?"

"I'm sure it looked impressive, but the innate skills and muscles I use for flying felt forced and unnatural. I could feel myself wobbling. So, I figured why not hit the gym and see how my strength is doing."

Sketch motioned to the bench press. "You first. How much weight to start?"

"One-thirty-five," said Sid, as they each loaded a 45 lb. plate onto the 45 lb. barbell.

After he finished a set of ten reps, Sketch took his turn, completing the same warmup.

"How'd it feel?" asked Sid.

"Honestly, like there was weight."

"It didn't feel easy?"

"Not really. But I'm sure that'll change. It's a matter of finding a zone. It comes from a motivational spark, either internal or external."

"Sounds pretty human to me."

"Trust me, the spark is of an inconceivable magnitude."

Sid increased the weight to 145 lbs., and did eight reps. Sketch did the same.

Next to them was another bench press where three male college students, back from the beach, took turns lifting 225 lbs. Heavily muscle-bound, their tans popped against brightly colored tank tops. The strongest of the three, Derek, had razor wire tattoos around both biceps, and another tattoo covering the side of his right shoulder that read: "BIG RULES". The loaded bar clamored against the rack as they finished each set with a resounding victory grunt. "Slap on another fifty," said Derek. "Today I'm going for four-hundred!"

After a set each of 155 lbs., Sid asked Sketch if he was in the zone yet, but before he could answer…

"Hey, pops," said Derek, "don't load that bar too heavy. Last thing you need is an injury."

Pops??

Sketch smiled at Sid, saying quietly, "You know how I just told you finding the zone can come from an external motivation? Well…"

"Seriously, pops…you ain't young anymore."

"Thanks for the advice," said Sketch, reaching out to shake his hand. "And you are…?"

"Derek."

"Nice to meet you, Derek."

"Did you lift weights back in the day?"

"Not really. I just pushed around tractors."

Derek laughed, looking to his friends. "Whatever that means."

Sketch leaned towards Sid, then said softly, "Let's put on four-hundred."

"Are you serious?"

"Yes. I've found the zone."

"If you say so."

Derek and his friends continued to take their turns as Sid and Sketch loaded the bar with 400 lbs. "Are you sure about this?" asked Sid.

Sketch nodded as he laid on the bench, then adjusted his grip around the bar. "You can move away, Sid. I've got this."

"Are you sure you don't need a spotter?"

"Positive."

Derek had been watching, amused. "That's it, Pops, you go for it."

"Derek…"

"Sir?"

"Give me just a moment here. I've got this little zone inside of me that I need to lock into. It's been forty years. So, bear with me for just a moment."

"Sure. Take all the time you need."

Sid stood by, anticipating what was to come, but unaware of what Sketch was truly capable of.

The zone was similar to Sketch receiving a call, but was triggered by neurotransmitters that immediately radiated tendrils of heat from his spine into his tendons, ligaments, and muscles. At once, there was a superhuman rigidity stiffening the connective chain of muscles summoned to lift the weight—a supernatural degree of tensile strength.

"Go for it," cheered Derek and his two buddies. "It's only four-hun—"

The barbell rose from the rack like a levitation magic trick, then lowered to his chest, calm and controlled. What should have passed as a well-rehearsed and explainable illusion, was nothing of the kind.

It was real. After completing three reps, he gently lowered the bar back to the rack. Derek and his buddies stood speechless, seemingly hypnotized. "Like I said, Derek, I had to find that zone. After all, pops needs all the help he can get."

"What the hell was that?!" said Derek. "How was that even possible?"

"I don't know, Derek. Sometimes I guess you're just born with it. Now, if you'll excuse me, we have to get going. Have a good day, guys!"

When they reached Sid's car in the parking lot, Sketch looked over the hood at Sid. "Hey, can I let you in on a little secret?"

"Sure. What's up?"

"The four-hundred pounds I just lifted…"

"Yeah, that was insane!"

"I did it all with just my right arm."

Sid's eyes widened. "Are you serious?"

"No joke. My left hand was around the bar, but was opened up just enough so it barely touched."

"That's unheard of! I mean, your right hand was off-center and the bar stayed level the entire time."

"I know, it's insane."

"But why didn't you let Derek know?"

"So I could pass on a life lesson to you."

"Which is?"

"Always stay humble."

Taking their seats in the car, Sid started the engine. "Now where?" he asked.

"To a quiet country road."

"And why?"

"I need to run."

"How far?"

"Not how far, but how fast."

"And how fast is fast?"

"Fast enough to catch your car."

Chapter 2
WHO AM I?

County Road 222, which was infrequently traveled, cut through an expanse of pecan tree orchards. The farmhouses sat at least a half-mile apart from each other and each was about a quarter-mile off the road. One homeowner stood on her front porch, watching a blue Ford Mustang drive by at 95 mph, but failed to notice the bearded gentleman running in grey sweats, approaching the car from behind, then slapping its front hood while passing by. Nor did she, or would she, have any idea that the bearded man felt this was reminiscent of a time, four decades prior, when he flew past an owl during his first flight.

A minute later, Sid pulled over to the shoulder as he came upon Sketch standing by the road. "I literally lost sight of you," he said, as Sketch opened the front door to get in. "You nearly vanished. Your acceleration was…"

"Superhuman?"

"Yes," chortled Sid. "Exactly! What's it like running that fast?"

"Like something is doing the work for me, as if I'm a passenger."

Sid looked out at the long rows of pecan trees, their bare limbs just beginning to bud. "This is going to take me some time to adjust to," he said. "You're not human and were never conceived, and yet you're here."

"I know exactly what you're saying. I often wonder just who am I? How is it possible that I have the inhuman qualities of a superhero, yet I live in the real world? I have a heart and a brain, and I laugh and cry, but I'm not human because my veins flow with ink."

"And because I traced the lines of your original drawing,

you can now outrun my car. I mean, this is a Mustang!"

Sketch chuckled, tapping the car's dashboard. "She's still a beauty, Sid."

"Yes, she is, but you hurt her pride."

"I think she'll heal," said Sketch tapping the dashboard again, then continued. "Look, I don't understand the science behind it all, or the magic for that matter. All that I know are the facts. I'm the result of your grandfather Charles' imagination, and my superpowers are now a result of yours. I am supernatural, transcending an origin in fiction to living in a nonfictional world, all the while still possessing what should be fictitious inhuman abilities."

"So, it truly is magic ink. There are no special effects?"

"None. This is no comic book. This is no TV show or big screen Hollywood production. It's a paradoxical life, and should be an impossible existence. But because of the unknown properties of some magical ink, I've had this transformation. I can't explain how I just outran your car, but I know one thing is for certain…I'm as real as you. Just different."

"It's so much to take in. But, you're right. The facts are the facts. So, what's next?"

"I say let's head back to my place," said Sketch. "There's still much more to tell you."

"What about Dwight Kellogg? You said you were going to teach him a lesson. Are you going to beat him up?"

"Beat him up?" laughed Sketch. "That's not quite what I had in mind. He just needs a good talking to, and I have an idea how to do that. You'll see."

Sid made a U-turn, then proceeded on the route taking them back to Sierra Oaks. Once they got to the main road, the pecan orchards faded behind them, replaced by small metal building businesses and lackluster student apartment complexes.

"So, Sketch, if you exist in this world as a superhero, then shouldn't there be a villain?"

Sketch looked out his window as the mundane scenery passed by. In comic books and movies, the villains were typically portrayed as characters who could cause global destruction. They often carried out their evil agendas through masterful and unsuspected plans. And they were often one step ahead of the superhero, who would eventually find a way to defeat the villain. But Sketch was living in a real world, and whether or not the villain was going to be defeated or be victorious was completely unknown. Especially since the whereabouts of the villain were unknown as well.

"Yes," said Sketch, "there is a villain. He calls himself the Finger Gunman."

"Awesome! Cool name!"

"Sid, he's nothing to get excited about. Remember, my existence is real, and so is his."

"Sorry. It's just hard to believe that all of this is really happening."

"The Finger Gunman is as real as my superpowers. While he, too, is immortal, the difference between us is that he wants to corrupt the magic ink and unleash evil acts."

"Like what?"

"We don't know yet."

"Who's we?"

"Heba and I."

"Ms. Habib?"

"Yes."

"Why is she in on all of this?"

"Because she's twenty-four-hundred years old."

Sid silently glanced at Sketch, then put his eyes back on the road.

"Like I said, Sid, there's much more to tell you."

Explaining everything to Sid meant untangling a web of information, but Sketch knew it was necessary since he was now in the know of the supernatural. So many players and layers that needed to be sifted through and explained. For a year and a half Sid had known Heba, but only as a polite, simple woman who lived with Sketch and had spent the majority of her life in Egypt. He knew she was a traveler and made baskets by hand. Beyond that, there was very little else since they rarely crossed paths. And he certainly didn't know her veins flowed with ink. But Sid would soon learn that his role of being Sketch's adjunct creator would now allow him to summon Sketch to threatening or perilous situations by initiating a "call", which had only been used one other time in his existence.

It was time Sketch and Heba divulged all.

Chapter 3

THE GREAT SIERRA OAKS FACE-OFF

The reason Dwight Kellogg won so many shuffle board games at Sierra Oaks was not because he was good at it, but because he was annoying. If he was losing, he'd make an excuse for everything. If he was winning, he'd gloat and boast about every shot that scored. It wasn't unusual to be halfway into the game when opponents became so tired of his complaining behavior, they found it far easier to concede victory to him. "You know what, Dwight…you win," they would say. And then he would pump his cue stick high in the air like a triumphant knight with his sword, while his poor wife—unconditionally loving Lola—sheepishly looked on.

Quiet, until the day Sketch showed up.

"Tisdale!" hollered Dwight, as Sketch and Sid exited the backside of Sierra Oaks. They entered an outdoor courtyard of six shuffleboard courts enclosed within a seven-foot-high stucco perimeter wall. "You up for a game?"

"Sure, Dwight. I'll give it a shot." Sketch then whispered to Sid, "Here I go."

Two couples were using the near court, while Dwight was practicing solo on a court furthest from the building. A mimosa tree offered shade where Lola sat on a bench by the wall.

Sketch selected a cue stick from a rack where they entered, then joined Dwight. Sid made his way to the mimosa tree and stood leaning on one hyperextended leg with his back against the trunk and the other leg bent beneath him.

"Feel free to sit here," Lola said to Sid, scooting down the bench. The dappled shade of the mimosa leaves shifted gray patches about her face. "It's Sid, right?"

"Yes, ma'am. Thank you, but I'm fine."

"My god, Lo'," groaned Dwight. "Let the boy be."

Lola turned her head away, briefly closing her eyes. *Why? Why?*

Eyeing Sketch's attire, Dwight smirked, "Sweats?"

"I was at the gym."

"Well, you aren't now."

"Dwight, please..." muttered Lola.

"Please, what?!" he snapped. She was all too familiar with his snaps. "He's wearing sweats in the summer. He should be questioned."

Lola turned to Sid. He saw in her a woman treading to keep her head above water, her eyes beseeching him for help.

"Haven't seen you much, Henry," said Dwight. "You still working at the comic store?"

"Yeah, I help out with inventory, checking in new shipments when they arrive." Sketch took a concerned glance at Lola. She was ashamedly embarrassed. He took a practice shot, positioning the claw of his cue stick behind a disc and sent it down the lane.

"Like superhero comics?" scoffed Dwight.

"A lot of it, yes."

"I've never understood people who get into that stuff. Especially adults. I say, get a life. You know what I mean?"

"Actually, no, I don't."

"Oh, come on. It's a fantasy world. A waste of time."

"Imagination is a waste of time?"

"When it comes to comic books, yes."

Sketch sent another disc down the court where it stopped next to the previous one; both were in the center of the triangular scoring zone. "I think superheroes are good reminders."

"Of what? That buying a comic book is a stupid purchase? Do you think superheroes can actually influence us when they're not even real?"

"They do influence us. They remind us that evil must be defeated."

"Henry, you're delusional. Superheroes do not exist. Period!"

Sergeant Perkins, who had exited the building, walked towards them, having heard Dwight's last comment. "Dwight, of course superheroes exist."

"Buzz off, Perkins! This doesn't concern you. And why are you even out here?"

Perkins rubbed his hands together in the sunlight. "It's cold inside. I need to thaw out. Why are you so sensitive about the topic of superheroes?"

Sketch smiled discretely at Perkins, then raising his hand said, "How 'bout we drop the superhero subject and play the game?"

"If that's what you want," said Dwight. "Sure, have it your way. But I don't think I like your tone."

"There was no tone. I was merely making a suggestion."

"You know what I meant!" Dwight said pointedly, but there were cracks in its boldness. His intention was always to control the dialogue, but he got flustered and had fallen short. Sketch was standing firm, not backing down. For a moment Dwight said nothing. An intense heat was building behind his eyes as he stared off into nowhere. He was visibly bothered. "We'll start after this split," he said, attempting to regain himself. Dragging a disk onto the playing area with the claw of his cue stick, he readied himself, then deliberately fired hard at his target. It struck sharp, sending Sketch's discs left and right off the court, while his disc stopped on impact. "Are you sure you want to play me?" His tone reeked of self-importance.

"Positive," said Sketch, stepping in front of Dwight to go next. He jabbed his cue stick hard into the court, bending it like a saber. "Now, let me take one last practice shot."

Barring a gunshot, compression molded phenolic resin shuffleboard discs are nearly impossible to fragment. Let alone, obliterate, which Sketch could easily have done. But he held back. He didn't want to raise Dwight's suspicions. Still, he needed to make a statement. Dwight was condescending, arrogant, pretentiously superior, and obnoxious. If you had to put him in one camp or the other—good or evil—he would clearly be in the latter. He did not hurt or maim people, but he sure could be a thorn. He needed to be taken down a notch or two, a taste of his own humiliation. Sketch fired off a disc, blurring it down the court, smarting the eardrums as it hit Dwight's disc. Dwight was left daunted and dumbfounded as his disc was broken in half.

"You split my disc in two. How's that even possible?!"

Perkins was standing to the side of them. "Damn!" he yelled, completely enjoying the show, then stepped forward and high-five'd Sketch.

Dwight rolled his eyes, annoyed.

"I don't know what got into me," said Sketch. "Maybe your disc was defective and I hit it at the right vulnerable spot. I would never do that on purpose. Unless…"

"Unless what?"

"Unless it was an act of my subconscious. Do you think that's possible, Dwight?"

Lola's ears perked up, as she curiously eyed Sketch.

"This is crazy!" said Dwight.

"Is it? I don't think it's crazy at all. I think what just happened is that my subconscious has become very tired of watching The Dwight Kellogg Show. Which, by the way, is getting horrible ratings. It's unfortunate that your performances aren't entertaining. You're a cancer of negativity. No one is impressed. It's time to cancel the show."

In a rare moment of tour de force, Lola popped up to her feet. "Mr. Tisdale, please! I think you've said enough."

"Ain't that the truth!" grumbled Dwight.

"You too, Dwight," said Lola, moving toward her husband.

"Lola," said Sketch, "I'm sorry if I—"

"Offended me?"

"Well, yes, I—"

"You didn't offend me," she said in a calmer tone.

Dwight blurted, "Well, he sure as hell offended me!"

Lola turned to Sketch. "A cancer of negativity?"

"It seemed appropriate."

"You're an ass!" shouted Dwight.

"Dwight!" yelled Lola. "For once, can't you just stop it?!"

"For once...?"

"You know what I mean."

Dwight stared curiously at Lola, uncertain of his place in the conversation. She was being assertive, something out of her character, and it bothered him. "No, please, tell me. What do you mean?"

"I don't want to get into it here."

"Into what?"

"Let's not make a scene, Dwight,"

"Over what?"

Lola could not ignore the veracity of Sketch's assessment of Dwight. It stung and penetrated, but it woke her up. No more refraining. No more fear of breaking the silence. Speak! "A cancer of negativity," she said.

"Oh, and now you're quoting him?"

"Dwight," said Lola, as she headed toward the building. "I'll meet you in our apartment. We have a lot to discuss."

Caught in a rift between frustration and a scolding, Dwight looked over at Sketch. "Are you happy?!"

"I'm staying out of it, Dwight. But you heard her. You might want to go to your room."

"You're an ass!" repeated Dwight, as he followed his wife leading him on the path of shame.

"Takes one to know one!" yelled Perkins.

"Bite me, Perkins!"

"In your dreams, baby!"

"Sarge," laughed Sketch, "let him be. He's in enough trouble as it is."

Sid's inner cheer rang *What a show! What a show!* as he had admired Sketch's ability to wield and control the Great Sierra Oaks Face-Off, as well as inspire Lola. The past few days had been filled with adjusting to the reality that Sketch was not human. Flying, unbelievable feats of strength, and chasing cars had proven he was not a hoax. But even with having witnessed those amazing acts, accepting them as real felt strange. It was as if an alien had landed and you didn't know if you should welcome it or fear it. Though Sid knew everything was still so novel and hadn't fully cemented, he had no doubt Sketch was as pure as truth.

His college art class assignment had taken a backseat to all of his curiosities regarding Sketch's existence, as well as being part of testing his supernatural abilities. He still had not talked with Heba, but was certainly anticipating her arrival.

As he took in the backyard debate between Sketch and Dwight, and as the tables turned in Sketch's favor, one thing became crystal clear: Sketch was Sid's $100,000 man.

He was his answer to what kind of original superhero to submit. A uniqueness not so much attributed to the abilities of the superhero, but about how the superhero came to be. There was no need to tell the truth by literally exposing the magic ink. But, rather, shroud the truth by suggesting the idea. He would "What if..." the idea.

What if there were a magic ink? What if an artist could will it to life? What if that life could be a superhero? And what if there was a contest searching for original superhero ideas, and the art student who submitted one kept his submission a secret to himself, so that if he were to win, the element of surprise would certainly be worthy of a huge celebration?

Lips sealed, Sid stuck to that plan.

Chapter 4
SOMETHING MEDIEVAL

When he first discussed the idea, the Finger Gunman told the engineers involved with the project that it was part of a high-energy acrobatic theatrical performance that would debut in Las Vegas. They said they had never heard of such a thing. Of course, the Finger Gunman applauded himself when hearing such a response.

The construction team gathered inside an old metal building located in the dense post oak and piney woods of East Texas, just shy of the Louisiana border, where the trees thrived in the sandy loam soil. The building's roof and sides were coated with aging streaks of rust. Inside, the air was damp and warm and smelled industrial from years of housing drilling equipment and oil pipes that had been altered with cutting torches. Oil stains and industrial solvents painted the cracked concrete floor, and tattered oil-soaked rags piled around an overflowing corner trash can.

There wasn't a single square inch that he wanted cleaned. The building was filthy—perfectly filthy.

"It's called The Trap," he told the group. "It's the climactic conclusion to a production called The Lure."

A welder tilted his head curiously. "The Lure?"

"Yes. A contest in search of the greatest talent who will be showcased in The Trap."

"It's going to be quite a contraption," said the welder.

"Yes, it is. And I can't wait to see its completion. I do have one question, though. Now that you know its design, do you feel confident that it will spin at least 120 revolutions per minute?"

"Meeting your specifications, yes," said one of the engineers.

"And its stabilizing anchors will be securely bolted into the floor?"

"Yes, sir. Solid."

"You're certain?"

"Mr. Fontaine, I've been in charge of anchoring roller coasters for years all over the world. This won't be a problem."

The welder was uncertain, concerned. "Mr. Fontaine…the chair you want built, with the straps and bolted inside the sphere…someone's going to sit in that while the sphere spins?"

"Please, refer to it as The Trap only."

The welder and the other crew members had sensed an oddness about the Finger Gunman. He was adamant about them calling it The Trap and not the sphere or the cage, as if it were the name of a newborn, and referring to it otherwise would be discourteous. They would pass skeptical glances amongst one another whenever he spoke in vague terms about why The Trap was being built. Telling them it was for Las Vegas didn't satiate their curiosities. But, as eccentric as he was, they couldn't rule out Las Vegas either. He wasn't breaching into illegal territory—at least not that they could tell—but his answers seemed evasive, as if he were suppressing some kind of dangerous motive. Still, they agreed to respect his need for holding back the details of the project and having them sign non-disclosure agreements to ensure that no one ran with the idea.

"Yes," said the Finger Gunman, "there will be someone strapped to the chair as The Trap spins."

"If I may ask," said the welder, "then what is the need for The Trap to spin so fast? Wouldn't 120 rpms be dangerous?"

The Finger Gunman had dealt with undesirable workers when he was scouting for explosives experts. It was always his bad luck to have to rely on someone who was exceptionally qualified, but who also asked too many prying questions. As much as he wanted to fire the welder on the spot for questioning the inherently dangerous design of The Trap, he opted against it to keep the peace. The welder was too valuable to let go.

But, of course it's dangerous, you fool! Of course, it's designed to make someone nauseous and terrified, and give in and tell the truth. And if they don't, then I'll turn the control knob again, spinning and spinning them until they vomit and lose consciousness, then later wake up with a shirt soaked with bile. And that my friend is the dangerous beauty of The Trap!!

It was a 20-foot diameter caged sphere that appeared to be floating six inches above the floor. It was made of a latticework of welded sturdy strips of hand-forged steel to give the effect of something medieval. A hinged hatch allowed access into The Trap where a steel chair was bolted to the latticework. Leather straps for securing a person's arms, legs, and torso were attached to the chair. Above the chair, a steel axle ran horizontally through the center of The Trap, one end connected to a floor-anchored motor that rotated the sphere about the axis.

Over the decades, the Finger Gunman funded The Trap by means of illegal activity. His ill-gotten gains came primarily from convenience store robberies, jewelry store heists, and car thefts. He once tried to make a living as an honest car salesman, but the term "honest" was nothing more than a spot-on oxymoron. So, he gave that up and resorted to the cash-cow industry of dependable crime.

So that his workers didn't think they were constructing some kind of torture device, he told them to think of The Trap as something for an escape artist to free himself from, like Houdini. "Remember," he'd say excitedly, holding to his story, "we're talkin' Las Vegas!"

Four months later, when construction of The Trap was completed, the welder asked eagerly, "Can I take it for a test ride?"

"Why, of course," said the Finger Gunman, looking at the welder's peers who were nodding approvingly. "Let's christen The Trap!"

After entering through the hatch, the Finger Gunman securely strapped the welder to the chair, then exited and went to the control box that had three options: a green start button, a black speed knob, and an emergency red stop button. "Okay. Here we go..."

As he slowly turned the speed knob, the only sound was a low hum coming from the two motors. All the welding joints held strong, nothing creaked. The welder rotated, fastened securely, 360 degrees like a Ferris wheel except he was upside-down when he passed over the top, above the axle.

"No photos, please," said the Finger Gunman as two workers took out their cell phones.

"I'm already feeling a little nauseous," said the welder. "Maybe this wasn't a great idea."

"I'm going to increase your speed just a little. See if it helps."

"I don't know, sir..."

"Juuuust a little faster..."

The increased speed was just fast enough for an observer to have difficulty tracking the welder, their eyes rotating as if without control.

"Mr. Fontaine! Please, stop!"

The Finger Gunman kept his hand on the knob. To the left, slower. To the right, faster. The welder shouted a second time. To the left, slower. To the right, faster. If he ever caught the person who had the magic ink, and if that person ever refused to talk, then The Trap would work. The knob had plenty of turn to the right. Vomiting and unconsciousness were there. Sure, he could put a gun to their head, but what fun is something without his spin of originality?

"Sir!" shouted the engineer.

The Finger Gunman hit the red button, slowing The Trap rather abruptly.

"I'm sorry," said the Finger Gunman, "the speed knob got jammed. I'll take a look at it later." He opened the hatch, then unstrapped the welder who stumbled his way out of The Trap. He found a wall, pushing his back against it, then slid down to the floor. There he hung his head between his knees and closed his eyes.

"Are you okay?" asked the Finger Gunman walking over to him.

The welder opened one eye and looked up. "You expect someone to actually escape from this thing?"

He knew his answer was obscure, and that no one would understand it but himself. And, really, that's all that mattered. So, with a smirk, he said, "Yes. And the truth shall set them free."

Chapter 5

KNOCK, KNOCK

Sid took his seat in the classroom, observing the drab mood of his fellow students trailing in, after reluctantly returning from the beach, ski slopes, or their hometowns. Across campus, the spring break exodus had been completely reversed, and the entire student body was moving with heavy feet and curbed enthusiasm.

"Good morning, everyone!" said Professor Collins, zestfully. "Welcome back to paradise! I'm sure you missed this place."

"Last week went way too fast," said a student.

"It's-like-we-never-left too fast," moaned another.

"Well," said Collins, "by the end of today's class, all of your depression will have vanished. You will have been restored to normal. That's the power of higher education!"

A student laughed, "I actually have a normal?"

"No, you don't," chuckled Collins. "You are the exception!" There was an energy in his step as he paced the front of the classroom, eager to kick off the new week. "Seriously, though, I want to welcome y'all back. As you know your superhero assignment is due this Friday. If you create a character who is original enough to catch the judges' attention at VIP Comics, then you just might win $100,000."

"Professor Collins," asked another student, "do you really think this is legit and not a scam?"

"I know that a lot of universities have researched the legitimacy of VIP and there've been no red flags."

"But I've searched for them on the web, and nothing comes up."

"I'm not surprised. They only communicate via email and phone with the universities," Collins acknowledged another student raising her hand.

"How long will it take them to make their selections?" she asked.

"There's really no telling. Weeks. Months. I can't say. But I do want to remind you to keep your ideas confidential. And by that I even mean amongst yourselves. Use this contest as good practice to not share what you're creating. The more people know of your idea, the greater the chances it might be pirated. Especially, do not go online with it. There are idea thieves in this world who could care less if you're the creator. If something looks profitable and new, they'll snatch it in a heartbeat and take it to the bank."

Sid listened intently, recalling the steps he had taken up to this point to keep his idea secret. But there was more to it than just keeping it hidden from others. Originally, he had thought he was gambling—taking a risk by telling of the magic ink in The Lure contest, even if in a roundabout, hypothetical way. But listening to Heba helped make his decision. He would never jeopardize himself or Charles, who, as Heba believed, was back.

For two days he had spent a considerable amount of time talking with her and Sketch, now that she had returned from her Texas hill country trip. Heba had experienced so much over the centuries. If she were to journal her travels, it could act as a reliable account of world history. A panel of historians would only need to interview Heba and no one else. "My memories never fade," she told Sid. "It is an immortal attribute. Everything is like yesterday." As she recounted many of the artists whom she had selected since her existence, Sid felt an honor to be among the privileged ranks. "But what makes you unique," she told him, "is that you and Charles are the first bloodline pairings to ever share the same creation. And I never knew it was possible until Anne gave birth to you and we began following your development. Sid, your personality and artistic talent are uncannily similar to Charles', and this includes your imaginative energy. Charles once asked me a question to which I had no absolute answer. He asked since he had the ability to bring an immortal into existence, whether it be an insect or human, did possessing that ability in some way make him supernatural?

"I had never thought of it that way. I had only seen it as a creative gift. But once Sketch and I began wondering if he would ever regain his superpowers, we eventually became curious about bloodlines, which Charles had once touched upon. And now, well, here we are, and our curiosities have been answered. Which has led me to believe two things. First, because of your abilities, I believe you and Charles are supernatural. And second, the reason I say 'are' and not 'was' regarding Charles, is because I believe he is alive within you. His imaginative energy is immortal. It just took you, a bloodline of equal creativity, to be his host. So, keep the ink alive and magical."

Heba then went on to tell Sid of Khepri and his wisdom.

"Be faithful to it," she said. "It knows good intent. It understands you. Try to fool it, and it will revert to being normal ink, and nothing else."

Sid needed the money. $100,000 would go a long way. A house down payment. Money to invest for future use. Children's education. Pay off his college loan. He would never disrespect the ink, and he knew this thought was pure. He was not trying to telepathically foil the ink with some hopeful message. He was not showing off the ink's magic. *The ink understands me.* So, he kept his idea a secret from everyone.

He mailed in his superhero submission to VIP Comics, titling it: *What If There Were A Magic Ink?*

One week later, at Sid's apartment on a quiet Wednesday evening, just as he was about to put in a frozen pizza and do some homework, there was a knock at the door.

Chapter 6
THE SHOE BOX

Before he drove off in the car he stole from the shadowy back alley behind a laundromat, the Finger Gunman had been in the restroom of a gas station, tending to an injury seeping silver ink.

The snake had struck his forehead hard like a staple gun. But it was his own fault for getting too close to it, talking to it, and thinking just because he was who he was, he had some kind of rite of passage, that he had been granted snake bite immunity.

But snakes didn't think that way, especially vipers.

And because he didn't have any bandages, his only option was an old gauze pad he found at the bottom of a small trash can. It was caked with dried blood and a scab from someone else's wound. He took a piece of duct tape that was holding a business card on a grimy, water-stained, mirror above the sink, stuck it to the gauze, then pressed both over the bite. Looking in the mirror he shouted jubilantly, "Hello, handsome!!"

In his younger years, his wounds healed within minutes. But as he grew older the healing process took longer. He had thought that the healing time would always be quick, but he had thought wrong.

Scars of other snake bites from months or years past dotted his arms and even neck. Most had dulled, but were raised and looked cancerous.

He combed his greasy black hair to the side, making a sharp part, then combed food particles out of an unkempt mustache. He wore black dress shoes and slacks, and a surprisingly clean and ironed white button-down shirt.

After driving to his destination, he sat in the dark in the stolen car, and waited until he felt he was ready, until he knew he couldn't mess up. Reaching into the back seat, he grabbed a brief case that was sitting next to a red shoe box. He lifted the box lid to be certain it still contained the syringes.

Stepping out of the car, he took a deep breath, followed the walkway to the apartment and knocked on Sid's door.

He heard footsteps from inside, and smiled.

Chapter 7
ITALY! ITALY!

A dark plum hue painted the sky's horizon, dissolving into the advancing night. Sid's apartment complex was relatively quiet with most students in for the evening. Having knocked, The Finger Gun man stood at Sid's front door, his briefcase in hand. The makeshift duct tape bandage stuck to his forehead like an unsightly eyesore. It was still too early to remove it, for fear of drawing too much attention with even a few drops of silver ink oozing out. The porch light turned on as Sid cautiously opened the door.

"Hello? May I help you?"

"Are you Sid Welch?"

"Yes."

The Finger Gunman smiled, his face lit with happiness. "At last! We meet!"

"Excuse me. Who are you?"

"Sid…let me introduce myself, I am Claude Fontaine, owner and founder of VIP Comics. And you, my friend, are a winner of The Lure contest!"

Sid opened the door further, his excitement forestalled with a puzzled hesitation.

"I…I'm a winner? At this hour?"

"Yes, sir! The first of nine more to come!"

"You caught me a little by surprise."

"I realize that, and I do apologize for this unexpected visit, but being the first winner, I couldn't resist bringing the news in person." He knelt down to open his briefcase, then took out some papers. "Here you go," he said, handing them to Sid, "these are the official winner's documents of The Lure."

"I can't believe I won."

"Well, believe it! After all, that was quite an original idea you submitted. Who would've ever thought of a superhero being created from a magic ink?"

"Yeah, it just kinda came to me one night."

"And imagine if there really were a magic ink, and because of it a superhero really did exist."

Sid was caught off guard, pausing for just a moment before he replied. But it was the pause the Finger Gunman was hoping for, as he noticed Sid's trepidation. A giveaway. Why else would Sid have hesitated? "And imagine," the Finger Gunman added, "if the ink were Egyptian."

Sid hadn't mentioned a word in his contest submission about the ink being from Egypt. He tried not to stumble, but he did, and the Finger Gunman caught it all. "I…I guess we'd finally have ourselves a real superhero."

The Finger Gunman looked to his left and right. The area was quiet. "Sid, do you mind if I come inside to go over the documents?"

A wave of ambivalence moved through Sid, not just because of the man's unannounced visit, but something seemed off. The duct tape on his forehead—what was up with that? It smeared a little tarnish on his credibility. However, as they talked more and the man mentioned professor Collins and cited noteworthy laurels about the art department, and the fact that he knew what Sid's superhero idea entailed, the more authentic the man became.

"Of course, Mr. Fontaine. Please, come in."

It was a small efficiency apartment, the kitchen barely able to accommodate two people. An adjoining living space had a small round wooden table with three chairs.

"This brings back fond memories. I lived in a place like this when I went to school."

"Where did you study?"

"In France."

"I thought you sounded French. What was your major?"

The Finger Gunman momentarily flipped through the papers, pretending to be occupied, giving himself time to think.

"Biology," he said.

"Biology?" said Sid. "How'd you end up in the comic book industry?"

"Oh, you know...life's twists and turns are always full of surprises."

"Why biology?"

The Finger Gunman casually touched one of the raised bites on his neck. "Snakes. I love snakes."

Sid squirmed in his seat. "You can keep 'em! I want nothing to do with snakes."

"I understand. It seems that most people fear them. But they fascinate me, especially the poisonous ones."

"Why's that?"

"Because they are masters at finding their prey." The Finger Gunman neatly stacked his papers, then lightly slapped the tabletop. "But enough about snakes!" he said, smiling. "Sid, have you had dinner?"

"I was about to throw in a frozen pizza."

"Frozen pizza? Oh, no, Sid...you're not having that tonight. We're going out to eat. We're going to celebrate! Do you like Italian?"

"Yes, but—"

"Sid, there will be no frozen pizza tonight. I know a little Italian restaurant named *Italy! Italy!* Have you eaten there before?"

"Once with my parents."

"Well, it'll now be twice. I insist. It's not every day you get to celebrate winning $100,000!"

"I can't argue with that, sir,"

The day before his arrival, The Finger Gunman had rehearsed, numerous times, executing the signing of the bogus paperwork. If he could get Sid to sign, then he knew he had him by the hook. He located the non-disclosure agreement and slid it over to Sid, along with a pen. "But, first things first," he said. "If you would, please, sign this. You're basically agreeing to not tell anyone about any ideas or projects that VIP Comics is involved with."

"Sounds pretty routine," said Sid, picking up the pen. "I do have a question, though. When do I get the money?"

"The funds will be transferred to your bank account within four weeks. But I can explain that and much more over dinner. You good to go?"

Sid nodded, grinning as he signed his name. "Yes, sir!"

Returning the documents to the briefcase, the Finger Gunman stood up and made his way toward the front door. "I'll drive," he said. "Besides, you're in college. Save yourself some gas. I don't mind bringing you back. It's my treat."

"Ok. If you say so."

As Sid led the way to the car, the Finger Gunman trailed a few feet behind, staring at the back of Sid's neck. Staring with a morbid smile, at the precise spot where he would inject the needle.

Buckling into their front seats, the light from a nearby telephone pole cast a soft glow over the Finger Gunman's face. Sid looked at him. "Mr. Fontaine, are you okay?"

"Why, of course. Why do you ask?"

"I don't know…it's the duct tape on your forehead. It looks loose and your wound looks red, like it's inflamed. And is that ointment?"

The Finger Gunman reached up and felt that the bandage had, indeed, loosened. He touched the wound with his finger, then looked at it, noticing silver ink that was still moist. "Ah, yes, just a little ointment."

"What happened? And why duct tape?"

"On my way over here, I hit my head on the corner of a cabinet in a gas station bathroom. I didn't have a bandage, so I had to make one. I know it's unsightly, but sometimes you just gotta make do."

"Well, as long as you're ok, that's what counts."

Do not mother me! Do not nurse me! Do not console me! Shut your fucking mouth!!

The Finger Gunman was about to start the car when he tapped the top of the steering wheel. "Sid! I almost forgot!"

"Sir?"

"Hang on a sec!" He hopped out, and circled around the car, opening the door behind Sid. "Sid," he said, positioning himself directly behind him with the opened red shoe box by his side, "do you like surprises?"

"Well—"

"Well, of course you do! Now, no looking! You're going to love this! Gimme just a sec. I brought it especially for you…"

This is odd, thought Sid. Like it was his birthday, and he was ten years old now and his parents were about to surprise him with a brand-new shiny bicycle. So odd, it felt uncomfortable, out of place and wrong. As he was about to turn to see what the big surprise was all about, the Finger Gunman's left arm quickly hooked around Sid's throat, leveraging him hard against the headrest. The chokehold made it impossible to yell at two students walking to their car just down the street. A stifled gurgle was all he had as he desperately tried to pull the Finger Gunman's arm down, clawing and grappling, and kicking the underside of the glove compartment. But he faded rapidly, his eyelids bouncing, and then his deadweight slumping against his door. His struggle was over almost as soon as it had started, because the needle had already been plunged into his neck, injecting the anesthesia.

"Cheer up, kiddo," smiled the Finger Gunman, as he returned to his seat and started the car. "We've got a big day tomorrow!!"

Chapter 8
THE SCENT

"He's still not answering," Sketch told Heba as he ended his phone call. They were sitting on the sofa in the living room with Khaldun stretched out between them. "It's been two days, but he's a student. I'm sure he has a lot going on."

"I am a little concerned," said Heba. "I think we should drive over there."

"Or we could fly," smiled Sketch.

"Oh, no, you are not flying me. You are not ready for a passenger."

"Are you kiddin'? I am back, baby!"

"Oh, you are back, alright. But it has been 40 years."

"Oh, c'mon. If you fall, I'll catch you before you hit the ground."

Heba smirked, shaking her head.

"Okay, okay," said Sketch. "I'll get the keys."

"And one more thing," said Heba. "Put your superhero outfit on under your clothes."

"And why?"

"Just in case, that is all."

On the way to the apartment, Heba's face wore a look of concern, as she gently stroked Khaldun who lay on her lap. "Something has happened," she said. "We have been talking daily. I just assumed he has been busy now that school is back in session. But I am not feeling that."

"What are you feeling?"

"A knot in my stomach."

When they arrived at the apartment, there was no answer at the front door, so Sketch opened it with the spare key that Sid had given him. Khaldun entered first, his nose immediately to the ground, sniffing quickly as he darted through the apartment. Heba feared that it would be upturned, that Sid's belongings would be in heaps of disarray. The forty-year memory of her personal experience of having been intruded upon came to mind. But that was the Finger Gunman, decades ago, and Sid's apartment appeared to be undisturbed. There was no intrusion here, no signs of a struggle. That was reassuring. There really was no need to be on edge.

"I see nothing out of the ordinary," said Sketch, walking about. "Looks like a normal college student's apartment. Unmade bed, dirty dishes, and dirty laundry. Though leaving out a frozen pizza is a little unlike him."

Heba went into Sid's bedroom to look around, but stopped as she stood over his drawing table. "Sketch, have you seen this? It is a paper he has written titled, *What If There Were A Magic Ink?*"

Sketch walked into the bedroom. "Sounds like something for a class assignment."

She noticed another paper next to it that read: *Contest Submission Form for Original Superhero Idea*. "It says here it is a contest sponsored by VIP Comics. Have you heard of VIP before?"

"Can't say that I have."

"These look like copies," she said. "I wonder if he submitted the originals."

They read the contest description together, then reread Sid's submission.

"The Lure is a peculiar title for a contest," said Heba. "And no phone number, just a post office box mailing address in Lake Cherokee, Texas, wherever that is." Heba set the papers down on the desk. "Sketch…the damage would easily have happened by now."

"What damage?"

"The damage to you if Sid went public about the magic ink. He may have jeopardized your superpowers. Remember, the ink detects being boastful."

"But it looks like he wrote the paper as something hypothetical. I think they're two different things."

Heba went into the kitchen and found a screwdriver on the countertop. "Here, bend this," she said. "We need to know."

Sketch took the screwdriver in both hands, instantly and effortlessly bending it end-to-end.

"Well, that is a relief," she said.

Sketch handed it back to her. "But you were right."

"About what?"

"Putting on my superhero outfit."

"I figured you might as well be prepared." Heba examined the screwdriver, but her attention was soon diverted to Khaldun who was hard-focused, rolling out a long, deep minacious growl, his snout hovering just above the chair where the Finger Gunman sat the night before.

"Khaldun," said Heba, "what is it?"

The intensity of the growling grew louder, and his inhalations quickened. Heba walked over to him, stroking the scruff of his taut neck.

"What's he doing?" asked Sketch.

"I am not sure, but he is definitely sensing something."

Khaldun escalated into a repetitive cadence of two drawn out growls followed by two sharp barks.

"He is acting very territorial," said Heba, kneeling on one knee, gently stroking Khaldun's head to calm him. "There you go, buddy. There you go," she said quietly. "Someone has been here. And whoever it was, sat in this chair."

"As insignificant as it may seem," said Sketch, walking into the kitchen and picking up the thawed, limp pizza box, "it's not like him to leave this out. Maybe he got distracted by something? A girl? A girl can do that, you know."

"I cannot argue with that, and I really hope we are just overthinking this, but Khaldun would not react that way without a reason," said Heba. "His behavior leads me to believe Sid is in trouble and he is unable to call us."

Sketch began scanning the area. "Are his sketch book and pen here? If he's in trouble, and if for some reason he has them, but not his phone, or if the battery is dead, he knows to draw me a call."

They thoroughly searched the apartment, including the obvious places around Sid's drawing table, but nothing surfaced, so they agreed to leave. Before meeting Heba at the car, Sketch tossed the thawed pizza in a large dumpster behind the apartment.

Khaldun laid down on the back seat, subtle growling murmured within him. Being eternal, he had the ability to recall even the most ancient memories as if they occurred yesterday, as long as the scent was embedded in clothing. A scent picked up from Khepri's loin cloth would be enough to identify his creator. Though Khepri was long deceased, a present-day scent could easily trigger the total recall of an ancient experience.

The chair inside Sid's apartment was different, as only a small residue of the Finger Gunman's scent remained. But the scent of the chair stimulated his olfactory receptors. Inside the apartment, as he barked, the source of the scent reeked of bad news—of something evil. How he discerned that was an immortal quality.

As he continued to inhale the scent that had enveloped him, the memory began to take shape, until, at last, he remembered being atop the table in the market, snarling aggressively at the Finger Gunman. Khaldun shifted his head forward, his eyes looking through Sid's front door, and zeroing in on the chair. Heba reached back to calm him, but his rage was too heightened. Khaldun jumped onto the console dividing Heba and Sketch, his front paws on the dashboard as he furiously barked against the windshield.

Sketch wrapped both arms around his torso, squeezing firmly as he pulled him away from the dashboard, then held him securely against his chest. "It's okay, boy. It's okay."

Khaldun fought to break free, but Sketch only tightened his hold, until eventually the dog surrendered.

Heba softly scratched his head. "Good, boy, good boy. There ya go. Calm down, Khal'."

Sketch relaxed his hold, patting Khaldun on the back, then guided him to the back seat, where he laid down.

Heba looked at Sketch, her face a composite of worry and sadness. She knew exactly who Khaldun had detected. Forty years of freedom from the Finger Gunman had now come to an end.

One question sill remained…

Where is Sid?

Chapter 9
EVIL

Sid's eyes struggled to open as he slowly woke up inside The Trap. A leather strap was being cinched tightly around his chest, jerking him in the process against the chair's solid wooden back. The anesthesia was wearing off, but his muzzy condition put a damper on the return of his consciousness, making it difficult to identify the Finger Gunman as he fastened him to the chair. Whistling jovially as he worked, he tightened a strap around each leg, then did the same to each wrist, affixing them to the chair's armrests. He placed a tied-off white nylon bag next to Sid's feet, but he was too groggy to notice it shifting slightly from side to side.

The room was dimly lit and smelled as industrial as ever, if not more since the welders had finished constructing The Trap.

The Finger Gunman double-checked that the leather straps were secure. "Good afternoon, Sid! How are you feeling?"

Sid continued to fight his heavy eyes, the lids fluttering as the anesthesia tried to pull him back under. He vaguely recognized the man's voice, but couldn't pinpoint it. The nylon bag, moving on its own accord, bumped against his feet.

"Hey, wake up!" said the Finger Gunman, lightly slapping Sid's face. "I need you to snap out of it. We've got things to discuss."

A couple more minutes passed until clarity and focus finally began to emerge through the dissipating fog of anesthesia. Sid squinted and blinked as his vision restored itself. "Mr. Fontaine...?"

The Finger Gunman stood before him, wearing a brown, short-sleeve, full-body canvas coverall with dirt stains up to his knees. On the back was embossed stitching of the head of a large silver-eyed viper. A metal snake bracelet coiled around both forearms from wrist to elbow.

Tugging his wrists, Sid made a futile attempt to break free. "What is this?" he asked, looking overhead at The Trap.

"This is the home of VIP Comics."

"No, what is *this*?"

"Oh!" he said, grandly, "This is The Trap! The final destination of The Lure! Isn't it beautiful?!"

"I don't understand."

"I wouldn't expect you to."

Sid became visibly concerned. "Why am I in here?"

"A better question might be, why would I want to rotate The Trap with you in it? That's simple...because you wouldn't be telling me the truth."

"Rotate? The truth?"

The Finger Gunman reached down and picked up the white bag, shook it next to Sid's ear, then smiled as the bag hissed. "In your apartment you told me you hated snakes. Well, did you know the best way to get over your fears is to confront them?"

Sid jerked his head away, his body nearly convulsing as the bag was pressed against the back of his neck. Inside, two snakes slithered faster, hissing louder. His eyes shut tight, Sid pleaded, "PLEASE, STOP!! PLEASE!!"

"Oh, Sid! Do you really think I would open this bag?"

"Please, sir, please! I don't know what this is about, but I'll tell you whatever I can."

"Answer my question, Sid!!"

"I...I'm afraid, yes. Yes, you would open the bag."

"Contestant #1...you...are...riiiiiiight!!"

"Mr. Fontaine—"

"Shut up!! SHUT UP!!" the Finger Gunman yelled, aggressively. "Claude Fontaine was another man, who I suspect, is dead by now.

I forged his identity on all necessary documents, including passport and driver's license. He was my alias and nothing more. I am the Finger Gunman!"

Sid pressed himself to the chair, his eyes now wide open, scanning The Trap and the room for exit points, fully aware of the monster he was up against.

"Have you seen a ghost? Are you frightened? What's up, Sid?" The Finger Gunman spoke as he left The Trap through the hatch, dead bolting it behind him. "You've heard my name before, haven't you?"

"I'm not sure, sir."

"Not sure?" He walked over to the operating controls that were positioned atop a podium, setting the bag of snakes on the floor. The controls wiring made its way through a conduit leading to the motor that powered The Trap. "Here's what disturbs me, Sid…I asked you a simple yes or no question, and you gave me an uncertain answer, which tells me, yes, you have heard my name before. All that I ask for is the truth." The Finger Gunman turned on the power by turning the speed knob to the right. "Sid! Hang on, ol' buddy! It's Trap time!!"

"Please, sir! Yes, I've heard of you!"

"A little late, Sid!"

The first two rotations were slow, but unnerving, since he had no idea what to expect. The anesthesia hadn't completely worn off, which, combined with the circular motion, worsened his nausea. He feared that pleading or protesting might only encourage the Finger Gunman to spin The Trap faster, so he remained silent. But talking or not talking didn't really matter. Sid knew the monster only played by his own rules. After six rotations, the Trap began its acceleration. At ten rotations, it spun at three-quarter speed, its motor whirring loudly. At fifteen, it began decelerating. At twenty, it stopped.

Eyes closed, Sid's head hung down, swimming in motion sickness. Dry heaving on an empty stomach only compounded his misery.

In a soft, psychotic voice the Finger Gunman said, "Hey, buddy…that was quite a show. Did ya have fun?"

Sid had broken into a cold sweat. A claustrophobic-like feeling washed over him, being so tightly confined to the chair. He knew it was best to answer him. "No, I did not have fun. There. There's your truth. Are you happy?"

"I love it! You have a little sarcastic fight in you. But I'm warning you…don't try to test me. Sometimes I have an anger switch that turns on. And, trust me, you don't want to see my bad side."

He untied the bag of snakes by the podium, then carefully reached in to take one out, but whipped his hand back out immediately.

"Dammit!! Bit me again!!" he hollered, shaking his hand, then sucking on the fang puncture where the venom seeped into his silver ink. "These are asp vipers. Wicked deadly. The duct tape you saw that was on my forehead…one of these bastards struck me. And, damn, their venom stings! However, because I am immortal, a poisonous snake delivers nothing more than a sharp bite."

Looking over the bag's opening, he poised his hand above it, then quickly jabbed downward, pulling out a viper. Holding it from behind its head, the snake aggressively wound itself around his forearm, intertwining with his bracelet, trying to break free. When the viper realized its struggle was futile, it began to relax as if some kind of kinship or mutual bond had formed.

"Sir…please," said Sid. "I don't understand why I'm here. What is it that you want from me? Haven't I answered everything you've asked?"

The Finger Gunman waved the snake in the air, gliding it side to side across his face, even pausing to meet it eye to eye.

"Yes, in fact, you have and that's why you're still here."

"And this is what I get for cooperating?"

"Sid, what do you think VIP stands for in VIP Comics?"

Sid sensed a change in the tone of their conversation, as if they were actually on the cusp of getting along, though he knew to beware of the calm before a storm. Still, for the time being, it was as good a place to be as he could ask for. "I've often wondered that," said Sid. "Is it as obvious as Very Important Person?"

"A likely guess, but no." The Finger Gunman bent over, returned the snake to the bag and tied it off, then walked up to The Trap. "VIP," he said, "stands for Viper In Pursuit."

"In pursuit of what?" asked Sid.

"In pursuit of you, though it could have been anyone. You just happened to be the one person to submit an idea about a magic ink. It took me years to formulate a plan that would appear so believable that no one would doubt its authenticity. I had to forge all documentation to pass through the required check points. Of course, The Lure was a deceptive scam. There is no money. There are no winners. For the participants, it was nothing more than a complete waste of time. The only person who will ever benefit from it is me. The Lure was certainly a gamble on my part. What if whoever has the magic ink never came forward, for fear that doing so might end their creative connection with the ink? I'm fully aware of the properties of the ink. But, I thought, what if someone presented the idea of the magic ink in a speculative, roundabout way? I knew it was a long shot, but when you're eternal, like me, you've got nothing but time, so what the hell. And then one day your submission arrived, and...well...here we are. And the question is: do you have the real magical Egyptian ink?"

Sid couldn't afford to hesitate. There was no telling what the man was capable of. Putting vipers down his shirt as The Trap spun—anything was possible. "Yes, I do," said Sid, ashamed of his answer.

"This is so exciting!! I'll be right back!" The Finger Gunman went through a nearby office door, then moments later returned, carrying his briefcase. He picked up the bag of snakes, carrying both as he reentered The Trap. Circling Sid, he once again dragged the bag of snakes along the back of his neck.

Petrified, Sid knew there would be no negotiating his way out of this situation. All that was left was hope. You aren't strapped to something that resembles a prison execution chair that revolves within something called The Trap for just friendly entertainment. Instead, the reason you're strapped in it is because the man circling you with snakes is a barbaric demon, and your chances of survival are slim.

The Finger Gunman stood in front of Sid. "I want to share a little something with you that no one else knows about. A little something to remind you just how volatile I can be."

Sid froze, not wanting to take any chances of lighting his captor's short fuse. If there was any chance of survival, he couldn't afford even a hint of one wrong move or wrong answer.

The Finger Gunman pointed at various areas of The Trap's steel latticework, making note of numerous dark red stains, as well as larger stains beneath, on the concrete floor. "A few days ago, I came up here late one night to do some work, when I heard the door open over there. It's got a real squeak to it. I thought, well, that's kinda strange. So, I came out here and found the welder who had helped build The Trap. He was with some girl about his age. Cute brunette, but walked funny. I think he was trying to impress her. I asked what the hell was he doing, entering without knocking? And, get this…he laughed and said he 'built this thing.' And I said 'you helped build it.' And he said 'whatever' and that he was the chief welder. Then I saw he was walking as funny as she was, and realized they had had a little too much to drink. So, I said, 'Chief, gimme a sec.'"

The Finger Gunman walked up to Sid, placing his briefcase on his lap, opened it, and took out a revolver. "Ain't she a beaut?" he said, holding it just above his head. "You like it, Sid?"

"Yes, I do, sir."

"You seem a little skittish, Sid."

"I'm ok."

"The hell if you're okay! I gotta loaded gun right here! You're not okay, now are you?"

"No, sir. To be honest, I'm scared, sir."

"Now, that's what I like!! Honesty!! Oh! And look what else I have in here…your sketchbook and this peculiar looking red pen. We'll address all of that later. But for now, back to my story…"

The Finger Gunman set the briefcase and gun down on The Trap's latticework, then continued…

"So, I came back out of the office with this gun and pointed it directly at him, and kept walking closer until I could smell him, and told him to get inside The Trap. His eyes got big. I yelled, 'NOW!!!' So he did, but he said something that really angered me. He said, 'Mr. Fontaine, I wasn't going to turn the cage on. I just wanted Shelby to see it. I'm sorry.' I told him I remembered once having to correct him for calling it a cage, and to never call it that ever again. Especially him, because he got under my skin more than anyone. I told him to sit in the chair, and to not touch the straps. He was scared, but I didn't care. My anger switch had now been turned on. I could see the girl looking around, like she was gonna bolt. I told her if she ran, she'd never run again. I told her to watch The Trap, to not take her eyes off of it. Then I turned it on to a low setting at first, watching the welder trying to grab hold of the latticework, but he would lose his grip and drop to the bottom of The Trap. A few rotations later, as I increased its speed, he tumbled and fell and hit his head on the axle. He landed at a weird angle on the chair, and I heard a bone crack, and then he went silent and became a sort of rag doll. And that's when I turned it to top speed, and he was lifeless, stuck to The Trap as it spun. Shelby was screaming, watching in horror. Of course, I couldn't afford a witness, so I made her get in The Trap as well. And I think you know what happened next. Two rag dolls. And now all these blood stains."

The Finger Gunman leaned his back against The Trap, letting out a sigh, then shaking his head with his eyes closed. "I wasn't always like this, Sid. For a few minutes I was Zenator. I was all about peace and love. There were these pulses of peace I was able to project at people. That was my superhero power. I remember it all. Then I was corrupted. I'll never go back. I am evil. I was altered to do no good. And that is why I killed the welder and the girl. And that is why there is dirt on my coveralls…I buried them far out back in the pines." He reached down and took out the sketchbook and pen from the briefcase, and set them on Sid's lap. "You now know the terror I can cause," he said. "Let me remind you to only tell me the truth, because I'm tired of burying bodies."

"What would you like me to do?" asked Sid.

The Finger Gunman took Sid's cell phone out of his front pocket. "I found this as well when I went back into your apartment. I want to thank you for not having a passcode, though I really haven't had much time to look through your contacts. So, answer me this... do you know a woman named Heba? And I strongly suggest you tell the truth. After all," he whispered ominously, "I am a cold-blooded murderer."

"Yes, I know her."

"Oh, Sid! You have no idea how happy I am! Let's call her!"

"Sorry, but I don't have her number."

The Finger Gunman leaned into Sid. "Listen to me. I have no problem stepping out of The Trap and turning it on again, and letting it run for a while. Hell, I might even toss a snake in your lap to go along for the ride. So, once again...what's her number?"

"I'm telling the truth. I don't know her number. I haven't known her very long."

"Dammit!!" he thrust his hand around Sid's neck, tightening his grip until he couldn't breathe, watching his eyes grow larger, "Do not play games with me!!" he said, relaxing his hand. "One snake bite followed by a spin in The Trap will fuck you up!! Talk to me, Sid! Give me a name to call who has access to the ink!"

Guilt and betrayal. Sid was swimming in both. He was cornered. He had no way out. "Sketch. Call Sketch. He knows her. He's in my contacts."

"And who is Sketch? That's an odd name."

Sid knew Sketch had suffered enough. He knew he wore the burden of blame for not having saved Charles' life. Then forty years later, Charles' bloodline restored his superpowers. Sid had no idea how any of this was going to play out. And at this moment, he had only one option: to speak the truth. "Sketch," he said, "is a superhero. He was created from the magic ink."

"HOLY SHIT!!!" The Finger Gunman threw his head back in celebration. "JACKPOT!!! You gotta admit, Sid, The Lure was a stroke of genius!" Flipping the phone open, he tapped the camera button, then aimed the phone at Sid. "Hey, buddy! Say, cheeeese!" Looking at the photo, he said, "Really? No smile? But I get it. Things aren't exactly going your way today. But that's okay, I'm going to send it to Sketch in a text."

As Sid looked around the room disbelieving where he was, a moment of profundity struck him. He was caught in the middle between good and evil, taking part in a comic book storyline where the villain unveils his darkest side, and, with a self-devised lure, forces good to play by his rules. Though the match between Sketch and the Finger Gunman was on the horizon, Sid feared he might fall along the way.

"He should be calling soon," said the Finger Gunman. "I texted him this: 'Having the time of my life. Sid.'"

When the phone rang, the Finger Gunman answered jubilantly, "Hello? Sketch?"

"Who is this?!"

"Oh, Sketch, I think you know who I am. And if not, then just ask Heba, who I suspect is there with you."

"I want to talk to Sid."

"You'll get your turn, but first—"

"Let me hear his voice, now!!" Enraged, Sketch wondered if the photo wasn't current, if Sid were even in a worse, tortured condition.

"Calm down, Sketch. Don't get me all riled up. You don't want that to happen, trust me. Here's your boy." The Finger Gunman put the phone on speaker holding it next to Sid's ear.

"Sketch! I'm just as the photo shows. I'm ok, but please do as he says. And I'm so sorry I got us in this mess."

"It's okay, Sid. Just do as he—"

The Finger Gunman pulled the phone away. "Sketch, what you need to do is very simple. In one hour bring me the magic ink, and Sid will be set free. Sid will call you through a sketch. I know how quickly you can travel. It is a five-hour drive here, and I do not want to wait that long. I have a gun. Don't forget that."

"Do not harm him, and you'll get the ink. I'll be there in an hour."

There was no reply. The Finger Gunman disconnected the line.

Heba had been listening intently, standing close to Sketch

throughout the call. Her greatest fear that one day the ink might end up in the hands of evil was now approaching.

"His game is not over yet," said Sketch. "You never know when he might stumble."

"Perhaps," said Heba, "but be certain his stumble is real, because you can never trust a snake."

Chapter 10
THE WINDOW

Heba and Sketch were seated at their coffee table at Sierra Oaks after having ended their call with the Finger Gunman. Before them was a burlap sack containing the wooden box with two bottles of magic ink, each within its own smaller burlap sack. An eye dropper was also being provided as Heba suspected the Finger Gunman might want to transfer the ink to an empty pen of his own.

"This is dangerous," she said. "There is no telling what he has planned for you when you arrive."

"We have no choice. Sid is strapped into that chair. It looks like he's in a round cage that rotates. Like some kind of torture machine."

Heba stood up and walked over to a picture window that overlooked a wooded view of majestic live oak trees. It was a haven for a commune of squirrels that were chasing one another around the tree trunks, as if playing tag. "For two centuries, the ink has withstood any kind of infection," she said. "It has never been tampered with. In the Cairo market the Finger Gunman had told me that the god Apep orchestrated the campaign to poison the ink. If, in fact, a crazed falcon did do the dirty work, I am bothered by an unknown—that there is something unique about his silver ink that I have no knowledge of."

"The possibility of superpowers?"

"No. If he had them, I do not think it would have taken him forty years to find us. My concern is not just his thirst for evil, but that there must be something about his immortality that makes him different from us due to his silver ink. When Zenator became no more, I think the Finger Gunman was cast into this world under a different set of rules."

Sketch went over and stood behind Heba, placing his hands on her shoulders. Turning her head up to him, she said, "He is a sick individual. It is anybody's guess what he might have up his sleeve."

"I'll be okay."

"But will you?"

"Heba, I wasn't given superpowers for no reason. If I see an opening, I'm going after him."

"But you must not risk Sid's life. Let him have a bottle of ink. The Finger Gunman has no knowledge of how much ink there is, and that is why we are keeping one for ourselves. I am sure he would not expect us to hand it all over. His objective is to get a reasonable amount of ink, enough to carry out whatever hell he is preparing."

"Like supervillains?"

"Anything is possible, because everything is unknown." Heba slammed her hand down on the countertop. "Dammit, Sketch!! He found us!! And poor Sid is caught in the middle." She wrapped her arms around Sketch, laying her head on his chest, listening to the immortal *thuh-thump…thump* beat of his heart. "Remember in Africa, watching the water buffalo, I told you to never die?"

"Yes. I promised I'd do my best. And I still promise."

Sketch smoothed back her midnight hair lined with thin streaks of gray, then kissed the top of her head. "I need to get my boots and mask, and prepare myself. The time will be here before we know it, and I want to stop by Sergeant Perkins' room before I go."

"He may be asleep. You know how he likes his afternoon naps."

"He won't care." Sketch made his way toward the bedroom, waking Khaldun who was napping on the bed. "Besides, I want him to see me fly. He's only seen evidence that I've flown, but has never actually seen me in action."

Heba followed him into the bedroom, troubled and apprehensive, wondering if Sketch was unsure if he would return from confronting the Finger Gunman. "Are you wondering if Perkins may never get another opportunity to see you fly and that you might not return to me?"

"No. He's old. He has known me since the very beginning of my existence and I have always insisted that flight was one of my special abilities. I want to make sure he sees me fly before he passes. Not that I think he's going to die soon, but I just want him to have the memory of witnessing me. Though there is one other detail."

"Which is?"

"You haven't seen me fly either. So, I'm killing two birds with one stone."

"No, I have not. I am sure it will be amazing, but I am more concerned for your safety—dealing with the Finger Gunman—than I am wanting to witness you flying. And I am certain Sergeant Perkins will feel the same."

"I see your point, and it's valid. Nonetheless, I exist to defend against adversity. I will return. The call will be coming soon. But before I go, give me a moment. I have a small order of business I must tend to."

Sketch disappeared into their bedroom bathroom, closing the door behind him. Soon, running water from the faucet could be heard and the occasional sharp tapping of metal on porcelain. Five minutes later he reemerged, his face completely shaven.

Heba's eyes grew large. "Sketch? Is that you? It has been decades!"

Sketch smiled, massaging his hands along his newly exposed jawline. "Figured if I'm a superhero, I should at least look like one. Besides, the beard creates too much drag. But enough about me. Time is ticking. We must go."

In a small bag, Sketch carried his boots and mask, while Heba carried the burlap sack containing the bottle of ink and the eye dropper.

Perkins' door was at the opposite end of the hallway. He was in full stretch of a long yawn when he answered Sketch's knock. "Excuse me," he said covering his mouth. "Long nap."

Heba playfully nudged Sketch in the side with an elbow. "I told you!"

"Oh, don't worry," said Perkins. "I needed to wake up."

Sketch nudged Heba in return. "I told you, too!"

"Come on in you two. Make yourself at home. Can I get you anything?"

"No thanks, Sarge," said Sketch, closing the door behind him.

The apartment's furnishings had been brought down from Illinois. Sofas, chairs, and beds that Sketch and Heba had occupied over their forty years gave Perkins' place more of a sense of home than their own.

Perkins opened the fridge. "Are you sure? I've got some cold 7-Ups."

Sketch made his way around a small kitchen island, facing Perkins. "Sarge, I don't have a lot of time to explain things, but Sid's in a potentially very bad situation."

Perkins closed the refrigerator door. His direct, sergeant tone rose to the surface. "Talk to me, Sketch. What's going on?"

"It's the Finger Gunman. He's here. He found us."

"Ah, Christ! I haven't heard that name in years. Where is the bastard?!"

"We don't know. We don't know much of anything, to be honest."

"Except we do know Sid is safe," said Heba. "At least for now."

"And what's that supposed to mean?"

"It means," said Sketch, "if we don't do as he says, Sid's life could be in danger."

"So, what does he want?"

"The magic ink," said Heba.

"You've got to be kidding me! How the hell did he find you guys?"

"Sarge, Heba can explain all that we know—The Lure, Sid's apartment, and even Khaldun's behavior."

"Khaldun's a part of this?!"

"Sarge, please. The time is nearing. Do you remember me explaining a 'call' to you…how Sid can summon me through a sketch?"

"Sure do."

"Any minute now he's going to call me, which will direct me to where he is. It's not an emergency call, but rather one ordered by the Finger Gunman for me to deliver the magic ink."

Sketch took off his everyday clothes, revealing his superhero outfit, then took out his boots and mask from the bag and put them on. Heba and Perkins followed him into the bedroom, where he opened a window, then took off its screen. The window opening was large enough for him to fit through, and launch himself into flight.

"You're serious, aren't you?" said Perkins.

"Yes. Sid is being held prisoner, strapped to a chair in what I think is some kind of spinning cage. The Finger Gunman texted me a photo, and that seems to be what's going on."

"I've never seen you fly."

Sketch looked at Heba as she raised her brow to him. "No, you haven't," said Sketch. "I would love to showcase it, but this is strictly about saving Sid."

Heba walked over to Sketch by the window, and handed him the burlap sack of magic ink. "I am nervous," she said. "I am afraid you are about to fly into a very sticky web. Remember, he is a snake. Trust nothing he says. And remember…I love you."

"I love—"

The call arrived sharply, like a dagger, piercing and unexpected, radiating hot from within him, erecting his body as a searing current fired outward. Before he left, an internal white flash fleetingly blinded his vision, unseen to anyone but himself. And then he was gone. Heba and Perkins witnessed his flight, at least all that they could make of it. Sketch had left so suddenly, it was as if he had slipped into a trance, departing without saying farewell. Flying high over the tree tops heading into far east Texas, the visual details of Sid's call became clear. He saw The Trap, sketched crudely, but well enough for him to discern the necessary details. He saw a gun and a woman. What details Sid didn't have time to draw, he made evident willing them into the call. The woman was pleading for mercy. But who was she? Sketch couldn't make her out.

There was much more to the call than just giving him Sid's location. Sid had willed a warning into his drawing, signaling through his imaginative energy that the rot of evil was awaiting him—that the Finger Gunman was nothing but darkness.

Chapter 11
THE ASSISTANT

The Finger Gunman had hired a middle-aged woman, whom he had known over the years, to assist with sorting through the large volume of original superhero submissions that were mailed to VIP Comics. She was out of work and needed money. Due to having no kind of relationship with almost every single person he'd ever met, he gave her a call since she was one of the few who barely tolerated him. She agreed to the job since he offered to pay for her travel expenses and lodging. She said she never knew he was interested in the comic book industry. He kept his reply simple, saying it was an entrepreneurship that he had always wanted to pursue, and that he loved comics as a kid. He told her if she found any submissions that even remotely suggested magical ink, that she should bring it to his attention immediately. She had no knowledge that The Lure was anything more than a travesty of a contest promising a lucrative prize. Nor did she realize that she was nothing more than a pawn, an office assistant never to be compensated for her time and effort under the facade of the nonexistent VIP Comics. He didn't care how long he'd known her; she was expendable.

When she first began working for him, and before the time that she came across Sid's submission, he couldn't resist showing her The Trap. After all, it was his baby.

"Impressive, isn't it?" he said, sticking to the lie, as he walked her into the dingy room. "It's called The Trap. It'll be debuting in Las Vegas. It's part of a show where an escape artist must break free while strapped in the chair as The Trap spins. It'll definitely give Cirque du Soleil a run for their money!" The Finger Gunman opened the hatch, then gestured to the chair, "Please, be my guest…have a seat."

There was something unpromising with a hint of eerie about his invitation. "You're not going to turn it on, are you?"

"Ha! Don't kid yourself. Of course not. But I understand. It's just you and I and this medieval contraption. I'm sorry if I scared you."

"I'll pass," she said politely. "I don't do well on carnival rides, even if they're not moving."

Insulted, but keeping his composure, he said, "I assure you, this is not a carnival ride. Not even close. But I do respect your choice. The last thing I want is to make you uncomfortable."

A few days later, while sifting through a batch of new submissions, she came across Sid's contest entry.

Finally, the pinnacle of his forty-year search for the ink was nearing. She, however, had no idea why any submission about magic ink was such a big deal, but what she did know was that it signaled an abrupt change in the civility of Mr. Fontaine's character. He not only became very territorial of The Trap, adamant that she never enter the room again, but he ended The Lure as well, declaring Sid the sole winner. There was no parting handshake, no thank you for her time and commitment. Instead, in true Finger Gunman fashion, he told her to collect her belongings and leave. He would pay her later. "I'll call you," he said. "Don't call me."

Two days later, he killed the welder and the girlfriend.

Three days after that, he was holding Sid captive in The Trap.

And it was then, as Sketch was flying to deliver the magic ink, that the Finger Gunman's assistant—angry about not being paid for her work—made the unfortunate mistake of entering The Trap room, unannounced.

"Mr. Fontaine!" she yelled, bursting into the room. "I insist you give me my pay!!…*WHAT…THE…HELL?!!*"

Chapter 12
THE SAFE

Flying through the cauliflower-shaped cumulus clouds, the mysterious characteristics of the ink within Sketch guided him to The Trap's location. His mind wandered as he thought about Heba's concern for his safety. She wasn't sure if the properties of the Finger Gunman's silver ink made his immortal existence different from hers, and Sketch's. She was convinced, though, that he had no superpowers, but, instead, had a mind saturated with evil. As Sketch neared his destination, he reminded himself that saving Sid was the primary focus while delivering the ink. Secondary, if the opportunity presented itself, was the destruction of the Finger Gunman. He would obliterate him.

A half-mile long caliche driveway S-curved its way through a dense forest. Sketch floated down from the tree tops, landing softly between two cars parked outside The Trap building. One was positioned at a sharp angle, close to the entrance, its driver's side door left wide open. Sketch figured either someone had forgotten something or was in a rush. He stood still, listening for anything, something stirring nearby. Something inadvertently giving itself away. He had seen nothing from above and now heard nothing from below.

He opened the front door, stepping into an office. There were two desks, each piled with large, unopened Manila envelopes—all VIP contest superhero submissions. Several cardboard boxes were lined against a wall, acting as makeshift trash bins where many torn or crumpled envelopes had been discarded. The only other items in the office were a file cabinet and a small safe that sat on the floor.

He walked over to the only other door, beyond which he heard a man's boisterous voice. There was a second voice as well, but much quieter, timid.

Sid.

Sketch turned the doorknob and entered The Trap room.

"LADIES AND GENTLEMEN!!!" cried out the Finger Gunman. "The man of the hour is here!! It's Sketch, here to save the world!! Such prompt service!!"

From Sketch's vantage point, The Trap was fifty feet away. To the right, the Finger Gunman was standing at the control podium that faced The Trap. At his feet was the bag of snakes and his briefcase. In his right hand he held the gun. Within arm's reach of the Finger Gunman was the hatch that was bolted shut. Inside The Trap and facing Sketch was Sid, his arms unstrapped. Sitting on the latticework next to him was the assistant.

"Sketch, let me make something very clear: I will not hesitate to shoot your boy. Do not try to be a hero."

"Sketch," said Sid, "please do as he says."

"See, even your boy agrees."

"Just as you've requested, I brought you the magic ink," said Sketch. "Now, set him free."

"First things first. I want you to stand on the other side of The Trap, across from me." He poked the gun's nozzle through the latticework, aiming it at Sid.

Sketch kept calm and walked to a spot opposite the Finger Gunman, noticing old blood stains on the floor beneath The Trap.

"I see your eyes, Sketch. That's the blood from two people, one of whom made a very costly mistake. I had no choice but to eliminate them, spinning them unstrapped." He chuckled, adding, "It was really quite entertaining the way they begged for their lives."

Sketch clenched his hands onto The Trap's steel latticework, subtly testing what it would take to pull it apart. The welded steel straps were heavy duty. He could muscle it apart, but it wouldn't be quick. "Please, take the gun off of Sid. I have brought the ink under your conditions. There is no need to drag this out. It is a fair exchange—the ink for Sid—then we shall be gone."

"Your boy won't be released until I have proof that the ink you brought is, indeed, magical. My assistant holds a pen that has an empty ink cartridge." Motioning for her to stand, he continued, "Sketch, I want you to hand her the ink."

"And I want you to lower that gun."

The Finger Gunman paused…then nodded. "Fair enough."

There was just enough room to pass the bottle through the latticework, as well as the eye-dropper used to transfer the ink.

Sketch asked the assistant, "Who are you?"

"I'm—"

"SHUT UP!!" snapped the Finger Gunman, raising the gun at her.

Her eyes were pleading Sketch to rescue her.

"She's nothing more than someone who just barged in here, interrupting my genius. She infuriated me!" The Finger Gunman told her to give the bottle and dropper to Sid, who then suctioned the ink and dispensed it into the pen's cartridge.

Sketch looked on, fully empowered with superhuman abilities, yet was powerless. The assistant's trembling hands had nearly dropped the bottle when he handed her the ink. "It's not helping, pointing the gun at them," said Sketch.

"I'll make the gun decisions! But I'll tell you what's not helping, and that's her being here in the first place."

The assistant turned slowly, timidly. "I only came to collect my pay, and then I heard voices. I had no idea something was going on."

The Finger Gunman lowered his head, shaking it side to side as he rubbed his eyes, then drew a deep breath. "I guess I wasn't clear," he said. "I guess I had no idea I had to spell things out. There is no pay. I paid for your travel and hotel. Other than that, there is nothing for you! NOTHING!!"

"I should've known better," she said, taking a brave step toward him. "I should've known not to trust you."

Without hesitation, the Finger Gunman looked down the barrel of the gun, then fired one deafening shot, passing just over her shoulder. The bullet bulls-eyed perfectly through an opening in the latticework before tearing into the galvanized steel wall, its impact reverberating sharply.

The assistant had dropped to her knees, shuddering, cowering next to Sid who was no better, shaken in the chair.

"You nearly killed her!" yelled Sketch, his frustration mounting as he, too, began feeling as if he were taken hostage.

"It's a warning shot. I will not hesitate to hit my target. Do not provoke me."

Sid interjected, his voice short of breath, startled from the gun shot. "An animal," he said. "I'll draw an animal to life to prove the ink is magical."

"Sketch, your boy is worth something! I was just about to suggest that. I like how you think, Sid. I really do. No large animals, please. An insect if you'd like." The Finger Gunman raised his arms high in a V, imagining he was leading a stadium of people. "All quiet please!"

Sid tilted his head down toward the assistant, and said softly, "For your safety, please stand behind me."

Rising to her feet, she did as requested. She was disoriented, though, with all that had transpired, unable to make sense of anything. Sid strapped to the chair, Mr. Fontaine firing a gun at her, and a man named Sketch, who, dressed like some kind of superhero, had supposedly flown like Superman. All that she had done was come to collect her money. Perhaps she did enter the room a bit forcefully. Maybe a more civil approach would have achieved her goal. Instead, her aggressive demeanor agitated the Finger Gunman, resulting in him pointing a gun at her and demanding she get inside The Trap. But then again, she knew Mr. Fontaine was unpredictable. She had known him for many years, and how he would sometimes brag about his spontaneous outbursts. He told her about a grocery store clerk in Cairo whom he forced to lie face down on the floor at gun point. The clerk cried and begged for his life. She asked him if the clerk survived. He said, "Yes, unfortunately." He delighted in retelling the story, as though he deserved adulation. She clearly knew his volatile potential. Yet when he contacted her to help sort through the VIP submissions, he caught her during a difficult time in her life. She was destitute and needed the money, so she agreed to help him. And now, as she stood behind Sid in The Trap, she knew she had made a horrible decision to be his assistant, and that she only had herself to blame if this were to be her last breathing hour.

"What are you going to draw?" she whispered.

"A surprise," said Sid.

"And it'll come to life?"

"I certainly hope so."

"Hey, you two," barked the Finger Gunman, "no secrets! Sid, just draw."

Sketch watched intriguingly, as he had never witnessed imaginative energy in action. He had seen Sid trace the original drawing of himself that Charles had drawn, but had never seen something come to life from scratch. He watched Sid stare intently, hovering the pen above the blank page, formulating an idea. Equally enthralled was the assistant, whose knowledge of the supernatural went only as far as the world of fiction could take her. Then, two minutes later, after Sid commenced drawing, willing the drawing to life, the animal appeared...outside The Trap.

It was almost as if the sound came before the animal arrived. It was the intense hissing of the snakes in the bag next to the Finger Gunman. They were on high alert. They could smell it—the one animal that truly stood its ground against them.

The Finger Gunman jumped aside as the mongoose crouched toward him. It sensed the reptile in him. It sensed his venomous serpentine soul. It also sensed his fear. Within striking distance, it jabbed at his ankles, throwing him into a frantic dance around the podium. "DESTROY IT, SID!!! DESTROY IT!!!"

"SKETCH!!" yelled Sid. "GET READY!!"

The Finger Gunman, backpedaling, stumbled over the conduit that housed The Trap's power wires, falling against the latticework with the gun still in-hand. His shoulder, taking the brunt of the fall, landed heavy and hard, causing a gash that bled silver ink. The mongoose leapt onto his chest, making hisses that sounded like sharp bursts of steam, then struck quickly, sinking its teeth into the side of his face, penetrating to his jaw bone. Grimacing in pain as his flesh was pulled and torn, he threw a fist, but it was no match against the animal's reflexes. The mongoose moved swiftly to his backside, continuing its onslaught, biting with full force and tearing into the base of his neck. An agonizing scream was proof that his immortality offered him no exemption from the fierce sting of pain. The snakes in the bag had gone silent, recognizing his suffering, but prepared to strike if discovered.

Sketch had been looking for a break to bolt toward the Finger Gunman, but it was his grip on the gun that concerned Sketch most.

Sid saw it differently. He saw an opening. "NOW, SKETCH!!! NOW!!!"

Managing to knock the mongoose off his neck, he laid flat like a sniper with one arm extended, steadying the gun's barrel through the latticework, aiming it at Sid. "Destroy the drawing!!" yelled the Finger Gunman. "Destroy it, or I will shoot!!" To his side, caught in his peripheral vision, he saw the mongoose preparing a second attack to his flesh-torn jaw.

"Sid!" said Sketch. "Do as he says! Destroy it!"

"But—"

"Destroy it! It's the only way!"

Dejected, Sid slumped in the chair. Hope was right there, within reach. But now, there was no telling. So close, he thought, so close. He held the drawing with both hands, closed his eyes, then tore it down the middle, splitting the mongoose drawing in half, forever vanishing it from existence.

The assistant looked on, speechless. Who were these people? An animal appears, then disappears. She watched it evaporate. The ink truly was magical. Why Sid? What gift did he possess to bring things to life from a drawing, from nothing?

Rising to his feet, the injuries sustained to his neck and jaw made it impossible for the Finger Gunman to get comfortable. With his free hand cradling his wounded chin, he motioned to the assistant, "Hand me everything—the ink, pen, and dropper."

She collected the items, returning the ink to the sack, then handed them to him through the latticework.

"My work is done here," he said, wincing. "It is time to bid you adieu." Keeping a close eye on Sketch, he opened the bag of snakes, deposited the ink items into it, then closed the bag. His face and neck throbbing and stinging as silver ink seeped from his wounds, he managed a kind of sickened, diseased laugh while brandishing the gun. "Sketch," he said, "you're superhuman, right?"

Sketch stood still, disgusted, not responding.

"Oh, come on. You know you are. But let's find out."

Sketch clenched his fists, his muscles charged, ready to erupt. "Stop your sick games!"

The Finger Gunman had positioned himself next to the control podium, exactly where he had hoped to be when he had finally taken possession of the ink. He hadn't built The Trap as some kind of design challenge to marvel at. He had built it for only one purpose: to torture in order to facilitate the ink transfer. And now he had an extra participant…his unstrapped assistant.

"This is no game, but rather a match between Good and Evil. LADIES AND GENTLEMEN!!…TAKE YOUR MARKS!!… GET SET!!…"

The Finger Gunman fired the gun into the air. And, with a sudden twist of his wrist, he simultaneously spun the speed knob to the FAST setting. Before he began his own escape, the last glimpse of his pet project was of his assistant clinging to Sid's chair while The Trap began to rotate. Her frightful voice calling out, "Please…stop it!! PLEASE!!" Turning away, as he heard her body drop, he grabbed the bag of snakes with the magic ink, and fled the room. He wanted to stay and watch the show—to savor their suffering—but he had far greater things to tend to.

On the second rotation, the assistant fell again, severely rolling an ankle, but landing close to Sid. Grabbing the chair, her body contorted and her legs dangled as she rotated back to the top, this time holding on.

As the fourth rotation began accelerating, heading toward an inevitable and lethal speed, the whir of the motor grew louder. And louder. Until The Trap jerked and stopped instantly, as if the emergency STOP button had been pressed. But no one was at the podium. Still, The Trap was defiant and inched forward, fighting something. Fighting Sketch.

His fingers intertwined with the latticework, every muscle in Sketch's body contributed in forcing The Trap to stop. The motor whirred louder, screaming as it fought against him. His feet sliding on the concrete floor, Sketch was slowly being pulled forward. The increasing volume from the motor gave Sketch some hope, though. It meant it was struggling. Tapping into his core and giving The Trap one final yank with his grip, he brought it to a standstill, then smelled it: burning oil from the hot metal of the turbine motor that was no match for his strength. The motor began smoking under the strain, then fell silent as it finally stopped. The Trap surrendered to Sketch, who ran over to the hatch and, ignoring the deadbolt, ripped it free from its hinges. "Ma'am, are you ok?"

The assistant was sitting down, holding her ankle. "I might've broken it," she said.

"What about your back? That was quite a first tumble you took."

"Pretty sore, but it'll be alright."

"Sid," he said, unstrapping him, "are you okay?"

"Yes, but you have to go get him. Rip him to shreds!! We can't let him get away!"

"I'll find him. But first, let's get out of this thing, before it decides to start back up on its own." Draping her legs over his arms, he effortlessly lifted the assistant and carried her out, setting her on her feet. "Can you put pressure on it?"

"Ouch!" she flinched, tapping her foot on the floor. "It's not good."

"Let's get you a seat in the office."

Helping her through the office door, Sketch placed a chair where she could prop her foot up on a desk.

Sid explored the room, flipping his fingers through the Manila envelopes. "Are these all superhero contest submissions?"

"Yes," she said. "And all for nothing. I can't believe I never caught on that it was a scam, a ploy to get the ink. It's all about the ink, right?"

"Yes, ma'am," said Sketch. "And I'm sure you're pretty confused."

"Yes, I am. But I feel somewhat responsible for this mess."

"For what reason?"

"Because I showed him Sid's submission."

"But you had no idea what he was up to."

"I should've suspected something. He's always had a history of being sly, and he's always prided himself for his bad behavior. I really never liked him, and it all began when I was a little girl. Over the years, he would occasionally line up jobs for me. I was grateful for that. So, when he called me up a few months ago and asked if I wanted to make some money, I said, sure, because times have been hard."

Sketch pulled aside a window curtain, and looked out at the parking lot. He noticed the car that had its doors closed was now gone. "If I may ask, ma'am, what happened when you were little?"

"I was probably five or so. I was in an open-air market in Cairo. My mom had just bought a glass lantern and asked me to hold it while she went to do something. Somehow it slipped out of my hands and shattered. She had met Mr. Fontaine the night before. And when she returned, he was with her. They were both very upset with me. Later, he called me worthless. I remember a nice man named Charles knelt down and told me that it was okay, because even he broke things. I remember it like it was yesterday. He was so kind and—"

Sketch had turned away from the window the moment she mentioned Cairo, listening intently as she spoke. "Excuse me," he interrupted, "but I know this story." His eyes welling, he said, "You're... you're Angie, aren't you?"

"Yes...I am...but, how would you know that?"

"Because Charles created me."

Angie sifted through the entanglement of her confusion. "With the ink?"

"Yes. He drew me. And it was from his imaginative energy that I came to life."

"And I," said Sid, his face flushed with emotion, "am Charles' grandson."

Blindsided by the revelation, Angie cautiously lowered her foot to the floor, then, hobbling, gave Sid and Sketch each a hug. "Oh, my god," she said, tearing, "there truly are no coincidences."

"Sketch," said Sid, "you must go find him. The Finger Gunman must be destroyed!"

"Angie," said Sketch, "Sid's right. I move quickly. I'll catch him, and—"

Angie raised a hand. "Finger Gunman…is that what you said?"

"Yes," said Sid. "Has he said it to you?"

"Has who said it to me?"

"Mr. Fontaine. He is the Finger Gunman. Has he ever referred to himself by that name to you?"

"No, but I've seen the name on a drawing."

Sketch and Sid looked at each other, both caught off-guard.

"What drawing?" said Sketch.

Angie pointed to the small safe on the floor that sat against the wall. "In there."

"Wait," said Sid. "You're telling me there's a drawing in there with the name Finger Gunman on it?"

"Yes. He keeps cash in there and some other stuff I'm not sure of. But a couple of weeks ago he left the door open, when he had to go out to his car, and I got curious and looked inside. I saw a drawing that looked like a younger version of him. And I also saw another name on the drawing."

"What was that?" asked Sketch.

"Zenator."

Sketch looked at Sid. "Could this actually be possible? Could it really be this easy? Angie, do you know the combination?"

"I'm afraid not, sorry."

"No problem. I've got a solution." Sketch pushed aside the desk to give himself some room, then picked up the safe as if it was an empty box. Finding a finger hold along one edge, he wedged his fingertips into the closed door and pried it open like a piece of tin. Setting the safe on the desk, he reached inside and took out the drawing of a younger version Finger Gunman. He handed it to Sid to inspect, who dragged his index finger over the drawing. "No doubt," he said, "it's an original."

"But, in his rush to leave," said Sketch, "did he really forget it? Or is it possible this is a copy he had made by some artist with no imaginative energy?" Studying it more closely, Sketch grew curious about the handwriting. "Notice how the names Zenator and Finger Gunman are written differently. Zenator looks like a woman's handwriting. I believe Genevieve wrote it. I believe this is the original drawing, and that the Finger Gunman, in his rush to leave, forgot it."

"If it is," said Angie, "does this mean, like the mongoose, if we tear it in half, the Finger Gunman will vanish and cease to exist?"

"Yes," said Sid. "Yes, it does."

"Tear it," said Sketch. "Both of you hold the drawing and tear it right down the middle. Then I'll search for signs of him missing. He took off in the car. I should find a crashed car if he vanishes while driving. He has no superpowers. He's dependent on normal transportation, or on foot."

Together, Sid and Angie held the drawing. They had suffered enough humiliation and mental anguish at the hands of the Finger Gunman. The moment they tore it in half was the moment Sketch departed, flying upward and over the treetops.

There was only one highway for Sketch to follow, and the Finger Gunman had either gone left or right coming out of the driveway. Sketch chose left. With a couple hours of daylight remaining, the dense forest of pine trees had begun casting a wall of shadows across the roadway. The area was primarily rural with only a couple of thinly populated farming communities.

Following the highway, Sketch noticed a group of bicycles lying on their sides on the outside of a hairpin curve, but saw no riders. Curious, he descended to a lower altitude where he hovered as if standing on air, hidden by a cluster of trees. He heard voices deeper into the forest, a hundred feet off the road. Then, through the branches, he saw the Finger Gunman's car upside down, nearly flattened, windows and windshield shattered, and the front crushed from colliding with a sturdy pine. Sketch drifted lower to hear their conversations, remaining hidden—motionless—and, through the branches, watched and listened...

"Shit!! Look at it...it's totaled!! It went airborne, right out of the ditch."

"Yeah. Crossed into our lane doing what, sixty? Seventy?"

"At least."

"I saw him coming, and thought for sure he's gonna slow down. But he barely missed us. And what's crazy, I didn't see a driver. I mean there was no one."

"Maybe he got distracted and was reaching for something on the floorboard."

"Maybe, but if that's so then where is the driver now?"

Sketch noticed a cyclist kneeling by the driver's side door, looking inside. "Guys! Come here! Check this out. There's nobody in it. I mean...nobody."

"What do you mean?"

"I mean, nobody."

"Do you think he bailed?"

"There's no way. We saw the car coming, and it's an uphill climb to this turn. It never slowed down. And what's strange was it stayed right in its lane, even during the subtle curves down there. It was too far to see a driver at that point. But there must have been one. And then something happened. Something unexplainable."

Intrigued, all the cyclists, but one, knelt around the car to take a look. The other walked beyond the impacted tree, seeing something on the ground.

"Hey, look at this!" he said, holding the gun in the air.

"Look what I found," said another, spotting the nylon bag. "Maybe a bag of money?"

"Open it!"

The cyclist undid the tie, then looked inside. "Shit!!" he said, his body flinching as he jumped back, dropping the bag. "Snakes!!"

"In the bag?"

"Yeah, two of 'em." He kept his distance, waiting for the bag to move. Using a broken tree branch he poked inside it. "They're dead," he said, as he reached down, pinching the bag by its ink-stained bottom, then dumped the snakes and the bag's contents.

Black ink spilled out, as well as pieces of broken glass, a crushed pen, and the dropper. The vipers were coated with ink, and pierced with fragments of glass.

"It's ink," observed one cyclist. "This is just too bizarre. Ink, snakes, a gun, and no driver."

"You called 9-1-1, right?"

"Sure did. They asked if the driver was injured. I said there was no driver. And if there were, he musta vanished into thin air."

"But, did you see this?" said a cyclist taking a longer look inside the car, particularly at the mangled steering wheel. "It's silver… like ink." He reached in and swiped his finger on it, then dragged it across his other hand. "Well, I'll be…it is ink, or sure seems like it."

Sketch had heard all he needed to hear, and had seen all he needed to see. Even if the Finger Gunman had jumped out of the car, he would never have done so without taking the bag, or, at the very least, the ink. His entire existence had been to secure and corrupt the ink, but he had failed.

Perhaps, though, there has always been another lure at work. Perhaps it was Charles all along who, despite his death, had triggered a chain of strangely connected events that would work in concert to eventually give the Finger Gunman the impression that he was in control. When, in fact, it was his very own Lure that sealed his fate, his vanishing point.

Rising out of the trees, Sketch began flying back to Sid and Angie. What a wonderful feeling it was to have closure, and to fly freely through the warm summer air, knowing there was no need to look back over his shoulder.

Chapter 13
BOXCAR

2066

Heba opened the cabin door and stepped out onto the front porch. Saluting her hand against her brow she shielded her eyes, squinting, looking up into the shower of falling snow with anticipation. The Montana air was still and cloudy-white, and the several feet of snow that had accumulated muffled the sounds of the day. It had been an hour since Sketch had heard the alert on the police scanner. Certainly, she thought, he had finished dealing with the bank robbers by now.

"HEADS UP!!" said the voice from above, beyond the point of visibility. "INCOMING!!"

Heba took cover underneath the porch eave as a barrage of snowballs pummeled the roof. Drifting down into view, Sketch laughed, "Sorry! I couldn't resist."

Heba shook her head, smiling. "Why do I put up with you?"

Sketch landed softly on the porch, then kissed her on the cheek. "Because you have a thing for immature guys who fly."

"I suppose," she chortled. "So, how was work today?"

"Freezing. I was in such a rush, I forgot to wear extra tights. Too bad Charles didn't make me impervious to the cold."

"Oh, my brave superhero!"

"I know. I do have my delicate side. I just hate the damn cold."

"Did the cold prevent you from finding the bank robbers?"

"Of course not. Duty before frostbite! I spotted their car traveling on a backroad that hadn't been plowed. They were moving slowly, about a half mile from the main road. I stayed low, and snuck up from behind them. I wish I could've seen their faces as I lifted it up off the road. I positioned myself underneath it in such a way so I could turn it, then speared it into a large snow bank. All that was visible was the back end and tires sticking out. When I heard the police sirens coming down the road, I hovered out of sight until they were discovered and apprehended."

"Well, come inside. I have got a fire going to warm you up."

"Has the game started?"

"Not yet. The holograms are having issues."

Sketch followed Heba into the cabin, taking off his silver boots and mask, then took a seat in the living room on the fireplace's stone hearth. Khaldun was sprawled out on the floor, his back against the hearth. Levitating halfway between the floor and ceiling, was a three-by-four-foot hologram, its three-dimensional image blinking erratically with static. The hologram was created by TracLasers—multiple laser ports positioned about the cabin that worked seamlessly with one another. Upon command, a technology called DriftMode allowed the hologram to move about the cabin with no reception interruption.

Heba walked into the living room and stood close to the hologram, observing its jittery image. "They are saying on TV that there is a technical problem with the Holo Tower signals. Nationwide, the holograms are experiencing excessive static. DriftMode is not working either. The holograms are not moving by voice or remote control. Of course, this being Super Bowl 100, they are not about to have the opening kickoff until the static issue is resolved."

Sketch warmed his hands close to the fire. "Can you believe the Honolulu Volcanos are in their third straight Super Bowl? And it's only their fifth year in the league. Do you think Berlin has a chance?"

Heba turned, taking a seat on the hearth. "The Badgers have only lost two games this season, so I certainly would not rule them out."

Sketch chuckled, "Listen to you talk football...who would ever have thought?"

"No kidding. But once the NFL expanded and went global, becoming the GFL, I got interested in international teams."

For a moment, the hologram disappeared, then, seconds later, reappeared, blinking on and off as it worked out its final kinks. Once the technical issue was resolved, the hologram displayed an apologetic broadcasting statement, then resumed with live coverage of an aerial view of the stadium. A baritone voice boomed, "WELCOME BACK TO THE GLOBAL FOOTBALL LEAGUE'S SUPER BOWL 100!!!"

"It's always a production," said Sketch as, minutes later, a hundred skydivers jumped from a fleet of lumbering airplanes, descending into the deafening roar of a hundred-and-sixty-thousand spectators chanting, "ONE HUNDRED!!!! ONE HUNDRED!!!! ONE HUNDRED!!!!..." The three-dimensional hologram technology was so advanced, so clear, Sketch felt like he could snatch the skydivers right out of the air, like the plane he snatched out of the air in Chicago in 2010.

It marked the beginning of many emergencies that Sketch would respond to after the last of the Finger Gunman. A private Lear jet had been stolen from a southern Wisconsin regional airport. The pilot—the only occupant on the plane—radioed one statement, then went silent: "Goodbye, John Hancock." With the memories of 9/11 still fresh on everyone's mind, the FAA didn't hesitate and immediately started diverting air traffic. Tracking its flight, authorities assumed the worst that the pilot was referring to Chicago's John Hancock building. Sergeant Perkins had stopped by the police station to say his final goodbyes before heading to Texas, when he heard the news. Unsure if military fighter jets could scramble in time to intercept the plane, he immediately alerted Sketch...

9/11 cannot happen again. Find the plane...Find the plane...FIND THE PLANE!!!...FIND THE...BINGO!!!

He was a twenty-three-year-old American who had a beef with the government. In the lawnmower shed behind his mother's house, he had a stockpile of weapons and ammunition, none of which he carried on the plane. The plane was his weapon. The John Hancock building was visible, eighteen miles away. One year ago, to the day, he had planned the mission, reminding himself that nothing is ever completely secure, therefore anything is possible. His plan was to knife the plane through the building's belly.

But he never got the chance.

Sketch seized it from the sky, maneuvering it away from the city, then drove it into Lake Michigan, skimming it just below the surface. He contemplated driving it deeper, into the lake's bottom, but, instead, he brought it to the surface, leaving it for the Coast Guard, then made his exit.

Whether he received his information from national or local news, or from the police scanner, Sketch was often in action, doing all he could to make things right. After all, he was created as a superhero to defend against evil, and to rescue those in need of help.

The list of accomplishments was long, including two boys trapped in an icy pond, a shooter at-large on a college campus, a raging father kidnapping his child, a fallen crane at a construction site, an escaped convict, and a life-threatening catastrophe on an off-shore oil rig.

His anonymous rescues and interventions were strategically managed. They had to be. He couldn't afford to be identified as "that masked man". He didn't want the status of becoming a global superhero celebrity, forever hunted by the international paparazzies. He wanted to throw playful snowballs at Heba in the open. He did not want their lives turned upside down. So, he tended to his heroic tasks very carefully. Besides, if his identity were to go public, it would put him one step closer to the world knowing his veins flowed with magic ink. And once that news broke, it would be the end of his superpowers. The ink has no tolerance for the disclosing of its secrecy. Only, under rare exceptions may an outsider be informed about the ink. Sergeant Perkins and Angie were the two exceptions due to the timing of their place in Sketch's life. As they say, Sketch and Heba lived the good life. Moving about the country as Sketch continued to uphold his duty, saving lives and combating evil.

It was their first time to winter in Montana, and, despite Sketch disliking the cold, the cabin did make for a cozy change of scenery.

A minute before the Badgers kicked off to the Volcanos, the rowdy stadium cheered like Roman spectators surrounding the pit of gladiators. Sketch and Heba moved from the hearth to a sofa, voice commanding the hologram to drift over to them. The 3-D hologram miniaturization of the game was so clear, so close to real, it made a mockery of a technology called HDTV that once dominated nearly every household.

As the Badgers' kicker sent the ball beyond the end zone, the police scanner sounded an alert:

"Attention all officers. A multi-vehicle pile-up has occurred on an icy stretch of northbound I-15, ten miles north of Great Falls. Several tractor trailers are involved. Serious injuries are to be expected, and possible fatalities. Approach the area using extreme caution."

"Well," said Sketch, standing up, "so much for the game."

Heba voice-commanded the hologram to turn off. "I cannot watch football knowing there might be children involved."

Sketch made his way back to their bedroom. "I'm putting on extra tights."

Heba followed him, stopping at the doorway. "But with so many people, how will you remain unseen?"

"Maybe this is the one that changes that."

"But the ink must remain a secret. Only under extreme circumstances—"

"I would say this one might be extreme."

"Sketch...you must be sure."

Heba walked back to the living room as her phone rang, retrieving it from a sofa-side table. "Hello?"

Sketch walked out from the bedroom, holding a pair of tights. Heba's back was turned to him, but there was something about her physical demeanor, a slump in her posture, that made him wonder who had called.

After a few short exchanges she hung up, then turned, sensing Sketch was in the room. Her usually cheerful expression had changed to one of sadness.

"There is no need to go to the accident," she said.

"Why's that?"

Heba moved forward, reaching out to Sketch as he took her in his arms. "Because, your powers are gone. Sid died."

On the day that Sid passed, Heba was 2,516 years old. Sketch was 99. Age was of no significance to them. What mattered was as long as their original drawings were never destroyed, they were destined to live eternal lives together. But how might that be accomplished? Where would the best place be to maximize the safety of their drawings?

For years, Sketch's original drawing was kept in a safety deposit box of a bank vault in Waterstone, while Heba and Khaldun's drawing remained in the Khepri Collection in the Egyptian Museum. Though their drawings were secure, they weren't together. If a drawing were to be destroyed, then they wished the other be destroyed as well. Neither wanted to experience eternity alone.

Sid was forty-four years old, married with two teenagers, when Sketch and Heba presented him with an idea to preserve their drawings. They had met the family when the kids were young, but over time had to stop due to the cessation of their physical aging. They continued to visit Sid, but only him, away from his home. He lived comfortably in San Antonio, working as a graphics designer for a large advertising company. They met him at a Denny's restaurant during his lunch hour, taking a booth by the front window.

"There is only one way to protect the integrity of our drawings," said Sketch, "and that is to have them buried with you in your casket, entombed and undisturbed."

Sid looked at Heba and said, "But your drawing is in Egypt."

"It was in Egypt. It has taken some time, but it turns out that many of Khepri's drawings were on loan to the museum as part of a private collection. It has been a tedious undertaking, but after finally contacting the owners, I approached them, asking to purchase just one drawing, and gave them a more than fair price to purchase it."

"And...?" said Sid.

Heba smiled, "And it is now in a bank vault with Sketch's."

"Odd as it may sound," said Sketch, "we want the origins of our existence to be buried with you. All you have to do is have it requested in your will and final testament."

Beyond that, there were no further questions. "Consider it done," said Sid. "I'll meet with my attorney this week and have it amended."

A large gathering of family and friends descended upon a Methodist church on the outskirts of San Antonio for Sid's Celebration of Life. Sketch and Heba stood in the back, making a quick exit just prior to the end of the service which was uncannily reminiscent of Charles'. Sid's qualities of kindness, humor, and integrity were equally as storied as his grandfather's.

They walked back to their car where Khaldun quietly anticipated their return. The windows had been cracked to allow the sixty-degree air to circulate. They drove to a small cafe called The Depot where they would meet Sid for lunch when they were passing through. Behind the cafe was a boarded-up railroad station, which explained The Depot's name and interior wall decor of photographs and paintings of trains throughout history, as well as maps of railways across the US. It was a small, but iconic eatery that withstood the test of time, and was still as popular as ever.

"Welcome back!" said an older waitress approaching their table. Her gray hair was pulled back into a bun, and bags beneath her eyes puffed like tiny pillows.

"You remember us?" said Sketch.

"How could I forget. You're the ageless couple. How do y'all do it? You must spend thousands on facial creams."

Heba glanced at Sketch. "I guess it is a gift," she said.

"Somethin' like that." The waitress smiled, handing them their menus.

"Plastic menus," said Sketch. "Will this place ever get holograms?"

"Ha! Are you kiddin' me? Hell, no. This place is old school."

"Well, we really don't need the menus. We'll each take the fried catfish platter."

"No problem," she said, "I'll get your order going." Turning to head to the kitchen, the waitress stopped, returning to their table. "Hey, just curious, but where is your friend…the gentleman you always met here?"

"I am impressed," said Heba. "You have quite a memory."

"I know my customers."

"His name was Sid. He died last week of a heart attack. We just came from his service, and thought we would come here to honor his memory. A small gesture."

"I'm so sorry to hear that. He was a sweet man. Y'all are good friends."

"It feels strange without Sid," said Sketch, as the waitress walked away. "I hate the void that comes with losing a close friend. It's been almost one hundred years since Charles died…and now his grandson. They, and Seargent Perkins, are the only true mortal friends I've ever had."

Heba extended her hands across the table for Sketch to hold. "Our drawings are safe now. They are together, as we are. For how long is unknown, but together is what matters."

"And what do we do with the magic ink? Even if one of Sid's kids shows artistic promise, I don't want to return to being a superhero. That's why I'm ok with my drawing being buried with Sid. I want to live a simpler life with you."

Heba leaned closer toward Sketch. "But what if we do come across another artist who is worthy of the ink? Should we include him or her in our little secret?"

"Honestly," said Sketch, "I say we give it a rest."

"Are you sure? What if an evil entity were to surface that only a superhero could defeat?"

"Then I guess we'll cross that bridge when we come to it."

They left the cafe after a parting conversation with the waitress, then went to the car and put a leash on Khaldun to go for a walk.

Passing between the cafe and a gas station, a narrow alley divided the two buildings, leading back to the abandoned railroad station.

"Let's get a little adventurous," said Sketch, holding the leash on Khaldun, then entered the alley. Its pavement was cracked and uneven, sprouting with overgrown weeds. Discarded beer cans and general trash cluttered the area.

Heba walked by his side, holding his hand, then stopped, pointing ahead. "Sketch…look…do you see it?"

From behind, came the sound of clanking pedals and chains as four young boys zipped past on bicycles, narrowly clipping them with their handle bars.

"Hey! Watch it!" yelled Sketch, as Khaldun barked jointly in protest.

"No barking, Khaldun!" ordered Heba, then repeated to Sketch, "Do you see it?"

"You mean the graffiti artist tagging the boxcar?"

"Well, yes, but do you see what he is painting?"

Exiting the alley, they noticed the boys' bicycles laying on their sides. An impromptu game of cops and robbers had ensued as they chased one another around the railroad station.

"Excuse me," said Heba, as they neared the artist, "but I could not help but notice what you are painting. What species is that?"

"Are you a bird lover?" asked the artist.

"I most certainly am."

"Ma'am, it's a falcon."

Heba turned to Sketch, her face taken aback, and said, "Do you believe in omens?"

Before he could answer, two boys ran past, one in pursuit of the other, with his arms extended. Khaldun's hair immediately spiked along the ridge of his back, as a deep growl murmured.

"POW!! POW!! You're dead!!" yelled the boy with piercing eyes. "I got you with my finger gun, man!!"

ACKNOWLEDGMENTS

I am beyond grateful to Britt Van Dine for the countless hours he spent helping me forge the pathways of *Sketch*. Thank you for wordsmithing the trouble spots. You played an integral part, helping bring the ink on these pages to life.

And thank you, Emily St. John Mandel, for writing your wonderful novel, *Station Eleven*. All that it took was one sentence, and, as inspiration goes, the idea of *Sketch* popped into my head.

ABOUT THE AUTHOR

ROS HILL grew up in Normal, Illinois. He is the author and illustrator of two children's books, *Shamoo: A Whale Of A Cow* and *Unexpected Tails.* He has also authored a collection of short stories about his observations on life, titled, *Taking Out The Trash. Sketch* is his first novel. He lives in San Marcos, Texas.

www.ingramcontent.com/pod-product-compliance
Lightning Source LLC
LaVergne TN
LVHW041146150826
845673LV00001B/83

* 9 7 9 8 9 9 9 2 5 1 3 0 5 *